IMHOTEP

ALSO BY W. J. CHERF

The Manuscripts of the Richards' Trust

Bow Tie
Recovery
Children of Ptah
Imhotep
Maat-ka-re. Memoirs of a Time Traveler
Iron from the Sky

The Adventures of J.J. Stone

The First Soul
The Lictor of Magic
I Am the Storm
Dark Blade

Adventures in Paranormal Archaeology

The Magician's Tomb
Netherworld's Gate
Dhampirica
Hallowed Promises

Twenty-Four Century Mercenaries

I Am Jonathan
I Am Gregory
I Am Krait
I Am Peter

IMHOTEP

THE FOURTH MANUSCRIPT
OF THE RICHARDS' TRUST

W. J. CHERF

Foxbat Publishing
ISBN: 978-0-9834814-4-7

Cover art. Adapted from a black and white Matrix background,
with the front cover's reversing clock image adapted from the
apple.com time machine logo. The back cover includes the
southern entrance to the Step Pyramid's underground maze of
passages. Imhotep's hidden tomb entrance is along the cut bedrock
to the left.

An author's first line of defense is made up by those brave souls who are willing to plow through the early drafts. They are a patient and hopeful lot, and without them, frankly, this book would have been a disaster. Consequently, it is with deep and heartfelt thanks to Joni and Jim that I dedicate this manuscript. Their honest assessments and observations were invaluable.

That is not to say that my ever-endearing wife, Sue, did not have a hand in the matter. In fact, it was her idea in the first place, after having read a very raw version, she firmly stated that "things just have to change." And, as usual, she was absolutely right. Bless you.

ABBREVIATIONS

Firth   Cecil M. Firth, J. E. Quibell. *Excavations at Saqqara. The Step Pyramid.* Vols. I-II. Cairo, 1935.

Hannig   Rainer Hannig. *Großes Handwörterbuch Ägyptisch-Deutsch (2800-950 v. Chr.).* Mainz, 1995. German dictionary of ancient Egyptian. A valuable resource for most aspects of the ancient Egyptian language that includes lists of gods, kings, weights and measures, abbreviations, toponyms, and maps.

Lauer   Jean-Philippe Lauer. *Saqqara. The Royal Cemetery of Memphis. Excavations and Discoveries since 1850.* London, 1976.

RUTI   *Rukovodyashiy Ukaeaniya dlya Tymporalie Eksploratsiya* (*Guidelines for Temporal Exploration*). Time travel protocol authored in former Soviet Union in 1941 by the famous Hour Glass Seminar. Chaired by the philosopher Gregor Survurov, its membership included: Victor Latysev, Byzantine papyrologist credited with first expressing concern for "the preservation of the delicate fabric of reality;" three theoretical mathematicians: Nikolai Federov, Alexandr Koslov, and Dmitrey Giga; and Pyotr Borov, theoretical engineer and quantum physicist. This document makes no reference to any political or governmental body and states that all temporal decisions must occur within the framework of an international, scientific forum outside of any religious, political, or ideological control. This apolitical ideological stance proved to be the Hour Glass Seminar's greatest achievement.

Wb Adolf Erman, Hermann Grapow. *Wörterbuch der Ägyptischen Sprache*. 4th ed. 7 vols. Berlin, 1982. Primary lexicon for the ancient Egyptian language includes context, sources, and a reverse Egyptian-German word list. Essential, but considered dated. Should be used in conjunction with more recent philological sources.

Editor's Note

My name is Paul Silas. I am both the editor and executor of the so-called Richards' Trust; so-called because the name behind the trust is a fiction. Nonetheless, I can assure you that the dynamic personality that lurks behind the *nom de plume* of Professor Joseph William Richards was a living and breathing individual of breathtaking capacity. You may accept this judgment based upon some thirty-odd years of association.

Per the instructions of the Richards' Trust, I was initially instructed to publish three manuscripts, but after Professor Richards' disappearance, the trust empowered me to sell his flat and all of its contents with the proceeds to be divided as specified below. During that liquidation process, all went well and according to plan, that is until I tried to move his old wooden desk.

What I discovered in it was a false bottom beneath the lower left-hand drawer. Upon removing said drawer, I spotted several items. The first was a green, rectangular cloth container labeled Remington Universal Fast Snap Cleaning System. Not knowing what that was, I sat down on the dusty hardwood floor to find out. Unzipping it along its upper perimeter, I was greeted with the smell of light oil, a neatly folded green microfiber cloth, small plastic bottles of Ultra-Lube and Shooter's Choice, and a grooved plastic piece that held several sizes of copper brushes and cloth plugs. Zippered into the cover were several knotted cables with odd attachments and small ziplock bags of what looked like small paper squares of various sizes. In short, it was a gun cleaning kit.

Putting aside this strange and arcane collection, I peered again into the dark niche and pulled out a small spray can of Break Free CLP – more gun cleaning paraphernalia. Again placing that aside, I began to wonder what else might be in this secret cache. Reaching in again, this time I snagged a largish rectangular black plastic box with a molded handle. On the lid beside a stamped seal that said "Military" and "Police," I read the words "Smith & Wesson." Opening the lid, nestled inside in foam cutouts lay an automatic pistol and three loaded magazines. Additionally, there was this strange-looking plastic device labeled an UpLULA that accompanied the lot in its own cutout. It opened and closed much like a child's toy, but its true function totally escaped me.

Closing the black plastic box, I laid that too aside, and now beginning to feel a bit like an archaeologist, I reached into the dark yet again and pulled out a weighty cardboard box that said "Federal Ammunition – 100 Round Value Pack." In all, there were five other such boxes. Then, on the seventh attempt, a lighter, flatter cardboard box was revealed that said "Federal Classic Pistol Cartridges 50." There were another two such boxes found within. Now hefting several of the ammunition boxes, I could easily see why my attempt to move Richards' desk had been so difficult, as this corner had been weighed down so.

Now with my backside sore and going numb, I was about to lever myself up off the floor, when I then noted, to my ever-continuing surprise, that something else lay within the darkness. Reaching in, I pulled out from the hidden compartment's floor an old and heavily flattened manila envelope with several stains that reeked of the aforementioned oils and lubricants. Opening it, I discovered a manuscript, a manuscript that Richards and I had never before discussed within the provisions of the trust agreement. Nonetheless, I decided to take this "orphaned" work under my wing and edit it as if it were part of my original mandate.

As for the weaponry and ammunition, I donated it all to the local Chicago Police Station on South Ellis Avenue with the stipulation that a full forensic analysis be made of them. That analysis revealed that the pistol, magazines, and carrying case were all covered with a single set of palm and fingerprints, those of Joseph Richards. The serial number on the weapon had been expertly removed, but through a trace placed upon the ammunitions' lot numbers, it was found that they were all purchased by the military. The analysis also mentioned that the weapon had been modified, its grip made smaller, its trigger pull lessened, and its hard-mounted sights replaced with green tritium ones. In summary, it was judged a well broken-in weapon "that was really sweet to fire" and was loaded "to pack a punch sufficient to drop an animal the size of a cow." This last assessment was based upon the fact that the pistol's three seventeen-round magazines were loaded with "nine-millimeter, 147 grain, Hi-Shok, hollow points," judged "a perfect load for home defense." As for the mysterious UpLULA, I was told that it was for the easy loading of magazines and that it was especially prized by those with arthritic hands.

Up until the discovery of this weapon and its associated items, I was not aware of any hard evidence whatsoever that might have lent any credence to the contents of the four manuscripts. Now, with this weapon in hand, so to speak, I am no longer all that sure. Consequently, I find myself entirely rethinking and reconsidering this series, and that troubles me.

I have mentioned already in the previous editorial notes of the first three manuscripts that while I am an editor of a university press, the subject matter of these narratives cannot be published under our house banner. So, I have again sought out the good graces of a local nonacademic publishing house. As a result of that collaboration, you now hold the fourth manuscript of the series, originally a trilogy, now clearly a quadrilogy.

As for this manuscript, and based upon its internal details, it is clear that the events described within occurred during Richards' eighth and ninth years of his university employment, just after the passing of Peter Borov and John Milson and his promotion from associate to full professor. As to why Richards did not incorporate these details toward the end of his third manuscript, *Children of Ptah*, I have not a clue, as that is where they naturally belong.

Furthermore, this manuscript, unlike the previous three, is far shorter, is a departure from the usual ancient Egyptian time travel fare, and offers a possible explanation for the course of some current events. Additionally, again unlike the others, this manuscript required a full-blown edit, as in its original state, it was a bit of a hash. So, I have taken full editorial license here and there to fill in and occasionally expand upon certain passages in order to assist the reader.

Since this manuscript's publication, Richards has been missing for some seven and a half years. His trail ends in Egypt with an empty hotel room and unused bed. His brownstone flat, now long sold, similarly offered no clues as to his whereabouts. It is as if the Egyptologist has fallen off the face of the earth.

So, as with the first three manuscripts, all advances and royalties from the publication of this fourth manuscript will be deposited into the Richards' Trust, where they will be divided equally among several designated funding instruments. Once any of these instruments reach a specified threshold, then that threshold is to be reduced by seventy-five percent, and the apportioned amount is to be distributed equally in the following manner: to a preexisting offshore bank account, as seed money for the establishment of an endowed chair in Egyptian philology at Richards' home institution, and as research grant funds to a West Coast prostate cancer research institute. Once the specified thresholds are again reached, then the cycle is to begin anew with an equal apportionment of funds to the same entities. Once the copyright limitation has been reached on this publication, then all instruments are to clear their accounts to the above established entities in one final, lump sum deposit, and the Richards' Trust extinguished.

PROLOGUE
April 2010. Shanghai, China

He didn't want to be at this international radiological congress, but his superiors had sent him to keep his eyes and ears open for any potential advances worthy of pursuing. He had endured the first two days well enough, but by the third, the agent's patience had worn thin. He had exhausted his inventory of professional small talk, and frankly, his face ached from all the polite smiling.

Then, at the end of the third day of sessions, he caught wind of a remark made by a retired Egyptian academic that was more than intriguing, something about an amputation performed by an industrial laser.

The agent sought out the aforementioned academic, suggested they have dinner to discuss mutual interests in radiological interpretation, and that the agent's home institution would cover the bill. Consequently, the invitation was accepted, and the evening's professional conversation went well, especially after the second round of martinis.

The Egyptian academic, the former chair of the Radiological Sciences Department at the Cairo University Medical School, was Professor Dr. Ali Hassan. And indeed it was true that he had seen the radiographs of an extraordinary amputation, which had cleanly removed a right hand at mid-wrist. As the third martini was deftly applied, the radiologist waxed lyrical about the limb's fused bone, the precision of the hand's removal, and the lack of evidence that would have pointed to a mechanical amputation.

"My friend," the retired professor embellished, "it must have been an accident involving a very powerful industrial laser, or a medical procedure using one, because I cannot think of any other kind of power that literally melts bone with such precision."

Nodding in thought, the agent probed a little harder.

"But professor, where was this procedure undertaken?"

"I have no idea," the academic replied. "Must have been at either a European or American operating theater. But . . ."

No longer pretending to hang onto the good professor's every word, the agent pushed a little more.

" 'But' what, sir?"

Shaking his head and examining his hands, the professor said, "It was very strange, this amputation, as it was not a recent procedure. In fact, the area in question was well healed, callused, and fully calcified, indicating that it was an old wound. My colleague, who had brought this case to my attention, was very mysterious about the origin of the radiographs in question. Afterward that troubled me.

"And there is more. I thought I saw some suspicious shadows in the radiographs that my colleague never addressed or commented upon."

Now genuinely curious, the agent prodded yet again, "What sort of shadows? Shadows from improper development? A miscalibrated X-ray machine perhaps?"

"No, no, I thought that too at first, but upon reflection, the shadows were too uniform to be produced by either of those issues."

Now leaning forward across the remains of what had been a sumptuous dinner, the Egyptian stated in a hoarse whisper, "The shadows looked to be bandages, as in mummy bandages. I well know that this sounds insane, but I have been reading X-rays for over fifty-five years."

Deeply immersed in the fantastic possibilities of this radiological mystery, the agent then absentmindedly asked,
"When did you last see these X-rays?"

"Some thirty years ago. Now do you have a better appreciation of my reticence regarding this subject?"

CHAPTER I
Philology Annex

Across the northern hemisphere that year, spring had been pleasantly mild with plenty of warm rain. As a result, the buds were exploding on the trees and well-manicured bushes of Chicago's south side university campus. Once brown lawns were turning green at least where the winter's street salt hadn't intruded. With a deep intake of breath, one would be rewarded with a loamy fragrance, proof positive that the Jack Frost's grip upon the city had ended. Here and there colorful perennials were poking through the heaving soil. Vagrant breezes off the lake had given up their north wind harshness and were actually warm. What a concept.

In the fading sunlight of that late afternoon, figures hurried across the campus, some to parties and others to catch an early dinner. Others had a more serious reason for being out and about, for a mandatory five-o'clock meeting had been scheduled at the Philology Annex. Such a summons from the dean of humanities was not to be trifled with.

As for the Philology Annex itself, it had been purchased from the university by a private party during a financial downturn. Upon approaching the three-story brownstone, one was first greeted by low wooden signage tastefully sized with well-polished brass roman letters. The structure's wood trim had been freshly painted the previous September in a dark brown that matched the brickwork. Four concrete steps led up to the centerpiece of the building's exterior: its architectural entrance and brass kick plate. One twist of the warm brass doorknob signaled that this was not a university-owned facility, for it wasn't a crash door or simple latch. It was instead the entrance to a home of sorts that beckoned and greeted its visitors.

Early on during the brownstone's purchase, the buyer had been portrayed as a friendly one that promised to benefit said institution. That benefit was delivered in the coin of a research institution dedicated to the ancient languages of Western Asia and the Near East. Both faculty and students were free to peruse the Annex's resources for the modest fee of fifty cents a semester.

The three floors of the Annex had their own kitchenette, lavatories, seminar room, and library holdings devoted to Phoenician and Aramaic, Persian, Akkadian, and Sumerian, and the various periods of Egyptian. Scattered about were gently sloped desks built of well-worn woods and individual light fixtures with various intensities. The aroma of fresh coffee and pipe tobaccos scented the air, while cigarettes were forbidden.

Throughout an emphasis was placed upon polished woods: the floors, staircases, moldings, window casements, chairs, and of course shelving. The whole glowed warm and invitingly, and the mildly pervasive smell of wood polish only reinforced the impression.

The entire ambiance seemed to deny the wearing of noisy street shoes. So the order of the day was slippers, either your own or temporary ones provided by the Annex, again for the modest fee of fifty cents. Needless to say, such an environment with so many convenient amenities invited their use. It was not uncommon to find a solitary library rat in earnest study or a couple huddled in quiet conversation at all hours of the day or night.

The Annex's foyer was dominated by a central reception desk, with the Head Librarian's milky white glass door directly behind it. To the left and right were individually labeled cubbyholes for the storage of street shoes and slippers. The staircase to the second floor was on the right, just past the entrance to the first floor's library. The floor's seminar room was to the left, opposite.

Since the reception desk was the first thing every visitor to the Philology Annex encountered, certainly the most memorable impression was made by its inhabitant, Ms. Jennifer Ann Kelly. A middle-aged, alpha cougar if there ever was one, this lean strawberry blond, with a dapple of freckles across her delicate nose and cheekbones, regularly froze with her measured gaze male underclassmen in their tracks, while earning the immediate ire of females that crossed her threshold. All others she coolly ignored. Originally from central Minnesota, Kelly was a secretarial dynamo without peer and a true managerial asset. Most believed that the Head Librarian reported to her, instead of the other way around, as she had been employed by the Annex since its inception.

However, there was another side to Ms. Kelly, a second employer, a very black one that was based in a Virginia suburb. Somehow, her second employer could not bring itself to trust what the American and Russian Academy of Sciences might be up to. Placed as Kelly was, Jennifer Ann Borgensen being her true name, her second job was to report back what she could about the everyday goings-on at the Annex.

Today was just one of those special days, when visitors would appear, walk into their respective washrooms, and disappear. While Jenny would pretend not to notice this odd behavior, she did note down the basics: who, when, and for how long. She had long suspected that the Annex had a secret basement conference room, but she had no clue how to access it. So she sat behind her massive flat screen, typing away at her e-mails, and sending them off to parts unknown.

During the natural course of events, Kelly's divided loyalties had been discovered by the Annex's security detail and its sophisticated monitoring system. Nonetheless, she was retained, as the security personnel were curious as to who planted her and why. What they did ascertain was that the comely Minnesotan, while quite a head turner, nonetheless performed her tasks in a remarkably efficient manner. So their final decision was simply, watch and wait.

Not everyone at the university and in the Philology Annex's employ could legitimately use the front entrance as easily as the humanists did. Instead, and much to their often expressed displeasure, the hard sciences faculty had to use a secret side entrance located in the windowless gangway shared by the next-door brownstone.

Despite all of these perceived privations, all twenty-two guests managed to arrive at the agreed upon location by five o'clock, with the exception of two: a certain physicist, Professor Dr. Ernst Jung, who was in Munich at the time, and the second temporal field operative, Vesna Gregorieva. But unknown to those in attendance, two others would be added to this select group, having fought their way from O'Hare Airport across town through the mid-day traffic and perennial road construction.

* * *

Ms. Kelly did not know that the Philology Annex actually had two sub-basement levels in addition to its original. These highly secured areas were dedicated to the grueling linguistic training that the Annex's temporal field operatives must undergo. After all, if you make a temporal drop, you need language training in order to blend in, per the rules established by "The Guidelines of Temporal Exploration," or *RUTI*. But if the language is a dead one, how can you possibly learn it? Put simply, you can't, unless of course you have a place to learn the language, or even better, someone to talk to.

Enter Alexander Andreovich Piankoff, the first temporal field agent of the Philology Annex and favored grandson of the famous Russian Egyptologist Alexandre Piankoff, who as a young boy developed a fluency in Middle Egyptian that was phenomenal. It was rumored that he and his grandfather spoke to one another in the tongue.

However, at the time his country had a dire need for soldiers instead of Egyptologists. So young Piankoff was slotted early on as a candidate for a special KGB department. Devoted to watching the *Rodina*'s own scientists, this department's mandate was to prevent defections, in addition to detecting any foreign or domestic espionage. That department was called the

Special Projects Directorate and Karlov Drazinzka was its director.

From its very infancy, the calibration of the temporal device, nicknamed the Soap Bubble, had remained the one core issue and stumbling block that had to be overcome. After all, what good is a time machine if you do not know *when* you are? After herculean effort, the device's calibration did progress, but only to a point, and a very crude one at that. During the early 1990s, the solution became apparent to all, and especially to the device's inventor, Peter Borov, himself a defector from the *Rodina* to the United States. The only way to achieve an accurate calibration was to send some brave soul back, who would then return with the much-needed astronomical data. So just after the breakup of the U.S.SR in January of 1992, Borov reached out to his former countrymen and colleagues, asking for help, and they sent Piankoff. This led to the early pact struck between the American and Russian Academies of Sciences.

The plan was to drop Piankoff into an ancient period well-known to modern Egyptology, *somewhen* during the long reign of the Pharaoh Amenhotep III. The Russian's rudimentary preparation included: a shaved head, the removal of all his stainless steel crowns, gold or silver teeth fillings, full body tanning, the attire of a *sem*-priest of Ptah, a forged papyrus that explained his scholarly quest, and a crudely fashioned sextant-like instrument made of tamarisk wood, a tree native to ancient Egypt. And one last thing, the Russian was to pose as a mute, hence removing his need to speak the long dead language.

His first drop was placed within the most holy of holies of the Karnak Temple devoted to the god Amen Re in ancient Thebes. It was judged that his sudden appearance on the scene would have no witnesses, just as would his sudden disappearance when he returned to his own time. Since this arrangement worked so well, more temporal drops and retrievals took place within that darkened, incense-filled chamber.

As a credentialed *sem*-priest of Ptah, Piankoff's scholarly mission was to collate on the behalf of his home temple in Memphis any and all king lists that might be present within the library archives, or *per ankh*, of the Karnak Temple. The high priests of Ptah and their scholarly order were well known and respected for their acumen. Consequently, this archival research was readily granted, and comfortable quarters, meals, and other amenities were provided to their scholarly visitor.

And so Piankoff's day was devoted to this scholarly pursuit, while his sensitively attuned ears recorded the rich sounds, guttural explosions, and near musical cadences of the late Eighteen Dynasty Egyptian dialect. Then, at night, he would visit the roof of a particular pylon within the temple's complex and from its unobstructed view would "shoot" a particular star's location in the sky, at approximately the same time, and dutifully record the results in his personal papyrus roll.

To Piankhotep's surprise, for that was his adopted Egyptian name, he found that his astronomical observations were not considered odd in any way, as nearly each and every night he was joined from an adjacent overlook by several priests, who performed their own observations of the Milky Way's stellar vastness. After one week's time, Piankoff was retrieved along with his papyrus of recorded stellar observations, his trusty wooden sextant, and a head full of the sounds of a dead language.

In all, Piankoff endured four drops as the mute priest, with each return and retrieval timed in such a way that his stay at the temple appeared to be seamless. By his fourth retrieval, Piankoff had amassed a sufficient body of linguistic material to create a series of language tapes, to train additional field operatives on how to speak the Egyptian dialect of the period. These language drills, exercises, and, yes, even tests, were recorded and stored in the second sublevel of the Philology Annex. Both Richards, and Piankoff's replacement, the lovely dancer Vesna Gregorieva, were the beneficiaries of this man's extraordinary linguistic gifts, not to mention extreme bravery.

As for the wily Russian, he was made the unprecedented sole recipient of two Lenin Crosses for valorous achievement in his service to his mother country and to mankind. He was made an honorary member of the Russian Academy of Sciences, and was posthumously promoted from Colonel to Major General of Special Operations by his proud superior, Drazinzka.

*　　*　　*

"Good evening, ladies and gentlemen," the Oxford accented voice of Dr. Paul Young, the Dean of Humanities, began. "If you look around you, you will see that we have two additional colleagues in our midst, none other than Dr. Charles O'Brian Naysmithe, the Director and Chief Investigator at Horizon Pass, and

Commander Charles Abraham "Tuna" Cartwright, retired."

A smattering of polite academic applause broke out.

"Ahem. Yes. Charlie and Tuna, no pun intended of course, have just flown in all the way from our Horizon Pass facility located in God-knows-where, New Mexico."

Bubbles of chuckles emanated from the assembled. Then Young continued.

"Given the full house, you are correct in assuming that today's discussion is of the utmost importance. I yield the floor first to Commander Cartwright."

Gathering some note cards before him in his thick and heavily callused hands, the former Special Forces officer and chief security officer settled himself in behind the podium. Now attired in a gray pin-striped suit instead of his usual army greens or desert cammies, Tuna unconsciously remembered to stand straight and tall. Nonetheless, a slim bead of sweat threaded its way down the side of his closely trimmed gray hair.

"Dear colleagues," he began, "I find it a bit rich that I am nervous standing before all of you brainy folks. I was trained to decisively act and give orders, not to discuss and ask for permission. But here goes.

"Frankly, we have several security problems that we need to discuss and address. What we decide today will have ramifications, which will have broad impacts upon how we will do business in the future.

"As you know, recently the temporal device and our very own temporal field assets have been threatened on two separate occasions by foreign interests. The first incident occurred in Icelandic airspace when our aircraft experienced a missile attack. The result of that encounter was the splashing of the unknown aggressor and the capture of five accomplices at an Icelandic airfield.

"The second incident was even more blatant. While preparing a temporal drop site in the open desert in Sakkara, Egypt, a highly trained and equipped death squad stalked and attempted to grab the Soap Bubble directly from my security force. A nighttime firefight commenced, while our temporal field personnel were on the scene. Twelve individuals were killed. We are fortunate that we did not suffer any casualties.

"As to who was behind these two attempts, on the Soap Bubble and our temporal field personnel, there can be no doubt. It was our Russian colleagues. We have evidence in hardware, tactics used, and personnel. Again, there can be no question. There can be no doubt."

At the enunciation of this verdict, silence filled the room, for many had already suspected who the culprits were. Nonetheless, a question was posed by an economics professor, well known for his progressive thinking and political preferences.

"Commander. Are you *absolutely* sure that it was the Russians?" he imperiously asked with an exaggerated raised right eyebrow. "Furthermore, I heard through the grapevine that the fighter jet who attacked ours was Syrian. Is that true?"

Seeing these queries as a classic softball opportunity, Cartwright decided to swing for the fence.

"First of all, thank you, sir, for your questions. I am *absolutely* sure that the threat was Russian. As for the aircraft itself, it was of Libyan origin and perhaps even its pilot as well. The missile that it deployed, however, was not, as it was a heat-seeking, air-to-air missile, either a medium- or long-range Vympel R-27TE, also known by its NATO designation as the AA-10 Alamo. Furthermore, the missile was a purpose-built dude that was designed to cripple our airframe, not kill it. This weapon is specifically designed for use on the Russian MIG, SU, and YAK fighter airframes.

"Next question."

However, the same professor was not sufficiently cowed by this masterful display of military arcana, even though he visibly winced at the commander's use of the word "kill." His still raised hand indicated that he wanted more clarification.

"Commander. You also mentioned in your remarks that your evidence, which *suggested* Russian involvement, included personnel. What did you mean by that?"

"Again, sir, thank you for your question. By personnel, I meant personal effects, body type, blood type, and of course, any identifying marks, specifically tattoos. In the Sakkara incident particularly, several of the aggressors had tattoos on their persons that established them as former Russian Special Forces."

The professor then followed up. "So, Commander, if the aggressors, as you put them, are former Russian Special Forces, what you are really saying is that you are not actually sure who they currently worked for?"

Stunned by the nature of the question, Cartwright forgot that he was miked as he glanced over at Dr. Young and murmured, "Just how did this puke get in here?"

Naturally, the entire audience heard his aside as a wave of hand-covered snickers erupted. As for the economics professor, his skin turned to a brilliant beet red at hearing the off-the-cuff remark.

Realizing too late his *faux pas*, Cartwright surged ahead.

"Ahem. My apologies, sir. The tattoos that we encountered were exclusively worn, and proudly I might add, by the Russian *Spetsnaz*, their elite military commando. Several examples were recovered from this death squad."

In response, the economics professor then retorted in triumph.

"So. Finally, Commander. Only 'several' out of the twelve you could positively identify as former Russian Special Forces!"

At this point, Cartwright had enough, rolled his eyes, and said, "Next question."

Fortunately, there were none, and so Cartwright summed up his presentation.

"In summation, ladies and gentlemen, we have to make a decision regarding the security of the temporal technology. Do we continue to deploy it around the globe as we have in the past? Or, since the Russians are so desperate to get their grubby meat hooks on the Soap Bubble, is now the time to mothball, or even shut down the project altogether?"

This news hit the audience hard, but not where one might first expect. Before anyone voiced an opinion on the matter, Dr. Young deftly introduced Charlie Naysmithe.

Tall, lean, and middle-aged, Naysmithe represented the second generation leadership of the Soap Bubble

Project. His long blondish hair, gathered neatly in a flowing ponytail, was the polar opposite of Cartwright's military bearing. But, as they so often say, appearances can be deceiving.

"Dear colleagues," Naysmithe began, "I suspect by your reactions to Commander Cartwright's closing remarks that many of you cannot believe your ears. So let me be clear, I totally agree with the commander. In fact, I firmly believe that our days as 'dabblers in time' are over. In point of fact, I believe our work is done, and the greatest task now before us is how to close down the project."

* * *

As Richards left the closed meeting, his mind was all abuzz. Closing down the project meant no more drops into another time, both for him and his partner, Vesna Gregorieva. Now, while the reality of that was a real stunner, the Egyptologist quickly rationalized that the gravy train had to end at some point. On the other hand, closing down the project also meant that he would not have to deal with the debilitating effects of the post-drop syndrome, or PDS, that even Doc Allen out at Horizon Pass was not able nail down. As best as the good doctor could surmise, passage through the extraordinarily powerful electromagnetic field of the temporal device caused his electrolytes to go on the fritz. Temporary bouts of dizziness, loss of balance, confusion, and blackouts occurred. Even more strangely, it seemed that the adverse symptoms only affected males, for only he and the late Piankoff suffered from them, but Gregorieva had not.

In the midst of these deep musings, as Richards made his way to the public entrance of the Annex, he spotted the comely secretary, and her, him. To chronicle the many dalliances that this pair had had over the past nine years would have filled a five hundred page novel, not to mention that intriguing 'interview' during his initial training as a temporal field operative. So impulsively, he stopped before her desk and asked with a grin, "Hey, Jenny, could I interest you in some dinner?"

Smiling broadly and wrinkling her pug nose in the process, she rather lazily performed a full body scan of the academic before she answered.

"I suppose. But just what did you have in mind?"

"Steak. I'm starved. How about you?"

"Hmmm," she purposefully drew out as she licked her lips.

"Let's see now," she said as she made quite a production of examining her watch. "It's only 6:35 and I'm due to be off at seven. Will that do? Or just how 'starved' are you?"

She parried as she slowly arched her back and stretched cat-like against her silk blouse. All that was missing was the extension of claws.

Ah, she thought, *boy, do I have him! Just look at those dilating pupils!*

Throughout this delicious performance of enticing body language and raging pheromone production, Richards could only continue to grin a goofy grin that went from ear to ear.

"Well, I guess that I am not that 'starved.' So I'll just hang out until seven up in the Egyptology carrel. I have some stuff that I want to look up."

"Yep, I'm totally dead meat," he said as he began to ascend the wooden stairs, full knowing that Kelly was watching his every tread.

* * *

It has to be recognized that pillow talk is as dangerous for the interviewer as the interviewee. It's a treacherous two-way street. Just one misstep, one slip of the tongue, and the jig's up. After the pair had thoroughly enjoyed their 'dessert' at Richards' flat following a marvelous steak dinner and two bottles of an Australian Shiraz, Kelly felt that it was high time to perform some good old-fashioned Mata Hari.

Mostly lost in a tangle of sheets and covers, Jenny peeked at her partner who was lying atop the same, buck naked.

"How can you do that?" she said from her den of warm cotton.

"Do what?"

"Just lay there out in the cold? Which reminds me, where's the heat in this place anyway? I'm freezing!"

"After what you just did to me, I just need to chill out. And it isn't that cold in here. Besides, aren't you from Minnesota?"

Silence.

"So, I have been wondering." Jenny said from the covers. "Ever since Mr. Piankoff was replaced with that insufferable worm Baxter, I often wondered why Mr. Piankoff left in the first place. One day he's its chief librarian and my boss, and the next, he's gone. Like poof! So what gives?"

The mention of Piankoff's name set off a firestorm of images in the Egyptologist's head. Initially, Piankoff was an insufferable jerk and S.O.B. Then during their first deployment, an understanding and basis of trust developed. During their subsequent adventures, a friendship had been forged from their many adversities, a true warrior's bond. Finally, unbidden, came the memory of his funeral beneath Red Square, which brought a moistness to Richards' eyes.

Ever the keen observer, Jenny took in the intake of breath and stiffness to a once very relaxed body, the faraway look that stared at the ceiling, a classic example of the thousand-yard stare, and even the falling of a tear.

My God, she thought, *that was a raw nerve I poked!*

And then, to her everlasting surprise, she got an answer. Stiffly, Richards choked out that the Russian had passed away rather suddenly several years back.

"How?" she dared.

"Bad water," was the initial laconic response that was quickly followed by the reason. "Parasites."

"Yuck!" Jenny genuinely gasped out.

Nonetheless, she now finally had absolute proof of the man's death, a bullet point that now could be permanently stricken from her long list of to-dos.

Now putting her to-do list aside, she returned to her favorite sport and began to delicately stroke a well-muscled thigh, idly allowed her fingers to wander, and suddenly, like a striking snake, she was again entwined in the Egyptologist's arms.

Richards whispered into her left ear as he nibbled on it.

"You talk too much."

Chapter II
Machinations

It was the thirty-fourth interview that the old imam conducted. The first thirty-three had yielded a mixture of ignorance and wishful thinking, but here and there were interspersed some intriguing rumors. Ever patient, ever persistent, the imam followed up on each of the leads, pulling at them as if they were the severed threads of a vast carpet that required repair. A carpet whose pattern and design were unclear, amorphous, and yet very, very tantalizing.

The trail had begun with a radiological academic who had an exceedingly elevated opinion of himself. Yet, his detailed knowledge of an improbably ancient mummy's X-ray was almost too good to be true, and just as unbelievable.

Could have an industrial laser accident occurred in 1980? Most certainly. CO_2 lasers were readily available by the 1970s. The problem was that while the mummy's X-ray dated to around 1980, the amputation itself occurred prior to that by some twenty to thirty years, at the very least!

This anomalous mummy amputation had led to an obscure, preliminary archaeological report by a Dutch university team. Within it was mentioned the discovery of a pristine mummy named Meryptah, a high priest of some god, no less. While the rest of his tomb had been lavishly published, there was no further mention of the mummy. Officially, the imam saw, the artifact seemed to disappear. Meanwhile, this same archaeological team seemed to have the Midas touch, for wherever they sank their spade, notoriety followed. First, they uncovered the Treasury of Amen-Re within the Karnak Temple's circuit. Then they found within it an intact glider and a manual for its operation.

While sourcing that team's membership, one individual, a young American Egyptologist, seemed the odd man out. But upon investigation, this same American turned out to be one very well-connected odd man. His name seemed to appear nearly everywhere, but always in a secondary role, buried in a footnote, making him a classic behind-the-scenes man. Yet, this youthful overnight sensation possessed an academic pedigree that was difficult to discern, a dissertation written on a knotty philological topic in a matter of months, then a sudden university appointment, and the production of a language textbook that was well received by the academic community. Strangely, it was his sporting background that had received more print.

While these threads were in and of themselves valueless, it turned out that the imam's meetings with several of the Egyptian Supreme Council of Antiquities support staff were quite interesting. Specifically with the guards themselves, those who secured Egypt's important cultural sites, they offered the most coherent insights.

Egypt, that vast open air museum, possessed a nearly endless supply of archaeological sites that were critical to its economy. Yet, clearly with the blessing of higher officials within the SCA bureaucracy, one such site was occasionally closed down, but only for brief periods. Even the French Archaeological Mission had been evicted for a time, an unprecedented act by the Egyptian archaeological authorities. Reportedly, over the last eight to ten years, strange nighttime events occurred within the Karnak Temple complex.

Then, in a flurry of recent activity, strange tales were told about the environs of Step Pyramid at Sakkara. Throughout all of these stories, mention was made of a particular truck, its striking, authoritative, and ranked American military driver, a Russian, the aforementioned young American, and once even the report of a breathtakingly beautiful woman. This last detail the imam had early on discounted as a pure fantasy, the stuff of a perverted watchman's daydreams.

Dressed in flowing religious robes and head wrapped in the appropriate manner, Aref Fardoust was the eldest son of Hussein Fardoust. Plump of face and with heavy eye folds like his father, Aref truly looked like an imam with his shaggy salt-and-pepper beard. An experienced and seasoned intelligence officer in Iran's Ministry of Intelligence and National Security, or SAVAMA, the successor institution to the infamous SAVAK of the Shah, Aref was a true credit to his ruthless late father's memory. While Hussein had led the SAVAMA, his only son, Aref, had implemented many of his father's intelligence gathering directives, creatively and with considerable success. In the process, Aref began to create his own following based upon his sheer reputation for acquiring sensitive data. When it came to divining what the Great Northern Satan of Russia or the Great Western Satan of the U.S. were up to, Aref would stop at nothing and seemed even to revel in the oftentimes gory details. So, when the strange rumors began to arrive at his section's desk about events in Egypt, Aref took the bit in his own teeth and began to search for the truth.

The current interview, as with the first thirty-three, began in an almost word-for-word, rote formulaic manner. Why, because Aref believed in consistency. *After all*, he concluded, *how else can one arrive at consistent data?* And so he began.

"May Allah bless you my son. I wish to thank you for your time to speak with me, an old man, as I know that it takes you away from your beloved family."

To the nodded response in acknowledgement, the imam then innocently asked, "Yousef Mohammed. Do you consider yourself a good Muslim?"

The question was designed to place the individual under examination on the defensive, and it always worked to some degree. It prompted quick professions of faith, shock at its cool directness, and sometimes even defensive body language. Usually, the eyes were the first hint of a potentially guilty individual. Sometimes nervousness with the question was betrayed by the hands or a simple bow of the head.

But to the imam's surprise, interviewee number thirty-four did not react as had the others. Instead, the security guard just sat there, confidently looking back directly and deeply into his interlocutor's eyes. After about twenty seconds of silence, he responded, and he did so with a polite certitude that was unnervingly noble in its manner.

"Indeed, Holy One, I am certain that I am a good Muslim. But I find the question posed an odd one, coming from you, as I am Sunni, and clearly, by your dialect, you are Shi'a. While we are both truly brothers of the Qur'an, we nonetheless occupy the opposite sides of a great philosophical rift."

Taking the time to gaze more fully into the guard's clear and unwavering brown eyes, the imam then unconsciously shifted in his robes in an attempt to disguise own his surprise and asked the guard directly, "I have been told that a great many strange things have occurred at Karnak while under your watch. Is that not so?"

Again the question was posed to place one on the defensive. But instead the blunt statement caused the fine laughing lines of the guard's face to wrinkle as he glanced down to briefly inspect his casually folded and relaxed hands. Again, after a brief pause, he looked up and said, "Indeed, Great One, 'a great many strange things' have occurred at Karnak. But they are merely a matter of record, as all of those disturbances were duly reported to the Luxor police authorities."

Hmmm, thought the imam, *was that a possible evasion? Still my subject remains calm. I see no sweat beads. His mouth remains relaxed. Is he slow of intellect? A mere simpleton? Given the nature of his position, that could be entirely possible.*

"Yes, yes. I know of those," the imam tersely stated, "for I have read them – several times. But what I am interested to know is what you might have seen with your own eyes or heard with your own ears during those disturbances."

After a moment, the guard asked with what he hoped would appear to be total, wide-eyed innocence, "Why?"

That one word, posed as it was, stopped the imam's interview dead in its tracks. Doubt now stood squarely before him as to whether any further pursuit of this interview would be even worth his time. Now tilting his head to one side, the imam asked again, while exposing the palms of his hands in near supplication.

"So, you claim to be a true pillar of Islam, a good family man, and yet you verbally spar with me. Why is that, my son? I am curious. What are you attempting to hide?" *And guess what, you moron, I am becoming more and more curious, and my questions are more than just ones of curiosity.*

To this the guard smoothly replied, "Holy One, your obvious curiosity is a natural thing. Truly a blessing from Allah himself. But still, Holy One, you refuse to answer my simple question of 'Why?' directly. And instead, you answer my question with one of your own. Now, Holy One, who truly is sparring with whom?"

This last verbal parry actually caused the imam to think, and in so doing his brow unconsciously became a deep and craggy furrow. This facial development was not lost on the guard, or for that matter the imam's previous nervous shifting beneath his robes, as he noted it and quietly thought, *Score one for my side. Now I have you really thinking.*

Now stroking his chin, the imam decided to play hard ball.

"You should know that this interview was arranged for by your superiors. I should advise you that your future career within the Supreme Council of Antiquities may be in the balance, may become precarious, as I was assured of your complete and total cooperation.

"Now, with that understanding made clear, let us begin again. Do you have anything to share with me about the strange things that were reported at Karnak?"

* * *

The director of the Egyptian National Museum in Cairo and her guest sat comfortably within a generously sized office that was brimming with overflowing bookshelves at every quadrant. The air was fresh and lightly perfumed as the cigar haze of her predecessor had been long removed.

Behind a proportionately massive desk sat an equally remarkable Egyptian woman. After all, she was the first woman to ever occupy that chair as the Director of the National Museum. Petite, lithe of form, and stunning enough to attract the persistent attentions of a global cosmetic empire, Dr. Sharil Moussa was a Cambridge University-trained specialist in Eighteenth Dynasty hieratic, the cursive scribal version of ancient Egyptian hieroglyphs. But Sharil was far more than an accomplished philologist. She was a seasoned field archaeologist as well, not to mention a maven of institutional organization and administration. Today, she was attired in a tailored black business suit with a skirt that ended just above her delicate ankles and low black pumps. The collar of her red silk blouse was worn high up against her regal neckline, the whole surrounded by a short strand of tasteful white pearls. Middle age had been kind to this accomplished woman, showing its mark only in a light graying of her once raven-black hair, which she wore in two sweeping shoulder length wings that framed her face. Leaning forward on her elbows, the director deliciously smirked.

"So, Joey, how'd it go?"

Sitting opposite Sharil, Joseph Richards had chosen to cover his taut, medium-sized frame with a tweed jacket and a pair of casual canvas pants. Open-collared and tieless, the American sat slouched to one side, while supporting his chin in his left palm.

With a slight sigh and a smile, he said, "I think that I confused and frustrated him. The best part was the dumb act that I played, which was taken hook, line, and sinker. But, Sharil, you were absolutely right. All those conversations, coincidences, and the diplomatic contact that you were privy to, they all were dead on. Knowledge of our activities, and in particular of a certain temporal device, has surfaced as subjects of interest. Clearly, a certain group with deep pockets is interested, and that big money would be awarded to anyone who could supply certain details. In all, I think that it's the Iranians who are behind this. His Farsi dialect was clear enough to my ears. If they are sniffing about, that really concerns me, and the folks back home.

"And then there are always the Russians. Are they not implicated as well in this nonsense?" Richards said with a dismissive shrug.

"Nevertheless, can you imagine what would happen if Iran somehow got the temporal device? The mere suggestion gives me the absolute willies!"

Nodding, the director agreed, "Yes. I too can only begin to imagine what they would do with it. No, this interested party is definitely not Russian. I also suspect that this group would dramatically change the course of history."

At first only silence came from the American, and then in a rush, "Sharil you have to be kidding! Are you referring to Charles Martel, the decisive clash of East versus West, and the resulting failure of the Umayyad conquest of Europe?"

"Indeed, Joey. And I am very pleased to see that your grasp of history extends beyond that of pharaonic Egypt. By the way, your willingness to turn actor and portray yourself as Yousef Mohammed to find out what that charlatan imam wanted was most brave of you. And Joey, you look quite handsome with that Egyptian moustache," she said with a dreamy sort of whimsical smile. She then thought to add, "I'm sure that my father would agree."

CHAPTER III
2689 BC. Mennefer

Nekhem was a born dreamer, a young man-child with exceptional eyesight and a strong and healthy frame. As for his name, it was the namesake of a far southern city. Yes, it was the place where he was conceived.

While still a lowly second-year *wab*-priest of the god Ptah, his dedication to this beloved deity had been established without question. Tangible proof of this was his quick mastery of the glyphs, especially for one so young, that assured his future within that scholarly temple community. Nekhem's family bubbled with pride at his achievement and was overjoyed at the many praises that the high priests and *sem*-priests of Ptah had heaped upon him.

Nekhem nonetheless remained a dreamer, and to harness and focus that marvelously energetic quality, one of his priestly mentors suggested a task befitting a dreamer with the eyes of a falcon: astronomy.

*   *   *

The young man's station was perched atop a tall, mud brick observation tower that was located within the whitewashed walls of the temple's precinct. From this lofty vantage, Nekhem enjoyed an unlimited view of the Lower Egyptian starscape from horizon to horizon. Even the many smoldering and aromatic cooking fires of Mennefer could not intrude upon his marvelous perch that faced the heavens.

Mounted at the tower's center was the delicate astronomical sighting tool that the *sem*-priest Sekemka had grudgingly entrusted to the youth. Quietly vexed at the combination of his own failing eyes and Nekhem's remarkable optics, the wizened astronomer priest had nonetheless taken a shine to the precocious youth and his seemingly boundless store of energy and curiosity.

Arranged along the upper surface of the tower's limestone parapet were 360 evenly spaced radiating grooves that pointed in all directions. A handy open wicker basket contained numerous smoothed river stones, each with meaningful markings carefully etched upon them.

Patiently tutored by Sekemka, Nekhem knew that he should first track and then mark with two stones whatever noteworthy event that might cross the evening sky. Once so marked, the sighting tool would then provide a precise astronomical bearing, which was to be recorded upon a potsherd with the carbonized end of a reed. And yes, Sekemka had even provided his charge with a wicker cylinder chock full of those.

With the brightening of the evening sky, Nekhem was to descend with his potsherds of stellar readings to the temple's *per ankh*, or House of Life. There they were laid out in their order of occurrence, discussed, interpreted, and then recorded in Sekemka's long astronomical journal of celestial observations. Before Nekhem could rest, however, the young astronomer-in-training had to wash all of his potsherds and lay them out to dry in the early morning sun.

It was on the seventeenth day of Ephiphi, third month of the harvest season, during the fifteenth year of the Pharaoh Khasekhemwy, the last king of the Second

Dynasty. On that evening Nekhem noted and dutifully recorded during the mid-passing of the night's cycle his first astronomical anomaly, not that the now-apprentice astronomer thought in those precise terms. For he had already witnessed with his young eyes the passing seasons of meteor showers and was familiar with the occasional rogue meteor, as well as the first appearance of the Dog Star. No. This was something new to his experience, something, frankly, quite odd. Perhaps the word "portent" would be more appropriate.

With mouth agape and eyes full of wonder, Nekhem witnessed the bright and clearly defined streak of light as it passed from the far horizon to a point overhead in what seemed a matter of moments. The brightness then continued on toward the opposite horizon. But what shocked the young man was that the bright streak descended into that vast, waterless wasteland known as the *deshret*, the Red Desert.

Automatically grabbing several stones from his basket, Nekhem expertly marked the course of the event. Then, with a quaver betrayed in his hands, he squared up his astronomical sighting tool and recorded what he had just seen.

I wonder if the venerable Sekemka has ever witnessed such a thing.

*   *   *

At its acme, the first capital of Egypt, Mennefer, later called by the Greeks, Memphis, was inhabited by perhaps as many as thirty thousand souls, a vast amount for such an ancient city. Yet, the importance of this urban complex was not based upon its much-revered temple to the god Ptah, but rather its location. This fact becomes clear when one recognizes that the town was situated astride the southern apex of the Nile's delta, making it an advantageous site for riverine commerce, the central administration of Egypt, and a strategic choke point that separated Upper from Lower Egypt. This last reality gave rise to Mennefer's well-known nickname "The Great White Wall" because of its soaring, whitewashed, and crenellated mud brick fortifications, which mimicked, if only in part, the high, white limestone desert escarpments that faced the settlement to the east and west.

Nonetheless, that early capital city during the late Second Dynasty supported a more modest population, perhaps only a couple of thousand strong, with modest accommodations, but still dominated by the Temple of Ptah at its center. But this early city was not alone, for it was surrounded by smaller agricultural hamlets that represented more a clustering of extended family units than anything else.

One of these settlements, Ankhtowe, "Life of the Lands," really a rural extension of Mennefer, was devoted to the fiercely protective lion goddess Bast. At the second hour of the morning market, a young man wandered into this helter-skelter gathering of mud brick structures and crudely delineated streets.

*   *   *

In another existence, another incarnation on this planet, I was called Ptah. I am what other space faring cultures call an Old One, one who observes, formulates, and acts as appropriate, occasionally planting some precious seeds of knowledge. My kind has worn countless faces, countless times, in countless places. In human terms, my kind is nearly immortal and we choose to nurture only those deserving, those with promise. Some might think of us as gods, but that would be a grand conceit, a far greater mistake.

After once sowing some rudimentary seeds on this third satellite, I then visited the rest of the system's orbiting planets and planetoids in the hopes of finding other opportunities for the encouragement of life, the sharing of knowledge, and perhaps even the development of something far greater, civilization.

Sadly, other than two frigid and icy moons of the fifth planet, my quest was empty, for all were lifeless. On the fourth satellite, where I spent considerable time on its examination, all I discovered was a dark reality. It had once harbored life abundant. But the fourth satellite's former inhabitants had chosen complete annihilation on such a scale that the satellite was nearly obliterated, its once cloudy atmosphere stripped away. It was made waste. How tragic.

As one can imagine, this careful sojourn took some time, and at its completion I decided to return to the third satellite because of a simple personal weakness, curiosity. I was eager to know whether my sown seeds had taken hold. I even dared to hope that they had flowered.

As I had centuries before, I, the Old One once called Ptah, again emerged from the Red Desert as a naked fair-skinned boy with hair the color of ripe wheat and eyes as green and brilliant as a wet lotus leaf. Reaching the brink of the rocky ledge that overlooked and separated that arid wasteland from the fertile river valley below, I stopped to take in the view and gasped.

It was breathtaking to behold how my seeds had grown! Oh, how they have progressed! The wild riverine jungle lands have been tamed. Now irrigated fields extend from the river to practically the base of this high and steep slope upon which I stand. And Mennefer is no longer just a rude collection of reed huts and a dozen cooking fires. It has grown into, dare I say, a small city. No, it's a walled and whitewashed city! I see everywhere evidence of population growth, centralized organization, and social complexity. I am again an explorer who must see with my own eyes what my heart yearns to see. And I am again a teacher, for they are clearly ready for the next lesson.

*   *   *

From that high prospect, the young man smiled and shook his head in frank admiration at the scene before him. He sadly realized that he could not return as his former self. So he decided to reinvent himself, and one with a worthy name.

As the young man carefully descended the slope toward the vast alluvial fields of cultivation, he ruminated on an appropriate name. And after a fashion, he again smiled.

I return in frank, peaceful, curiosity, ever the patient teacher of lessons. No, better, I am he who comes in peace. Yes, I am pleased with that formulation. Thus, they shall know me as Imhotep.

*   *   *

Sensitive in ways that few could understand, the young, naked, and sunburned Imhotep, searched among the streets of Ankhtowe for a childless couple to adopt as his surrogate parents. It did not take long for this powerful empath to find what he was looking for. As it turned out, the household was better than most: a two-story whitewashed mud brick structure complete with a baked brick first floor and a modest central courtyard. What had attracted the youth to this particular household was the sound of gentle singing that he vaguely recognized as the traditional bread dough-making song.

Daring to peek inside the drawn reed matting of the shadow-darkened doorway, Imhotep saw a middle-aged woman on her knees kneading a heavy mound of dough on a slab of smoothed limestone shaped for the purpose. She was heaving her way through the process with obviously painful and arthritic hands. Entering, he croaked out with his dry throat the needed words in the regional Predynastic dialect that he had previously acquired.

"Venerable One, mightest I haveth a portion of water?"

Surprised by this sudden intrusion into her wandering thoughts, Khereduankh nearly jumped out of her skin. But upon seeing just who had done so, a very dusty and sunburned young boy, she broke into a broad smile.

Pointing, she said, "There, child. The open beaker. Drink your fill."

Crossing from the threshold to the container indicated, Imhotep drank dry its cool contents, smacking his cracked lips with delight.

While he was so engaged, Khereduankh observed him. *Who is this strange boy that I have never before seen? With his odd words? Is he a runaway from one of the tribes of the Western Desert? His fair hair and complexion would easily mark him as one of their own. Perhaps he is instead the son of a merchant trader, who has become lost within the maze of our settlement or that of nearby Mennefer. Or is he just an orphan?*

These thoughts were broken when Imhotep, now finished with the reused beer jar, for that was what it was, wiped his hand across his mouth, grinned, and then ran out of the house.

Shocked yet again, Khereduankh, still kneeling and far too stiff to rise, could only blurt out, "You ungrateful scamp! Come back with my water jar!"

Refusing to be so easily pillaged, the thirty-year-old woman dusted off her hands and began levering herself up on two legs that had unfortunately gone asleep. Finally struggling into a standing position, the much beloved wife of the master architect Kanofer began to stagger badly yet again, but did not fall as a cool wet hand was there to steady her. Startled yet again, she found that the young scamp was back at her side. Holding under one arm a refilled jar, upon his return, he caught her with his other.

"Careful, Venerable One. Dost thou think so ill of me that I wouldst not return thine kindness with a fresh fill of water?"

Khereduankh, stunned still by the youth's dialect, for the first time looked deeply into his striking green eyes with her squinting eyes and wrinkled brow. While understanding the gist of the young one's speech, she could not for the life of her place it.

Imhotep, mistaking her demeanor as anger, countered with a bowed head, "Venerable One, mayest

I help knead the bread dough in payment for thine generosity?"

Again understanding what was said, but not how it was said, Khereduankh nodded in the direction of the still rising dough. And as if the many surprises of the day would not end, she saw the boy first place the water jar back in its place and then proceed to wash his face, arms, and hands in the basin nearby. Once so cleansed, Imhotep plopped down, sitting on his ankles, and got down to work.

*   *   *

"Who is this?" whispered her husband Kanofer, the architect, in genuine curiosity.

"I do not know my husband. It is strange. He appeared at the entrance of our household begging for water during the first hour after the midday meal. And before I knew it, he was preparing the bread for our evening meal, and then straightened up the kitchen as if he knew where everything was meant to be placed. But even stranger is how well behaved he is and what a calming nature he possesses. It is as if he were our own son assisting his mother."

Throughout this explanation, Kanofer, with his callused hands resting on his hips, listened while he watched the lad in the kitchen area cut up a bunch of ripe figs with the household's prize obsidian knife.

"So, what's his name?"

"My husband, I do not know. He has been so busy, so helpful, that I forgot to ask."

CHAPTER IV
A Blast from the Past

Professor Joseph William Richards sat at his desk poring over his latest edits to the third edition of his textbook, *The Scribe's Way*. This remarkable grammar of the ancient Egyptian's language, which had been his dissertation and his first professional publication, had launched his academic career. Uncannily popular with students and even some of his colleagues, Richards found himself tweaking the manuscript here and polishing it there, as if he was a jeweler buffing a beautiful gem.

One new innovation was the inclusion of oral dictation exercises that both challenged and demanded of the student a thorough mastery of the glyphs and their grammar. Richards would never forget that first surprise dictation exercise he had sprung upon his students. What he had witnessed was absolute, wide-eyed panic that resulted in a marked and renewed vigor in their industry. No doubt as a consequence, there occurred an outbreak of some rather imaginative and colorful Egyptian graffiti on campus, which was strategically chalked onto walls and sidewalks where he was known to pass, near the Near Eastern Institute and Faculty Club. Universally, they revealed what his charges thought of his "innovative" teaching methods.

Perhaps it was only natural, but two of his colleagues found the phenomena humorous, good PR for the department, and queried Richards on whether or not these extracurricular efforts should not be considered gradable. In particular, two rather bawdy ditties came to mind that caused Richards to chuckle at their appropriateness. But that train of thought was shattered by a polite knock on his open doorframe.

"Excuse me, but I'm your ten-o'clock appointment," said the brown-haired man in sneakers, careworn blue jeans, a bright orange Chicago Bears tee-shirt, and an open, dark blue Patagonia shell vest.

Peering through his round, wire-rimmed reading glasses, Richards took in the local newspaper reporter, flashed a grin, and waved in his former student.

"Take a chair, Jake. It's damn good to see you again," he said, rising and extending his best welcoming handshake from across the mound of paper on his desk. "So what's it been? A couple of semesters since we last spoke?"

Jake Greenwood, now displaying on his patented, sheepish grin at Richard's pointed directness, shrugged his narrow shoulders.

"Nope Doc. More like only ten months. Right after you got back from Egypt and the opening of the Amen Re Treasury. Now that was that some interview! My editor at the *Chicago Tribune* was really stoked when I pitched it to him. It got me a raise and a minor promotion too."

Richards also remembered that interview, all the flashy newsprint it had generated, the effusive praise from the humanities dean, and then all the carefully veiled heat and animosity that had been directed his way by some of his colleagues. Even the chair had chosen to ignore the publicity, but did not once regret the uptick in departmental enrollments, even if it had meant overloading young Richards' introductory classes in ancient Egyptian, which represented a sizable departmental windfall.

Seeing the faraway look, Jake asked, "So, Doc, after all the fuss and feathers, all the hoopla, how are things – *really*?"

Snapping out of his thoughts, Richards replied, "So Jake, now you're my shrink too?"

"No, not really. It's just that I saw one of your classic thousand-yard stares. That's all. I don't know if you know this, but there were a handful of times in class, when you did drift off into space."

Smiling back at the young reporter with a crocodile grin, Richards stated the obvious, "Okay Jake. Enough with pleasantries and the all-too-happy school memories. What's up my friend?"

"Well, Doc, I'm here fishing. That's all," he said with an infectious grin as broad as the Mississippi.

"Just hoping to find another blockbuster story from my blockbuster source. So, what do ya' have for me?"

"Jake. Dude! Do you have any idea what happened around here the last time I gave you a 'blockbuster' interview?"

Now with eyes wide with innocence.

"No, Doc. Did you get a raise? A promotion? Or better, laid by some fawning movie star?"

Richards, with his eyes rolling, could only shake his head.

"No, Jake. You're not getting *that* story. But do you know about that recent discovery at Memphis? The one about the Austrian excavation at the Temple of Ptah?"

"Yeah. How couldn't I? It was all over the Internet, the print media, and the cable news. So what about it?"

"Well, specifically this: did you know that the lead archaeologist, a guy named Ulrich Schachermeyr, was a close friend of our own department's Professor John Milson?"

"Nope."

"Did you know that John influenced Schachermeyr at a very young age to go into Egyptology?"

"Nope."

"Did you know that Schachermeyr's father was a big-time Classicist?"

"Nope."

"Then start looking around. You will get quite an interesting story, and more importantly, one that does not include me."

Now it was Jake's turn to wear the thousand-yard stare. Richards did not dare move a muscle in fear that he would break that spell until the young man had returned to the here and now.

Finally, Jake asked, "You know. Doc, about this god Ptah. I seem to remember that he was thought to be an actual person who was later deified. Is that right?"

"Yep, you remember right. You must've been taking notes that day instead of sleeping," Richards replied with a smirk.

"Did that happen a lot in ancient Egypt? What I mean is, did other normal folks get deified too?"

With his chin in hand, Richards considered the question, paused two seconds, and then said, "To pharaohs, all the time. But to commoners, not often. In fact, I can think of only one other, a fellow named Imhotep."

"You mean that evil mummy guy with all the flesh-eating blue beetles!" Jake exclaimed excitedly, linking the name to several movie baddies. In response, Richards pummeled him with a wadded up paper ball.

"No, you wild man. I mean Imhotep the architect. Imhotep the physician. Imhotep of Memphis. The god Imhotep."

After a thoughtful pause, Jake said, "So. Both Ptah and Imhotep were from the same hometown then?"

"Seems so."

"How interesting. Didn't know that. Thanks, Doc. I think I have all I need. See ya. And thanks."

As the reporter took his leave, Richards looked down and pretended to return to his editing, but his trained and drug-enhanced eidetic mind was elsewhere and in high gear.

What is it about Memphis? First Ptah, and then Imhotep. I wonder if there is some sort of a connection?

*   *   *

It was getting on toward early evening, and Richards' stomach had already spoken about its neglected condition. Finished with the editing of his book, he had moved on to a mound of midterm blue books that seemed to be multiplying, instead of declining. His eyes were shot from reading them, deciphering their god-awful handwriting, and trying to grasp their oftentimes convoluted logic.

I just got to get these exams online somehow. And while that idea was still bouncing around in his head, he thought he heard something.

A moment later, he again heard it. It was a gentle knock on the milky glass of his office door. Looking up from his grading, Richards said simply, "Enter."

Sighing and looking down at his wristwatch, the Egyptologist figured that anyone visiting him at this hour had to be desperate for a grade. Holding his head in his hands as a hunger headache was beginning to brew between his temples, he said, a bit muffled, "Can I help you?"

"Perhaps," returned a voice rich and full of life.

Now looking up to see just who his visitor was, the Egyptologist went slack-jawed, for he recognized those green eyes. *Green eyes that no one else could possibly possess. But*, he rationalized, *that just can't be. I must be mistaken.* So he winged it.

Half-standing behind the barrier of his desk, he gestured and said without preamble, "Please take a seat."

At the courteous offer, his visitor sat. He was a middle-aged man of slight build with tawny hair worn at a roguish length that tumbled over his ears. It was further messed up as he had just removed his Panama fedora, which he held in clean, but heavily callused hands. The man must have liked the rumpled hat as there were sweat stains on its broad cloth band. His clothes were foreign to typical American tastes, being made of wool blends by the look of them. The gray baggy cuffed pants and lived-in overcoat of a dark tweed and undetermined style were definitely not domestic. A white shirt collar poked out vertically from his burgundy sweater. His shoes, well, they were worn black leather and sorely needed a shine.

"Now, what can I do for you?" the academic bravely said with his hands tightly clasped before him as if in prayer.

With those damnable smiling green eyes, the visitor then said in an odd accent, "Professore Richards. *Ciao bello!* I haf come all de vay from Roma to speak with you."

That odd accent was distinctly Italian to Richards' ears, but that boyishly unwrinkled face, those eyes, were all owned by someone else. So Richards stood, rounded his desk, and closed the office door, all the while observing his visitor from 360 degrees.

Again sitting, the Egyptologist decided to pop the question and said in the ancient Egyptian tongue, "So, Great One. It has been some time since we last spoke. Since *you* last disappeared. I trust that your health has been good?"

Now smiling a truly memorable smile, the visitor's green eyes seemed to dance and crinkle in pleasure at the sound of that most ancient Egyptian of dialects.

"Thank you, most noble Mayneken, for honoring me so. You are most perceptive. The old tongue is much easier for me to speak. And yes, it has indeed been some time since we last spoke. What, some five thousand rotations by your reckoning? And as for my sudden departure, well, my work was finished. My seeds were sown. The presence of you and the most beautiful Maatkare was ample proof of that. And finally, as for my health, I am."

"So why are you here? Now? In Chicago? And why from Rome?"

Sitting back, the visitor showed his open hands, palms forward.

"So many questions, so many questions!

"Well, where do I begin? I suppose curiosity. I do not know whether you know it or not, but this is my third visit to your marvelously beautiful land, so full of wonder, promise. The first time is when we met in old Mennefer. I had adopted the name Ptah at the time. I was a teacher. It was there and then that I sowed my first seeds: the necessity of good hygiene, rudimentary medicine, and irrigation agriculture. My second visit was several hundred cycles later. Then I adopted the name of Imhotep, an architect by trade, and sowed more seeds, but specifically the notion that Egypt should become unified, instead of a collection of minor and competing communities."

To this revelation, Richards unconsciously jerked in his chair and took a deep breath of pure disbelief.

The visitor, noting this, innocently asked, "Noble Mayneken, do you know of this?"

"Oh, yes. Oh, yes indeed. Trust me when I tell you that you made quite an impression in that incarnation. Bad enough you were worshipped as a god in your first. As Imhotep, your name was forever after held in quite high regard. You, after all, were the one who built the Step Pyramid of the Great Horus Djoser! You were even later deified, again, I might add," Richards remarked with a smirk.

"Hmmm. How strange. I would never have guessed that such things would come to pass. Does that sacred place on the western horizon still stand that my adopted father and I caused to build?"

"Indeed it does, even if the passage of time has been occasionally cruel. A Frenchman named Lauer devoted his entire life in its restoration. Today, it is a famous tourist destination."

Again that smile, and then he continued, "But once again, Mayneken, I have returned to see how my seeds have grown. Again, my curiosity. And now, there are many things that I like, and as it must be, much that I dislike. So it goes as that is the way of things. The way civilization develops. Many times it is like a young one struggling to walk. Sometimes it is funny, sometimes not.

"But to answer your question, your world has learned the unification lesson very well, perhaps too well. It is now time that the simple lesson of sharing must be taught and learned. And, by now, I would have thought that this new lesson had been learned. After all, my galleries and the tomb of my adopted parents have been found. This I know, because while at the Vatican I read about the discovery of my galleries by a man called Schachermeyr. Yet, despite his best efforts, my carefully guarded gift to your world was not found. How heavy my heart has become on account of this."

His mind boggled, Richards asked, intellectually holding his breath, "So what is this gift?"

"Something that must be found, must be shared with all," came the laconic reply.

Now shifting gears, Richards queried, "So what, may I ask, is your name now?"

"Oh, that," said the man as he rummaged about in his side jacket pocket.

"Here I am," he said as he presented to Richards a plastic laminated ID card complete with a color photograph and an unreadable signature.

Examining it closely, the Egyptologist gasped.

"Why, this is an official pass to Vatican Library made out to one Alfonso Ricardo Russo. How did you get this?" Richards barely squeaked out.

"It is a long story, as you say, but one worth telling. When I returned to your land this time, so much had changed. I did not recognize anything, only the land masses and even some of those had changed. But when I examined the land called Italia, I saw Vatican City, with its obelisk, with its grand architecture. I felt at ease there, even more so than in the ruins of old *Kemet*. So I went there. I saw their gardens with all their lovely living things. I offered myself as a gardener and worked, what, two years tending those magnificent gardens, tilling their rich soils. I made them better. Noble Mayneken, I was useful.

"Then I heard that the Vatican had its own *per ankh*, how you say, eh, *biblioteca*. And so I went to the head of the gardeners, a *sem*-priest, eh, *monsignore*, and asked if this were so and whether I might visit it. I admit that I must have surprised him quite a bit. That's when I got what you are now holding. So, whenever my day was complete, I would visit the *per ankh* and what I beheld was beyond my wildest dreams! Myriads of works on myriads of subjects and in so many languages! I could not believe my eyes that my seeds had produced such an abundance! And, noble Mayneken, I did not know where to begin. Then a very helpful *wab*-priest appeared, and he showed me where all the most recent books were kept. He then asked me what kind of subjects I was interested in, and I told him of my longing for, eh, *Aegyptos*. I remember him quite distinctly smiling and then showing me where those books were kept.

"I spent many hours at that place, reading everything on old *Kemet*. And then one day, while I was perusing for a new book of interest, I saw a grammar book, and so I sat and read it. I thought that it was a good book. Unlike many of the others with their fanciful ideas, this book spoke truth to my heart. But when I saw your very image on the book's cover, then I knew that I had to find you. To tell you what a fine book it is. And in this the kindly *wab*-priest assisted me as well. It was he who found your address."

Sitting back in his chair, Richards was quite sure that no Egyptian philologist in history had ever had his textbook read, and then praised by an Old One. And then to listen to this tale of a sojourning entity, who yearned for a sacred temple to return to, who then selected Vatican City, was most telling. And then his stomach really growled and quite loudly. Glancing down at his watch, the reason was clear, as a full hour had passed.

"Noble Mayneken, I remember well that sound. Your body has spoken. Let us continue our discussion at a place where we can silence that sound, and with some beer perhaps?"

* * *

While walking across campus on their way to the local steakhouse that Richards favored, Alfonso said in his broken, but very understandable, English, "What is this place where you work? Do you teach?"

Smiling broadly, the Egyptologist went on to explain what a modern university campus was, what he taught, and why. During the entire oration, the former god and once royal architect just listened with his head down and hands gripped behind his back in total and rapt concentration. If you happened to be a passerby, you would have thought nothing of the pair, for you would have seen such deep conversations between two close colleagues before. In this case, however, it was one clearly between an American and his European counterpart. In short, Alfonso fit right in, as always.

Having secured a table in the back of the tavern where the din was not quite so harsh, Richards ordered two large Weissbiers from the wait staff.

"Alfonso, you mentioned beer earlier. I just ordered us a round that comes close to one that you might have sampled once upon a time."

"Joseph. What does this 'once upon a time' mean?"

*   *   *

Given Richards' natural hunger, now whetted with the extraordinary excitement of his Italian colleague's surprise appearance, the American ordered for the two of them. The dinner began with a salad and a roll of hot black bread and butter. Next came the second round of beer. Apparently, Alfonso's hearty thirst had not slackened over the millennia. Then the steaks arrived, each with a baked potato. They too disappeared with gusto. Then arrived the third round of beer. At this point, Alfonso released a massive burp, much to Richards' delight and great amusement from a neighboring table of football players.

"Good out, dude!" one of them wryly commented as he extended a virtual clinking toast toward Alfonso.

Now satisfied and with a good buzz going, Richards asked his dinner guest where he was spending the night, did he have a hotel booked, the usual drill. But before Alfonso could reply to any of these particulars, a very odd thing happened.

"Well, well, what a surprise. Hello there, Professor Richards," cooed none other than Ms. Jennifer Ann Kelly, the secretary of the Philology Annex. This drop-dead gorgeous thirty-something, and as the Richards could readily attest, was pure trouble on roller skates, and a known security risk, not to mention a serious nymphomaniac.

There she stood, wine glass in one hand, hand on hip with the other, as her eyes devoured Richards. But then she got a real shock, for sitting opposite her usual thrill was this intriguing little guy with the most beautiful green eyes that she had ever seen in her life. And here she thought hers were the best!

"Well," she again cooed, "what does a girl have to do to get a seat at this party?"

Jolted out of his initial surprise at her surprise appearance and the assault of her pheromones, Richards jumped out of his chair and seated the smoldering woman between them. This development too was noticed by the neighboring table of jocks, for several pairs of eyes bulged.

For Alfonso, the pleasant appearance of this woman was intriguing, for this hypersensitive empath was receiving a reading from her that was simply going off the charts. As he observed her, she was pointedly observing him, while surrendering herself to his guileless eyes. Somehow, someway, she finally got out with a coquettish tilt of her head, "Hi there. My name's Jenny. What's yours?"

And in his broken English and Italian accent, he responded with a warm smile, "I am Alfonso."

The effect was immediate. Jenny's eyes dilated and her skin blushed as she let out a quiet moan.

"Oh, but of course you are. . . ."

And with that sudden chain reaction of physiological events, Alfonso's head jerked back in surprise.

Richards, who had been observing Jenny observe Alfonso, who had been closely observing Jenny, knew the signs well and hid a grin behind his beer glass.

What fireworks! He thought. *And she's only been at the table, what, thirty seconds. Time to bail out my old buddy.*

"Alfonso." The sound of Richards' voice was enough to break his lock on the woman as he turned his head toward the Egyptologist.

"Jenny here works at a small research library devoted to ancient languages. Isn't that right, Jenny?"

Trying really hard to rally as she attempted to brush back a loose strand of her naturally strawberry blond hair, the woman said, "Ah, yeah. That's right. It's open to the campus. Anyone can use the, ah, facility."

"That's great, as Alfonso here is a colleague of mine from Rome. His special interests are in ancient Egypt as well," Richards said with some license.

Then like a honeybee attracted to a flower, she dared again to look deeply into Alfonso's eyes.

"Jenny?"

"Ah, yes, Joey," the secretary said as she again snapped out of it.

"How many glasses of wine have you had tonight?"

"Ah, just a couple," she said with an all-too-quick shrug of one shoulder and a broad, inviting smile. "Why do you ask, you rock hard hunk of protein candy?"

*   *   *

Somehow, someway, Richards left the steak house alone that night. All he could remember was drilling into Jenny's head that she had to deliver Alfonso to his office by ten the next morning, no excuses. So the following morning he was again attempting to get through all of his midterm blue books, but this time with a brain that was a bit fuzzy from the previous evening's revelry. Promptly at ten, a knock was heard at his office door. Looking up, there was Alfonso beaming, his rumpled clothes looking exactly the same as before.

"So, my friend," Richards began, "did you sleep well?"

"*Grazie tanto!* Yes, I did. I did well. Your friend Jenny. She is remarkable woman. And good cook."

Richards found it remarkable as well, as he took in the Old One, mixing the languages, being the dirty dog. *But I didn't know that Jenny was a good cook!*

"Now what happens, Alfonso? What do you want to do? You have seen some of the campus. Can I offer you another tour? Perhaps meet some people, people who would find you of considerable interest?"

Now it was Alfonso's turn to get up and close the office door. Upon returning to his chair, he began in the old tongue, "My dear friend Mayneken. Your hospitality truly knows no bounds, but I am a very particular sort of . . . man. I truly require very little. Yet I am again most grateful for your hospitality. But no. Sadly, I must go as I came. Quietly. It is my way. It has always been so.

"But before I leave, I ask of you, my dear Mayneken, to go to Sakkara. Find my gift for your world. Make sure that it and its gifts are shared. That, truly, is all that I desire. Your world must learn its lesson in sharing. My gift will greatly cause that to happen. Otherwise, I fear the worst for your world's future development."

Nodding in understanding, now perplexed even more about the "gift," Richards then asked a favor.

"May I keep your Vatican ID as a souvenir of your visit?"

"Yes, noble Mayneken, you may keep it, as I will surely no longer have need of it."

And with that, Alfonso stood up, rummaged around in his coat, produced the ID, smiled, nodded his head in farewell, and left the office never to return.

For Richards, the moment was filled with a deep and quiet melancholy. He felt like jumping up and stopping the man, but he couldn't. It was like a warm, serene, and pleasing buzz had been removed from the air. It was what he always imagined it would be like if he had a brother to say good-bye to. He felt that something great had just passed him by far too quickly. He had many questions to ask, but right now he knew that he could never ask them. He felt, somehow, incomplete, and empty. And so he did the sensible thing. He wept.

*   *   *

Ruben was an elderly black man who had been raised as a kid on a north Georgia farm. When he had reached an age where he thought that he could make his own way in the world, he did, by riding trains and hitchhiking, and by taking on odd jobs to get by. His many travels took him far and wide, but somehow, someway, he ended up in this town of Big Shoulders. *Must have been all the trains*, he commiserated with himself. In short, this was a proud, self-made man with six wonderful grandchildren that he loved to death. Up until this day, he also thought that he had seen it all.

Sitting on his favorite green collapsible camping stool, the one that he had many times mended with some spare fishing line, near his favorite willow tree, Ruben was transported back to his youth. He didn't know just what it was about the smell of the pond, its surrounding thickets of cottontails, and the trees and flowering bushes, but here he was at peace. So he cast his line out again into the murky green water, delicately holding the bamboo pole in his arthritic left hand. Then he reached down with the other into his cooler for a cold one. As he intently watched the red and white bobber for any telltale signs of a nibble, he took a long pull, and then saw that ripples were disturbing and intruding upon his tranquil green universe.

Looking to his left for the source of his annoyance, he saw a naked white dude walking slowly and purposefully into the pond. Looking closer, he then noticed that the naked white dude had even left his clothes neatly folded on the bank. Looking back to the naked white dude, the water had quickly reached head level, and then his head just disappeared under the water. Now staring with his mouth wide open in total disbelief, Ruben noted that the ripples had begun to fade away, as if nothing of any consequence just had happened. There were no bubbles either, just a lonesome stack of neatly folded clothing.

"What the dickens!" he exclaimed as he rose from his seat, as if standing would somehow give him a better perspective on the now smooth green pond.

"Well, I'll be!" breathed the now very troubled man and elder of his Baptist church.

And as if his concern had been heard by the Almighty Himself, a large underwater disturbance commenced right before Ruben's very eyes as a shiny, silvery globe, the size of an old Cadillac, slowly emerged from the pond, rose above it, and then silently shot straight up into the sky where it disappeared.

The displacement of the pond water had totally doused Ruben's shoes and pants up to the calf of his legs, but he didn't pay it no mind. He didn't even realize that he had dropped his beer either.

*   *   *

What to do? So Richards picked up his office phone and called the dean's office. At the other end of the line, a pleasant and efficient voice answered. He stated his business and in mere moments had an appointment for later that day at three forty-five.

That chore accomplished, he fingered the Vatican ID card for what must have been the umpteenth time. Such a neutral face looked back at him.

Sigh.

Time to grade some more blue books before I go over to the administration building.

It was not often that a professor suddenly schedules a visit with a high university administrator seeking wisdom. But Richards thought that the situation required it. Dr. Paul Allister Young, grandson of an English viscount, university dean of humanities, and occasionally an insufferable Brit, also was the man who hired him at the counsel of his old friend, John Milson. As was his style, he felt that he owed the man.

He entered the dean's outside office chambers and presented himself before the secretary's desk. There, behind a shield fortification comprised of two computer monitors, the young woman looked up and smiled with genuine warmth.

"So you must be Professor Richards. I will inform Dr. Young." Her sightless fingers furiously typed out his guest's arrival.

"You know, I am a real fan of yours."

"How so?" replied the surprised Egyptologist.

"Oh, all those TV specials about you in Egypt. All of that was really cool."

Now mildly blushing, all Richards could say was, "Thanks."

At that moment, a quiet chime rang from the computer's screen.

"Dr. Young is ready for you. Just walk in."

"Thanks again."

As the conflicted Egyptologist turned away and strode purposefully across the lush Persian floor covering, past the elegant mahogany paneling, toward the massive mahogany double doors of the dean's office, a certain secretary's eyes glazed over and dilated ever so slightly.

What a hunk! She thought. *And so humble as well. I could just hug him to death.*

Young's office, as with all high administrative dignitaries of old and established universities, was a splendid example of naturally aged woodwork, paneling, tastefully appropriate period furniture, bookshelves, and the luscious smell of their contents. The desk, the sacred altar of university status and power, was center stage, and Young was comfortably ensconced behind his. Let there be no mistake, each and every executive office and boardroom in the business world, no matter how well appointed, can ape nothing more than a pale reflection of such grounded institutional power, such gravitas. Without question, this was Young's turf.

Putting down his pen and rising to greet Richards, Young, now in his early fifties and graying gracefully, still looked fit and trim. As he rounded the aircraft carrier that was his desk, he offered his colleague a chair and then sat opposite him in the other, smoothly crossing one leg over the other.

"So, Joseph. What can I do for you? The urgency of your message with Ms. Robertson was clear enough, but not the reason. So, as you Americans like to say, 'what's up?'"

Leaning forward with his elbows on his knees and feet flat on the floor, Richards looked the man straight in the eye.

"Dr. Young. During the past twenty-four hours or so, our campus has hosted a rather distinguished visitor. Do you remember my last deployment with Vesna Gregorieva? The one back to Predynastic Memphis?"

Frowning slightly in thought, Young said, "Was that the one with that rather dreadful dust up in the open desert?"

"Precisely, that was the one. But more to the point, that deployment's agenda was to find and interview a man called Ptah. Do you remember that?"

The dean, now pinching his lower lip in concentration.

"Why, yes, yes I do. Where are you going with this, Joseph?"

"Well, during that deployment, we did indeed find and meet with the entity called Ptah. Furthermore, we were able to identify him as an Old One just prior to his rather sudden departure."

Now with widened eyes.

"That is correct. Yes. But why—"

Richards rarely interrupted anyone, but with the news that he was carrying, he just had to get it out. Raising his open hand for the dean's silence, he began,

"Dr. Young, this campus has just been visited by that very same entity, quite literally an encounter of the third kind. Yesterday afternoon, he came to my office. Last night, we went to dinner. Last evening, he spent the night with Jennifer Kelly. And this morning, he again came to my office to say good-bye."

To say Young was stunned at the news would have been an extreme understatement. Initially he had found young Richards' interruption rude, but given what he had just related, well, Young found it in himself to forgive the young man. But to have had such a visitor on campus, and so recently, left him speechless.

"What do you want me to do?" the bewildered dean finally asked.

"Well, as of this moment, there is nothing anyone can do. By the way, here is what he looks like."

Young, now holding the Vatican Library pass, found that his hands were shaking with emotion.

"My God, man! A bona fide extraterrestrial has just traipsed across my campus, visited with one of my illustrious faculty, had dinner, and then was shagged by our biggest security risk. Then the very next day, the same chap has the polite decency to say toodle-doo! And now I am in the possession of his library card to the Vatican Library of all places. What in God's name is this world coming to?"

For the next thirty seconds, the dean's office was a place of silent disbelief, if not outright confusion.

Now waving the library card in one hand and pointing at Richards with the other, the dean then said, "Okay. Are you absolutely sure of a positive ID on this bloke?"

"Without question, sir. In fact, much of our conversation was in ancient Egyptian. And his eyes were green in a way that made them unforgettable. They were the same back in predynastic Memphis. And his empathic powers had quite an effect on Jennifer Kelly, by the way. Dr. Young, again without question, this was the same entity."

Now steepling his hands in thought, Dr. Young said. "So, you say that he had sexual relations with Ms. Kelly?"

"I would suppose so, but that would be just an educated guess on my part."

"Is Ms. Kelly currently at the Philology Annex?"

"Again, I would suppose so."

"Dr. Richards, is there anything else that you would like to share?"

"Yes. Yes, there is. I have been given a quest. Ptah/Imhotep/Alfonso left a gift for the world to share at Sakkara. It apparently has not been found, but the entity was very specific that it must be found, and then shared with the global community."

"'Shared' you say," Young whispered.

"Yes, sir. The entity was quite specific. He practically begged me to find it."

"Dr. Richards, thank you for coming to me with this matter. I will look into it immediately."

* * *

Jenny was still all aglow from last night's simply amazing tryst. Never before had a man reached her in quite the same way Alfonso had. In every way, she had never felt so alive, so vibrant, so whole, and so complete. It had been marvelous, and to think that Richards had even been a part of it just made her smile and appreciate the man even more than she had before. While she was still daydreaming about last night's encounter, a strapping, no-nonsense security type about six foot two came through the Philology Annex's front door. Stopping before her secretarial desk, he stated, "Excuse me, but are you Ms. Jennifer Ann Kelly?"

Jenny could feel her adrenaline rise as she said, "Why, yes. Yes, I am. Can I help you?"

"Yes, Ms. Kelly, you certainly can. Would you be so kind to grab your coat and come with me?"

Coolly.

"May I see some ID?"

"Yes, indeed you may." As he reached inside his dark blue suit coat past a concealed weapon, he withdrew his identification jacket and passed it to her.

"Here it is."

Now freezingly chilly.

"Yes, I see.

"Now, Officer Callahan. Why is the Center for Disease Control interested in me? What is this all about?"

"Ms. Kelly, that question is way above my pay grade. I am just here to take you to the university hospital as quickly as I can."

*   *   *

"Ms. Kelly, my name is Dr. Jeremy Simon," said the fatherly, white-haired man in the green scrubs and white lab coat with a laminated ID tag that confirmed just who he said he was.

"Is it possible that you encountered this man recently?" he said as he showed her of all things a Vatican Library card.

Looking at it carefully, Jenny bobbed her head in the affirmative and then asked why.

"Well, Ms. Kelly, it is suspected that Mr. Russo is carrying a virulent, ahem, social disease that is currently raising cane in Central Italy, Rome in particular. Since his passport did not have the required vaccination stamp, we have been interviewing people left and right who may have come in contact with him. Then we have been examining them for any possible disease transmission. In fact, Dr. Joseph Richards was just released after he submitted himself to an examination and blood draws. He was just as shocked about all of this as you probably are. So that is why you're here. Do you fully understand what I have just said and its potential magnitude?"

Dr. Simon said this advisedly, because as soon as he had mentioned "social disease," Jenny had turned white and had actually shuddered a bit in her chair.

"Yes, Doctor. I understand you perfectly. I took him home and had sex with him last night. Now what am I in for? What can I expect?" she said with pleading eyes for help.

"I see," he began with great sympathy. "In that case, we'll want to draw some blood for a couple of bioactive panels and then have a gynecologist look you over. The gyno, by the way, that is on staff is a woman. Ms. Kelly, I cannot force you to comply with any of this, but for your own sake, do you wish to proceed?"

"Absolutely, Doctor. Time's a-wasting!"

*　　*　　*

By nine o'clock the next morning, Dean Young had the lab results before him, delivered personally by Dr. Jeremy Simon, an award-winning human geneticist and longtime member of the Philology Annex. In fact, Simon had collaborated on the lab results with Dr. James H. Allen, the chief physician at Horizon Pass, the Annex's technical sister institution in New Mexico. Lieutenant Callahan, the chief security officer for the two facilities, who had escorted Kelly to the hospital, was also present.

"So, Jeremy, what do you have for me?" an atypically nervous Young demanded.

"Well, it's hard to say. The mouth swabs of the subject came back negative with anything out of the ordinary. The subject's vaginal swabs also were negative for any SDs. But we were fortunate to harvest some samples of seminal fluid. So I ordered a full diagnostic panel, and right now we are awaiting the gen lab's results.

"That's it?"

"I am afraid so, regarding the sample analysis," said an almost apologetic Simon.

"Even given our special relationship with the hospital and its laboratories, these sensitive tests still require time to complete.

"But there is one thing more that you should know about that the subject that Ms. Kelly volunteered. She noted that her sexual experience with the vector was 'psychologically transformational.' Her words. Now what that precisely means, I'm not sure, but I would strongly suggest that she gets a new psy-panel workup. It might be revealing."

"I see. Thank you, Doctor. Leftenant Callahan. Is there any trace of our visitor?"

"None, sir. It's like he just walked into Lake Michigan."

"Damnation!"

"But, Dr. Young, I did hear on the police scanner that an old guy reported seeing 'a white dude' walk 'stark naked' into one of the Chicago Park District's ponds. Then he claims that he saw a UFO fly out of the same pond."

"Oh!"

* * *

Four days later, a courier dropped off at the Philology Annex a registered letter from the university hospital addressed to J. A. Kelly. In it, she was informed that all of her laboratory tests were negative. Additionally, Dr. Simon stated that he had informed the CDC that Mr. Alfonso Russo could not have been the pathogen that they thought he was. This news brought an immense sense of relief to Jenny, not only for her own well-being, but also for her Alfonso, a man who had reached her to her very core.

On that same day, the same courier then delivered a sealed package to the dean's office. Usually, Ms. Robertson opened all of the dean's mail, but quite clearly this piece of mail from the university hospital was one of those that fell under the "do not open" category. So, helpfully, she placed it atop the day's mail, walked the pile into his office, and deposited the mass in the center of his otherwise immaculate desktop.

Meetings prevented Dr. Young from getting in as early as he preferred, so by the time he could focus on his mound of mail, it was lunch time. But his secretary's sense of priority got the better of him. He ripped open the package from the university's genetics lab. As he read each and every word of the report, the color from his face faded.

VECTOR DNA ANALYSIS
PRELIMINARY RESULTS

Summary: DNA analysis is atypical (see below).

Procedure: Samples per laboratory protocol are divided into three separate analyses. Each sample analysis is subjected to identical procedures and practices.

Results: Macro examination of the vector's DNA samples reveal fifty-six chromosomal bodies. Micro examination of the vector's DNA structure revealed a quad-helical matrix made up of Thymine, Cytosine, Guanine, and Adenine. Purines, Pyrimidines, Deoxyribose Sugars, Nucleosides, and Nucleotides have also been identified.

Interpretation: The vector's DNA is extremely atypical:

a) The presence of fifty-six chromosomal bodies is unknown within the human genome.

b) Human DNA is constructed around a double helical structure, while the vector's DNA exhibits a symmetrical quad-helical arrangement.

c) Te presence of the Thymine, Cytosine, Guanine, and Adenine components point to the possibility of genetic engineering.

d) The presence of the Purines, Pyramidines, Deoxyribose Sugars, Nucleosides, and Nucleotides suggest similar intracellular interactions and functions as found in human cytology, but will require further study.

e) Determination of sexual assignment is not possible at this time.

My God in heaven! Young thought. *Richards was spot on! He was visited by an alien life-form.* Now holding his head in his hands, the dean just kept shaking his head.

Ms. Kelly even had sex with it and now claims that she is somehow a changed woman. And then there is the question of why it was even here? Yet, Richards claims that it told him that it was just curious as to how we were progressing as a sentient species, but was extremely concerned about our ability to share. And the Egyptologist specifically mentioned something about a gift for humanity that had to be found. Which leads me next to the following logical question: Just how are we doing if we need to learn how to share?

CHAPTER V
The Milk Run

Remote facilities such as Horizon Pass are hostage to their logistical support. Such remote *and* secret installations must provide for many situations that go far beyond the normal going to the local grocery or convenience store for a gallon of milk. While it might take a Black Hawk just fourteen minutes to fly from Holloman airfield to Horizon Pass, it takes a darn sight longer for an eighteen-wheeler running on unimproved dirt tracks. Nonetheless, the trip was made twice a week come hell or high water to keep the inhabitants of Horizon Pass happy in beer, eggs, milk, and anything else that a big truck could haul. Tuesdays were the refrigerated runs. Fridays carried everything else. Both returned with the trash.

As truck cabs went, they were certainly special but were put together to look as ordinary and vanilla as possible. They were Kenworth C500s minus the rear living quarters, built with twin steering, wide wheels and massive knobby tires, and sure-footed and agile air suspensions allowed for the occasional off-road excursion. Painted white to reflect the heat and with oversize radiators, these Kirkland, Washington, specials were fully armored with bulletproof glass and shrouded and raised puncture-proof fuel bladders. Sixteen liters of straight diesel motor motivated these monsters.

As one might expect, their drivers were special too, all being security-vetted ex-military, who were trained and experienced in tanks or other heavy machinery. Each carried personal defense as the cab provided the always-loaded pump assault shotgun. To land a slot on this twice-a-week milk run between Alamogordo and Horizon Pass was considered a really sweet deal, as the pay was for full week's time. Consequently, second jobs in Alamogordo or at the airbase were not uncommon.

Raybob Smith was an ex-Abrams guy, who usually was scheduled for the Tuesday haul with the reefer. Tall, lanky, and calling home College Station, Texas, he relished driving his C500 and cared for it in ways that would have put a typical car owner to shame. He even named the truck Sally. This last detail, in particular, had initially gotten him into some trouble at a few local establishments, until he had set several individuals straight. Thereafter, not a catcall was heard, although whenever he was in a certain local establishment sipping a cold one, a song by Johnny Cash often "magically" seemed to be selected.

What was loaded into the trailers that Raybob hauled, he rightly considered none of his darn business. Loaded and sealed at a secure warehouse, all he had to do was sign the paperwork, hitch up, and attach his brake lines.

*   *   *

On this particular Tuesday morning in early May, the sky was robin's egg blue, and the Weather Channel promised relatively mild temperatures. For Alamogordo, Gordo to the locals, that meant mid-eighties. But once in the upcountry, as Raybob thought of it, by noon it could be warmer than that.

Slipping the cab into gear, he was off and heading toward Highway 54 South and the Air Force base.

Leaving that sprawling complex in his wake, Raybob slowed and eased over onto the gravely siding near mile marker thirty-two. At the third reflector, he turned onto a scrabble desert dirt track and headed for the foothills. From here on, it would take him some fifty-four minutes of dusty and bumpy driving before arriving at his destination. The route, if you wanted to call it that, was literally over hill and dale, through scrub bush, tumbleweed, and cacti.

But unknown to the driver, he was being shadowed by a helmeted fifteen-year-old on a dirt bike. His motivation was simple, money. And the money offered was extraordinarily good. Otherwise, he would never have considered such a daring stunt. Besides, the biker didn't care why the man had challenged him to parallel the truck in the desert. The man just wanted to know where it was going. Why? Because he had his orders to find out. And, oh yes, his money was green.

*   *   *

There were three ways into Horizon Pass: at the rundown lean-to shack where personnel deposited on the chopper pad usually gained access; on the opposite side of the outcrop where a hidden secondary personnel gate, rarely used, existed; or, the truck dock that was located under a rock overhang that shaded and shielded its presence from any overhead surveillance. The raised dock and its roll-up door were spray-painted with a gritty epoxy paint that matched the color and texture of the surrounding rock perfectly. As Raybob began to maneuver his rig to back in, he stopped, checked his watch, and noted on his paperwork his arrival time. It was well within the window before the next satellite flyover. Coming to a halt against the flexible backstop of the dock, he thought that he saw something glint out of the corner of his eye. Now that he was holding still, he saw the reflection again, and then recognized it as a dirt bike's tailpipe rapidly fleeing the area.

"Oh shit," were the first words out of his mouth before he could key the mike of his radio.

"Tombstone, this is the grocery man. I just spotted a dirt bike that is rapidly leaving the area. It looks like I was tailed again. Better alert the flyboys back at the ranch. Over."

"Message received, grocery man. Flyboys will be informed. Good eyes, grocery man. Over."

A minute and a half later, an unmarked, black helicopter was scrambled from Holloman Air Force Base. The four men aboard were the pilot, copilot, and two gunners amidships. Being as close to the border as the base was, such a sudden and unscheduled departure went unnoticed. Even though it was late morning, the copilot had on his infrared visor. While the team knew the course of the delivery route like the back of their hands, all four sets of eyes were scanning for any signs of movement or anything out of the ordinary.

After being airborne for six minutes, it was the copilot who first spotted the deep red signature of the bike's motor, and then only secondarily its rider's bouncing pink blob.

"Tango at zero-one-zero," the copilot called out to the crew.

"Roger that," the pilot automatically responded.

Simultaneously, the starboard gunner swiveled his six-barreled M134 minigun to cover that quadrant. Firing 7.62 mm shells at a rate of fire between two to six thousand rounds a minute, that one gun alone could easily dismantle a small hillside. Flying purposely low, to take full advantage of the machine's muffled blades and near silent approach, the pilot tried to startle the biker off of his mount. He failed, but he had sure gotten the biker's attention as several handgun rounds flew their way.

"Shooter! Shooter!" called out the copilot.

Noting this, the pilot announced, "Shots fired! Shots fired! Guns free! I repeat. Guns free!"

As the helicopter passed over the bike's position, the pilot pivoted it to come around. Meanwhile, the port gunner briefly opened fire, registered as a short rumble in the cockpit. The return fire spilled the rider in a rag doll tumble, head over heels, and over the front end of the bike. Hovering now very low over the crooked form, the starboard gunner jumped to the ground, while his twin covered him. Rifling through the biker's pockets, he gathered all that he found, put it in a zippered pouch, and returned to the chopper.

Once airborne again, the pilot got on the horn and laconically stated, "Black Three is returning to base.

"Now just what the hell is going on? That's the third intruder this month alone. What gives?" said the pilot conversationally to his copilot.

*   *   *

Unloaded and already rolling on his way back to Gordo, Raybob watched in his side mirror as three men with backpack leaf blowers began to totally obliterate all trace of his rig's tire tracks.

They're damn efficient, he thought, as he reached for his second low gear with the reefer now stuffed to the gills with trash and recyclables. *Food in and garbage out. What a living I'm making.* Then those thoughts were broken with a radio transmission.

"Garbage man, FYI. The flyboys are on their way back to the nest. Scratch another tango. Over."

"Tombstone. Message received. Over. *Is it just my imagination or was that the third this month?"*

*   *   *

La Luz was a tiny suburb located north of Alamogordo. A quiet location on the western slopes of the Sacramento Mountains, it was a perfect place to set up an overwatch in a nondescript house on a neatly manicured street.

The owners of the house were Native American, but who were of the belief that their Mescalero Apache tribal rights had been trampled upon, their culture taken advantage of, and their blood defiled by the evil White Man. Worst of all, they had their land taken away from them, even though they had been paid for it. Because of this, they had remained angry, bitter, and directionless, until a dark-skinned man arrived with a big bag of money. He had offered to make their life better and suggested some ways to perhaps regain some of their pride, which the couple felt had been rudely taken away from them. Before the generous man left, he promised to write to them, make sure that they remained financially secure, and requested a few favors along the way. To this, the couple had agreed as the favors seemed so inconsequential, the money was in cash, and so was tax free. Screw the White Man.

The husband spoke. "That young man with the dirt bike is late my bride, just like the other ones. I fear for his life, as I have for the other ones. Just what is going on in the white desert?" he concluded with a slow shake of his head.

The wife replied. "My husband, what shall we write to our dark-skinned friend? That the white desert takes all that we send into it? No, we must try again. This time we must send someone older and wiser in the ways of the white desert. Not just another hooligan with a dirt bike and a gun. We know well the schedule. We should send a tracker, but this time on foot."

"On foot! Who would we find to do that?" said the incredulous husband.

"I think I know one. I have seen him at mass at Our Lady of the Light. He's a veteran, and I believe, by the look of his clothing, that he is in need."

"Do you have a name for me to look into?"

"Yep. His name's Johnny Lee Blackfeather."

"Well, well. I used to know his father before he passed. A good man. Where do you think I might find him?"

"I'm not sure, but I thought that I saw him working at the market on Alamo Street."

"Well, I guess that I'm going to have to look him up tomorrow."

*   *   *

Three days later, on a Friday, J. L. Blackfeather, formerly a squad leader of the 1st Army, 120th Brigade out of Fort Hood, Texas, lay in wait under a desert gillie suit, alongside a certain desert track off Highway 54 South. His contact in La Luz had dropped him off an hour before sunrise, and that gave this savvy desert tracker enough time to find what he was looking for, dig in, and wait.

As he had been briefed, a mammoth-looking white rig pulling a trailer blew past him leaving a rooster tail of dust almost the length of a football field. The time was nine thirteen. Counting slowly to thirty, only then did Blackfeather begin to stir himself to his feet. Crossing over from the scrub to the track itself, he got down and closely inspected the tire markings in the dust, memorizing them, making them his friend. Looking up from under the brim of his desert canvas hat, he set off after the rapidly disappearing transport. Under his gillie, he carried four liters of water and enough food for four days in the open. He also brought along a GPS, an assault knife, and a 9mm Glock with several spare magazines. Fit and used to forty-mile hikes with a hell of a lot more on his back, Blackfeather broke into a lazy, easy trot, figuring that it was best to make the most of it in the relative coolness of the early morning. Besides, in another two or so hours, he'd have to dig in again, when the big rig made its return run.

At eleven, the tracker selected a bush to set up beneath and began his patient wait for the returning transport. Seventeen minutes later, he felt its approach through his belly and moments later was buffeted by the roar of its exhaust and tires as it passed within twenty feet of him, trailing, as before, a rooster tail of dust and grit. Waiting again for the dust to settle, he slithered out from beneath his hide and continued his trek into the desert with the foothills in the background.

Pace was key. Blackfeather knew how to monitor that critical factor. He figured that he had already covered a good ten miles before his last hide. Now, with the track all his to command, he set off at a walk, following the unmistakable tire marks in the dust. His goal was to settle down in the foothills some twenty to thirty miles distant, get some rest, and continue again at first light. It was a sound plan, and one that he had done dozens of times in as many foreign deserts. What could possibly go wrong?

*   *   *

Blackfeather's first suspicion that his goal was that distant and distinct solitary rock outcropping was the way the track ran toward it, all the time following below the ridgeline in a natural shadow. To him, it made absolute sense, if you were trying to hide the route from overhead observation. Sternly warned by his contact that this was a high security installation, the tracker kept something between him and that outcropping at all times. That tactic was relatively easy as he paralleled the desert track with its obvious tire prints. While his progress was slowed somewhat, Blackfeather figured his probability of detection was proportionately reduced.

About a quarter of a mile out, he stopped under cover to assess how to best approach the suspected installation, suspected because he had not yet traced the tire tracks up to those rocks. For all he knew, they just might continue on. Furthermore, he had not encountered any security measures, fencing, and the like. In short, he had not found the front door.

Given that it was just a little past noon, he drank some water and munched on a power bar, while he took in the situation and thought about it. A slow crawl was always possible, but what the former recon soldier did not know was what sorts of passive detection equipment might be out there to snare him. If there were any infrared detectors, then a recon in the heat of the day had a better chance for success than one during the cool of the night. Pressure plates, on the other hand, out in a vast wasteland like this, just didn't seem practical. Ditto on trip lines and flares, as there was just too much wild game to trigger them, not to mention the potential for starting a brush fire. So, in the end, he decided on infrared as being their first line of defense, and that meant he was about to start a long, slow crawl.

Blackfeather was always amazed during a gillie crawl how insignificant bushes and imperfections in the terrain could be used to one's advantage. In this case, the very edge of the desert track itself, worn down by the bi-weekly passage of the transports, had created for him a low wall to hide behind. This mundane feature allowed him to safely crawl to within one hundred yards of the outcropping, close enough for Blackfeather to see an oddly out of place squarish-shaped feature under the rock overhang to his left, while to his right stood, no, leaned against a rock face a battered and worn-down shack-like structure. Crawling on a bit farther, he encountered the edge of a slab of heavily weathered concrete and found, much to his surprise, the embedded lens of a landing light! And from this vantage point, the odd feature to his left, now only about fifty feet away, was clearly a cleverly camouflaged truck dock.

Damn, he thought. *Was that slick!*

But Blackfeather did not move one inch more, for he quite distinctly felt the end of a rifle barrel pressing against the back of his head. Confirmation of that fact shortly followed with a firm voice.

"Freeze, mister. Don't you dare move a muscle or I'll blow your fucking head off."

*　　*　　*

"Lieutenant Callahan, sir, we just caught a creeper wearing a gillie outside of the installation," the roving security squad leader reported in over his personal radio.

"Yes, sir. We bagged and tagged him."

"Yes, sir, he was armed and he had a GPS on his person as well."

"Yes, sir."

Now looking over at Blackfeather meaningfully, the squad leader continued, "Sir, what do you want us to do with him?"

At this point, the tracker was sure that he was a dead man. Never before had anyone got the drop on him like these dudes had. And he wasn't surprised, because their camouflage was like nothing he had ever seen before. As they moved about, their uniforms sort of rippled through the air, blending into the environment, and making them invisible. Twice now, Blackfeather had focused on one of them. And twice he had lost sight of him not forty feet away. It was downright spooky. It was just like those old stories of the spirit walkers that he remembered hearing as a boy. *Just who are these guys?*

"Bring him in, Corporal. I want to talk to this joker."

"Yes, sir. Advise the portal that we will be arriving, three plus one. Over."

*　　*　　*

Hooded, frisked of all his belongings, and with his hands double zip-tied behind him, Blackfeather was led shuffling into an air-conditioned room that smelled vaguely antiseptic. Guided by hands on his shoulders, he was made to sit on a firm chair. With his ankles shackled to the chair legs, he was left to sit, think, and contemplate his future.

"Well, Corporal," said Callahan, "how has our guest behaved?"

"Very cool, Lieutenant. It's almost like he has been through this before. Without doubt, he's ex-military and knows what he's doing. In fact, we didn't pick him up until he had reached the southern edge of the helicopter pad."

"You're kidding!"

"No, sir. He was a real snake out there. Jonesy even back tracked his trail a quarter of a mile. He did all that on his belly."

"Interesting. Well, I think it's high time to meet our guest."

Blackfeather heard the knob on the door turn and three pairs of boots crunch toward him.

"Okay, friend," a voice said. "Mind your eyes as I am taking off your hood."

Even with his eyes closed, the glare through his lids was bright. Soon enough, the Apache had partial vision, but what he saw was nothing but white. White table, door, walls, ceiling, even the cameras mounted above in the corners, all white and bright as the entire ceiling was illuminated.

From behind him, that voice returned.

"Okay, who are you, and why were you messing around in my sandbox?"

Silence.

"Okay, slim, you asked for it." And a thin-needled hypodermic was pressed against his neck.

Still more silence and then Blackfeather's neck seemed to turn into jelly as his head began to sag this way and that as his neck muscles relaxed.

"Okay, slim, let's start this again. What's your name?"

"B-b-blackfeather . . . Johnny Lee B-blackfeather."

"Who do you work for?"

"M-myself."

"Who did you used to work for?"

"1st Army, 120th Brigade, out of Hood."

"What was your rank, soldier?"

"Corporal, s-sir."

"All right, Corporal Blackfeather. Why were you crawling around in my desert?"

"Recon, s-sir. Recon. I'm the best recon in the 120th."

"Recon on what, Corporal?"

"Don't really know. S-some secret squirrel location."

"Who sent you, Corporal?"

"S-some nice folks. Generous. Wanted to pay me a shit-load to locate s-s-some secret squirrel location."

"How much were the 'nice folks' gonna pay you?"

"Ten large."

"Corporal, do you mean ten thousand dollars?"

"Yessiree, sir!"

"Why do you want the money, Corporal?"

"No job, sir. Can't find a job. A man needs to make a living, sir."

"Corporal, could you identify these 'nice folks' of yours?"

"Yes, sir. Absolutely, sir!"

"Well, that's good to hear. Now, Corporal, would you like some water?"

"That would be outstanding, s-sir!"

As a flexible tube was placed in Blackfeather's mouth, he sucked on it greedily and quickly emptied the half liter of water that contained a mild sedative. Now licking his lips, the tracker contentedly exhaled, and fell into a deep sleep.

"Okay, that should do it," said Callahan.

"And thanks, Doc, for your assistance on this one. We're going to scan him for his military chip, if he still has one, clean him up, and put him in the brig. Then I want to talk to this guy as soon as he's sober again."

*   *   *

Blackfeather's mouth was so dry that he thought that he couldn't swallow. It was a sort of drowning sensation, one that he couldn't run from in his dreams. Then, with a snort, he was awake, thirsty for sure, but awake, and for the first time in a long time, not hung over.

Sitting up, he saw that he was clean and clothed in one of those pansy-assed hospital gowns that was open at the back. Worst of all, it was bright pink. Strangely, they hadn't shaved him.

Putting a hand to his shaking head, Blackfeather tried to remember just what had happened to him, and as he tried even harder, the fog began to clear. He had been caught, cuffed, and hooded. And now he was here, wherever here was.

As if in a psychic response to that question, the door to his white-on-white room opened and in walked two men. As Blackfeather struggled to focus his eyes, he saw one in a white starched medical coat complete with a stethoscope and the other a soldier in desert cammies, a lieutenant. Continuing to blink his eyes, Blackfeather tried to say something, but his voice box wouldn't function.

Observing this, Doc Allen pulled a small bottle of water out of his pocket and gave it to his patient.

"Drink, soldier. It will help a lot."

Blackfeather didn't need to be told twice, and so he drained the bottle.

And as Blackfeather was wiping his mouth with the back of his hand, the soldier said, "So, Corporal Blackfeather, here's the deal. We know from your Army jacket that you were twice awarded a Purple Heart while en route to that Bronze Star for Valor. We also know that you received an Honorable Discharge and subsequently had some recurring medical issues that the VA failed to completely solve. Then Doc here tells me that your blood work is in a shambles, as you are a borderline alcoholic. A real sad and sorry state for a former soldier so honorably decorated. So again, as I said, here's the deal.

"Either you work for us, get paid, get relocated to a decent, permanent job, and tell us just who put you up to this, or you go to the stockade for a long time on the charge of trespassing on federal property. Those are your options, mister. So what's it gonna be?"

Shocked, confused, powerless, and more than a bit disoriented, Blackfeather went with door number one. In his mind, it was a no-brainer.

The second sentence that he managed to enunciate was a simple request. "Where are my clothes? This all-pink shit just isn't me."

*   *   *

"Okay, so, once again, when were they supposed to pick you up?" Callahan asked.

"In four days. On the fourth, early, before dawn, next to the highway where I was first dropped off." Blackfeather answered.

"And again, their vehicle, can you describe it? The lieutenant prodded.

"A white Cherokee pickup. An old one. In good shape. With a spare tire on the rear gate."

"Okay, Mr. Blackfeather. Are you absolutely sure that you want to be bait to catch these S.O.B.s?"

"Yes, sir. I do. I really do."

Six hours later, Blackfeather, with all his gear including his knife and handgun, stood by the side of Highway 54 at the agreed upon location. To complete the scene, he had rolled and crawled around in the desert. In short, he looked the part. For his protection, Callahan had arrayed around him and on both sides of the road his men in their adaptive camouflage and armed to the teeth.

Around four o'clock, a white Cherokee drove right past Blackfeather with its high beams on. Then, after about a quarter of a mile, the same vehicle stopped. It turned around, and returned, stopping opposite the tracker on the northbound side of the highway. As

Blackfeather crossed the road to meet up with the vehicle, Callahan's men surrounded it, and its lone driver was taken into custody.

*   *   *

Like clockwork, on every Tuesday, Mr. Jonathan Roots went to his Washington, DC, post office box to pick up his mail. This time, the batch was thicker than most, as the junk mail this time of year just seemed to proliferate like bunny rabbits. Strolling over toward the trash bin, Roots began the much-needed sorting process and in the end had only two pieces of mail left that were even worth the effort to open.

The first was a bill, the second a handwritten letter from La Luz, New Mexico. Folding them in half and stuffing both into one of his outer suit coat pockets, the handsome and dark olive-complexioned man with a big smile exited the post office and got into his light green Toyota Camry that was parked outside. Opening the letter from New Mexico, he smiled as his friends out there had found something that he just had to see for himself.

Running through the week's schedule in his well-ordered mind, Roots quickly realized that he could be on a plane the following day. Pleased with himself, he went to work and during his lunch hour made his arrangements. Unfortunately, there weren't any direct flights to El Paso, Texas, but his frequent flier status with American would make the five-plus hour journey pleasant. With the short drive north in a rental car, the transaction couldn't be easier, as he would be back the late same day.

*   *   *

At the specific request of the husband, his wife would not be present at their house during the sting. With the structure now rigged to the gills with video and audio recording devices, even in the bathroom, Callahan had his command center, a white Tahoe parked on the next street over. His men he had placed around the house and neighborhood. While they knew which day to expect the man with all the money to arrive, they didn't know when, and so the tense wait began.

Just before noon, a white Impala pulled into the neighborhood and unerringly went into the driveway of the couple. A well-dressed man of medium height, dark olive complexion, and looking to be in a bit of a hurry, rang the doorbell, and was recognized and greeted by the husband. Once inside, the soldiers closed in, and Callahan and three of his men took the heavily protesting man into custody. On his person was found ten thousand dollars in cash, a wallet with a driver's license and three credit cards belonging to a Jonathan M. Roots, a Meisterstück Classique Montblanc fountain pen, a very pricey, white-gold Cartier wristwatch, and a hidden passport identifying him as Jahan Manu Rabiei, a diplomatic functionary of the Islamic Republic of Iran.

This last detail floored the husband as Mr. Roots/ Rabiei had portrayed himself as a wealthy east coast American Indian who owned several casinos.

Callahan just grimly smiled.

*   *   *

Much to his surprise, fourteen hours later, Rabiei found himself booked on another flight, this one a bit longer in duration, as he had been very publicly expelled from the United States on several charges, and espionage was the least of them. His future career in the Iranian secret service was dashed, as before he departed the States, several domestic governmental agencies had him fingerprinted, photographed, and sampled for his DNA. Unknown to Rabiei was that during that intake process a chip had been surreptitiously implanted in his arm just for good measure.

*　　*　　*

The sudden and much-publicized arrival of Rabiei in Tehran caused quite a stir among the strategic planners of SAVAMA. To lose a domestic cell was one thing, but to have its directing field officer uncovered and expelled was quite another. Hardly a career enhancement, Rabiei's career as a field officer in the West was over, as Britain, France, Germany, and Israel now had his particulars, courtesy of the United States.

But one man in that black ministry was inwardly pleased at the outcome, because it clearly proved to him, at least in a general sense, where the secret research facility was located.

The detection, capture, and very public expulsion of a spy caught red-handed, however, were very rare occurrences. It didn't follow the usual heavy-handed fickleness and desire for convoluted intrigue that were trademarks of the American government. No, Aref reasoned. This expulsion was executed by a very different sort of organization. One that thought deeper and was more Russian in its chess moves than the heavily inbred, predictable, and shameless politically motivated U.S. State Department.

Then an odd thought occurred to Aref. Could it be that this research organization was so powerful that it could actually implement its own rules for dealing with foreign spies? Was it also in a position to bend the law of the land to its own will? Even more formidable, would that satanic cabal form its own destiny? Now that was something to consider, because if that was true, then that would explain much, so very, very much.

* * *

It hadn't been particularly difficult to get a hold of the Rabiei file and discern the take from his recently burned U.S. cell. As Aref pored over it, he soon realized that Rabiei had been very close to providing a GPS location for this super-secret research installation. Furthermore, Rabiei's strategy of following the logistical trail had been a very sound one, just one that had not been brought to fruition.

So, what do we know? He asked himself.

We know that every Tuesday and Friday, provisions are transported overland. We know, because of an analysis of their trash, that approximately twenty-five to forty-five people are based there. We know the warehouse where said provisions are prepared and loaded for transport. That means that the installation and its warehouse are in constant communications. We know that the installation cannot be more than sixty miles from its warehouse as the travel times recorded did not allow for a greater distance. We know from hard experience that terrestrial reconnaissance of the area is especially hard to do. That means they must have an efficient tactical security force. So where is there a chink in their armor? And then, for some reason, an ancient story came to him, a story about a horse gifted to the victors.

CHAPTER VI
Tehran, Iran. Niroo Research Institute (NRI)

They met in a smallish seminar room located on the Niroo Research Institute campus, one of Iran's innovative energy research centers. While NRI is not exactly a household name, it is perhaps best known for the highly publicized disruption of its website by an Israeli hacker. Located at the western end of Shahid Dadman Boulevard in Tehran's northwestern quadrant, the god-awful sulfur dioxide smog on that day in May obscured anyone on campus from seeing the rest of the city's skyline, much less its distinctive Milad Tower.

In all there were three of them, all dressed in generic dark suit coats, open collared shirts, and slacks. All were heavily bearded. After a male assistant had left with their orders of tea or juice, some standard formulaic pleasantries were recited, and then the trio got down to business. As had become custom, Aref Fardoust began the discussion.

"As you know, I have been away to do some research. After many, many interviews, it has become eminently clear to me that something very odd has been going on in Egypt, and for some time, perhaps as long as the past ten to fifteen years."

This news was greeted with sagacious nods and grunts of acknowledgement.

"It also concerns the Americans and the Russians."

This revelation was met by the other men with negative head shakes, and elicited from the second man a mumble and curl of the lip, who voiced, "Both Great Satans! I am not at all surprised."

Waiting for the pair to refocus, Aref continued.

"This last detail of the American and Russian involvement was only confirmed after the administration of sodium pentothal to a highly placed Egyptian bureaucrat. Additionally, I also learned from him that experiments in high energy physics were involved, the precise details of which he did not possess. Further, this same bureaucrat claimed that it was through the practical application of high energy physics that men were actually traveling back and forth in history, in time."

"My esteemed brother, are you quite certain of this?" stated the third man with more than a bit of disbelief.

"This is what the man stated. And for the record, he even sang to me his favorite song in the ancient Egyptian tongue, which was first sung to him by one of these time travelers!"

"Needless to say," began the second man, "what you have just reported as practical fact is at the very least extraordinary and scientifically quite controversial as well. In fact, some physicists would tell you outright that practical time travel just cannot be. But for the moment, let us suspend that discussion. For what intrigues me, while I know that the Two Great Satans have worked together in the past, is why they would do so now and with such a critical and ground-breaking technology. Would not one, instead of both, be the master of such technology?"

In answer, Aref could only first shrug his shoulders in ignorance before he responded, "Holy One, I am only reporting what I have discovered to date. I cannot answer such intimate questions of science or international relations. What I can say is that it is most unfortunate that this same bureaucrat's daughter was not available to confirm his story."

"And why is that?" asked the third man, his voice still betraying his total incredulity.

"Frankly," Aref said, "I think she somehow received word of her father's abduction and went into hiding."

"And what is the current state of her father?" the third man again queried, this time with a hard voice and eyes.

"Oh, he's alive, if that is what you mean. But just barely. When we were finished with him, we dropped him off at a neighborhood clinic. It seems that his heart was just not up to the sodium pentothal. Perhaps it had reacted poorly with some other medications that he was taking. I do not know. He was barely conscious when we left him."

"And do you think that was the wisest course?" yet again asked the third man.

After a dramatic pause for reflection, Aref said, "Yes. Yes, I do. He was old, harmless, and a bit befuddled. Besides, he was a good Muslim, even if a Sunni."

"I am concerned, Aref, that your late father would not have approved of your decision-making in this matter," pressed the third man. "Are you getting soft in your advancing years?"

Bristling internally at being second-guessed by this self-professed fanatical cleric, one who had repeatedly preached for further suicide attacks, but would never participate himself. Aref first smiled benignly, bowed his head, and said, "Holy One. Thank you for blessing the name of my late father by remembering him and all that he has done for our great and just cause. But as for the Egyptian, I had no cause to spill his blood. No reason whatsoever, for he has no face to remember, as we all wore hoods. Kindly remember, he is a former member of the Supreme Council of Antiquities and a well-known personality to the Egyptian administration. To spill his blood could potentially be harmful to our countries' relations. Besides, Allah is often merciful. And at times, so am I."

"But that nation is allied with the accursed nation, whose name I will not even speak! So who really cares about the spilling of one man's blood?" heatedly replied the third man.

Bowing his head during this ridiculous and often repeated tirade, Aref remained humbly silent as he prayed that he had his knife to silence this idiot. But at this point, the second man, wishing to move on, opined, "So how are you to proceed if this missing daughter cannot be found?"

Now looking down on his folded hands as they rested relaxed upon the table, Aref knew that he was in a bind, and so followed what his father had always taught him in such cases: lie and lie well.

"Fortunately, Holy One, I have several options that are still available to me. Options that I wish to examine. That is all that I can say at this point in my investigation."

"That sounds like a blatant evasion," the third man said.

"Yes, Holy One, it may well be. But a man such as I always has resources at his disposal that can shed light upon a particular matter. I just wish the time to make sure before I speak."

"Time travel," the second and younger of the two clerics mused. "Now that would be a most powerful tool for the advancement of Shi'a Islam! I can easily imagine many points in history when, instead of a defeat, a victory would have been most helpful. . . ."

*   *   *

Professor Jamal al-Ibin sat in his office, rereading a book written by an enlightened Westerner by the name of Montgomery Watt. *The Majesty That Was Islam,* an intellectual *tour de force*, still stirred the scholar's heart at its very core, even if it was for the fourth time. So deep was he in his focus upon the text that he failed to hear the respectful knock upon his door. It was only a loud clearing of a throat that finally snapped Jamal out of his reverie. It was his assistant, a thin young man with an enlarged Adam's apple. To Jamal, whenever the man spoke, it was as if he was watching a giraffe swallow.

"Excuse me for disturbing you, Holy One, but there is a man from the Ministry of Intelligence and National Security that wishes a brief moment of your time. May I say that you are available?"

The mention of that particular ministry caused Jamal's stomach to tighten and mouth to turn dry. Looking down, he placed a bookmark where he had been reading, closed the forbidden Western author's book, and placed it on the shelf behind him among the other hundred or so books.

Choosing now to acknowledge his assistant, he just nodded his head in assent, who then scampered off to fetch the unexpected visitor.

While Aref Fardoust was not a patient man by inclination, he was nonetheless one who had learned the skill. He was fully prepared to wait for an audience with this supposedly learned historian of Islam, so he was surprised when the lackey returned so quickly, bowed, and led him down the hall.

Well, that's a first, he thought. *Would that my colleagues back at the ministry behaved so politely!*

Upon entering the scholar's inner sanctum, Aref was assaulted by the smell of ink and books. Books covered the walls and even stood in two neat stacks to the right of a modestly sized wooden desk, before which the lackey had just thoughtfully placed a chair. As for the inhabitant of this minor library collection, he was a man of short stature with a round, bearded face of salt-and-pepper. Aref guessed his age at being somewhere in his sixties, making him a man who had known prerevolutionary Iran.

Standing behind his desk, Jamal stated the proscribed Muslim welcome. Aref, standing opposite, by rote recited its proper reply. Introductions were made and accepted. A courteous offer was extended that the ministry official make himself comfortable, followed shortly with a polite offer of some tea or juice. "No thank you," was the equally polite response. For Aref, it was as if he had been transported back in time to the nineteenth century. All that was missing was the reek of camel dung, some sand underfoot, and the wind whipping at a tent flap.

"Sir," Jamal began, "how might a historian be of service to a member of the Ministry of Intelligence and National Security?"

The clarity and directness of the question was a pleasure for Aref, who after those dreary interviews in Egypt, was aching to get to the crux of the mysterious events that had taken place at Karnak and Sakkara.

"Holy One, I wish to first thank you for meeting with me and on such short notice."

Notice? What notice? Jamal thought. *Just what does this silver-tongued bureaucrat want of me?*

"I was hoping to find out which battles against the infidels, in your learned opinion, were the most crucial to the course of Islamic expansion? While I am not a historian, I am nonetheless curious to know what would have happened if this battle or that had not gone badly for the faithful of Allah, what perhaps would have been the long term result."

Jamal's eyes widened at the question, no, the series of logically intelligent questions that had just been uttered.

"So, you are interested in the crucial battles that occurred during the Umayyad Caliphate. Most likely battles that took place on European soil. Let me see now," pinching his lower lip between his thumb and forefinger, "I think that I have just the source. One moment, please."

At that, Jamal stood up and went to the bookshelves on Aref's right. Standing on his tiptoes, the scholar reached up and plucked a volume by its spine from the second shelf from the top. Returning to his desk, he quickly paged through the text, clearly one that he was familiar with, and stopping at a page, he smiled and said. "There are precisely eight such battles: at Avignon, Narbonne, Nîmes, the River Garonne, the River Berre, Simancas, Toulouse, and, of course, Tours."

"Holy One, if you were to choose any one of those, which infidel commander played the most decisive role?"

Without skipping a beat, the imam declared, "Why, the Frankish nobleman Charles Martel, of course, also known as Charles the Hammer. Because he, without question, led his Frankish troops the best, and played multiple roles in many of the battles that I have just mentioned. Without him, I think that I can say with some authority, Western Europe would have surely fallen to the Caliphate. And who knows, perhaps the Mediterranean may even have been renamed, Allah's Own Sea.

"But also of note, my son, is the fact that this Charles Martel was the founder of the Carolingian Dynasty, making him the grandfather of Charlemagne, the man who launched Europe into the High Middle Ages. To be blunt, Charles Martel is a macro-historical figure. He occupies a fundamental historical pivot point in history. Without him, the entire historical landscape of Europe changes."

*　　*　　*

While Aref drove himself back to the Niroo Research Institute, a plan began to form in his mind as he now had a distinct target. As his thoughts tumbled this way and that, he began to formulate a strategy, and then the tactics, to do what Allah justly commanded him.

The institute, as with all research institutes throughout the world, had its own computer science department that acted as a teaching facility, a research department, and a functional service and maintenance arm of the NRI. It was to the research area that Aref made his unannounced visit in the hopes of finding someone who might be of service. In the Western vernacular, he went phishing. And as before, he was resigned to the inevitable circuitous departmental meanderings until he found that one personality upon whom he could make a special request.

It wasn't as if he did not have readily at hand such resources within his own ministry. But like his taste in fish, Aref preferred his data fresh and unadulterated. He was so successful precisely because he was the consummate loner. If he had ever played cards, he would always have closely breasted them. Besides, ever the maverick, this meandering research project was personal, off the books, and therefore unauthorized by his own ministry. Only two others even knew of it, and it was for financial reasons that they did, as his investigations cost money. But, for a man like Aref, even two was far too many for his tastes.

In all, his quest took three introductions before he had found his man. Javed Habibi, a graduate assistant, once he saw the ministry badge, was nervously eager to please his unexpected visitor.

"Mr. Habibi, to be blunt, I require information on an American, a Professor Joseph Richards. I know that he is an Egyptologist at an American university. What I want you to do is to find his e-mail address. Then I want you to break into his university's e-mail server.

What I want is a copy of the American's e-mails, as many as the server contains. Can you do this for me?"

"Oh, yes, sir. I can. E-mail servers at universities are very susceptible to, ah, external examination. Do you wish the e-mails printed out or copied to disk?"

"Disk would be best."

"Ah, ah, when do you want this task completed?"

Now with a smile that was most disarming, Aref said, "Yesterday would be fine, but, that would be most impolite. So, how about in two days' time?"

*   *   *

As it turned out, the disk so kindly provided by the graduate assistant contained six years' worth of the American's e-mails and took up Allah only knows how much storage. Clearly, Aref did not intend to cull through each and every one of this academic's incessant prattle, but a thought did occur to him. The FIND function just might be the way to tease a thread free from this vast tapestry of correspondence! But upon carefully examining the very first record, it was the e-mail addresses themselves that caught the Iranian agent's eye. Then Aref made a prescient, intuitive leap, typed into the FIND function's search box the name Moussa, and pressed the ENTER key.

"By Allah's own beard!" he exclaimed, for there was no fewer than fifty separate correspondences: one for a "smoussa" and another for an "imoussa". Emboldened, Aref scanned down through the list, and another address appeared. Lo and behold, it was linked to "smoussa"'s e-mail address, and this time with over two hundred hits.

Now sitting back in his chair, the Iranian intelligence agent knew that he had what he was looking for, as both of the Moussas he suspected were highly involved in the Russian and American time machine operations in Egypt.

This will clearly take time to reconstruct. I will begin chronologically. In the process, more names will be caught in my web, which will only fill out the picture more completely.

*　　*　　*

After four days of intensive analysis, Aref now possessed the picture that he so dearly wanted. The potential scope of the operation was breathtaking. So much so that the Iranian intelligence officer had to lay it out piece by piece on the table before him, and even then more and more connections began to show themselves. There were two primary facilities: one clearly quite secret in New Mexico, and the other quite public, called the Philology Annex, located in Chicago and on a university campus. *What an audacious cover!* The Chicago location appeared to be an administrative training center of some kind, while the New Mexican site, by the very nature of its secrecy, must be where the technology resides.

Travel arrangements to New Mexico, as mentioned by Richards, began as early as 2000 and as late as 2006. This period of time corresponded well to the reports in Egypt of odd or suspicious activities. Several mentions of artifact retrievals occurred also during this period. On the basis of pure context, several nondescript e-mail addresses must be addresses of the New Mexican facility.

So, now I have at last something more to hack, and Allah only knows what I might find.

* * *

"Hello, my good friend! Do you have a moment for me?" asked the Iranian security officer of the suddenly nervous graduate assistant.

Obviously trapped, with Javed Habibi's eyes darting this way and that for some possible means of escape, but obviously finding none since he was sitting in his cubical, a stuttering reply was all that he could manage.

"Ah, why, yes! Yes, I do." Now standing, he indicated to a chair. "Kindly sit and be at peace."

"Why, thank you. I just wanted you to know that your research has exceeded all expectations. Would you be so kind and tell me who your supervisor is so that I can personally put in a good word for you."

Now frantically waving his hands in negation, the assistant blurted out, "No. No. That will not be necessary. As it is, I am behind in my research, and I do not want to attract any unusual notice."

Then realizing who he was talking to, he recovered and said, "But I do appreciate your most kind offer. Sincerely. But now I must get back to work." That last said in the sincerest of hopes that the intelligence officer would get the hint.

"I am truly sorry, Javed, but you see, you have talent. True talent. And right now, talent that I require, the ministry requires. Do you fully understand me?" Aref stated with a stone-like firmness.

Again trapped, the assistant just shook his head in negation. "No. One small favor perhaps, but not two.

You will have to discuss this with my supervisor as my schedule is such that my hands are tied."

"You say that your hands are tied. What an interesting metaphor," cooed Aref with a sinister tone. "That is one of my special skills.

"So, I will ask you to reconsider only once more your most ardent desire to assist me. Otherwise, I will present to your superior graphic and plentiful evidence of Western pornography that you downloaded from the Internet. I think that this should go a long way in explaining to him why you are so far behind in your research.

"So, Javed, what's your answer? You hold your future in your hands."

Truly scared, but even more so angry at his predicament, the assistant did not at first say one word. Then he said quite clearly and distinctly as if into a microphone, "Sir. This entire conversation has been recorded. It is you who have overstepped your bounds, and your childish threats are worthless to me. Why? Because, Mr. Aref Fardoust of the SAVAMA, eldest son of the late Hussein Fardoust, I have reported you to your ministry. They were most interested in your first request, as much as your current whereabouts. So, leave now, before I call security."

Aref, stunned by this development, looked first to his right and then left, and seeing no one, swiftly and silently killed the assistant with his bare hands. Looking down on Javed's crumpled and disfigured form, the Iranian official thought, *Fine. Your choice. Now tape that!*

*   *   *

99

At that precise moment and not two stories above the now late Javed's cubical in the very same NRI administrative building, two men were conducting a serious discussion about what to do about Fardoust.

"He is an unmanageable asset who, because he carries his father's good name, thinks that he can run his own private operations. While I recognize his instincts do border on the paranormal, his lack of obedience to authority and disregard for protocol is legendary. And now he browbeats a research assistant into hacking for him. And why? Because he doesn't want to go through our dedicated personnel. And why? Because he has inherited his father's own well-known paranoia."

Stopping only to take a deep breath, his colleague then joined in, interrupting the other's near tirade midcourse.

"I must agree with you. Aref is quite abrasive, but he is also effective. Is it your wish to dull his keen edge? Look how far and how fast he has progressed on this investigation by himself. Why, two months ago, we both thought that he was crazy – time travel of all things! But now, with just a small effort, we have the truth of it buried in some American academic's e-mails.

"So, may I suggest that we bring him in, visit with our cyber-oriented colleagues at the ministry, and really come up with some results?"

* * *

While his colleagues in the ministry were furiously trying to get in contact with their wayward agent, the personnel of the Computer Technology and Research Department were greedily dissecting, parsing, and reconstituting the disk of e-mails that Javed Habibi had provided them. They too created their own scenarios as to the e-mails' significance. What they did not have, however, was Aref Fardoust's insights that he had gained through all the interviews and interrogations that he had held. In short, they did not have a context for place these correspondences. Hence the reason behind the all-points bulletin on Fardoust's whereabouts.

So, when Aref blundered into the ministry's complex of his own accord, his colleagues were most appreciative of the fact, as the agent was placed in an interrogation room. Ten hours later and feeling like a wrung-out dishrag, Aref emerged victorious as his head remained on his shoulders and he was still considered a vital asset. His leash, however, had become far shorter. Now with the full force of the Iranian ministry's CTR Department behind him, the cyber onslaught began in earnest on a handful of promising e-mail addresses.

CHAPTER VII
1992-1996. Sakkara

It was a Monday afternoon, and Salah was trudging away with his basket of debris from the Sakkara excavation to mindlessly and mechanically dump his burden at the designated spoil site. Once there, he knew that it would be sifted. This he remembered with a wince as he had once performed that god-awful, dusty chore. *All that effort expended for just the recovery of some worthless chunk of rock, piece of pottery, or sliver of bone. These archaeologists, whether European or Egyptian, were a very crazy bunch!*

While the money was good and the work remained tolerable, Salah felt that he was just an ant toiling away in the hot sun beneath the grand remains of the Step Pyramid. Per his habit, and to help pass the time more quickly, Salah began to daydream about what it must have been like for his distant ancestors, who had no doubt toiled during the construction of this vast architectural wonder. Despite his remarkably active imagination, this particular day seemed to pass with glacial speed. It was as if there was something ominous in the air.

Then it happened. At precisely at 3:09 p.m. local time, a deafening roar was heard that lasted for some twenty-odd seconds. Now finding himself sitting on his backside, Salah was terrified beyond belief as he found that his entire world was in motion. Earthquakes that are 5.9 on the Richter scale do that, especially if you are practically standing, or in this case sitting, directly over its epicenter. Little did Salah know, but what he had just experienced on that October day in 1992 had not struck Egypt with such force, a force of over seven kilotons of TNT, since 1847. Once his head cleared and his senses began to register, he then heard the many screams and, to his horror, witnessed four of his companions being swallowed up in the liquefaction of a sandy depression. In mere moments, they were no more, not even a single trace.

*   *   *

It had finally occurred. The recent seismic event had dislodged the shard of plaster that had been first cracked in the earthquake of 1847. As fragments go, it could have easily rested in the palm of a child's hand with its one smoothed side and its opposite molded into a raised, T-shaped configuration almost a quarter of an inch tall. As it fell away from the wall that it had faithfully chinked for more than forty-six centuries, it exposed a precisely carved horizontal groove some four centimeters long.

*   *   *

As a consequence of the 1992 seismic event, the many subterranean passages of the Sakkara Plateau were closed, much to the tourism administration's dismay. Leading that list was the vast and subway-like Serapeum, followed closely by the Ptolemaic upper and lower baboon catacombs, and the contemporaneous ibis galleries. Not overlooked in that same governmental embargo were the nearly 3.5 kilometers of tunnels beneath the Step Pyramid complex. In many respects, the financial impact of that geological event was greater and far more lasting upon the well-being of the nation's balance sheet than upon its ancient monuments.

* * *

As Richards removed the three volumes from the NEI's archive, he hefted their weight in both hands and noted that he had a long read ahead of him. Entitled *The Galleries of Imhotep. An Investigation Beneath the Step Pyramid at Sakkara*, volume one, edited by Ulrich Schachermayr, was the narrative. Volume two contained the line drawings of many inscriptions, ostraka, finds, and architectural plans. While volume three was a copiously illustrated photographic record, both in black-and-white and color plates. Curious, Richards looked for and found the list of donors on its separate page. It read like a *Wall Street Journal* blue-chip stock listing. *So that is where he got all of his funding for this lavish publication!*

So Ulli, Richards mused, *this was your first major publication. Impressive indeed, my friend. And from Sakkara to now digging at the Temple of Ptah in Memphis. Impressive indeed!*

Being that it was late afternoon, the Egyptologist gravitated over to his favorite spot, and settled himself down for the duration.

To his great pleasure, Schachermayr's writing style, while direct, was clear and lively for such an archaeological publication, which by definition tend to be as dry as dirt. What Richards soon found was the fascinating tale of serendipity and dogged persistence, an earthquake that loosened a plaster layer that camouflaged a hidden doorway, a mildly claustrophobic archaeologist working in tight quarters, and a remarkably collegial relationship between a green-as-grass Austrian archaeologist and an old master of the trade, the Frenchman, Jean-Philippe Lauer.

*   *   *

In 1925, Cecil Firth, a man of considerable vigor and girth, had begun clearing the Step Pyramid complex and discovered that it was the work of the Third Dynasty Pharaoh Djoser. With much of this ancient monument found in ruin, the Englishman realized that a considerable clearance and restoration effort was required and that he needed an architect on his staff in order to undertake this massive task. After having made several inquiries within the Egyptian Antiquities Service, its then Director Pierre Lacau assigned to Firth for the next archaeological season a young twenty-four-year-old Frenchman named Jean-Philippe Lauer. At the time, Lauer's initial contract was only for an eight-month period. Little did anyone know, however, that the contract would be renewed, re-renewed, and renewed yet again until Firth's untimely death in 1931.

Then, when another Englishman succeeded Firth, a man named James Edward Quibell, Lauer was again at the scene, no doubt providing some much needed stability during that sudden transition. Lauer would remain working at the Step Pyramid up until the outbreak of World War II, but would return to his labors in 1946. In fact, only one more break would occur in this man's devotion to that most ancient archaeological site, and that was during a brief period during 1956 to 1959, the early years of the Gamal Abdel Nassar administration.

With archaeology, there was always politics. So from 1959 onwards, when Lauer was allowed to return, he remained at the Step Pyramid of Djoser as it slowly, inexorably, began to emerge from the sands of Sakkara. Throughout it all, several generations of Egyptian laborers, who had worked with Lauer side-by-side, had considered the slight and soft-spoken man first as their "brother," then "father," and eventually "grandfather." But above all, for his lifelong toil at the pyramid, he was assigned the nickname "the forgotten one of God."

*　　*　　*

As Richards continued with Schachermayr's narrative, the excitement and sheer electricity that he and Lauer shared at his chance discovery made was abundantly clear. And, perhaps perversely, Richards had a thought and put down the heavy tome so that he could scratch a growing intellectual itch that was bothering him.

So I wonder what does modern scholarship thinks about Imhotep. I'll just bet that my good friend Alphonso would be embarrassed.

*　　*　　*

Licking the tip of his thumb, Richards flicked his way through the third volume of the *Lexikon der Ägyptologie*. Acting on a hunch, his fingers stopped once they found the citation "Imhotep," and he scanned through the volume's narrow columns of dense and laconic academic German. Several items caught his eye.

Imhotep is often represented as a man wearing a skull cap that identifies him as a follower of Ptah. The Turin Papyrus refers to him with the epithet "son of Ptah." He sometimes wears an archaic linen kilt indicating his religious purity. Typically is depicted as a priest with a shaved head, seated on a chair with an open papyrus across his lap. Later, his statuettes show him standing with a divine beard and carrying an ankh and scepter. Little is known of I[mhotep's] life, but was an influential official during the reign of Djoser. He designed and built the Step Pyramid complex. He may have been responsible for the first known use of extensive stone blocks and drummed columns in architecture. As a royal architect, I[mhotep] must have had contact with the royal family, and on the basis of his many titles (Chancellor of the King of Egypt, High Priest of Heliopolis, Hereditary nobleman, Doctor, First in line after the King of Upper Egypt, Administrator of the Great Palace, Hereditary nobleman, High Priest of Heliopolis, Builder, Chief Carpenter, Chief Sculptor, and Maker of Vases in Chief.), probably even lived within the royal palace. He was the earliest mortal to be mentioned on a pharaonic statue (Cairo JE 49889). On the basis of a graffito found within the enclosure wall of Sekhemkhet's unfinished pyramid, it appears that I[mhotep] may have outlived Djoser by several years. Supposedly was a font of priestly wisdom and magic and was famous during antiquity for his contributions to the disciplines of architecture and medicine. His title as the high priest of Heliopolis (Chief of Observers) implies that he was an astronomer as well. It has been surmised that I[mhotep] was the author of an encyclopedia that provided the basis for Egyptian architecture for the next thousand years. His tomb's location is unknown, but is suspected to be found somewhere in the Sakkaran region.

So, Richards summarized, *the historical Imhotep was an architect, healer, and astronomer – not to mention quite a social chameleon. No kidding! And what a lothario!*

In short, an early Renaissance man. But a man with such a resume had to have had quite a tomb. Still, it is yet to be found at the time of this publication's printing, and God only knows how hard Walter Emery, to name only one of many, searched high and low for it.

And then a thought occurred to the Egyptologist. *Imhotep was heavily involved with the royal family, most likely was a guest of the palace, and obviously worked closely with his Pharaoh Djoser, so my guess is that while everyone was grubbing all over the Sakkara plateau outside the Step Pyramid complex in search for his tomb, they really should be looking on the inside. After all, he designed the damn thing and oversaw its construction.*

Grunting to himself at that satisfied conclusion, Richards again summarized. *Yes, that must be how it was. Imhotep built his tomb somewhere within the complex, most likely in a location that would not attract much attention. I can see it all now. Just as with any magician worth his salt, Imhotep had his primary work crews working in one area, while another one – smaller and hand-picked – was busy elsewhere.*

* * *

With the particulars on Imhotep now squared away in his mind, Richards returned to Schachermayr's lucid account of the exposure of the entrance door and the remarkable discovery of its intact and pristine Third Dynasty door seals, arranged in neat vertical registers, which the editor pointed out, were

> Not royal and were only vaguely religious in nature; instead (they) were purely secular and administrative.

In fact, the entire central register of seals repeatedly said,

> Imhotep instructed that this sacred place be made secure.

As for the other graffito present, they all were proud proclamations of a work gang's name, those who apparently had constructed the gallery.

Schachermayr then revealed another first in Egyptian archaeology, when he described the discovery of ostraka in the door plug's fill, which had been found while sieving the debris. The forty-two ostraka recovered, one each from every *sepat*, or administrative district of Egypt, were densely covered with crudely etched hieroglyphic characters. Their content, while expressed uniquely in every case, wished "Imhotep and his parents, life eternal."

Glancing now over at the open architectural plans of the Austrian excavation, Richards saw that these ostraka came from the first plug of the gallery, the first of two, which blocked the entrance passage of the upper gallery.

Richards read on about the breakthrough of the second plug and the discovery of thirty-two more ostraka, all dedicated by the individual men of the excavation crews. What was notable about these heart-felt mementos was that they all had been written by the same hand, suggesting that one scribe had taken direct dictation from each individual. Again, something that Egyptian archaeology had never before encountered.

But all was not jubilation, for beyond the second plug, a modern workman lost his life when he fell through a plaster false floor into a twenty foot deep pit trap. It was the first of four that were encountered on the upper gallery.

So Ulli found some mantraps too!

Richards, having finished reading the narrative on the first season of the excavation, saw nothing that deserved world-wide sharing had been found. So, glancing at his watch and noting that it was dinner time, he took a break.

*   *   *

The second season of the Austrian excavation beneath the Southern Superstructure of the Step Pyramid Complex was inaugurated in 1994. Because of their extraordinary nature, the oldest and most prestigious journal of Egyptology, the *Zeitschrift für die Ägyptische Sprache*, published the door seals that were encountered. Best of all, Schachermayr and Lauer had insisted that Nicole Golvin, the graduate student who was studying these inscriptions for her dissertation, should enjoy the lead editorial position on the publication.

As for the addition of the entrance doorway to the architectural site map, the Frenchman Lauer had this to say about it:

Regarding the new doorway's dimensions and its continuing corridor, they measure precisely 2.10 meters wide by 2.62 meters tall. This calculates out to four royal cubits wide by five tall. This is very significant as Imhotep's version of the royal cubit was 52.5 centimeters long. Furthermore, the cutting of the passageway itself is remarkably true and does not deviate by more than one degree, which is a significant observation. What is even more intriguing is that this doorway matches in dimension that of Door M directly opposite it in the Beta Corridor. So, even if we did not enjoy the benefit of the door seals and ostraka found by Mlle. Golvin, we could still cogently argue for a contemporaneous date for Door M and what is now called Door Z.

*   *   *

The Austrian team penetrated the entranceway, the first blocking plug of rubble, a pit trap, and yet another blocking plug, now encountered a T-intersection. Proceeding with care, three more pit traps were detected as the intersection led to a continuous rectangular passage that surrounded a central chamber, the entrance of which was guarded by one of the traps.

Directly opposite the central chamber's entrance, against the far wall, stood an exquisite life-sized statue. Carved of rich cedarwood, its lifelike ivory eyes and ebony pupils seemed to blink in curiosity in the lamp light of the new arrivals. The chamber's walls that surrounded this formally posed figure were covered with beautifully executed black hieroglyphics in vertical registers against a stark, whitewashed surface.

Other than the lone statue, the room was empty, except for a stone rectangle that was embedded flush into the center of the floor. Upon its examination, the rectangle turned out to be of white alabaster covered in columns of beautifully executed hieroglyphs cut in sunken relief. The following is a translation of the slab's ten line inscription.

[I am] Imhotep, son of Kanofer [and] Khereduankh the glorified, |

Chancellor of the King of Egypt, Doctor, First in line after the King of Upper Egypt, |

Administrator of the Great Palace, Hereditary nobleman, High Priest of Heliopolis, Builder, Chief Carpenter, |

Chief Sculptor, Chief Maker of Vases, and the most trusted architect [and] beloved companion |

of Hor-Netjerikhet Nub-Re Nisut-Bity-Neby-Netjerikhetnebu Djoser, ||

who granted me this sacred place for my beloved parents |

within his most sacred precinct. All that I am is contained within this most perfect of places. |

That which is obvious is not. To find that which is most valuable, things of the intellect, |

seek where Re makes his first appearance. [Established on the] nineteenth year of the Horus Netjerikhet, |

[the fourth season of] Shemu, [second month of]
Iepet-Hemet. ||

Richards' reaction to this inscription was a mix of
historical interest and outright, surprised fascination.
Initially, the text began with stock biographical themes,
the full content of which were quite extraordinary in
their own right. What followed was Imhotep's
dedication to his parents, which suggested that they are
buried beneath this alabaster slab. And then it was as if
Imhotep was speaking directly to the reader,
challenging the reader, most extraordinary. Finally, his
message became a riddle of some kind. There was even
a clue provided so one can find "that which is most
valuable – things of the intellect."

Finally, Richards thought. *Now we're getting
somewhere!*

Beneath the slab, once it was raised with the aid of
wooden scaffolding and block and tackle, was found a
rubble-filled shaft that no doubt led to the tomb of
Imhotep's parents. Upon its clearing, the rectangular
shaft measured some seven meters straight down and
behind a plaster layer of camouflage, its northern face
contained a doorway. And just like the plaster door
seals that had covered the entranceway above, the exact
same ones and their arrangement were found impressed
into the doorway at the bottom of the shaft.

The breeching of this doorway opened to a modest
burial chamber that contained two pristine Third
Dynasty wooden coffins and a scatter of grave goods
that covered its floor. Undisturbed since the early Third
Dynasty, this chamber was cleared and sent to the Cairo
Museum's Department of Conservation.

Drat! Richards thought. *It's not here either*. But as he sat in the archives, the Egyptologist nonetheless found himself captivated by the last register of that curious inscription from the alabaster lid. The glyphs just seemed to dance before his eyes teasing him, poking at his brain. While he thoroughly understood their grammatical underpinnings, what the individual consonant clusters meant, it was the inscription's contextual meaning that eluded him.

> All that I am is contained within this most perfect of places. That which is obvious is not. To find that which is most valuable, things of the intellect, seek where Re makes his first appearance.

Okay. Fine, Richards thought. I suppose that the daring unsupported design of the chamber would fit that first line, for I know of no subterranean chamber built by the Egyptians in any period that did not have pillars bracing its ceiling. Yet, this chamber had none across its nearly seven-by-five-meter expanse. Then again, to my best knowledge, the four pit traps are another first at Sakkara and only to be copied thousands of years later in the Valley of the Kings and the Treasury of Amen Re.

Beyond those two architectural features, this monument was constructed not for himself, but for his parents, or should I say, adopted parents on the basis of the chamber's wall inscription in the appendix. How selfless. How tender his detailed chronicle of his adoption, education, and loving care by his mother, Khereduankh, and his overflowing pride to stand beside his father, Kanofer, as his apprentice.

Then there is that marvelously executed three-dimensional self-portrait in flawless cedarwood. Itself a statement of supreme confidence, authority, and humanity, as he strode ever forward with a staff of office in his right hand and a roll of papyrus gripped in his left. And then there is the statue's satisfied smile produced by just the slightest of upturns at the corner of the lips. That too is a first, as it resembles more an archaic Greek form than an Egyptian one. But all in all, the whole is just breathtaking. "All that I am," indeed.

As for that next enigmatic line, "That which is obvious is not." Sigh. *Now just what am I to make of that?*

The Egyptologist considered. *It's hard enough to grasp its meaning, much less make heads or tails of what it refers to. So, Richards, spin this sentence around. So, something is not obvious? So what does that mean? That the tomb is not a tomb? That the laudatory inscription to his parents is something else entirely? No. That cannot be right. So, that means that something which is out in the open is not what it seems to be. The question then becomes: what is obvious that can in some way be turned around to be not obvious?*

For the moment baffled, the American refused to be defeated, but realized that he would have to place this conundrum aside for the moment. *Best sleep on that one. That now leaves us with the riddle about "those valuable things of the intellect" that can be found "where Re makes his first appearance." Well, one thing seems clear. Re's first appearance must be a directional reference, specifically to the east, where the sun first makes its appearance. So, the "most valuable things of the intellect" are to be found along an eastern bearing.*

That line of deductive thinking got Richards to pull out the publication's architectural plan. Spinning the schematic around so the top of it was oriented north, Richards realized that the directional referent indicated either the eastern wall of the central chamber or the easternmost wall of the encircling corridor.

Clever, he thought. *So Imhotep has hidden something of intellectual value probably in the eastern wall of the outside corridor, as the eastern wall thickness of the chamber is very doubtful, due to its narrow thickness. So, it has to be either a niche or another chamber hidden in the corridor.* And sure enough, a small niche was so indicated on the architectural plan.

Okay. I have now understood most of this most vexing inscription, but "that which is obvious is not" still remains elusive.

*   *   *

"Chapter III, Season Three (1995)" and Richards began anew the next day, in search of something worth sharing with all of humanity. As he read, several items jumped out at him.

The first was the niche, whose location he had figured out on his own, which had contained a domed cedarwood chest of exquisite workmanship. The volume had described it as having "Bands of gold leaf, tasteful ivory inlays, and delicately carved hieroglyphs." Within it lay sixteen papyrus rolls that were the architectural plans of the entire Step Pyramid Complex, and nothing else.

The second item that caught Richards' eye was the discovery on the opposite side of the semitransparent alabaster lid of an inscription that could only be read if illuminated through the opposite side. Considering this was a first in Egyptian archaeology, Richards found himself at a crossroads. Given the recto inscription on the alabaster lid, which was obvious, the verso inscription and its solution were decidedly not. Curious for sure, and clever on top of that, this still was not worth sharing with all of mankind. But the words of the composite recto/verso inscription seemed to hint at something more.

[I am] Imhotep, son of Kanofer [and] Khereduankh the glorified, |

(vac.) |

(vac.) |

(vac.) |

[I the] most trusted architect of Djoser made below for ||

(vac.) |

my beloved parents their most sacred precinct for eternity. |

[I] made below a sacred place that is not obvious. |

To read these words is to know the way of this stone's brilliance in Re's presence. |

(vac.) ||

(vac.) |

"Well, well," softly said a deeply thoughtful Richards, "it seems that the meaning of that penultimate line: 'I made below a sacred place that is not obvious,' clearly hints at something more to come."

He paused to stretch his mind.

"Could that line be referring again to his parents' tomb? I don't think so." Then Richards noted something. Imhotep used the verbal form *ir*, 'to make,' twice.

"No, sir, I read this as Imhotep making a point of emphasis that there is a separate, second sacred place."

And his pulse again began to rise in anticipation, and Schachermayr's narrative soon satisfied this drama with the discovery of yet again another plaster camouflaged doorway that had been cut into the back wall of Imhotep's parents' tomb chamber, one that was broader than any thus far encountered in Imhotep's Galleries.

At this point, Richards found himself grinning as Schachermayr stated:

> Yet another doorway! This must be some sort of arcane archaeological record. In actual fact, this series of chambers that Imhotep had commissioned resembles more a mine than a tomb.

How apt! When yet another set of door seals were found impressed into the plaster covering this doorway, the Egyptologist just threw up his hands, as if to say, "no kidding, what a surprise." But then Schachermayr's narrative sobered the American.

> Clearly, and these seals are just further evidence, Imhotep himself was directly involved in this

construction process. From everything that we have seen in this gallery, he was very hands on. He worked closely with these work gangs and clearly trusted them enough to construct his own parents' tomb. But perhaps even more than that, there was a partnership, a bond between him, a high administrative official of the king, and the common workmen.

What followed was the careful removal of yet another rubble barrier, a barrier that protected none other than the intact funerary deposit of the Pharaoh Djoser himself. The clearing of this chamber would require the construction of a massive restoration and storage magazine before one item could be removed. And as had occurred so many times before, an international effort built one, a state-of-the-art prototype, within the span of one year's time. Appropriately, it came to be known as the Great Magazine.

CHAPTER VIII
Rescue Flight

Lamkin is an itty-bitty Louisiana town located north of the Monroe city limits. Face it. It's a fly-spec of a town. If you were doing sixty-five on Highway 165 and sneezed real hard, you could miss its turnoff. What is mighty convenient, however, is that situated nearby is Black Bayou Lake, a sportsman's dream, a body of water with more interesting nooks and crannies than the hide of an elephant. On Stevenson Drive, not far from the aforementioned lake, more like a hard nine-iron away, Commander Charles Abraham "Tuna" Cartwright had built his handsome retirement home complete with an in-ground pool, a three-car garage, and a shed for all his guns and fishing tackle. Life was good, and with access to 165 so handy, the many shops in neighboring Monroe made it even better for his wife, Lucille.

Richards' plane, that very special Gulf Stream V owned and maintained by the Horizon Pass facility, landed at the Monroe Regional Airport three days after having flown all the way back from Cairo to Chicago. Truly not knowing just which time zone he was in, the Egyptologist staggered off the plane and was outright cold cocked by the region's bright sun and heavy humidity. Carrying an overnight bag over his shoulder and needing a shave, Richards walked the hundred or so steps from the plane's stairs to the corporate arrivals building.

Tuna watched the approach of the Egyptologist with his practiced eye.

Yep, he thought, *he's still ripped as ever. But by that stagger to his gait, he's bushed. Mostly likely heavily jet-lagged*, he silently diagnosed. *Yet, given his fancy ride, whatever he wanted to talk about that he couldn't on the phone must be really hot. Whatever it is, it's got to be really good or really, really bad. Probably the latter.*

Entering through the automatic sliding glass doors, the heavily air-conditioned atmosphere of the building hit the traveler hard. Although Richards involuntarily shivered, he was instantly warmed by the generous handshake and man-hug that the Louisianan offered.

"Well, Doc. Welcome to nowheresville. Did you remember to bring along yer fishin' pole?"

With a smile as broad as a house, the academic gave the former Special Forces officer a crushing squeeze and said, "Nope, Tuna, I did not. But I know for a fact that you have a spare that you might lend me, because we have a whole bunch to jaw about."

*   *   *

After a delicious home-prepared lunch of fresh fried catfish sandwiches and sweet tea, the pair found themselves fifteen minutes later floating in the shade of a long dead silver-trunked tree covered in Spanish moss. Flicking out their unbaited lures into the brackish green water, the silent men methodically popped open ice cold beers, sat back, and only then "commenced to jaw."

"You know, Tuna, during that firefight back at Sakkara, when Calli had Vesna and I huddled into those shallow depressions, I felt quite useless, exposed, and powerless. Hand to hand, I know that I'm lethal. That training at Fort Bragg ensured that. Practice, and some scraps on deployment, proved that training's worth in spades. Now, do you have any good Dutch Uncle advice for me? About guns, that is."

Examining his old and salt rusty spinning reel, the former special operations officer could only shake his well-trimmed head.

"You know, Joey my boy, this talk has been a long time coming. You're darn right about your close quarter's skills. They're honed to a fine, dark, and dangerous edge. Frankly, none of my boys never ever wanted to pick a fight with you, even the bigger ones. Calli's even a bit shy about you. They could tell, especially after your first retrieval, that you had changed, become something more, something not to be messed with, something far more than your name, 'young lion.' Something more like 'cobra' seemed more appropriate. Something coiled and ready to strike.

"But to get back to what you have in mind, remember that your training was purposeful. Back there in the *somewhen*, you had to rely on your wits and reflexes. Your body had to become a lethal weapon to give you any chance of survival. And damned if you didn't! Frankly, I'm quite proud of you, son. Especially how you handled yourself through some seriously tough times. Joey, my boy, you're quite the wonder in my book.

"As to that dust up in the Sakkaran desert, well, while unexpected, we were still ready for it, and we made damn well sure that the bad guys paid in full.

"So . . ."

Richards' cell phone rang. Looking down to see who it was, the Egyptologist smiled, raised his index finger to Tuna in apology, and promptly answered it.

*   *   *

The times were not auspicious ones for those in the Egyptian government's bureaucracy with all the political and civil unrest in the streets. And then there was the international press, who fanned the confusion and mayhem that seemed to flower in every corner once that little red light of their cameras appeared. Consequently, the director of the National Museum in Cairo decided to once again spend the night in her office. After all, she believed that it was safer here within its massive pink walls than to chance it in the streets. Tahrir Square was not all that far away.

Besides, Sharil rationalized to herself, the museum had its own security staff, who had been placed on high alert to prevent any further looting from occurring. That one incident was sufficient, and she had made that point absolutely clear by firing on the spot two suspected extremist sympathizers. The rest of the staff took note of their mistress's extreme ire, cinched in their pistol belts another notch, and began drinking coffee.

Glancing at her watch and making a quick calculation, Sharil picked up the phone and began to dial a number from memory. After two rings, a male voice answered.

"This is Dr. Richards. How may I help you?"

Letting out an unbidden deep and throaty chuckle, the usually formal director said, "Well now, Professor Richards, how courteous of you to offer so freely your assistance."

"Sharil! How are you! It's been so long since we last talked. Richards wisecracked, as it had only been, what, forty-eight hours?

And then remembering where she was calling from, and glancing at his wristwatch, what time she was calling. "Are you okay, as in safe and sound, over there?"

Pleased at Richards' concern for her well-being, Sharil quickly replied, "Yes, Joey. I'm still in one piece. But I must admit that this will be my last overnight in my office."

"Oh yeah? That bad, is it?"

"Well, let us just say that the streets of Cairo are not as hospitable as you might have once recalled."

Richards then shifted gears.

"So how's your father doing? I trust that he is well."

Again pleased with the American's appropriate sense of priorities, the question nonetheless caused a sudden ache in her chest.

"Indeed, Joey. I wish I could tell you that he is very well, and is resting nicely in his Alexandrian retirement. But I must say that I worry about him. He does not like one bit what has become of Egypt. Even his friends at the university are fearful of a government crackdown. And knowing my father, if that happens, he will throw himself right into the middle of it."

As Sharil's voice trailed off, Richards then decided to ask, "All right, Madam Director, what is the real reason for this call? Just a bit of international chitchat? Or is there something specific that is troubling you so much that you would chance the shaky security of an international cell phone connection?"

Silence. Then a quiet sigh.

"Joey. You know me far, far too well. Sometimes I think that you can almost read my mind. But since you asked, and since it was I who called you, just listen."

Needless to say, the news removed all the blood from Richards' face.

"Who's behind all of this?"

"I frankly do not know. But whoever they are, they currently are holding my father as a chess piece, so to speak. By the look of things, they probably have already drained from his mind everything that he knew, which while damning enough, fortunately, was precious little. But I am a different story, Joey. I frankly know far, far too much. So, would it be possible to send that very special jet of yours over to pick me up before they do?"

*　*　*

Snapping his cell phone closed, Richards just sat there for a moment with his eyes squeezed close. Then he just murmured to Tuna, "Well, that was quick. The bad guys have abducted Dr. Ibrahim Moussa in Alexandria, and now Sharil wants us to fly over with the GV and pick her up before the bad guys latch on to her."

With eyes that were angry slits, Tuna snarled, "Well, Joey! Don't just sit there like a bump on a log. Call up Horizon Pass and have them task the jet for departure for Cairo. While you're doing that, dump that crap fishing rig over the side, like pronto, as I get us ashore!"

And while the commander busied himself with the oars, causing them to creak with all the strain that his powerful shoulders and back were putting into the effort, he continued, "Fortunately for you, I have a spare deployment duffle that you can have. And by the way, I am coming with you on this gig. No argument. I owe Dr. Moussa big time. I owe Sharil big time. So be sure to tell Naysmithe that I'm going, like pronto!"

*　*　*

During their flight over to Egypt, Tuna and Richards continued their jawing session, and as it turned out, that spare deployment duffle included a Smith and Wesson M&P 9mm automatic along with several loaded magazines. By the time they landed, the Egyptologist had been grilled by one of the best in weapons' safety and etiquette. But the schooling hardly ended there, for the ever-patient Tuna had Joey aim and dry fire the weapon at least one hundred times.

As he explained to the philologist the various hand holds and stances, Tuna had to think in reverse when he discovered that Joey was a natural lefty. To end it all, the former Special Forces officer had Joey field strip the weapon seven times, clean it twice, and finally reassemble it four times blindfolded. When the plane had come to a stop at the corporate terminal at Cairo International, the Louisianan just handed the Egyptologist three loaded seventeen-round magazines.

"Okay, Joey. Here's your graduation gift: fifty-one Lake City 147 grain hollow points. Each one is the wrath of God. Place one well and it will instantly put down a full grown steer, like, to its knees. Do you read me, Joey? Good. Now, if you have to use them, use them judiciously."

*   *   *

The usual indestructible GM pickup truck that Tuna drove while in Egypt, and was so inexplicably fond of, was not deemed appropriate for this trip. Instead, Horizon Pass had arranged for another GM product, but one that possessed a bit more presence, and a bit more muscle, a white Tahoe. Jumping in and belting up, Tuna took the wheel and began to drive like the madman he always was. Having to stop briefly at two airport security checkpoints, they then entered the snarl that is typical Egyptian traffic.

"Damn, this is a sweet ride," Tuna crowed from the driver's seat. "But this thing is big!"

"Is it as wide as the truck?" Richards queried.

"No, I guess not," the Louisianan allowed. "But I would really hate to get a dent or mar on this pretty thing because of some dumbass blind mule, an errant pushcart, or some cocky Egyptian NASCAR-wannabe taxi driver!"

And then Tuna just shut up as he applied himself to the task of getting from the airport to the Cairo National Museum, "like pronto."

After some thirty minutes of truly hair-raising vehicle maneuvers, the raging Cajun said, "Joey. Give Sharil a call. Tell her we'll meet her at the loading dock in ten minutes. But tell her to stay out of sight until we back up to the dock. Oh, and tell her what we're driving."

And by the Egyptologist's wristwatch, they did indeed arrive at the appointed place at the predicted time. Getting out of the SUV, they both hopped up onto the dock with their side arms and banged noisily on its vertical door. A face briefly flashed in the window of the adjacent door, a slide lock was heard, and the door cracked open, allowing them to pass within. Now inside, Richards and Cartwright thought that it would be most wise to put their hands up as four very serious museum guards had their guns out. Then a commanding voice ordered them to stand down from a hidden position behind a massive crate. Striding forward in her tan archaeological gear, Sharil greeted them.

"Well, that didn't take long," she said as she embraced each in turn. "And welcome back, Joey."

"Madam Director," Cartwright now all-business said, "Your aerial chariot awaits. May I suggest that we bug out as soon as possible?"

Smiling back at the serious soldier, Sharil responded, "I'm all set, Commander," as she indicated with a shrug a small overnight bag over her shoulder. "Kindly lead on."

Then turning to one of the four museum guards.

"Mustafa. The museum is now in your hands. Protect it like your own beloved daughters."

"Absolutely, Dr. Moussa!"

The drive back to Cairo International seemed to take forever for Richards, now that they had Sharil with them. Tuna, noticing his fidgeting and constant peering into the mirrors, stated, "Okay, folks, we can all relax now. I lost our tail about a kilometer back."

"Our tail?" Sharil repeated in confusion at the slang expression.

"Yes, Dr. Moussa, the car who was attempting to follow us," Tuna answered, and then thought to add, "And by the way, folks, this vehicle is armored, so not to worry."

CHAPTER IX
Undeclared Warfare

Once the Internet came into existence, an undeclared war began to rage over objectives as old as humanity itself. Specifically, the insatiable desire to know secrets, to lie, cheat, sneak a peek over someone's shoulder, acquire, steal, and of course, to manipulate the simpleminded, gullible, and the uniformed and ill-educated masses. This was an entirely new sort of conflict, one never before experienced in the history of mankind, one that recognized no national boundaries, and was devoid of rules, much less the Geneva Convention.

The stakes could be corporate survival, stellar box office revenues, nuclear proliferation, a national election, or as pedestrian as a well-placed book review. The gamut of this incessant competition was truly infinite and just as frightening. The "infantry" of this conflict typically did not wear uniforms (except for perhaps the PLA's Unit 61398 of cyber-hackers near Shanghai, if all the reports are accurate), were male and female, in the main tend to be under thirty, and thrive on caffeinated and sugared beverages of all types.

Their moniker, "hacker," invoked a subliminal image of geeky, rumpled figures within messy dark dens illuminated by the photons of multiple LED flat screens. Oddly, unless organized into coven-like groups, hackers usually were introverted loners, free-thinkers, gamers, and puzzle fanatics. Their carefully constructed digital packets of zeros and ones were always badged with idiosyncratic markers that proudly declared their pride of place within the ether. And as one might expect, the results of their highly creative conquests were often cryptically paraded across the blogosphere for all to see.

From this pool, inevitably, as with cream in a bottle of fresh milk, a select handful rose to the surface. In the process, they became the well-known heroes, gods, and goddesses of this technological subculture. They were looked up to for sage programming or gaming advice, that is, if one was confident enough to ask and they were willing to share. These select eventually became targets themselves as well-grounded and financially well-funded entities aggressively recruited them to join their team, to become members of their cyber army.

*   *   *

"So," he began, "tell me all about this candidate that you are so keen on."

"Well, sir, this one is really kinda scary. She has a real gift, actually more of a knack, that allows her to de-engineer a string of security code, understand it and its triggers, and then get in and out without a ripple. Like I said, kinda scary.'"

Dr. Charles O'Brian Naysmithe, the head of research and the man who was solely responsible for all aspects of the care and feeding of the Horizon Pass facility, just shook his long blond mane, looked over his wire-rimmed reading glasses, and snorted.

"Buddy, don't give me that. Every hack leaves a signature of some sort, some minor disparity in character spacing or a time stamp anomaly, even if it is only an electromagnetic shadow. No hack is without a ripple."

Robert James "Buddy" McGuire just took a deep breath and let it slowly out. As the Head of Database Security, he knew what his boss Charlie was saying. Still and all, he believed in the candidate, so much so that he was willing to make a friendly wager in order to get his point across.

"Okay, Charlie. Here's how serious, like a heart attack, I am about this candidate. We lock her in a room with a laptop with Internet access and give her an hour's time to hack any database of your choosing. If she breaks in, then you owe me a week's supply of Rambo Juice. If she doesn't, then I'll go cold turkey for a week. Whaddya say?" said the man from Queens, New York.

Naysmithe was surprised by McGuire's hard sell, for it told him something. If Buddy was willing to forgo his near addiction to Rambo Juice for a week, then this candidate must be the real thing.

"Okay, Buddy. I accept. If you are so hot to trot over this candidate, then sit her down in a Pasadena hotel with a high-speed DSL line. Rig it up special if you have to. Give her all the technical advantage that you dare, but only one thing – no thumb drives."

"But, boss. That's not fair! A thumb drive is a hacker's toolbox. You can't do that!"

Momentary silence broke out before Buddy attempted a resale.

"I'll tell you what, boss. We'll limit the drive to only twenty megs. How about that?"

Pursing his lips, Naysmithe knew that what Buddy was saying was true.

"Okay then. Twenty megs, and not one byte more."

Slapping his massive hand on Naysmithe's desktop, Buddy said. "Done! I'll set her up with a super quick landline. Now boss, what's the target?"

Now it was the physicist's turn to grin a Cheshire grin.

"I want the candidate to break into the e-mail of the NRI. And once in there, she is to look for anything having to do with high energy physics or electromagnetism. Why that particular institution, you ask? Because, and I don't know if you know this, but they're our chief cyber enemy. So, needless to say, I am damn curious about them and what they're up to."

With a deep furrow across his shiny, shaved pate, Buddy pointed out, "But, Charlie, let's be fair here. The Niroo Research Institute has already been famously hacked by the Israelis and probably for the same reasons. Its defenses now, after that well-publicized scandal, will be epic and in Farsi as well. So what you want is a hack and a translation then?"

"Yep. A successful hack will ensure your supply of Rambo Juice. A hack and a translation, and I will authorize the candidate's papers like yesterday."

*   *   *

It was Thursday and already the campus was rocking. In one third-floor dorm room that overlooked the quad's inner courtyard, a warm orange glow pierced the Midwestern night. That was because its enterprising inhabitant had strung up an orange parachute across the room's ceiling. The effect within was a womb-like flashback. The wall hangings, some painted, some photographic, were an eclectic mix of sixties acid rock luminaries and bare-chested C & W hunks, a speed blurred Porsche 917 at Le Mans that was a precious gift from her Uncle Bill, various posters that announced the annual campus bicycling event, and a massive hand-painted acrylic of a brightly colored scene that covered an entire wall. The made bed, sans frame, sat on the floor. The desk, a sacramental altar to technology with its dual flat LED screens, looked to be overgrown with tangles of wires and cables. Add all the lit candles and their intertwining aromas, and you have a techno crash pad to end all pads. And it was as neat as a pin as its owner did not allow candy wrappers to fall anywhere else except in the trash can.

At the desk sat a lanky, cross-legged, and huddled creature, who was intently typing away on one screen while monitoring the other. This extreme concentration had been going on since dinner and it was now nearing nine o'clock. It was a game of sorts, multi-tasking and a thorough exercise of her peripheral vision.

A knock on the door caused the head to rise, and in so doing several cricks and pops in the neck and back sounded.

"Ouch!" Marla von Epping squeaked out. "Come in. The door's open."

As the relatively harsh light and sound of the common hallway penetrated the silent orange grotto, a familiar manta was heard.

"Darn it all, Marla. It's Thursday night, for Christ's sake. And here you are holed up in your womb again! Shut it down, girl. It's time to party," stated with complete conviction her next-door neighbor, an Anthropology major.

"Not tonight, Jeannie," said a fully stretching von Epping, who reached for the ceiling with her fingers spread and an arched back that caused her luxuriant and flowing black hair to fall like a silken wave.

"Besides, I have a project due Monday in random computer processing to skull out. I have this really cool idea about content reconstruction, but that will require several algorithmic engines to make it all happen. Then I'll have to compile all of it somehow. . . ."

Her neighbor just stood there, scowling and shaking her head, because Marla still had not moved from her chair.

Giving up, she said, "Perfect. That's just perfect. Hole up in here all you want. But don't come crying to me ever again about being one lonely girl. Marla, you're hopeless. You're married to that damn perfect computer of yours. That's it! Good night! The end!"

And the door slammed shut.

Marla, even while the impact of the solid door to frame was still echoing in her ears, just smiled.

Yes, she thought, *I do need a break*. So she unfolded herself, stood up, and plucked a frosty Diet Coke from her refrigerator. Max, a tiny thing of marvelous regenerative coolness, could only hold twenty-four cans, and then it would take a day to chill them properly. At the moment, Marla counted eighteen, good enough to get her through the weekend, she reckoned.

At the sounding of her e-mail chime, the near-six-foot junior in computer science padded back over to her chair and found a message from mom and dad. Opening the e-mail, Marla quickly read through it, stopped, and reread it once more. Frankly, she missed them dearly, but this message was curious, as a firm in Pasadena had contacted dad directly about her whereabouts and whether she might be interested in a summer internship.

A summer internship in Pasadena! Wow! How cool would that be! But that sudden euphoria was quickly tempered by the cold shower of reality. Pasadena for the summer would mean little or no time at home, no evening concert picnics at Ravinia, no water skiing adventures on the Fox River with the gang, and no race weekends tinkering with the computer on Uncle Bill's Corvette, or fooling around with his racing buddies Kent, Raybob, Too-Fast Tommy, or Scott. That really sucked as the Sheboygan brats at Elkhart Lake were to die for, not to mention the beer.

So what to do? Marla, ever practical, decided to split the difference and told her dad to forward her the e-mail. *What the heck*, she rationalized. *I'll respond. What have I to lose? Besides, what are the odds that I'll get an interview as a junior, much less make the cut?*

*   *   *

As proof that it is not what you know, but rather who you know, just try to follow this tenuous thread. Marla von Epping accepted a full academic scholarship to a Big Ten school that was located in south central Indiana. The big factors that had earned her that ride were all the advanced placement science courses that she had taken in high school. But what had really opened the door was that during her junior year in high school, she had devised a computer database security system that was state-of-the-art and, at the high school principal's prescient suggestion, had it patented. Then, during her senior year, a software giant out of Seattle made the von Eppings an offer on the system, which after some legal wrangling, she and her parents eventually accepted. The final arrangement was for an initial lump sum to be followed for the next five years with an annual royalty payment based upon two and a half percent of sales. Needless to say, that near blockbuster deal really caught the attention of the major technical colleges and universities across the nation. In the end, her final selection was based on the campus's beautiful trees, rolling landscape, and its commitment to the sciences *and* humanities. Marla knew that she was already a bit too geeky, and that's why she purposely shunned the more tech-oriented universities.

Then there was her father, Jack von Epping, who himself was more than a bit of a technical geek himself, known from his many convention and professional presentations as an energetic, creative, and persuasive freethinker. Once the word had gotten out what Jack's little girl had come up with, Marla's intellectual stock had gone through the roof. Now both academe and industry were aware of her. Consequently, Marla von Epping's name was flagged in several security-oriented databases as someone of interest, someone worth following, someone definitely worth acquiring.

This was where Buddy McGuire entered the picture, as he had heard Jack von Epping speak on several occasions, at several prestigious venues. Buddy first heard the gossip about Marla, firsthand, via the usual cocktail chatter. Interested, he looked her up, as he had access to several "promising candidate" databases as well. As a result, Buddy had taken the bait, hook, line, and sinker. He just had to have Marla as the lead architect on his security team.

*   *   *

"Ms. von Epping?" said the driver in the black suit, who held the sign that announced, "von Epping – Horizon Pass."

"That's me," said the tan, smiling, and duly impressed college junior.

"May I see some identification please?"

"Sure. Here it is."

"Thank you, Ms. von Epping. Do you have any checked luggage? No? Okay, then please just follow me."

As Marla tried to tag along, she noticed that her driver looked a lot like a NFL linebacker. Big, erect, fit, and a brisk walker. In fact, he reminded her a lot of her two older brothers, both hulks, but this one had a cat-like quality that she couldn't quite place. Holding the rear passenger door open, she easily ducked into the big shiny black Buick and was greeted by the rich aroma of its leather seats. But during that quick entry, her driver's suit coat had billowed open slightly, giving Marla a clear view of a holstered automatic.

As they exited the airport area, the driver toggled the privacy window into its up position and then reported in.

"Base, this is Corporal Brown. I have picked up Ms. von Epping and am underway to the hotel. I should arrive in about fourteen minutes, per the plan."

"Copy that. Callahan out."

From the lush confines of the backseat area, in near total isolation, Marla noted that the driver was talking to someone, and then she saw the squiggly wire at his collar that led to his left ear.

Well, doofus, she thought, *this is after all a security company interview. All I know is that I would want that big guy on my side if the stuff hit the fan!*

So Marla sat back in glorious contentment, seemingly floating on air, feeling like a movie star, and thoroughly enjoying the sight of all those palm trees through the heavily darkened windows. And then, far too suddenly, they had arrived on a curving cobblestone driveway that led to a magnificent hotel.

Opening the passenger door, the driver announced, "Okay, Ms. von Epping. Here's your hotel. Just go up to the reception desk through those double glass doors over there and check in. Everything has been arranged for. Have a great day."

As the driver remained standing now by his vehicle, he watched as the Midwesterner slowly sauntered with her head a-swivel toward the indicated entrance. Smiling, he just shook his head. *Yep! She's a real looker. But she also doesn't miss much either. I'm gonna have to get me a rear holster.*

Once she cleared the massive sliding doors, Brown got back on the radio.

"Base. The pretty chickadee is in the nest. But be sure to let Buddy know that this one is very sharp, very observant, and a knock-out."

"Copy that. Callahan out."

Letting out a sigh, First Lieutenant Patrick Doyle Callahan, the chief security officer responsible for both Horizon Pass and the Philology Annex, smiled to himself.

Okay, Calli, he began, *now all we have to do is get her back on the plane and on her way home by this afternoon. Then we pack up Buddy and his gear and get back to New Mexico. Should be a piece of cake.*

And then Calli's focus drifted a bit, back to a time when he and Sancho Sanchez had provided street security for that Russian vixen, Vesna Gregorieva.

So, I wonder what von Epping looks like? Must be good, because even big, bad Brownie had been moved enough to mention it.

*   *   *

To his everlasting surprise, it was like a battle of wills. He sat on one side of the conference table, and she on the other. He reiterated the rules. She just stipulated that she already knew what they were per his e-mail. He nonetheless asked to examine her thumb drive to confirm its specified twenty meg capacity. She asked him if he was testing her honesty or was just trying to figure out whether she was literate.

With those preliminaries over, he then placed before her a confidentiality agreement to sign. She said that she wouldn't until she read it and spoke with her father. In short, it was one of those ugly, prickly, testy encounters that no one likes, but everyone must endure at least once in their life.

"Fine," said McGuire. "For the record, I will accept your word on the thumb drive's specs. And by all means, please do read the legalese. I think that you will find it quite specific. And if you still wish to speak with your father afterwards, that's fine as well."

He then pushed an old-fashioned clam-shell phone across the table and crossed his arms. By his wristwatch, it took the candidate some thirteen minutes to wade through the boilerplate, four-page document, while she circled this and underlined that.

"Okay. I want to talk to Dad now. May I do so in private?"

So McGuire left the room.

"Daddy?"

"Yes, Daddy. I'm just fine, as was the flight in, but this hammerhead of an interviewer wants me to sign this legal document called a Confidentiality Agreement before we even begin.

"Should I?"

"Uh-huh . . ."

"Oh, really!"

"Uh-huh . . ."

"Okay . . ."

"Love you too, Daddy! See you and Mom for dinner."

And she signed the agreement.

Two minutes later, her tormentor had returned and put down on the table a sheet of paper with a neatly printed URL on it.

Then he said after picking up the agreement and checking to make sure that she signed, initialed, and dated all the required places.

"All right, Ms. von Epping, here's the deal. You have one hour to break into the e-mail server of this website, and once in, if you even can get in, find all references during the past six months to high energy physics and electromagnetism. Then translate what you get. The point of this exercise is stealth. I want no footprints left anywhere. See you in an hour."

Pulling out of his pocket an old-fashioned egg timer, he gave it a wrenching, savage twist and placed it next to the sheet of paper.

"Go!"

As he left, he quietly closed the door behind him, as he did not want to damage the conference room's sensitive microphones. Forty paces later, he joined Calli in one of the flanking conference rooms that the security team had booked. While she was surrounded, she was also protected by sixteen of Calli's best troopers, as Buddy did not want one hair on her pretty little head messed with.

"Damn, Buddy, did you have to be such a first-class ass with her?" Quipped Calli, who was seated in front of his video feeds that monitored Marla's room and several others where his boys were positioned.

Grimacing a bit, the native from New Jersey answered, "Calli, you know me better than that. I'm a teddy bear, a big, cuddly teddy bear. But this is serious business. I want the best for us, and I want someone who is tough as nails. So far by my book, she's held her own."

And with that said, he sat down before his laptop, which paralleled Marla's, as he wanted to see each and every one of her keystrokes. And what he saw was a blur.

Marla was pissed off, and she was using each and every one of her keystrokes, at ninety plus per minute, like daggers stabbing into her interviewer's heart.

*   *   *

It began as a series of surprised murmurs, a sudden shifting in his chair, followed by a voiced expletive or two. Then some thoughtful grunts mixed in with some nonverbal facial expressions that displayed wonder and pleasure. All through this emotional roller coaster, McGuire took notes, penned exclamation points, and even five-pointed stars. As one might expect, there were several question marks as well, but not many.

Calli, who was sitting opposite the database chief, just watched. Only thirteen minutes into the trial, he could see that McGuire was already in awe.

Thirty seconds later, Marla was in through a rabbit hole that some brilliant in-house programmer thought he had sufficiently hidden among convoluted code. How she had divined that was unfathomable. Nonetheless, Marla had entered the e-mail server through the provided dummy maintenance program, and once in, she copied to her hard drive the entire log of the last six months, some three hundred thousand records in all.

That task was completed around twenty minutes into the test. She deftly exited the website and began browsing the Internet for free Farsi–English translation algorithms.

At twenty-nine minutes in, she began testing several translation candidates that she had found with some random file samples copied from her recent heist.

At thirty-six minutes in, Marla stopped typing and sat back for a moment to watch her laptop begin its crunching on the three hundred thousand records. Then she opened another window and began coding search parameters into a simple SQL macro statement, based on a combination of twenty-five word keys.

At the fifty-three minute mark, when the crunching had stopped, Marla then launched the SQL macro, which not only found files of interest based upon her keywords, but also segregated them in a separate file in chronological order. That took just a handful of seconds.

By the fifty-four minute mark, Marla began, just for fun, reading what these e-mails contained, and at that point McGuire returned to her conference room, carrying in one hand his notes and in the other a small cooler.

She just looked up in triumph and stated, "You're late."

He sat down, smiled, pocketed the still ticking egg timer, and said, "Marla that was simply brilliant. I don't know where to start," while looking down at his notes, "but, well, let's just say that I am very impressed.

"So how many files did you manage to find and translate?" McGuire politely queried as he brought the cooler to the tabletop and then innocently asked, "Beer, anyone?"

"Three hundred and seventeen. But they all have to be read before we really know what the value of the harvest truly is. And yes. Any PBR or Bush?"

"Nope, just Bud."

"Close enough."

Popping a can and then handing it over to Marla, he said, "By the way, my name's Buddy."

CHAPTER X
Horizon Pass

"Charlie, you must be some kind of a mind reader, because there are close to sixty e-mails that Marla's interview found that went in and out of Niroo Research Institute that refer to us, the Russians, and theoretical discussions of time travel. It seems that the Iranians have been nosing around more than we had ever expected."

With a not-so-happy face, Naysmithe rubbed his eyes and let out a quiet moan.

"Buddy, that's not good news. Have you passed on that info to Calli yet?"

"Nope, I thought it best that you should make that call."

"Yeah, I suppose you're right. Please do pass on what you currently have. Have them try to make heads or tails of it all. Tell them that I need their thoughts, in writing, in two days' time."

"Got it."

"Now, what about the candidate? How'd she do?"

"Boss. Marla von Epping is the real deal. Period. End of story. We should make her an offer for the summer and see how she does. Then we fall back and reassess this situation."

"Sounds good. Run with it, and be sure to keep me in the loop."

"Boss. What about her package?"

"Make it competitive. Honest. Let her know what she is worth. Has she passed all the security screens?"

"Yep. Clean as a whistle."

"Then you have my authorization to go full steam ahead on this."

"Got it."

*   *   *

"Daddy, I really don't know what I should do!" the frustrated junior moaned with the employment package arrayed before her on the kitchen table.

"Okay, pumpkin, what's eating you?" her father said over his half-glasses.

"It's all so sudden! Spending the summer in New Mexico away from you and mom. I don't know. It's just all so sudden. That's all."

Chuckling, Jack von Epping was reminded of his first job offer, how he had practically the same discussion with his dad at the dinner table. What goes around comes around.

"Now, Daddy! What's so funny?"

"Well, pumpkin, I was just thinking. How many of your friends have a summer job yet?"

"I don't think any of them have. No, wait. I think Jody has – at the Burger King on Lake Avenue."

"And, pumpkin, what are they paying Jody for flipping burgers and frying fries?"

"Not much."

"And what is this summer job offering you?"

"About seventy-three dollars an hour."

"Ah-ha! I'm pleased that you have done that calculation already. Good. So is money the problem?"

"No."

"Have you ever been to New Mexico?"

"No."

"Will you be flipping burgers or will you be messing with computers?"

"Messing with computers."

"So, there's no problem?"

"No."

"So, pumpkin, to review, money's excellent, a new place to explore, and the job is right up your alley. You will even earn a college credit per week while on the job, plus all the bucks. As a bonus, you get all of this real-world experience. And finally, and I just cannot believe this one, free travel to and from, free room and board, plus full medical insurance.

"Pumpkin, what's not to like, girl?"

*   *   *

The departure from O'Hare International Airport had been for the entire family a teary-eyed one, and a bit odd as well, for Marla's flight originated on the military side of the airport. The approximately four-hour flight from Chicago to New Mexico was to be Marla's first visit to that southwestern Sun State of the Union. As for the flight itself, its flight log would never see the light of day, for its final destination did not officially exist.

Needless to say, the airframe that Marla rode in was not a commercial Gulf Stream V. With its tall T-shaped tail and its swept wings ending in graceful canards, the aircraft looked like it was doing .87 Mach just sitting on the tarmac. However, the plane was extremely modified, something that for Marla remained utterly opaque, for she did not know what a normal business jet even looked like. But once she entered the fuselage, the reality of the situation became eminently clear, for the usual commercial interior airplane panels, baffles, and partitions were all missing. The practical effect was an opening up of the plane's light tan interior. The seating for sixteen, however, was pure military transport, comfortable but ugly, quick-release aluminum frames entwined with olive green webbing. Massive but comfortable head and neck padding, five-point harnesses, and all arranged in two staggered rows with a wide common central aisle. General interior lighting was battle-station red with convenient reading lights mounted to the hull next to grounded, twelve-volt outlets and an adjustable ventilation port.

At a glance, Marla suspected that this was a military aircraft, just like in the movies. But it was one that sure did not look like it from the outside, and that fact alone started her mind to thinking that maybe she had made a really bad decision on this summer internship. After all, she reasoned, if my employers went to such lengths to gut and modify this interior for a specific purpose, what else might be so very different about this supposedly normal looking commuter jet?

Noting Marla's momentarily frozen stare at the plane's entrance, followed by her darting eyes glazed over in thoughtful contemplation, the copilot that greeted her at the forward hatch did his best not to break out laughing. For it was natural. He had exactly the same reaction upon seeing the jet's interior for the first time. And so he decided to soften the blow.

"Welcome, Ms. von Epping to the U.S. Army's very best accommodations in commercial aircraft. Allow me to help you stow your gear and get you safely strapped in. We can leave nothing loose, as loose stuff tends to be dangerous while flying upside down."

"What!?"

"Indeed. In fact, I suspect that the pilot just might want to show off for you, as you are the new greenhorn aboard."

"Greenhorn?"

"Yessiree. Greenhorn as in first-timer, novice, and sucker-bait," he declared with a wicked grin.

"Oh, that's just great. What's it like, anyways?"

'What?"

"Flying inverted."

Now with a full grin, "You'll just love it!"

*   *   *

Quiet and remote, Holloman Air Force Base is located about ten miles west as the crow flies from the New Mexican town of Alamogordo. Nearby White Sands, where the atomic bomb was first built and tested, officially, and publicly was closed down lock, stock, and barrel decades ago. Still, few can refute that an extremely low-profile, high-security installation did in fact still exist out there somewhere in the region. But where, nobody knew, and frankly, nobody cared. The territory was just too vast, wide open, desolate, rugged, and forbidding. One might just get lost or go missing.

Although the Gulf Stream would indeed land, refuel, and depart from the Holloman en route back to O'Hare, Marla did not. Nor did said passenger dawdle at the base. Instead, she was whisked away and strapped into the back of a waiting Sikorsky H-60 Black Hawk helicopter. Its undocumented departure from the base could only be described as having headed sort of northwest and toward the setting sun, deep desert, and its backlit scrub that covered the mountain range. Its flight record would be described as sort of north and through the vast desert flats of the White Sands Missile Range, sort of south of Lumley Lake, and heading toward the foothills of Strawberry Peak, trending in the general direction of the desert metropolis of Truth or Consequences.

As the helicopter zoomed on a WNW beeline into the late afternoon sun, Marla took in the remarkable dullness of the vacant desert flats. But those flats soon gave way to foothills, mesmerizing the young woman with its rugged beauty and surprising colorfulness of this southwestern desert. The earth tones, juxtaposed as they were one atop the other, were breathtaking sights for the Midwestern flatlander. Skimming just south of Strawberry Peak, the chopper rose and fell as it followed the hills and contours of Parson Canyon. Such roller coaster flying made Marla feel like a falcon soaring on the thermals looking for prey.

Then, as the canyon opened up at Sulphur Pass, she saw a curious split-fingered, rock in the distance. Surrounded by brush, yucca, and stunted pine, she guessed that was her destination.

As the helicopter neared the outcropping, it slowed, flared, and descended over a dimly lit, cement helicopter pad that magically appeared out of the shadows. With a jarring jolt, they had landed. Glancing at her watch, Marla calculated that the entire trip from O'Hare to touchdown had taken about four and a half hours. The chopper segment itself had been a breathtaking, fourteen-minute roller coaster ride. And all of that just to deposit her here. But where's here?

Once the blades had ceased their churning, the chopper's copilot helped her out of the restraints and hefted her two bags over the edge, where they dropped unceremoniously several feet to the ground. Next, he took both of her hands, pulled her out of the snug seat, and helped her down from the unmarked and flat dark gray Sikorsky. The pair, including the copilot with her bags, then made their way out from under the broad and sagging blades. Returning to his craft, the helpful copilot strapped himself in as the pilot restarted, throttled his collector and began his ascent to return to base.

As the dust cleared and the sound of the chopper blades' soft whoop-whooping faded off into the distance, Marla, now covered in fine dust, with her bags at her sides, became aware of several things. The silence, the distinctive smell of desert sage brush, the crystal clear air high elevation, and the incongruous sight of a ponytailed, blond-haired gentleman wearing goggles, standing just outside of the pad's sand eroded yellow safety line. Walking over, he extended his hand and introduced himself.

"Hello there and welcome to Horizon Pass. I'm Dr. Charles Naysmithe. I'm its director."

Still very jazzed from the aerobatic helicopter ride, the young woman smiled, took his hand, and said, "Hi. I'm Marla von Epping, hacker extraordinaire."

"Yeah, I know. And from now on, you can call me Charlie."

Now looking at his smart phone, Charlie said, "Well, it's time to quickly get inside before that nosey Russian bird flies overhead."

Confused, Marla said, "What?"

"A Russian recon satellite. It's due overhead in about four minutes. We need to get under cover, so let's move."

"Oh!"

At Charlie's announcement, he briskly led her toward a ramshackle structure at the base of the rocky formation that Marla had noted earlier on the helicopter ride in.

The complex at Horizon Pass, as are the great majority of government facilities in the southwest, was a subterranean one that took advantage of the native rock formations. In many ways, the complex used nature for its camouflaged. Its entrance was comprised of a rickety lean-to shack of weathered silver pine that backed up against a sheer two hundred-foot rock face overhang. Once inside, a gray, featureless, and hardened steel door greeted Marla. The shack itself, an oversize and sophisticated X-ray booth, scanned all who stood before the steel door's frame. Charlie, with Marla in tow, just seemed to wave at the entrance, and it opened broadly to accept their passage.

Greeted by a pair of Callahan's security guards who nodded in their direction, the bright white of the entrance vestibule momentarily dazzled Marla's eyes after the relative darkness of the entranceway shack.

"Marla," Charlie Naysmithe began. "I think that it is time for you to appreciate what you and your talents in security systems will be protecting. So, before I take you on a tour of this joint, let's step into the visitor's lounge, grab a coke, and have a chat."

While his visitor practically drained the icy cold drink in one gulp, the scientist just smiled. "Want another?"

"Sure, that would be great."

Sitting in an overstuffed and ridiculously comfortable chair, Marla almost had to fight away a sudden sleepiness. Naysmithe noted this and, realizing all the excitement and perhaps the effects of the local elevation, said, "Okay. Today has been a busy and exciting day for you, and so I will try to make this introductory briefing as brief as I can."

Naysmithe then paused to lick his lips and collect his thoughts.

"Marla, what we do here at Horizon Pass, in a nutshell, is top-secret research in temporal exploration."

That pronouncement caused the young woman's mouth to sag and eyes to widen. Marla also noted that Charlie now had morphed into a deadly serious man. Legs crossed over one another, hands steepled before him, and his eyes steady and penetrating, no, boring, right through her.

"Yes, Marla. You heard me right the first time, 'temporal exploration.' Horizon Pass is a fully operational time travel research facility."

Now raising the index finger of his right hand for emphasis, he continued, "Please note, Marla, that we are an autonomous entity. We are not a government facility. We quite literally take our orders, our direction, from a panel of scientists specially selected from the Russian and American Academy of Sciences. Do you have any questions?"

Gulping like a fish out of water, Marla figured that she had a million of them, but for some reason her head just slowly shook in the negative. Only then did she find her tongue.

"Alright. So all of this, that special military jet, that blacked-out helicopter, and this facility, all supports your temporal research."

Nodding and then responding, "Yes, they provide our transport and are part of our security arrangements. But also included, that you have yet to see, is an ancient language institute on a major Midwestern campus. That is the language-training facility for our temporal field operatives."

Naysmithe paused to allow Marla to digest.

"So just to be clear, Charlie, you guys perform temporal research, and, you are fully operational."

"Totally."

"Jeez."

"Now Marla, think in our terms. We run everything on computers, even the Soap Bubble – that's our time machine's nickname, by the way, – our e-mail, our HR files, our medical files, our security, our training programs, our HVAC, everything.

"Now let me ask you. If you were an Iranian terrorist, what would be sweeter than to hack our mainframes and steal the Soap Bubble's blueprints? What would be slicker than to have some super-wealthy Near Eastern power fund and build a Soap Bubble clone, and then proceed change willy-nilly Western History with it? Are you now beginning to appreciate just how important it is for us to secure our intra and Internet networks?

"Marla. We quite literally work to preserve reality as we know it. What on God's green Earth could be more important than that?

"Now, Marla. While I have just told you a shitload, you can still back out with no questions asked. You'll still be bound, however, by that confidentiality agreement that you signed in Pasadena, and that applies to everything that you have seen and heard today. Absolutely everything. But once you step out of this room," Naysmithe decreed, with his arm extended and pointing at the lounge's door, "your life will change and change radically. While you will discover that all of this facility's personnel are the salt of the earth, this place is nonetheless a very serious one, and a very exciting one as well.

"So, Marla. Are you our new cyber security architect? Or should I recall the chopper?"

Stunned at the scientist's message would have been an understatement, but after a pause, the young woman asked, "All right. I'll stay, but it's only for the summer, correct?"

"Yes. That is correct. You are only a summer intern."

"But how do I become full time?"

Now smiling broadly, Naysmithe answered with an endearing tilt of his head and with hands opened wide.

"Marla, Marla. Don't you think that you're getting a bit ahead of yourself?"

*　　*　　*

In truth, Horizon Pass was an underground lair, a grade B movie's notion of what an underground missile site must have looked like. And it was, for the installation had been constructed in the late 1960s. Rough concrete walls painted bright reflective white; exposed piping and tubes of all kinds, shapes, and colors ran along the ceiling and walls of every corridor and tunnel; everywhere emergency phones and lighting fixtures; fire extinguishers every fifty feet; caged overhead fluorescent lighting; bright yellow painted stripes running down the center of the twenty-foot-wide corridors and tunnels; convex traffic mirrors at every intersection.

It would have been very confusing to navigate such a maze if it were not for the fact that each corridor, intersection, and tunnel was branded in huge stenciled letters on the floor. Marla would learn that the late founder of Horizon Pass, Dr. Peter Borov, had a wicked sense of humor. The dormitory area was named The Swamp after the *M.A.S.H.* television series, the mess hall, bakery, and kitchen – Betty Crocker's, the gym – Venice Beach, and the main lab complex – Frank's, after Frankenstein's Castle. Marla's digs were located in a far more serious place that bore the name Tombstone. There was secreted the testing and storage area of the Soap Bubble and the facility's cyber core.

*   *   *

Buddy, Ron, and Marla were heads down in Tombstone's conference room as they pored over the facility's digital security schematics and protocols. What they were looking for were potential attack points where a cyber assault might occur. To date, Buddy and his CalTech second, Ron Marston, had the system running on pretty much off-the-shelf software, but given the current climate, something special, something in-house, was envisioned to be developed and take its place.

So Marla began with what she called a brain dump.

"Okay, so let's pretend that we are going to start with a totally blank sheet of paper. Let's also start with the macro view and then work down to the micro. Up front, we are like any other business. That means we purchase stuff, inventory it, and have to figure out what we spent and how. So on a purely operational level, we are a business.

"But for this business, we have to consciously build security into our system by design. We do that by instituting system-wide the principle of least privilege, meaning that you are only granted access to a portion of the system. For example, medical staff has access to only medical files. In essence, they have limited access by design to a portion and not the whole of the system.

"Next, we think in terms of deep defense, or defense-in-depth, so that if a break-in does occur, it only happens to a portion of the system. Again, the idea is to limit the damage to a portion and not the whole.

"Once we have designed a deep defense, we then implement default secure settings that when they fail, they fail secure, rather than insecure. In other words, let's build this so that only bona fide users can make the system insecure.

"To make sure that all is well, we will need to monitor the system. In essence, take its pulse. We will do this system diagnosis via audit trails. This way if any hacker breaks in, we will be able to find their tracks, where they broke in, and ultimately, how they did it. In short, we learn from our weaknesses.

"Okay now, that's the big picture, the design piece. Whatever we decide to implement, our security architecture will define our system's controls and countermeasures, and those features must provide us, at a minimum, with confidentiality, integrity, availability, and accountability.

"As for our hardware, from everything that I've seen, it all looks fine. But if we are to take into account a cyber attack from the inside, which in this place seems unlikely, then we will have to add to the design spec drive locks and the disablement of U.S.B ports and the like.

"Another avenue that we might follow is to build our own operating system that is based on kernel technology to absolutely, positively, provide a secure environment. While such a route might be considered crazy insane to build, guess what, absolutely no one on the outside will know how to hack it. Such operating systems usually are considered high-assurance systems, meaning that they are robust enough to keep the Department of Defense happy. Just an idea to consider.

"A good thing to have is a way to provide secure coding. That specifically means that access to the actual system code is itself secured by some means. That means we move away from the more commonly used C and C++ coding languages and adopt something that literally no one teaches anymore, RPG for example, and then we encrypt it just for fun at a 256-bit level.

"Now for the really fun stuff. This place is not an island unto itself. It needs to communicate with the outside world, and that is where the wolves will most likely try to enter our system. What I propose here is to segregate all incoming and outgoing e-mail traffic into separate virtual spaces, a sort of super firewall. These virtual spaces will then allow us to isolate an intruder long before any attack can be attempted on our robust, kick-ass system. This is also a great place to detect, contain, and control any malware, viruses, or pings, as it is a dead end. Or if we wish to be extremely devious, we can set up a honey pot that is purposefully vulnerable within one of the virtual spaces. That way we can crack back on any hacker.

"One item is a must. We have no rabbit holes, no back doors into the system, not even when we are just testing. Period. End of story. While they are neat and nifty to have, they are tremendous liabilities. In fact, I heard of an instance where this guy put in a temporary back door, finished the job, left the site, and then totally forgot about it. In two weeks' time, the system that he had designed had crashed to a hacker, all because he forgot about his back door.

"Well, that about does it for me. What about you guys?"

*   *   *

One very frazzled and traumatized Buddy McGuire sat before his boss with his virtual hat in hand.

"Charlie. I just don't know if I can do this anymore."

"Whaddya mean, Buddy? What happened?" said Naysmithe with a deeply furrowed brow as he peeked over his wire-rimmed reading glasses, "This isn't like you. You're supposed to be the one eating glass and nails and taking names. So what gives?"

"Well, Ron and I just had this little security design meeting with Marla. You know, a kinda get-to-know-you sort of meeting. A sort of an introduction to our system to get her feet wet. Well, what happened instead was that the two of us got a lecture on security that was so fucking mind-blowing that Ron, who is always such a gabby Gus, was rendered totally speechless. I mean, he was a mummy! As for myself, all that I kept thinking was of our budget, and then how I could find the resources to do all the coding. It was a frickin' nightmare."

Hiding his smile behind his fist, the director of Horizon Pass could only sympathize with his subordinate, for that was precisely how he had felt under the tutelage of Peter Borov, the then living legend. Underwater was the best way to describe the feeling. Gasping and fighting for air, looking for any sort of relief from the pressure of responsibility. Change and growth will do that to you. It forces you out of your comfortable cocoon.

"Buddy, don't worry about the budget or where you can find the necessary resources. That's my headache. What I want to know is this. Is Marla's vision feasible?"

With his two big excuses removed from the table, the man from New Jersey knew that he had to confront his true fear. Can I deliver?

"Boss," shaking his head, "I just don't know. Marla's vision is just flat-out breathtaking. Is it feasible? I believe so, but I am not the man to implement it. I . . . I just don't have the intellectual horsepower to see it through."

Ah-ha! I got him to admit it.

"Buddy, you're a damn good geek. And by the way, you're a damn good administrator as well. Are you telling me that you think you're all washed up, because a cyber genius just waltzed in and schooled you a bit?

"I'll tell you what I see. I see a very talented guy who has just realized that he is about to be pulled out of a comfortable nest, a predictable environment, one that is warm and cozy. Buddy, this is all about progress, change, whatever you want to call it. So, you can chicken out and bail, or you could instead ride this wild filly for all it's worth and learn something new along the way. It's your call. And whatever you decide will be okay by me. But there is nothing wrong with being a project manager, who can also play second fiddle to the first chair. So, Buddy, whaddya say?"

Several thoughtful moments of silence passed as Naysmithe hoped that Buddy would take the bait.

"Boss, you have a point. I am a damn good administrator, and no, I don't have to know absolutely every little thing about the system to be effective. I guess, down deep, Marla sort of freaks me out. She's so young, so bright, and thinks so differently from me. Like I said, she freaks me out. I guess it all comes down to trust in somebody that I just don't know."

"Well then, Buddy, that's your answer. Why don't you and Marla get some coffee and just talk, probe around, and get to know each other. And tell her why. That is how trust is built, not only for you, but for her as well. Now get your lard ass out of here and get Marla some coffee."

*   *   *

Two weeks later and after countless skull sessions, Buddy, Ron, and Marla sat before Naysmithe with their recommendations for going forward on the revamp of Horizon Pass' security platform. As the presentation progressed, the director was pleased that while Buddy had made the opening remarks, it was Ron and Marla who then presented the bulk of the design spec. What was also of interest to the scientist was the team's desire to patch, plug, and retain as much of the legacy system as possible. This clearly was Buddy's budget-minded contribution, while Ron's nearly encyclopedic line-by-line knowledge of how the legacy system really worked provided Marla with the firmly grounded basis from which she could patch and plug from a purely security standpoint. All in all, what they had presented was easily understood, practical, and doable in-house, without the need for any further resources. Needless to say, Naysmithe was very pleased with the exercise and authorized the project on the spot, much to the elation of the three grinning geeks before him.

Suddenly Buddy's cell phone began sounding off rather distinctively, for anything originating from a specific source triggered a ringtone that sounded like a submarine's emergency klaxon diving horn.

Immediately, an "Oh shit!" unconsciously escaped his lips.

"McGuire here," he quickly answered.

"Uh-huh.

"You're absolutely sure?"

"Uh-huh.

"I'm on it!

"Okay, everyone. All hands on deck. Someone is probing us big time from the Internet. That was Stan, and he is fast running out of fingers to stick in the dike. Let's get moving!"

At that directive, Buddy, Marla and Ron left Naysmithe's office at a run for Tombstone. Thinking ahead, Ron called up Tombstone's security office to get them to begin cranking open its four ton doors.

Dutifully following Buddy through the many maze-like corridor's, the trio found themselves before a slowly opening, vertically splitting, circular double-door that looked like the entrance to a bank vault, complete with a short, low ramp leading up to it.

While the cyber trio ran up to the vault's entrance, four security cameras trained on them, taking in their every move.

Guard One: "Here they come. Right on time. Ron must be really bugged about something. He's never before asked for a 'Blitz Opening' of the vault."

Guard Two: "Yeah, I know. He's a good guy nonetheless. Buddy, however, he can be a real pain sometimes. As for the chick, she's hot."

Stepping through the massively thick doors of Tombstone's entrance, the threesome were running across a steel grated landing that stood about fifty feet above floor level. Marla, who had been stunned by the volume of the area the first time that she had toured it, now raced down the spiraling ramp anchored into the outer wall of what once had been a fair-sized cavern. Below was a massive engineering bay with workshop, a climate-controlled computer room, and a generator area. But in the center of it all stood the current version of the Soap Bubble, the Mark VI B.

The device consisted of four black rectangular pylons, each about six feet tall, arranged symmetrically like the cardinal points of a compass that outlined a circle about twenty feet in diameter. Each pylon had its own thick power cable and attached at their tops were short, horn-like devices that were oriented inward, which also had their own power cables. In the center of this circle of pylons and horns, a thick, white, hula-hoop-like object, about four feet in diameter, floated horizontally and absolutely still about five feet off the ground. As magical as this may seem, the trio totally ignored the Mark VI B as they ran for the computer room.

"What ya have, Stan?" a puffing Buddy gasped out.

Sitting behind a pair of flat screens, the hulk that was Stan Fielding said nothing, but pointed to a continuous spike of graphed activity that appeared rather prominently on his diagnostic window.

"What is it?" Buddy wanted to know.

A negative shake from Stan's bald head was his only answer.

Meanwhile, Marla, who had brought along her laptop, now had it open before her and was furiously typing on its keyboard. Moments later, both Buddy and Ron were doing the same, but from their nearby offices that shared a glass partition with the main room.

And then the spike disappeared. Total lapse time of the cyber event: twelve minutes, thirty-four seconds. In short, an eternity in cyber terms.

"Are we nominal?" Buddy called out from his office.

"Seems so," Ron answered guardedly.

Stan signaled a thumbs-up, while he kept monitoring the system at large, looking for any evidence of a breech.

One minute later, Marla snarled out, "They got in, but I found 'em! I got the bastards!"

Instantly Ron and Buddy were hovering over her.

"Whaddya got, Marla?" the threesome asked in unison.

"I isolated three of the pings and followed them on a bounce trail from Chicago to Toronto, to Cambridge,

England, and from there to Marseilles, Athens, and Damascus. And, Buddy, you won't believe this. Our intruders used spoofed e-mails that targeted three of our own e-mail addresses."

Highlighting the addresses in her code, Marla cut and pasted them into a separate screen. Turning in her chair, she faced Buddy, and asked, "Okay, Buddy, who owns these e-mails at Horizon Pass?"

Peering down and studying the text before him, he shook his head and said, "One is Doc Allen's, our facility's medical officer. The second one is Naysmithe's. And the third one is a real ghost. It's Dr. Borov's old e-mail."

Silence. Then Marla perked up.

"Okay. That means that the bad guys somehow got two current and one dead e-mail address. That means that they got a hold of a file that is at least as old as Dr. Borov. When did he pass away?"

"A year and a half ago," said Ron.

Silence again. And again Marla spoke up.

"What we're looking at is the result of a hack. That means that someone probably broke into a poorly secured e-mail server and, for whatever reason, decided to pluck out these three e-mail addresses. And what they found is that only two of the three are current. So, for the moment, we're still secure. But if I had to put money on the table, they're coming back, and this time, with a battering ram."

Another voice stated with authority.

"Marla, another spike just started, but this one is very small." It was Stan.

"Can you tell me whose e-mail address is being called?"

"I think so," Stan replied as his fingers turned into a blur. Thirty second later, he said, "Not good news. Doc Allen and Naysmithe both just received an e-mail from the same source. Can you track it back, Marla?"

Back at her screen, Marla interrogated the two new e-mails, began her search, and then screamed, "Pull the damn plug!"

"What!?" Buddy and Ron simultaneously cried.

"Just do it!" Marla repeated.

And to his credit, Stan killed the power to the e-mail servers and then jumped up and physically began pulling cables from the back of the server racks themselves. When he was finished, he had a fist full of bright yellow cables in both of his two hands. Marla could see that Stan, while a quiet guy, was a thoughtful man of action. Late middle-aged, fit, and with a totally no-nonsense attitude. *Military*, she thought. *No, ex-military, he probably once was a kick-ass noncommissioned officer. He just has that economy of movement thing down just too pat.*

As the Internet connection throughout Horizon Pass was suddenly severed, people lost their unfinished e-mail messages, downloads, and website purchases. And who knows how many gaming sessions were ruined as well in the process. The result was instantaneous. The help line began to ring off the hook.

"What possessed you to do that?" a florid-faced Buddy ranted at Marla.

"Actually, sir. I did it," a calm, cool, and collected Stan observed.

Whirling around at him, the hot-headed director said, "Stan. You better stay out of this."

Wheeling back around to a surprised Marla.

"Well, sister! Why did you tell Stan to do that?"

Marla was amazed at Buddy's reaction. It was so childish, so inappropriate, and so very wrong. And her furrowed brow reflected her serious concern for the guy who had just hired her. His reaction also caused her to reflect. Just how shallow is this guy? Or better, just how deep are his issues?

"Well? I'm waiting."

A pregnant pause broke out. It was not quite a staring contest, but it was getting close, all the while the help line's phone kept ringing.

"Priorities, Mr. McGuire. Priorities. Consider, which is worse. The potential for someone cracking your current Internet security protocols, or the temporary inconvenience of a lost Internet connection?"

McGuire, who's mercurial Irish temper had cost him his last gig, thought, considered, and realized his mistake. More importantly, he now looked at von Epping with far more appreciative eyes. *Here is this young whippersnapper outthinking me again, and with such rapid dispatch, who is now so coolly informing me of what my priorities should be. Buddy, my boy, you know that she's right. Now be a man and admit it.*

Swallowing, Buddy did just that.

"Marla, you crazy . . . you're absolutely right. I apologize. I just lost it there. Good call. And thank you, Stan, for acting so swiftly on Marla's snap analysis."

Sigh and a nervous scratch of the head.

"Okay, now. Let's do a damage assessment. Let's see if we have been perforated in any way. In the meantime, I will get on the phone to all the department heads and explain the situation."

Sigh.

"Marla. In case you haven't noticed, I have a bit of a temper. I sometimes jump to conclusions that just aren't there. Again, I thank you."

And with that the man retreated to his office and began dialing.

Ron was the first to break the silence.

"Good job, Marla. Damn good quick thinking. I flat out froze. And by the way, after the way that you just handled that event, you're Number-One material in my book."

Stan just got up and held out his massively powerful hand, and Marla took it and found it to be remarkable soft.

"Missy, I have seen Buddy blow several times since I've been here, but you are the first to face him down. Just give him a chance, and he'll come around. All dinosaurs eventually do. Now Missy would you do me a big favor?"

"Sure!"

"Why don't you track down all those bounce points that you called out. Try to see what those IP addresses represent in terms of real world brick and mortar storefronts. I have this suspicion that will tell us a bunch."

*   *   *

While that conversation took place, and before Stan had torn out the e-mail servers' cabling, four viruses successfully insinuated their way into Horizon Pass' system from the e-mail server. As they were looking for something specific, they avoided the well-understood and off-the-shelf security package that was currently in place, which had been positively identified during the initial twelve plus minute interrogation of the system. After about thirty seconds, the viruses had found what they were tasked to find, copies of files were made, and those copies would now be seamlessly and surreptitiously sent back to their creators once the system was back up and the first outbound e-mail was sent.

* * *

"Stan, this is really troubling.' Marla said. "Just like you asked, I traced the e-mails back to the IP addresses located in Chicago, Toronto, Cambridge, Marseilles, Athens, Damascus, and there it ends. But now, as of this very moment, each IP now no longer exists. All have been scrubbed."

A grunt followed by a reply.

"Well, Missy, what does that tell you?"

"That the pings and e-mails originated, probably, somewhere in the Near East. And, that whoever was doing this was damn good. And, given the elaborate bounce trail, they have resources, so that almost certainly aces out an individual hacker."

A pair of soft brown eyes now gently prodded her.

"That's good, Missy. Now extrapolate on what you have just told me. Just swing for the fences and let it all hang out."

Smiling at the gentle challenge, Marla obliged.

"Near East, big resources, that could describe any of several governments."

"Yes, now think hostile."

"Syria – no. Iraq – no . . ." Then her face lit up. "IRAN! It's got to be Iran."

"Marla, I noticed that you did not mention Egypt, or Jordan, or Yemen, or even Saudi. Why?"

"Jordan is not hostile to the United States. Egypt and Yemen don't have the resources. Saudi Arabia? Stan, I don't know, but the Kingdom just didn't feel right."

"Marla. You have a fine mind and an even better intuition. Couple those with your proven cyber abilities. Have you ever considered working for an intelligence agency?"

Now Marla knew where Stan was ex-ed from. It wasn't the military.

*   *   *

While Stan and Marla were deep in their analysis of the take, Buddy had been busy as well.

"Ty. Hi. It's me, Buddy. How are your systems doing? Anything odd happen to you folks recently? Like in the past week?"

"Uh-huh."

"Uh-huh."

"Uh-huh. Really! How bad? Uh-huh."

"Do you know who was affected?""

"No kidding!"

"So, what are you guys going to be doing about it?"

"Uh-huh. Yeah. That should do it. But . . ."

"Uh-huh. Understood."

"Yeah. Best of luck on that."

"Yeah. You too! It's been a slice."

Now sitting back in his office chair, Buddy could feel the hair on the back of his arms tingle and chill.

Yep, he thought, *that is one damn interesting coincidence.*

Looking out into the main conference room, the native from New Jersey saw that Stan the Man and Marla were in a deep conversation. Smiling to himself, Buddy then decided to share with the rest of the team just what he found out.

"Okay, everybody. Let's form up for a chat," he began as Ron, Stan, and Marla joined him at the large circular conference table. "Ron, what do you have so far?"

Looking down at his yellow legal pad, Ron was all smiles.

"We look to be good to go. I have found nothing amiss with the e-mail servers. It seems that the rogue e-mails were stopped at the firewalls, at least for now. But who knows whether they would have held if Stan had not acted as quickly as he had."

"Well, that's some good news. But, Ron, do you think that this is a good time to shift our firewalls around a bit now that the bad guys have had a peek at our defenses?"

"Sounds good, Buddy, but that will only be a temporary fix. It would be like shifting our phaser frequencies against Borg force fields. They would work for a time, but we really need to get that new security design in place and up and running."

"I totally agree, but for the moment, set up some new wrinkles for our inquisitive friends."

"Will do. Just give me a couple of hours, and we can open up again, perhaps before noon." As Ron began to stand up, Buddy motioned him to stay. Ron, with a bit of a perplexed look on his face, sat down with a plop.

"Stan, Marla, I saw you two putting your heads together. What do you guys have?"

Stan just pointed his finger at Marla, and Marla took the hint.

"Well, we did some analysis on the IP bounce points that I initially recorded. Believe it or not, they no longer exist."

This fact raised both Buddy's and Ron's eyebrows.

"And since they no longer exist, that means that whoever successfully pinged us was really good. I mean really good. Remember, they routed those e-mails through six IP locations, across several continents, all to dead end in Damascus. That took considerable coordination and resources, resources far beyond an individual hacker, but not beyond those of a nation state."

"Okay, Marla, I'm intrigued, so who's our peeping tom?" Ron piped.

"Iran."

"Marla! Are you sure!" Buddy exclaimed.

"No, she is not sure, Buddy." Stan firmly stated for the record. "But her geopolitical assessment of the situation makes a whole load of sense."

"Iran. Damn. Come to think of it, it actually makes a whole lot of sense. . . ." Buddy said as he quickly glanced at Marla and then drifted off into a thought. Quickly returning to the here and now, he said, "Well, all the department heads now have the scoop and at least for the moment are cool with the situation.

"But, on a hunch, I decided to call up our sister institution in Chicago. What prompted me to give them a call was something you said, Marla. Something about our attack being the result of a hack. So, it turns out that four days ago, one of their academic e-mail servers was broken into. They even know who the target was. To make a long story short, someone copied six years' worth of e-mails."

Gasps.

"Well, our Chicago colleagues have since beefed up their security. It seems that it was on the maintenance schedule anyways. But unlike our hack, the guy who busted into Chicago's server did so rather carelessly, or else, the guy was just in a rush."

"And," Marla prodded.

"The hack originated from Tehran and the IP address pointed to the Niroo Research Institute. Now, does that institution sound familiar to anyone?"

CHAPTER XI
Taking Stock

On the return leg back to the States on the Gulf Stream, Sharil, Tuna, and Richards had plenty to talk about. First and foremost on everyone's mind was the unknown state and condition of Sharil's missing father. As they crossed the Atlantic, they had no way of knowing that his captors had dropped off the heavily drugged man at a local Alexandrian medical clinic. Admitted initially as a John Doe, he had been rendered invisible to the system. And as far as experience in these sorts of matters went, while no one dared express it, he was presumed dead.

As for Sharil's own fears of a kidnapping or worse, those were never questioned, although her chilling accounts of seeing black sedans made those fears quite concrete in the minds of Tuna and Richards.

But the tie that bound both of these events together rather neatly, perhaps too much so, was the retelling of Richards' own interview with the mysterious imam with a Farsi accent. Tuna, outright, was floored that the Egyptologist had so cavalierly placed himself in such potential jeopardy. And he in no uncertain terms said so.

"Joey, boy! You total idiot! You are not trained for undercover work. And what would you have done if things had gone south? Just what in God's green acre were you thinking? That you were Superman or James Bond? Christ All Mighty! And here I just gave you a lesson in gun safety!"

With his hands up in surrender to one very pissed off retired army officer, Richards tried to explain, while speaking very slowly.

"Tuna, with all due respect, if I had not done that interview, we would not have known that a Farsi speaker was interviewing select Egyptian Antiquities personnel. Personnel who were responsible specifically for the Step Pyramid's and Karnak Temple's security.

"We would not have known that this same joker was not so subtly threatening the same individuals, all in order to get them to talk about you, your team, Piankoff, Gregorieva, myself, and any odd events that took place at those archaeological sites.

"Furthermore, we would not have known just how thorough this prankster was. 'Christ All Mighty,' your words, he spoke with security guard starting with Piankoff's first deployment at Karnak.

"So, no, I'm not trained in undercover work, but I am a trained and experienced temporal field operative, which is not all that different if you stop and think about it."

Now somewhat cooled, but still mad as hell, Tuna blurted out, "Okay wise guy, I'll buy that you got real lucky. And come to think of it, that bushy caterpillar under your nose does make you look sort of Egyptian. But damn it all, Joey, that stunt just wasn't smart. This time you managed to get away with it, but next time, and I can see with you there will always be a next time, you just could find yourself royally screwed.

"You dig!" Tuna emphasized by sticking his finger hard into Richards' solid chest.

The contrite Egyptologist said, "Yes, sir. I dig."

"Okay then, let's move on."

Now focusing upon Sharil, who had become a bit wide-eyed during Tuna's dressing down of Richards.

"Dr. Moussa. I apologize sincerely for anything that might have offended you. But this lunk head clearly deserved it. We've an expression in Louisiana. If you want to get a mule's attention, first hit him across the head with a two-by-four. And I hope and pray that I have accomplished that."

Pausing to impressively crack his knuckles, Tuna then shifted gears.

"You know, Joey, that intel that you collected is very interesting stuff. We already know that the Russians have tried twice to heist the device and blessedly both times were unsuccessful. And now you tell me that the Iranians are in the picture. But for the life of me, I can't figure out why."

"Charles. If I may," Sharil said. "I think that I may be able to enlighten you as to what the Iranians are precisely interested in."

*   *   *

Upon landing in Chicago and deplaning on the military side of the airport, the very grim but determined trio made their way directly to the Philology Annex. Rumpled, unshaven, short on sleep that would never come, and jet-lagged out of their minds, they nonetheless had an important meeting to make. But as is so often quoted, "Allah is merciful," and from the airport to the campus, all three crashed once they hit the big Buick's comfortable leather seats. The next thing that they knew, their driver was politely jostling them awake.

Somewhat refreshed and mounting the cement steps of the Annex, Richards suddenly realized that it was a gorgeous, sunny spring day. Looking down at his watch, his still fuzzy head could not figure out the local time, but his ever reliable stomach did, as it growled loudly. Embarrassed, the Egyptologist said, "Sorry about that, folks. Must have been something I ate."

Growling back, Tuna confirmed what Richards had not been able to.

"No, Joey. More precisely, it was something that you haven't eaten. I'm starved, and I am sure that Sharil here is too, but is too much of a lady to complain. But I'm sure as hell going to devour a steak once this dog and pony show is over. Joey. Do you know of a local steak joint nearby?"

"Fear not, Tuna. I got that one covered," Richards stated with granite finality as he held the Annex's heavy wooden entrance door open for them.

Once inside, all were efficiently greeted by the receptionist, who helpfully explained to Sharil the bedroom slipper protocol, with which all visitors to the Philology Annex must abide. Richards and Tuna just pulled their own foot coverings from their shelved nooks. Looking down, Richards smiled at Tuna's green BDUs.

But something was amiss. Scanning around, Richards saw it. For the first time in his memory, Jenny had her beautiful, long hair pulled back in an attractive, but tight, bun. *Odd*, he thought. Then he noted as well the conservative, high-necked pant suit in a tasteful dark gray. As she interacted with the Egyptian, he also sensed a professional and neutral quality about her, and not the usual warm sensuousness on the edge of breakout.

As all three moved on to the first floor cloak room, the secret elevator to the Annex's subfloors, Richards watched the receptionist and never once did she look up at him. Instead, she was thoroughly glued to her flat screen. It caused him to blink in disbelief.

I wonder what's up?

Arriving to an already packed room, Tuna spied the three empty chairs in the first row and tried to steer everyone to them. Dean Young, however, had other ideas as he had never before met Sharil and welcomed her warmly.

"Good afternoon, everyone, and thank you once again for coming on such short notice," Dr. Young began as he addressed the entire room.

"Shortly, you will be hearing about some serious developments that have been occurring in Egypt and elsewhere. As I am sure that you have noticed, we have two additions in our midst, Commander Charles Abraham Cartwright, retired, and Dr. Sharil Moussa, the Director of the National Museum in Cairo. So, without any further ado, Commander Cartwright."

Grizzled, stiff, and short on sleep, the ex-army officer still managed to stand erect and command his audience.

"Dear colleagues. First, I wish to apologize to all of you for my shoddy appearance, as we have just arrived direct from Cairo, Egypt. In the past, I have briefed you on the two occasions when elements originating from within the Russian Republic attempted to outright steal the Soap Bubble."

One member of the audience chose to snort rather pointedly at that accusation to which a very jet-lagged and short-fused Cartwright retaliated.

"Zip it, bud. You're way out of your depth," Followed by a second of slit-eyed contact to make sure that the miscreant got the message. The rest of the audience smirked at his self-inflicted discomfort.

Sigh. *I don't need this now*, Tuna internally moaned.

"Recently, as in the past week, the ante has been considerably raised on our temporal device, as the Islamic Republic of Iran has now expressed considerable interest in it."

Audible gasps.

"Intelligence gathered from various sources has shown this assessment to be reliable. Specifically, the aggressive interviewing of over thirty Egyptian Antiquities personnel by an Iranian agent posing as an imam, the abduction of Dr. Ibrahim Moussa, whose current whereabouts are unknown, and the stalking of Dr. Sharil Moussa by similar elements, all prove that the Iranians' interest is more than just academic."

An extremely urgent hand shot up from the audience.

"Yes, sir," Cartwright acknowledged.

"Commander Cartwright. My name is Ty Lawson, and I oversee the cyber systems here in Chicago. Recently, as in the past week as well, our academic e-mail servers were hacked. Specifically, the e-mail files of Professor Richards were affected. And from everything that we can tell, nearly all of his e-mails were copied, some six years' worth.

"Not only that, the hack was an amateurish one, meaning that we could trace it back to its source computer. The source of the hack was located in Tehran and specifically originated from an Iranian research think tank called the Niroo Research Institute.

"Since the hack, we have upgraded our security on the e-mail servers considerably. But what just occurred to Professor Richards' e-mail files and what you have just told us, I cannot believe are coincidental."

During this revelation, the audience squirmed. One of their own had had his e-mails hacked!

"Thank you, Mr. Lawson. That intel is indeed most helpful, and I would like to discuss it with you further after this briefing."

But Lawson remained standing, and Cartwright noted this.

"Yes, Mr. Lawson. Do you have something further to add?"

"Indeed, I do. Just yesterday the e-mail servers at Horizon Pass were seriously pinged. Buddy McGuire, the director of cyber security out there, called me about it, and asked me whether anything odd had happened in Chicago.

"My guess is that someone mined Professor Richards' e-mail files, selected some e-mail addresses to test, and did so."

The clear linkage between Chicago and Horizon Pass, both under a cyber siege as it were, took the air out of the conference room.

"Finally," Lawson concluded, "this is why all cyber communications, both in and out of Horizon Pass, have been temporarily terminated. McGuire quite literally pulled the plug in a last ditch effort to seal themselves off. Incidentally, they, as were we, were in the process of a cyber security upgrade. In short, the Iranians hit us with our pants down."

Stunned silence reigned until Cartwright stated, "Dr. Young, if you do not mind, I think that this is a good time for Dr. Moussa to say a few words."

Sitting off to the side, the dean nodded in agreement.

As Sharil Moussa arranged herself behind the podium, she smiled wearily at the gathering and began.

"Ladies and gentlemen, I am Dr. Sharil Moussa. Since I was a young girl of fifteen, I have worked with my father, Dr. Ibrahim Moussa, first as his assistant at the museum, then as his assistant when he became the director of the Supreme Council of Antiquities. Now, I am the director of the National Museum in Cairo. During that period, my father and I have faithfully supported the Soap Bubble project. One week ago, my father was abducted by agents unknown, and his current location and disposition are also unknown. I too, was under surveillance by agents unknown, until Commander Cartwright and Professor Richards snatched me up out of their grasping hands. And now, here I stand before you.

"I wish to impress upon all of you how much my father and I know about the Soap Bubble Project and about all the deployments that have occurred in my country. I truly am in fear of what that knowledge could do if it fell into the wrong hands.

"As has been already mentioned here today, it is now quite apparent that the Iranians have designs on your temporal technology. Fine, so do the Russians. But the motivation as to why the Iranians want that technology, I believe I can offer an opinion."

At this point in Moussa's presentation, the impact of a falling pin on the conference room's carpeting could have been clearly heard.

"Put in the simplest of terms: temporal terrorism. What do I mean by this? Again, simply, the Iranians wish to alter time. The Iranians wish to erase the European Middle Ages. If they were given their druthers, they would want the European continent speaking Arabic. They would transform the entire Mediterranean Basin into one single Islamic lake.

"That, ladies and gentlemen, is what is at stake."

*   *   *

On his way out of the meeting, Richards decided to pay a friendly visit with the receptionist. Stopping at her desk, Ms. Kelly looked up, smiled, and said, "Why, Professor Richards. What a surprise. May I help you?"

"Yes, Ms. Kelly, you perhaps can. Can I interest you in a double date steak dinner perhaps?"

Tilting her head to one side, Jenny finally emerged with a warm smile.

"Why, yes you can. But what took you so long, handsome?"

Richards smiled his big goofy smile and thought, *Yep! I've got my old Jenny back!*

*   *   *

Also on their way out of the meeting, two other travelers were sorely in search of sustenance, Cartwright and Moussa. Severely drained from their travels, both looked ready to fall over. Waiting as they were for Richards and Kelly to join them on the front stoop of the Annex, Sharil's cell began to ring.

Plucking it out of her coat pocket, she wearily flipped it open and said, "Dr. Moussa. May I help you?"

Listening, her eyes widened, and a flood of tears began to fall down her cheeks. Cartwright seeing this, moved to her side in support as the Egyptian began bobbing her head up and down.

Finally, she choked out, "Poppy, is that really you?"

CHAPTER XII
The First Teleconference

In this day and age of near instantaneous teleconferencing on a planet-wide scale via Skype, Face Time, Zoom, and other platforms, truly secure methods for such communications have long been in place via dedicated satellites. One such network was established by the U.S. Air Force for just that purpose, and upon occasion, they lent out network access to organizations that required draconian security. When one adds instantaneous two-way idiomatic language translation, then individuals can communicate without the vagaries of interpreters or inconvenience of disparate time zones.

Needless to say, this was one of those instances, when a select panel of the American Academy of Sciences requested of their Russian counterparts a few moments of their time. What the Russians found so intriguing was the urgency of their request. So in a show of international cooperation, the Russian panel acquiesced.

Seated before the video camera in Chicago were Dr. Paul Young, Dean of Humanities, administrative head of the Philology Annex, and *ex officio* of Horizon Pass. As had become custom, Young held center stage. To his left sat Dr. Charles Naysmithe, theoretical physicist and director of Horizon Pass, while to his right was Commander Charles Cartwright, retired. Meanwhile in Moscow sat center stage Stefan Rosovec, Director of Advanced and Theoretical Technological Research for the Russian Academy of Sciences, while Gregorii Popev, Head of the Special Projects

Directorate, was ensconced to his left, and Viktor
Sokolovska, Director of the Theoretical Biology and
Special Projects Directorates, to his right.

As introductions by Dr. Young were made, it
became abundantly clear to two of the Russians that
Cartwright had to have been the one who had thwarted
their two attempts on acquiring the Soap Bubble. Popev
recognized him from the start as a worthy foe, Rosovec
bristled, and Sokolovska remained curious as to what
the conference was all about.

As per usual, Young kicked off the agenda.

"We have called this meeting as something
recently has been brought to our attention that we
believe you should be apprised of. Specifically, we
have experienced multiple instances of cyber intrusions
on sensitive network systems. These attacks were made
by intelligence assets of the Islamic Republic of Iran.
Additionally, corroborative human intelligence has
confirmed an intense interest in a joint project that our
two academies have engaged in for the past fifteen-odd
years. In all, some thirty-odd Egyptian Antiquities
personnel have been intensely interviewed on the
subject, one key official of the Supreme Council of
Antiquities has been abducted, and another barely
escaped the Iranian intelligence dragnet. It is our belief
that your networks may be next."

My God, thought Rosovec. *The Iranians have
beaten us to the punch! I can imagine what that nation
would want to do with the Soap Bubble. It really makes
their troublesome nuclear program look harmless in
comparison.*

And then Young gave voice to what specifically
the American fears were.

"Gentlemen. The government of Iran is very interested in the Soap Bubble, no doubt to produce their own clone of it. Why? Allow me to be crystal clear. They wish to prosecute a reign of temporal terrorism. And by that, I mean the drastic alteration of the historical timeline in such a way that Europe, as we know it today, would cease to exist. What we calculate Iran has in mind would be a Mediterranean Basin that speaks Arabic and a Continent that worships Allah.

"So, we have come to you today, hat in hand, so to speak, to request your assistance. I do not believe that I have to remind you that it was your scientists, men of sound conscience, who first enunciated the *RUTI* – "The Guidelines for Temporal Exploration". Your culture, chess masters all, should well appreciate the domino effect of an Islamic Mediterranean and what that would mean for the history of Western Asia."

After that preamble, the Americans sat, grim-faced, and patiently waited for their Russian counterparts to reply. After a few thoughtful moments, Rosovec leaned forward, apologized to his U.S. audience, and begged for several minutes of privacy, after which he turned and signaled the videographer to kill the feed.

Now staring at a silent screen of white static, Cartwright murmured to their in-house technician, "Is audio feed off?"

"Yes, sir."

"Okay. I can understand this desire of theirs to go offline, but I wonder just how shocked they really are. From the look on Rosovec's face, you would have thought that he had just lost the Super Bowl."

Naysmithe, nodding in agreement, also observed, "I agree with you, Tuna. That Russian definitely had a jealous look on his face, like someone had just stolen his last piece of candy. In fact, that big redheaded dude, Popev, actually glanced over at him as if to say, 'Shit, they beat us to it.'"

After a moment of silence, Young piped up, "You know, their biologist Sokolovska seemed genuinely concerned about our appeal. He fully understood the magnitude of the threat. Is it possible that he represents the odd man out of that trio?"

*   *   *

"Popev," Rosovec ordered. "Kill that operation that we discussed yesterday."

"Are you certain? We could reroute the investigation through our embassy in Tehran and make it look like the Iranians."

"No. Let's keep our hands clean on this one. Our cooperation now may lead to a future opportunity. Let's not risk it."

Popev looked down, sighed theatrically, and then got out his cell phone.

Now florid red, Sokolovska, with a voice that trembled with anger, said, "Director Rosovec, have I not been informed about yet another adventurous undertaking on the part of Director Popev and yourself?"

Pursing his lips in resignation, Rosovec replied, "*Da*, Sokolovska. Just yesterday we began a preliminary cyber exercise against the Americans. One, I might add, that we have just halted. So Viktor, what of it?"

Sitting back, Sokolovska shook his head once in a sign of negation, and to his credit, he stood, and left the teleconference.

Just wonderful, thought Rosovec. *I suspect when I get back to my office his resignation will be on my desk.*

Pause.

In some ways, I really don't blame him, as he is a truly an honest man and this business is anything but.

Snapping closed his cell, Popev asked Rosovec, "Where did Victor go?"

"Probably to clean out his office. Now, what are we prepared to do for the Americans?"

"What is logical. I suggest that we focus on Tehran. Perhaps we will get lucky and find out what they have learned. Then we can sit on the intel and use it in the future for our own ends."

Smiling at his colleague.

"Clever and cunning. I like that.

"Restore the link," he ordered their videographer.

*   *   *

When the transmission was reestablished, the Americans saw that only two Russians remained. None of the Americans commented on the fact nor inquired as to why, as they already suspected as much. Inwardly, Young just preened. *He had been dead on. The Russian team was split and may have even sundered itself.* But the continuation of that thought was interrupted by Rosovec's voice.

"Gentlemen, again, please accept my apologies and for the sudden absence of my colleague. He has just been informed of an emergency that he must attend to."

Bullshit on that, all three Americans thought.

"But before he left, we unanimously agreed that we will assist you in any way that we can. Just let us know how we may help."

*   *   *

"Well, now, that was a big waste of time," Naysmithe concluded. "We'll get help from them when hell freezes over."

"Now, now, Charles," Young said with a soothing voice. "Actually, I suspect that their team is now one fewer. In my book, that is a victory from within."

"I totally agree with that assessment, Dr. Young," Cartwright stated with certainty.

"In fact, I think that we just might have headed off a Russian cyber attack. Now, wouldn't that have been ducky, both the Iranians *and* the Russians with a Soap Bubble!"

CHAPTER XIII
The Great Clearance of '96

As Richards raised the heavy tome once again, he looked for the scrap of paper that he had inserted as a bookmark. Finding it, he began reading about the fourth Austrian excavation season of 1996.

* * *

With the Great Magazine operational and staffed with a small international army of restoration personnel, the great clearance began of the funerary deposit of King Djoser. After five weeks of efficient labor, the first chamber had been cleared and some 5,016 objects had been processed. With the first chamber swept clean, its next door neighbor now beckoned. And it too was staked from floor to ceiling with the dead king's grave goods.

This second adjoining chamber took another six full weeks to clear, to the tune of 4,305 objects. All, just as with its previous twin, were meticulously recorded and photographed *in situ*, before they were removed and transported to the Great Magazine.

Fully one-fifth of the artifacts inventoried contained or were made of precious or semiprecious materials. The next largest proportion was principally made up of beautifully fashioned stone dishes, craters, and containers in a multitude of sizes and shapes. But by far the greatest amount of the artifacts retrieved were of a more utilitarian variety, composed of woven wicker baskets, containers, and then all of the ceramic jugs of beer, jars of oils, and storage amphorae of grain.

To beat all, nearly all were inscribed with some name, message, or date. In short, a historical treasure trove of information.

Schachermayr then stated for the record that with these last two chambers the Galleries of Imhotep now extended under the southern courtyard, almost to its center, halfway to the pyramid itself. The Austrian then queried whether or not there may be yet another hidden doorway. Perhaps one that connected to one of the three kilometers of underground warrens beneath the pyramid itself.

It was with this thought in mind that the Austrian searched the back wall of the second chamber. What was found was again hidden by a plaster layer, but this time only the size of a modern window frame, placed within the center of the back wall. Again, as so many times before, the rubble plug of this small chamber or cache was adorned with sixteen identical plaster seals, all neatly arranged in four vertical registers. The seals were those of Imhotep. And within the photograph of the shallow niche was found a linen-covered object that was spherical in shape. The find number assigned to it was 9321.

Richards, curious about this object and itching to find out what it was, could find nowhere its description, not a line drawing or photograph, except for the one taken *in situ* and with the linen shrouding in place. In fact, much to the Egyptologist's surprise, the object was not even listed in the many indexes of the three volumes. While a total of over 9,300 other objects were otherwise carefully recorded, the very last one was not. Just its niche, and that really got Richards' attention.

This is damn odd, he thought. *Yet Schachermayr made sure that the find number did appear in print as some sort of backhanded record of the artifact. This is just too weird.*

Now pulling out his cell, Richards checked, and yes, he did still have Schachermayr's number, which Sharil had given him a couple of years back.

Well, now, let's just call up Ulli and find out what's up with artifact 9321.

*   *   *

While Dr. Ahmed Rashid had agreed to spend the entire 1996 season getting the Great Magazine up and running like a well-oiled machine, his presence at the opening of the 1997 season was more of a ceremonial act than anything else. The vast majority of the recovered antiquities were either in storage, in process to be stored, or in the skilled hands of the many restoration teams. Really, he did not know why he had even agreed to show up, much less supervise this first week of the Sakkaran archaeological season.

Rashid, when later asked about the particulars of that day, recalls that the roundish, linen-covered object arrived at the Great Magazine's intake processing around eleven thirty on a Monday morning. Its find number was first recorded by one of the restoration staff, while Rashid looked on. It was a generic form, where other details such as the object's find location, condition, material analysis, special notes, and eventual storage location would be found.

What struck Rashid was the globular shape of the object beneath its linen shrouding. Once the initial intake details were completed, the director of the

National Museum's Department of Conservation directed that the surprisingly heavy artifact be placed on a nearby empty table, where he himself could examine it and its shroud.

Resting upon a bed of native cotton batting, Rashid, now with a pair of Latex gloves on, began to delicately probe this way and that at the shrouding with a pair of tweezers. This hands-on activity pleased the Egyptian, for in his heart of hearts, he was not an administrator. He was first and foremost a chemist and a scientific investigator, when it came to the restoration of delicate artifacts.

After some work, this dedicated man of science found an edge, followed that edge, and with that discovery, began to peel away the dried out and stiff linen that encapsulated the object. And in so doing, Rashid was rewarded with a peek here, a portion there, of what looked like an oxidized bronze surface, a surface that was rounded. With fully one-third of the object revealed, the telltale greenish-blue hue of bronze was very apparent, but even more so was the presence of grooves in its surface, curves, curlicues, and unadorned areas as well.

Several moments later, the clearly spherical nature of the object revealed, Rashid removed his pen from his shirt pocket and noted on its accompanying information sheet the object's suspected bronze construction, shape, and odd surface features. With the shrouding now fully separated from the object, the Egyptian lifted the object clear and away from the linen beneath.

While heavy, Rashid lifted the spherical object and set it back down on the cotton batting with a slight grunt. Then, upon realizing what he was looking at, the elderly scientist gripped the edge of the work table in a death grip as his mind screamed in total denial.

It cannot be! How can I be looking at a perfect outline of the African continent! As his eyes began to wander, Rashid easily identified the Arabian Peninsula, the boundaries of the Mediterranean Sea, and the British Isles. Daring gently to roll the sphere to the right, the Indian subcontinent appeared, as did the island of Sri Lanka. And as the scientist continued to examine the entire surface of the sphere, the more his battered brain had to accept that he was looking at a very precise geographical representation of the Earth.

Looking around and noting that there was no one nearby, Rashid, in a moment of prescience, covered the nearly fourteen-inch diameter representation of the planet with a large microfiber cloth. Calling for a small, wheeled cart, the Egyptian then requested an artifact location in an empty container. Lifting the obscured globe to the cart, Rashid then quickly proceeded to the assigned container, and once he rolled the cart within, he sealed it, and pocketed the key.

Leaning heavily against the steel door of the container, the Egyptian reached into his back pocket for his handkerchief and began wiping away his nervous perspiration. Then he pulled out his cell phone.

I must call Sharil immediately! She will know what to do.

*   *   *

After waiting through four panicky rings, Dr. Sharil Moussa, the director of the National Museum, finally answered her phone.

"Dr. Moussa here. How may I assist you?"

A deep sigh of relief.

"Sharil, this is Dr. Rashid. Praise be to Allah that I reached you!"

Quite alarmed by the panicked sound of her father's good friend and lifelong colleague, Sharil replied, "Uncle Ahmed! What is wrong? Are you all right?"

"Sharil. Listen and listen to me very carefully. Do you remember the X-rays of a very special mummy that the Dutch team discovered?"

"Well, yes, but what does that—"

Interrupting her answer in mid-sentence.

"Sharil. Sharil. Again, listen to me very, very carefully. The Lauer-Schachermayr excavation has just discovered something that is very, very sensitive in nature. Do you now know what I mean? Sharil? How quickly can you get to Sakkara?"

"What?!"

"Sharil. Allow me to be plain. This is a true emergency. Cancel all of your appointments and get down here today. I have things to secure at my end. Good-bye."

Now staring at her silent receiver, Sharil could feel the panic tightening her chest. In that moment, looking up at the milky glass of her office door, she decided to act. She had to go to Sakkara, right now. Dr. Rashid needs me. So Sharil lifted her phone and called the motor pool. Then, standing, she put on a windbreaker, then, took the jacket off.

"Sharil. You don't know what all of this is leading to, but it might be a good time to change into your field gear."

*   *   *

To Dr. Rashid's everlasting relief, the Sharil Moussa arrived in her tan departmental Land Rover in an hour flat. In the process, she was quite sure that she had broken easily a dozen traffic laws, not that they were usually followed in Egypt. But none of that mattered. Just seeing the absolute joy and relief on Uncle Ahmed's face had told Sharil more than words could have expressed.

In the meantime, while he was waiting for Sharil Moussa, Rashid had furloughed the entire staff at the Great Magazine. To ensure a total lockdown on the object's intake, he collected all of its documentation, and placed them in the object's container as well.

Greeting her, the chemist then silently led her back into the depths of the facility to Container 43. Unlocking the door and opening it, Rashid flipped on the interior lighting of the space and stood behind the wheeled cart with its covered object. He then said, "Sharil, this object was delivered today from the Lauer-Schachermayr excavation. It was taken from a small niche located in the depths of the limestone bedrock."

And with that, he rather theatrically removed the microfiber cloth from the tarnished, bronze sphere and stood back to allow her to inspect it.

After a few moments of intense scrutiny, Sharil put on her reading glasses, circled around, and openly gaped at the sphere's details from every angle. As the magnitude of the shock took hold, Rashid knew that sooner or later she would find her tongue, and so he just waited for that moment to arrive.

"Extraordinary," whispered Sharil.

"But is this real?" she challenged in the next breath.

"Yes, Sharil, it is indeed real, and yes, it is indeed extraordinary. Now. What are we to do? Place an embargo on it, the same way we did on the Meryptah mummy?"

After the passing of several tense moments of thought, Sharil stated with certainty, "Yes, without question. This artifact has to disappear without a trace along with all of its records. In fact, we will take it back to the museum today in my vehicle. So, my good friend, let's pack this up for transport. Then, once it is at the museum, we will place it within your own department where it can be investigated in relative secrecy."

* * *

Dr. Ahmed Rashid sat in his office planning his assault on object 9321. Being a chemist, his first thoughts turned to an analysis of the artifact's alloy, but before that could be performed, the scientist needed to know precisely what he was dealing with. And that meant he needed some noninvasive way to peer into the object's interior, some way to gauge the shell's thickness, short of brutishly drilling a hole into it.

Smiling to himself, Rashid remembered a man that had not once, but twice, helped him with such a need, a man who had proven his trustworthiness over the years with his stunning silence. And so, he looked through his Rolodex and called the number. A pleasant female voice answered.

"Radiology. May I be of service?"

"Yes, yes, indeed. May I be connected to Dr. Hosny Zaaki, please?"

"Oh, I am very sorry, but Dr. Zaaki no longer is with us."

"Would you happen to know how I might reach him? Kindly allow me to introduce myself. My name is Dr. Ahmed Rashid. I am the head conservationist over at the National Museum. Dr. Zaaki and I have collaborated several times in the past, and I wish to do so in the future."

"Dr. Rashid, in that case, please hold for one moment."

By his wall clock, a full four minutes of nervous waiting expired before the disembodied voice on the other end of the line was again heard.

"Hello. Dr. Rashid. Are you still on the line?"

The relieved man answered in the affirmative.

"Dr. Zaaki is currently the chairman of the Radiological Sciences Department at the Cairo University Medical School. Would you like his phone number?"

"Yes! Please!"

Now armed with a new number, the scientist started his quest again.

"May I speak with Dr. Zaaki? This is Dr. Ahmed Rashid at the National Museum."

"One moment please."

"Radiology. How may I help you?"

"This is Dr. Ahmed Rashid of the National Museum. I wish to speak with Dr. Hosny Zaaki."

"Is this an emergency?"

Pause, and then, "Yes, it is."

"One moment while I transfer you."

Oh great, here we go again.

"Dr. Zaaki here."

"Dr. Zaaki! Good afternoon. This is Dr. Ahmed Rashid at the National Museum. Do you have a moment, sir?"

Pause. And then with a voice that dripped with sarcasm, "Dr. Rashid, do you wish me to irradiate yet another mummy or a cedarwood box?"

"No, Dr. Zaaki. Not this time. But I think that you will be most interested in the present object. It was discovered only three days ago at Sakkara. A very early tomb, Third Dynasty. Perhaps we could meet for lunch tomorrow? I would be more than happy to have you as my guest."

The sound of flipping pages in the background.

"Nope, I'm sorry, tomorrow won't do, but how about late this afternoon? I'll just meet you in front of the museum. Say around five. I have just finished my rounds and, as you well know, I am always interested in your mysteries. Then we can catch dinner afterwards."

*   *   *

Because of Rashid's sketchy memory of what Dr. Zaaki looked like, he decided to greet the man himself on the steps of the massive pink edifice that is the National Museum. Just to make sure that he would not miss the man, Ahmed was there, in position, at four forty-five. Not five minutes later, he recognized his guest striding purposefully through the entrance gates, and upon seeing him on the steps, the man waved in greeting.

"Dr. Rashid," he exclaimed, "how good it is to see you again."

Blushing from ear to ear, Rashid did not know what to say.

"Dr. Rashid, ever since our two collaborations several years ago, I have become an avid follower of archaeology. And now I cannot wait to see what you might have in store for me!" the head of radiology gushed as they began making their way to Rashid's office.

"Please, Dr. Zaaki. You are most kind, but I am only a conservator, not an archaeologist."

"Nonsense, Dr. Rashid. Your face was splashed all over the cable networks. Now, what have you for me?"

Instead of guiding the radiologist to his office, Rashid instead took him directly into the secured and caged area of the conservation laboratory itself. While the cage was a bit cramped for two, they nonetheless made do as they stood on opposite sides of a stainless steel table with a shrouded object.

"Dr. Zaaki. Before I show you what has caused me so much anxiety, I must, for the record, insist upon your cooperation and silence once again."

"Dr. Rashid. You have my word, sworn on my beloved parents' memory."

"Thank you, Dr. Zaaki. I knew that I could again depend on you." And as he removed the microfiber shroud, he said, "Here it is."

"By Allah's own beard! Is that a globe with all the continents?"

"Sadly, yes. I suspect that it is a hollow casting of bronze or copper. But I cannot remove a sample to analyze until I know how thick its shell is. Not to mention, whether there might be something contained within that shell as well. So here is my question to you,

Dr. Zaaki. How can we scan this artifact to see into it? To get an accurate cross section of it?"

Examining 9321 this way and that, but taking care to keep his hands in his pockets so as to not accidentally touch it, Dr. Zaaki replied with a sad smile, "Well, my friend, my radiology department will not be able to help you in any way. Both MRI and traditional X-ray will be totally useless. However, I suspect that one of my colleagues in Obstetrics might be of help, or perhaps someone over in the Physics Department."

"What do you mean, Dr. Zaaki?"

"What I mean is that you need an ultrasound probe. That's what will give you the shell's wall thickness and maybe even a shadow image of whatever you think might be suspended inside."

*   *   *

After a marvelously satisfying dinner, Dr. Zaaki, true to his word, arranged for a portable, handheld ultrasound unit to be delivered the very next morning to Rashid's office, complete with its lubricating gel and a step-by-step instruction manual. Confirming that the gel's components would not harm the metal or its beautiful patina, the scientist, with an amused smile on his face, began his sonic probing and confirmed that the sphere appeared to be of a hollow construction with a shell of uniform thickness, about four centimeters thick, but a shell made of two distinct layers. Nowhere could the man detect either a join or solder joint. Somehow, someway, it was cast as a hollow sphere of two layers. This fact alone caused the scientist to furrow his brow. Putting away the ultrasonic probe and its accompanying paraphernalia, the scientist began recording its other physical characteristics.

After about an hour's time, he discovered that the sphere was not truly a sphere, it was an ellipsoid or a geoid, an earth-shaped form, as it measured precisely 26.25 centimeters at its equator and only 26.16 centimeters from pole to pole. In other words, the globe had the subtle appearance of having been squashed from above, which caused a slight swelling at its middle. And while not a mathematician by trade, the ratio was 0.99679. Precisely the same ratio, if one bothered to calculate the Earth's equatorial swelling.

That fact outright troubled the chemist, as if the delineated seven continents on its surface were not enough. Next, Rashid placed the artifact upon a digital scale, which read 8.61 kilograms, about 18.98 pounds. But the chemist realized that if the globe was made of nothing but bronze, then it was far, far too light in weight. So whatever made up its inner layer had to be a lighter material, like aluminum or titanium. Again, something impossible for the Third Dynasty.

Satisfied now that he could coax a minute sample from the object, he did so using a small deburring attachment on his jeweler's drill. With the tiny fragments carefully collected in a test tube, Rashid ran the metallurgical analysis himself, which revealed that 9321 was indeed made of a copper alloy – bronze, but one with only trace arsenic and an unusually high percentage of tin for a supposedly Third Dynasty artifact. This detail caused the man some heartburn. As for the object's inner layer, Rashid thought it best to leave that well alone for the moment, as he already had sufficient fish to fry.

Finished with his preliminary analysis and before he would begin the laborious process of removing any injurious corrosion, he sat back, and for the first time in a very long time, lit a cigarette. He regretted doing so, for the tobacco was stale, as it had come from a stash that he had long ago squirreled away. Disappointed, he ruthlessly crushed it out after only two puffs.

Face it, Ahmed. *Just face it. This object is just like that most troublesome Meryptah mummy. Such a perplexing anomaly. And now this globe! Another godforsaken anomaly! But I am a scientist, and scientists need answers. Now just where in Allah's name can I get those answers!*

* * *

A day later, a thoroughly vexed Rashid received a phone call, while he was carefully dabbing away at the tarnished surface of object 9321. Locked away as he was in the peace and solitude of his laboratory, the intrusion seemed to rile the usually laid-back scientist even more, and it showed in his voice, when he finally answered on the fifth ring.

"Rashid here."

"Uncle Ahmed?"

Hearing Sharil's voice rather quickly snapped the conservator's attitude back to a more civil state.

"Yes, Sharil. How might I help you?

"Uh-huh."

"I see."

"Well, in that case, I will join you in about five minutes time."

"Good-bye."

Now that was odd, Rashid thought. *I have never before been invited for lunch by Sharil Moussa.* Quickly glancing at his wristwatch, the scientist nonetheless realized that he had to be fed and so began to seal up his chemicals and locked up the anomalous and weighty globe in the secured cage.

Throwing on his suit coat and locking his laboratory's door behind him, he strode off rather purposefully toward his luncheon meeting, with many questions buzzing around in his head.

*   *   *

Much to Rashid's surprise, the so-called luncheon was booked at the very exclusive Mina House that was situated near the base of the Great Pyramid. While the small talk during the taxi ride over had not betrayed their final destination, once they arrived, the scientist began to wonder who else would they be meeting up with. But again to his surprise, it was just the two of them.

Once seated at a secluded table that overlooked the hotel's gardens and pools, Sharil ordered a round of chilled, fresh juice drinks and then, once the two were alone, got down to business.

"Uncle Ahmed," she began, "for the longest of time, I have considered you a close and dear colleague, a true friend, and in some ways, part of my family. I know that my father feels the same."

What is this preamble leading to? Thought the suddenly nervous scientist. My retirement?

The museum director continued, "Now Uncle Ahmed, by the worried look on your face, this meeting is not about your retirement. That is a matter that my father has already taken care of in some detail. So relax and be at ease.

"But what this meeting is really all about is your incredible ability to act under extraordinary pressure. Your ability to recognize, as just proven again, when a situation is a most sensitive one. I am referring to the round object that the Lauer-Schachermayr team just uncovered. But even before that, I remember how well you handled the Meryptah mummy and its strange X-ray films, not to mention a certain cedar wood box.

"Well, Uncle Ahmed, I believe that it is high time that you are made aware of one other secret, one that will offer you a partial explanation of what is going on, an inkling that only a scientist would truly appreciate."

With his eyes wide and mind completely open, Rashid listened while his director spun a fantastic tale of a Russian boy-genius, his defection to the United States, and his prize project. The scientist then heard of the recent adventures risked by a gifted linguist into his own land's distant past, all just to calibrate the temporal device. While the museum director was not absolutely sure, she suspected that the extraordinary injury to that certain high priest that Ahmed had X-rayed, and now the true origin of the bronze globe, were somehow connected.

"So," began a dazed Rashid, "are you saying that this Russian linguist made all of these things happen?"

"No, I do not think so. But what I am saying is that the entire story has yet to be told. And that we must remain vigilant for any more strange objects that may come to light, just the way you did most recently with the globe. That act alone was truly one of prescient insight."

CHAPTER XIV
SAVAMA Computer Technology & Research

Delirious jubilation broke out in Tehran, after the first e-mail was sent from Horizon Pass after its cyber attack. Unknown to its author, that e-mail triggered the start of a very ambitious download.

For Aref, he could not believe the good news. It had all come together so quickly and after so many failed attempts to even locate the highly secretive facility. Now the accursed installation was his to cybernetically rape.

"*Allahu akbar!*" he joyfully shouted to all in the SAVAMA computer complex.

"Now," he ranted with tight fists to the three operators around him, "let us drain their databases as dry as the Maghreb!"

*   *   *

The following day at Horizon Pass, Stan noticed an odd, low-grade trend of activity on his security monitor. Before the hack, he wouldn't have given it a thought, but now he questioned everything he saw, no matter how insignificant. Checking back into the log, he saw that it had begun right after the e-mail servers went live yesterday with their new configuration. No, check that. Right after the first transmission of an e-mail, his in fact, letting Chicago know that they were again up and running and ready for business. It had been a long time since the ex-spook felt the hair on the back of his head stand up, and so he did the sensible thing. He called

Buddy, Marla, and Ron over to take a hard look at this innocent squiggle on his load graph.

After a good forty minutes of intense investigation, Marla spoke the words that no one wanted to hear.

"Dudes, we've been hacked. And hacked bad, like a raped ape. Stan, that activity was an internal download of God only knows what, and it ran, according to the log's internal clock, for some ten plus hours. Geez Louise! Our bottoms have been bared! And guess what? We gotta do something about it!"

*   *   *

"So Aref, how did the experiment go? Well, I trust?"

Impatient as ever, but also quite elated, the Iranian agent managed to hide both of those feelings from his departmental superior.

"Sir, we learned much about the target's security, but as we speak our worms are at work, and the downloading process has begun. I have been told that the information is coming in at a trickle in order to confound its detection. While we still know only that their secret facility is located in the deserts of New Mexico, we are slowly bleeding their database dry. As with everything, there is always a way."

The superior, pleased at the upbeat vibe that he was getting from his subordinate, approved the next day's activities on the necessary requisition sheet, with a red stamp no less. And while the reverberation of the stamp was still echoing, the superior asked, "And, Aref, do you truly believe that this effort will prove what your investigations have suggested?"

Still with the smug disbelief, Aref grimaced to himself. *These bureaucrats cannot think themselves out of a tent, much less grasp the very physics that make their beloved cell phones work!*

*   *   *

Three days later, Aref delivered to the Niroo Research Institute the temporal device's schematics, its operational logs, computerized calibration algorithms, and historical files, which had been acquired from the slow and steady hack of the Horizon Pass' system. Needless to say, the building of the device would take a bit longer, maybe four and a half weeks. The most difficult item on the list was the specially crafted drop ring, as its ferric ring was composed of a unique alloy. Meanwhile, an analysis of the stolen operational logs revealed many of the pitfalls that the Americans had overcome during the device's developmental evolution. As for the calibration algorithms, they were the true gold mine, as the device would have been useless without them.

What had stunned the development team the most, however, were the contents of the historical files, in which was chronicled the goals and results of each and every one of the joint Russian/American deployments. To the Iranians, it seemed that the Great Satans thought nothing of carrying out multiple pharaonic assassinations, the mass murder of whole populations with bioagents, the shoddy leaving behind of evidence of their presence, the tampering with the cultural development of a culture, and execution of personal vendetta killings, not to mention the stealing of artifacts.

But balanced against such obvious atrocities, there was this most curious document called the *RUTI*, a Russian anagram that translated into English as "Guidelines for Temporal Exploration." Apparently, this was the guide that the Great Satans supposedly followed so as to not affect the current reality or timeline. The brief document read as follows:

RUTI

Rukovodyashiy Ukaeaniya dlya Tymporalie Eksploratsiya
(*Guidelines for Temporal Exploration*)

1. TIME AS A SINGLE INSTANCE, ALTERABLE DIMENSION. Time is not immutable, nor is it subject to multiple parallel iterations. This position is not one shared by many theoretical physicists, mathematicians, and philosophers. So, the conservative position adopted by the Hourglass Seminar was not to offer a theoretical exercise, but rather to provide guidelines for the practical use of a temporal device.

2. AVOID TEMPORAL PARADOXES. Avoid any situation where two propositions are simultaneously true and false.

   2a. DO NO HARM. Do not terminate yourself or your immediate ancestors. Do not injure indiscriminately or consciously instigate change.

3. OPERATIONAL AUTHORIZATION TO USE THE TEMPORAL DEVICE. All temporal insertions must be authorized by designated representatives of the scientific communities of at least two national entities.

4. THE TEMPORAL DEVICE. While the initial design and development of the temporal device was funded by the government of the United States, the temporal device is not the property, nor is under the control of, any national entity; rather, it is the property of the American Academy of Sciences in cooperation with the Russian Academy of Sciences.

   4a. SAFEGUARDS. All temporal devices are equipped with self-destruct devices and protocols to prevent their falling into the hands of unauthorized persons, organizations, or national entities.

5. TEMPORAL INSERTIONS. Authorized temporal insertions are to be unobtrusive events designed to avoid an unintentional temporal alteration. All authorized insertions must be judiciously planned with specific scientific or operational tasks that are designed to produce specific results. The calibration of the temporal device was the primary reason for the initial temporal insertions.

   5a. INTRODUCTION OF CULTURAL ELEMENTS. Minor cultural impacts are inevitable; major ones are to be avoided at all costs (see 2a above), since any alteration may have temporal impact. Ripple effects will occur as changes to the past propagate into the present – the so-called "butterfly effect."

   5b. LEAVE NO TRACE. All temporal field agents must seamlessly blend into the temporal horizon into which they are deployed. They must be provided with a full briefing on the period, wear appropriate clothing, speak the language of the period, and assume an unremarkable persona.

5c. PROCREATION. Procreation during a temporal deployment represents a major alteration to the temporal flow with the introduction of a person who should not exist.

5d. INSERTED OBJECTS. All objects and temporal field agents must be retrieved or returned to their own time period, whether damaged, alive, or dead. Objects are not to be inserted or extracted from their rightful place in time.

5e. AGING. All objects that pass through the temporal device continue to age per their original timeline.

Needless to say, the document left the Iranian development team confused, for clearly the two Great Satans had not followed it. Instead they had wantonly broken codicils 2a, 5a, and 5b multiple times. So they began to wonder. What truly is our reality? Is it a purely Western European construct?

*   *   *

As with the American version of the Soap Bubble, the Iranians also had to find out that any living organic material that came into contact with metal tended to spontaneously burn, if not totally cremate the victim. This fact was learned the hard way, on no fewer than four occasions, until the Iranian development team began to seriously look into the biology of the matter. If their hackers had bothered to raid the medical files at Horizon Pass, they would have had their answer. Instead, four brave souls had been horribly martyred in the unquenchable fires of a temporal quantum field.

*   *   *

Despite the technical and rather grisly delays, Aref nonetheless was ecstatic at the rapid progress that the Niroo research and development team had made. Admittedly, there had been some casualties, but he reasoned that they had died for a far greater good – Islamic world supremacy. But now that they had successfully built the prototype, he pushed for a portable version that he could take into the field. Only then, he reasoned, could he strike at the very heart of Western Christendom.

*   *   *

"My brothers, it is time for us to prepare. While our journey will be a brief one, it will be an adventure unlike any other. For tomorrow, we will join with our distant cousins. For tomorrow, we will remove from the pages of history Islam's greatest foe.

"Fear not, my brothers, for he, this pig Frank, is just a man. This pig of a Frank bleeds just like other men. This Charles Martel, this pig Frank, breathes just like other men.

"Trust in me, my brothers, when I say that we will kill this Satan who walks the Earth.

"*Allahu akbar!*"

*   *   *

Horizon Pass had the time, leisure, and interest to borrow and then develop a compact backpack power source for their portable temporal device. The Iranians did not. From the very start, the Iranian device had only one purpose – the simple deployment of an assassination team. There were to be no retrievals, as their logic dictated that if the team was successful, then current reality would cease to exist. In their minds, it was just that simple. So, in order to make that one way deployment possible, two items had to be acquired. A flatbed truck was sourced along with diesel generators and a well-placed and secluded property.

Four brand-new Cummins Onan 12000 generators were purchased for the purpose and mounted on the wooden flatbed of a venerable 1987 Mercedes-Benz 814 truck. Each generator was rated at twelve thousand watts at one hundred amps, but for this exercise, their governors had been removed so that each could generate, on a one-time basis, close to fourteen thousand watts each. Eight heavy duty cables would run from these units, which were dedicated to each of the four electromagnetic pylons and their ion horns. As each of the nearly eight-hundred-pound units created their own electromagnetic field, this necessitated the parking of the flatbed truck that carried them on the opposite side of the property's main stone building to act as a shield, so as to not conflict with the temporal field itself.

As for the property from where the deployment would take place, Aref volunteered to reconnoiter the neighborhood. And what he found, just west of

Vouneil-sur-Vienne at the intersection of Highway D15 and Fonbrede, was the perfect spot. Located barely four-tenths of a mile from the village's center, the property was situated along the roadway's south side. It contained a two-story stone house and two outbuildings arranged in an L-shape, the entire lot encircled by a stone wall fronted by high hedges. A parking area along the roadway in front of the main house was of an ideal size for the flatbed.

Noting the lone Audi parked in front of the stone two-story, Aref recognized that, if necessary, his small band of assassins could easily dispatch the owners without much fuss, when the blessed time arrived. And if they were not at home, so much the better.

CHAPTER XV
Remote Sensing

As a determined Naysmithe scanned the faces of a very select group of satellite engineers, he then challenged them, "Here's what I need to know, like yesterday, can the specific intensity of a Soap Bubble field be detected from space? That's what I want to know right now. And if so, then how quickly can we configure satellites and get those birds on permanent station over Tehran and western France?"

To the specific question "can the Soap Bubble field be detected?" was answered two days later as the portable Soap Bubble had been set up out in the open in New Mexico, when it produced, at random, twelve different temporal energy fields. From the drone flying overhead at fifty thousand feet, the electromagnetic field was seen by a special sensor as clear as a firefly's light in a pitch black cave. Additionally, all twelve field intensities were correctly identified to an astonishing accuracy of four decimals to the right.

Fortunately, the sensor aboard the USAF drone out of Nellis was a well-known and understood unit, which had been already deployed in orbit for the detection of electromagnetic pulses produced by unauthorized, illegal underground nuclear tests. The sensor in question that came with the highly imaginative name, Special Electromagnetic Sensor, or SES, was currently being flown aboard all of the USAF Defense Meteorological Satellites, which are scattered about the earth in stationary orbits. Satellite EF-3, in stationary orbit some 450 miles over Tehran, watched for any evidence of the specified electromagnetic field, as it was believed that the Iranian device would be first developed somewhere within that city's vicinity. Satellite BD-2, in stationary orbit some 450 miles above Bourges, France, was their ideal candidate as the cities of Poitiers and Tours were well within its sensor's window. Now all that had to be arranged was a considerable narrowing of the sensors' wavelengths to specifically match those of the Soap Bubble's range. Once that focusing of the sensors was accomplished, then a painful and numbing waiting game began.

*   *   *

Three weeks later and only after some very energetic conversations with several irate global warming scientists, Horizon Pass had their two dedicated look-down electromagnetic sensors fully operational. Secretly, the USAF had been long looking for any excuse to rid themselves of those "quacks from East Anglia," so when Horizon Pass made their mildly odd request, the Air Force had jumped at the opportunity to assist their countrymen.

*   *   *

Live feeds from the EF-3 and BD-2 satellites were shared and recorded within Horizon Pass' Tombstone facility. In fact, a dedicated screen was installed on Stan's desk, right next to his daily interface. And in the possible event that Stan was not at his desk, when an event detection took place, he had rigged up an alarm so as to alert the rest of the computer department.

The first event detection alarm occurred about five weeks after the detection of the cyber break-in at Horizon Pass. EF-3 detected the brief emission of the unique Soap Bubble energy signature within Tehran and specifically from within the main building of the Niroo Research Institute. Over the next several weeks, six more detections were recorded, each of varying strengths and amplitudes. Clearly, the Iranians were making progress and at a rapid rate.

*   *   *

Perhaps it was inevitable, but seven weeks later Stan's BD-2 alarm screamed its head off at precisely four a.m. on a Saturday morning. Disturbing about the event detection was its location, a point some twenty kilometers northeast of Poitiers near the village of Vouneuil-sur-Vienne. The precise location seemed to be just west of the village, about a quarter mile along the D15 Highway. The local time was high noon, Sunday. As for the electromagnetic field frequency reading of the event, it calibrated to 12:03 p.m., October 2, AD 732. Apparently, the Iranians had decided to arrive early as the actual battle took place on Monday, October 10th. Then, rather suddenly, the field's frequency violently spiked and winked out altogether.

While the village's name did not ring a bell with anyone, Marla quickly cross-checked it and discovered that the area's name was once the hamlet of Moussais, better known later when it was renamed *Moussais-la-Bataille*, "The Battle of Moussais." In other words, this was the actual location of the famous battle in October of AD 732.

Chapter XVI
Special Training

It was a short walk down University Avenue from the Near Eastern Institute to the Social Sciences building on 59th Street. For Richards, this was to be his first investigative foray to the university's History Department to visit with one Colin Wentworth, Professor Emeritus of Western Medieval History. From everything that the Egyptologist had heard, Wentworth was the grand old man of the period, having written some fourteen books on the subject. With a no-nonsense reputation, Wentworth was a blood-and-guts military historian, a big fan of historical reenactments, and this native of Kentucky could ride a horse and swing a mean broadsword. Consequently, whenever he offered a medieval history course, which was not often at this point in his career, the lecture hall was packed as Wentworth was a sterling speaker, a great storyteller, and an easy grade.

As Richards approached the gray limestone Gothic edifice, he smiled, as it was often told that Wentworth could defend it all on his own. Mounting the three entrance steps that led to a spacious interior hall and an ascending staircase to the right, the young scholar did so, taking two steps at a time, until he had reached the building's third floor, or Keep. There, the second door on the left, was Wentworth's office. Firmly knocking twice on the door's hardwood surface, a bellow was heard from within. Taking that as a greeting, Richards entered and was transported to another place and time.

There was a solid-looking desk and behind it hung a magnificent and enormous copy of the Bayeux Tapestry depicting the Norman conquest of Britain. To the right were bookshelves crammed with books, to the left the same, except for the portly fellow on a ladder with an armful of books in one arm and his head within a thick cloud of pipe smoke.

"I'll be right down, Professor Richards. Just make yourself at home," the fellow said.

Looking around, the Egyptologist plopped himself down in the lone guest chair.

"All these damn books," growled his host. "I just can't seem to find enough room for them all – ever."

Descending from the heights with a bit of a blush to his ruddy face, Wentworth stuck out his full-sized hand and greeted his visitor.

"Frankly, sir, it is not often that a for-real Egyptologist wishes to speak with a Western Medievalist, so let's have at it."

Now sitting behind his desk, Wentworth, with his hands behind his head, the easily two-hundred-pound redhead said, "Now, Professor Richards, you mentioned in your e-mail that you were interested in Charles Martel, isn't that right?"

"Ah, yes, sir. That's correct. As I mentioned in my e-mail, I have been doing some research into Charles Martel and have come to the conclusion that he was a quite a guy, a nobleman, duke, prince, and mayor of the palace of Francia. Then there are all of his military exploits and victories. But in particular, I am extremely interested in his physical characteristics, his size, hair color, eye color, that sort of thing."

During this entire discourse, Wentworth listened carefully, nodding here and there.

"Well now, Professor Richards, about all that I can tell you for sure about Karl the Hammer is that he was a Frank, a battle-hardened Frank, a brilliant strategist and field tactician, and a damn good administrator as well, as you have already noted. As for his appearance, well, that I'll leave alone, as nobody really knows, but I'll wager that he was better than average in height and built like a brick house."

Shocked, Richards retorted, "You mean that we have no coins with his image? No depictions of him in manuscripts? No statues? Nothing?"

Smiling and opening his arms expansively.

"Professor Richards, Karl was a disowned bastard of a king's concubine, who rather brilliantly turned that colorful heritage into a strength. He was a soldier first and administrator second, first and always. He consistently represented the hidden power behind the throne, while never taking it directly. So, no, Professor Richards, there are no images of the man that I can place before you, no text that physically describes him.

"But given his life and his many battles, you can bet the house that his nose was broken countless times, that he wore his helmet so long that he was balding, and I wouldn't be surprised if his face was scared many times, just like today's hockey players. Why, you ask? Because a facial scar was a trophy that proved you didn't run in the heat of battle. That was Karl to the max.

"Besides, I remember that you were once a football player for this august institution. So, if you need a truly visceral image, latch onto this one: a middle linebacker, who is quick as a cat, tough as nails, and possesses a keen and agile mind. You know, like a George, a Butkus, a Singletary, or an Urlacher. Now, that my friend, was Karl in a nutshell."

Now pausing in thought, Richards then unleashed his next question.

"Alright, Professor, I can see the linebacker image. It's a good one. But in general, regarding his troops, his regular ones that is, how would you physically characterize them? And for that matter, the men of his heavy cavalry as well?"

Now rubbing his chin in thought, Wentworth pondered on this for a while.

"Well, in answer to this question, this too is a guess on my part and here is why. Karl's heavy infantry fought in a tight and intimate phalanx formation. Each man wore and carried some seventy to eighty pounds of gear. They fought close in and eye-to-eye, with large wooden shields, axes, Roman short swords, and spears. Their battles lasted hours on end, and still the Saracen heavy cavalry could not breech their lines. So, what kind of men does that suggest to you: offensive and defensive linemen? Big, heavy fellows, possessing brutish strength and incredible endurance? That would be my guess.

"As for the horsemen, the Frankish heavy cavalry, those guys had to be of a different breed, if you know what I mean. First, you had to learn to ride and ride well, not a Frankish strong suit. Then you add all the Saracen-inspired chain mail and armor. While atop the steed, you're now top heavy and need the gift of balance. Then somewhere along the line, you have to be able to swing a broadsword or an ax and somehow defend yourself with a shield, all while peering through a helmet visor. I don't know about you, but I would have preferred a place in the phalanx to that exposed position atop a warhorse."

Seeing Richards' highly focused thousand-yard stare, Wentworth went on.

"Then you have all the sweat that gets in your eyes, the blood flying everywhere, the sheer noise of metal on metal, the screams of the wounded and dying – both horse and men – and finally the sheer smell of it all. Without question, it was a dirty and serious business.

"What many do not tell you was that Karl's first battle was a rout. He was woefully unprepared, and he never, ever forgot that lesson. So Karl henceforth was always the prepared one, even while most of the time outmanned. Without question, he always, always was unpredictable, did things that were not supposed to happen, arrived early, attacked from an unexpected direction, or performed some tactical maneuver never seen before. He vexed his opponents and purposefully got into their heads. In short, he was a master of medieval psy-ops, as he outright owned, through his fierce reputation and force of will, the battlefield. Needless to say, his regular troops would follow him anywhere, at any time, even to the very gates of Hell, if so commanded."

Stunned by the sheer imagery of Wentworth's passionate oratory, Richards just nodded in admiration, for now he had a sense of what he must do to prepare.

*   *   *

"I have a good colleague," Dean Young began, "who really wants to learn how to ride."

"No, he has no experience whatsoever."

"Bareback."

"Yes, that is correct."

"Balance? I haven't the faintest idea. All that I know about his physical capabilities is that he was once an American footballer, and he is built like a tree."

"About two hundred pounds, I would think."

"Thank you, Charles. You're a good man. I knew that I could depend upon you in a pinch."

"Yes, and my best to your Margaret as well.

"Good-bye."

*　*　*

Charles Goodwin was once a champion jockey of some renown in Britain, at least until he suffered a tragic spill in the middle of a muddy turn. To make a long and painful story blessedly short, after two horses had trampled him, it was a miracle that the man could still walk. While his racing days were behind him, Goodwin felt that his training days were fully in front of him. Then came an opportunity he just could not ignore, a call from the owner of a Nashville-based horse-racing farm that inquired as to his availability. And as they say, "the rest was history."

The ginger-haired Goodwin knew Paul Young from their prep school days at the Christ Church Cathedral School in Oxford. As the pair both loved history and classics, they tended to hang together to the exclusion of the others. And since both boys were rather on the smallish side, rugby and soccer were avoided at all costs, but riding, as taught by Goodwin's father, had filled that void quite nicely. So while Young had pursued his father's wishes, Goodwin had done the same as an expert horseman and jockey.

And here stood before him, green as grass, his boyhood friend's colleague, clearly a sturdy chap, with an eager and ready grin.

"Hello, Mr. Goodwin!" Glad-handing the equestrian firmly. "My name's Joey Richards. Paul Young has told me all about you."

"Oh, he has now? So how is Paul these days?"

"He's doing quite well. He's the Dean of Humanities at a big school in Chicago."

Tilting his head to the left, as if the trainer had not heard that right.

"The dean of a prep school of all things?"

"No, Mr. Goodwin. He's a dean at a university."

"Oh, right! That's ever so much better." Then shifting gears, he asked. "So Mr. Richards, what can I do for you?" said Goodwin, glancing down toward the philologist's overnight duffle on the ground.

"Well, sir, I'm here to learn to ride."

"Is that all?"

"Well, Mr. Goodwin, that alone seems quite a lot in itself, don't you think?"

Now allowing a wrinkle of a smile to crease his weathered and heavily tanned face. "Why, yes, Mr. Richards, it is. It surely is. Now, tell me about your sense of balance," he said as he took off his wire-rimmed glasses to polish up their lenses.

And so the conversation went, with one asking and the other answering as best he could. What Goodwin got out of it was the impression of a man on a mission to conquer something. That same man was honest and open, not prone to exaggeration, just a man who wanted to learn to ride bareback, and was highly motivated to do so. Goodwin thought that this enthusiasm needed some tempering, and so he led Richards over to a small fenced in corral. Within it were two things: a short tree stump that stood in the center and a black Arabian gelding that was standing opposite against the fence.

As the pair leaned against the heavily painted white fencing, Goodwin narrated, "Mr. Richards, you were correct, riding is indeed quite a lot. It's a partnership between yourself and your mount, where the two forget and become one. But before that can happen, you have to know and command your horse. And, before that can happen, you have to extend yourself to the horse. Give it your respect, and only when you do that, God willing, will the horse respect you.

"Mr. Richards, that animal over there across the pen is a highly intelligent creature. It's smarter than a dog, has a greater memory, and an amazing sense of hearing and smell. Get within twenty feet of him, and Khan can hear your heartbeat and smell your fear.

"So, if you are ever to earn a horse's respect, you must grant it your respect first. It all starts right now. That animal is your emotional mirror. It likes to please, but only whom it wishes to please."

Now reaching into the pockets of his tan windbreaker, Goodwin pulled out a small pocketknife and a shiny red apple.

"All right, Mr. Richards, take these. Very slowly enter the pen and saunter up to that stump and go no further. Your task is to get Khan to come to you, and remember what I told you about how he's just your emotional mirror."

Taking the proffered knife and apple, Richards looked Goodwin straight in the eye, smiled, and in so doing, relaxed his face and entire demeanor. The Egyptologist then bent over, smoothly slid under the top rail to gain entry to the corral, and strolled over to the stump.

This entire process took a good two minutes by Goodwin's reckoning, and the Englishman was amazed at how smooth and fearless this youngster Richards' body language was.

Once Richards had reached the stump, only Khan's ears twitched in his direction, but other than that, the horse actually moved its rear quarters over toward that direction showing his total disinterest, if not disdain. A flick of the tail seemed to punctuate that assessment.

Much to Goodwin's surprise, Richards just patiently sat down on the stump, opened his knife, and began to carve the apple into six sections. Finished, the man then popped one into his mouth and began to rather noisily chew it.

These sounds were not missed by Khan, as his ears twitched again in Richards' direction, but the rest of him did not stir. So, Richards ate another section, this time even smacking his lips and making deep throaty groans of sheer pleasure.

This did get Khan stirring, and for the first time, he actually looked Richards' way. For his part, the academic slowly waved an apple section enticing Khan to move. He didn't. So Richards brazenly ate that one too. This caused the horse to actually snort, turn, and take one step forward, to which Richards said in a soft and gentle voice, "Hey there, big boy. Do you want some apple?"

He wagged the fourth section at the animal, which now bobbed its head twice, took another two steps forward, and stopped again. So Richards just smiled and ate that one too. That earned another snort and two steps closer.

Now within six feet of the sitting man, Khan carefully studied him and what was in his hands, just two sections of precious apple. The sitting man just stared back smiling, with a calm heartbeat and not a bit of nervous sweat about him. Now very curious, Khan's head tilted to the right with interest and took three steps forward, well within the stranger's reach. And then to Khan's surprise, the stranger offered him not one, but both of the remaining apple sections, which he then gently nibbled from the palm of his outstretched, open hand.

*   *   *

Never before had Goodwin seen the like, a total greenhorn so casually enter a corral and then communicate with such a spirited horse like Ghenghis Khan! And now to beat all, he's standing beside him, whispering into his ear, all the time stroking his nose and neck.

Now shaking his head in a mixture of amazement and amusement, he thought, *Paul always was such a prankster! Here he sends me a seasoned horse whisperer posing as an amateur! That son of a bitch!*

*   *   *

For the entire three weeks while Richards was on the property, Goodwin had the Egyptologist spending his entire day with Khan. He fed him, washed him, brushed him down, and of course, mucked out his stall. By the end of the second week, Richards was riding Khan bareback and at a full gallop. It seemed to Goodwin that the man's powerful thighs seemed to lock into his mount's barrel in a way that he had never seen before. His flowing shaggy black hair almost seemed to perfectly mimic Khan's mane as the pair moved, pivoted, and turned. It was just beautiful to watch them cavort together across the rolling fields of the farm. They had bonded.

*   *   *

When Richards returned from his equestrian experience in the rolling green hills of Tennessee, he knew that he still had a long way to go before he could pass as a Frankish military recruit. He needed to adequately grasp at least two languages, Latin and Frankish, attain some familiarity with the bow, and submerge into a brutal refresher course on hand-to-hand fighting. Fortunately for him, Richards knew just who to talk to regarding the languages and street thuggery, but was at a total loss regarding the bow. So he paid another visit to Professor Wentworth, full knowing the man's passion for historical medieval reenactments.

"So, Professor Wentworth, where would one learn how to properly draw a medieval compound bow?"

Staring at Richards again from across his desk, the academician furrowed his brow in thought, and after several moments of deep concentration, brightened and said, "You know Professor Richards, you do ask the most interesting questions. First, it was Karl Martel. Now, it's early medieval bowmanship. Most intriguing.

If I didn't know any better, I would have thought you to be a most promising graduate candidate in Medieval History. But, alas, I know that that is not the case.

"So, kindly allow me to rummage around for a moment as I find a telephone number."

And rummage Wentworth did, as he pulled out one of his desk drawers and dumped its contents on his desk's leather blotter with a crash. Richards, having never before seen such a solution, just sat there in rapt amusement as the emeritus professor pulled, pried, and sorted through an amazing assortment of tither that had managed to populate said drawer. But in moments, or so it seemed, a smile appeared as Wentworth withdrew a soiled and folded ivory-colored business card from the morass.

"Ah, here we go: Claude Depuy's Sporting Goods, Artillator & Bowyer, Peoria, Illinois. And there is even a telephone number, but I don't know if it is still current.

"So here you go," he said as he passed the card to Richards. "You can keep it. Without question, old Claude is the man that you should see about everything regarding medieval archery training. He's the best, that is, if he is still walks among the living."

*   *   *

The trek down I-55 to Peoria took Richards a little over three hours. Wentworth had been partially right. The telephone number worked, but the sporting goods store had morphed into a gun and ammunition establishment, complete with its own firing range. Nonetheless, the current owner knew Depuy and agreed to contact the old coot on Richards' behalf. After several more telephone calls, a date and time were arranged to the meet with the bowman.

Located on Peoria's north side on University Drive, the store was a low structure with a sloped metal roof. Richards had been told to expect a parked dark green pickup. Pulling into the tarmac parking lot, the old Chevy was indeed there, and someone was sitting it. Getting out of his black Corvette Z06, the Egyptologist sauntered up to the driver's side door and gently rapped on the window, startling the dozing occupant. With a snort, he shook his long white mane, blinked his robin's egg blue eyes, and rubbed his large hawk-like nose. Swallowing hard, Claude energetically wound down his window.

"Now that was cruel."

Smiling back, "Well, should I have honked?"

"No, no, I suppose not. So, are you that Richards fellow from the big city?"

"Yes, sir. And you are Claude Depuy, I presume?"

Now through slightly squinted eyes, "Indeed, you presume correctly. How did you get my name?"

"A certain Professor Colin Wentworth. It seems he holds you in considerably high regard, especially when it comes to medieval bows and their use. He told me to look you up, and so here I am."

"Wentworth you say! That old battle-ax! Why didn't you mention his name earlier? Or maybe you did. I tend to be more than a bit forgetful lately. Well, why don't you jump into that pretty little pocket rocket of yours and follow me out to my place? I have something that you will think is pretty neat!"

*   *   *

It was a classic Midwestern clapboard farmhouse with a large red-and-white barn out back. The two-story house was painted white and appeared in every way immaculate, down to its lace curtains hung just so in their squeaky-clean windows, a detail that Richards found to be remarkable given the dusty road up to the place. It was like stepping back in time to a far simpler era, another detail that was not lost on the Egyptologist. Upon mounting the traditional three-stepped entrance and entering the house, the smell of freshly brewed coffee met his nose as did the unmistakable lingering aroma of maple bacon.

"Penny, dear, we have some company from the big city," Claude announced as he made his way back toward the kitchen area with Richards in tow.

The hardwood passage from the front door to the kitchen passed by a modest dining room on the right and a comfortable living room opposite. Once at the threshold of the kitchen, windows greeted Richards that offered wide views of the gardens and greenery out back. Next to the left corner bank of windows sat on the massive wooden table a heating pad, a dented aluminum pot, and next to it, a still steaming mound of blueberry muffins, all flanked by a hulk of butter, its knife, three coffee mugs, and several serving dishes.

Penny, still wiping her hands dry near the sink, stood about five foot nothing, probably weighed an even hundred, and had a smile that could illuminate half of New York City.

"Welcome," she simply said. "Please sit down and help yourself. The coffee's fresh."

At the invitation, Richards' washboard gut growled loudly, much to his embarrassment.

"Well, now, I will take that as a yes." She chuckled.

* * *

"Colin and I go way back," Claude began. "We were graduate students together at the U of I, both of us in history. It all started when we were reading some historical sources that described some battle, I recall it as being Agincourt. Colin got into his head that he wanted to figure it all out, all the maneuvers, where everybody was, in short, the usual for him. But to do that, we needed to know the potential range of a longbow. Nobody really knew, so I sort of took the bit in my teeth and began fooling around building my own longbow, and before you knew it, one thing had led to another, and suddenly I was writing my dissertation on bow building and design.

"Then when it came time to find a job, I found myself out on a limb that no one really cared about. So I expanded my horizons, so to speak, opened a modest sporting goods store back in town, and surprised myself with how well it did. When the news got out that I was a bowyer, I found that I needed help with the store as the orders began to pour in from around the state, then the country. I even had a bunch of orders from some Frenchies who wanted longbows made for a history exhibit. Funny thing is, never heard from them if they ever used those three bows. It would be a real pity if they didn't.

"Then, somehow, Hollywood got my name as the go-to guy for bows. So my first movie was *The Ten Commandments*. DeMille had to have everything authentic. He insisted on it. So the pharaoh's chariot bow was mine. The next movie where my bows appeared was *The Vikings*, with Kirk Douglas and Tony Curtis. To this day, I still love that scene where Douglas is dancing on the extended oars. Well, as you can probably imagine, the list goes on. It was all good and honest money, and it helped a lot. The last movie that I did was *Robin and Marian*. I vividly remember teaching Sean Connery, James Bond himself, how to string a bow and then shoot it properly. Now that was a joy that I will never forget.

"But enough about me. So, Dr. Richards, now that my wife has finally silenced that stomach of yours, what do you want with me?"

Staring briefly at his hands, Richards made a very deliberate decision and a potentially very dangerous one as well, but sitting where he was sitting, and with whom he was sitting, the academic felt secure enough to explain his situation.

"Well, Dr. Depuy, here's the situation and it's a tough one. I'm a historian, just like Professor Wentworth, but I am a historian with a side job, you could say. That side job requires me to learn how to be a bowman, specifically of the longbow and the shorter recurve bow as well. I need to learn how these bows work and how to use them. And unfortunately, just like Hollywood, I have to learn how to use them quickly. My bosses have given me three weeks to become adequate."

While Richards stated his requirements, Depuy's eyes had glazed over in deep thought and concentration.

"Well, Dr. Richards, that's quite a lot to take on in only three weeks' time," Depuy stated, while scratching the back of his head.

"Quite a lot," he repeated for emphasis. "Typically, a reasonable longbow man takes several years to master his bow, to be able to judge the flight and the range of his arrows. The recurve, well, it's pretty much the same, except that you typically fire it from horseback, one rather salient detail that you did not choose to mention.

"So basically, what we're really talking about is two fifteen-day periods of intensive instruction and practice. To become 'adequate,' your words, will be more a matter of your own focus and desire to meet your bosses' deadline than anything else.

"Now, Dr. Richards, just how serious is all of this?"

"Actually, very."

"I see. Well, my fee is based by the hour. That's two hundred dollars an hour. Are you still that serious?"

"Yes, sir. Can we start today?"

"Yes, we can, and yes, we have a guest bedroom upstairs that you can move into."

*   *   *

As it turned out, Claude's barn was a mixture of garage, gym, and a well-appointed woodworking shop – not that Norm Abram would be jealous of it, just that Norm would appreciate all of its quaint touches and frontier solutions.

Lesson one started out as a familiarization of the bows themselves, what they were made of, their strengths and weaknesses, their construction, the names of their parts, what strings were made of, how moisture affected them, what made a sound arrow, how the feather fletching was attached, and the kinds of points or arrowheads. It was a lot to absorb, but Richards put his enhanced memory to good use and retained everything that Depuy said, every bit of it.

"So, Dr. Depuy, the string is made of hemp, which in turn is dipped in a vegetable glue to protect it from the damp or to strengthen it?"

Both surprised and pleased that his apprentice had been paying attention, he said, "Actually, both. Always remember that moisture is the bane of any ancient or medieval archer. The string, if not protected, loses its tension, as do the arms of the bow.

"So, my friend, if you really want to take advantage of your opponent who is armed with a bow, then attack him during a driving rain storm."

*   *   *

During the course of the next twenty-nine days, Richards learned about a brand new set of muscles that he was not used to using, specifically, in the forearms, wrists, and the center two fingers of the left hand – his draw side. Next came the many forearm abrasions caused by a lazy or collapsed wrist, which was quickly followed by a newfound appreciation for the leather forearm guard. Above all, it was the repetitive discipline of the draw, the kissing of the string, and the skill of the shallow breath before releasing the arrow, which took the most thought and patience to achieve.

But Richards' concentration and sheer doggedness quickly earned the respect of his mentor, who found himself divulging lifelong, near-spiritual secrets about the bow, its draw, the string, and the arrow's flight.

"Always remember, Joey. You and the bow are one. The draw is the simple intake of breathe and the expansion of the chest. The string's release, your exhale. A good longbow man could fire eight to ten arrows a minute, just by breathing naturally, calmly, smoothly. These are very difficult things to do during the hectic course of a battle, but they mastered it nonetheless. They had no choice and far too much depended upon it."

Finally, the last day arrived. For Depuy, Richards had been his finest student. Immensely strong and blessed with physical stamina, he had practiced from practically dawn to dusk with patience and without complaint. For Richards, Depuy, while initially a cool character, had warmed nicely by the third day. But today was to be graduation day and with it came a formal test of his abilities.

"Okay, Joey, that hay bale over there with the target is two hundred paces away. Stuck in the ground before you are ten arrows. Here is your longbow, the one that you first learned on, so you should be pretty familiar with it. I am going to crank up Penny's egg timer to one minute.

"Now I want you to acquire the target in your mind and when you are ready, just begin."

What Richards didn't know was that Depuy had a pack of Black Cats at the ready as well.

Richards, in his left-handed stance facing the target, just stared over his right shoulder for a good fifteen seconds with his arms relaxed and at his sides.

Then he suddenly *moved.* Plucking the nock of his first arrow with his left hand, it was on its way almost instantly, and so effortlessly.

The speed at which Richards was releasing his arrows had so mesmerized Depuy that he had almost forgotten to light the firecrackers. Quickly finding their wick, they began firing off, creating quite a racket.

But Richards' concentration had been so deep, he had not heard a single one of them. All he saw was that before the egg timer had dinged, eight of the ten arrows were in the target, and two had creased the outline of the bull's-eye. Only then did his nostrils register the stink of the expended gunpowder.

Depuy, who could not believe his eyes, saw that Joey had fired all ten arrows in about forty-five seconds flat.

"Joey, my boy, that there was some fancy shooting. Your only misses were the first and second. But once you found your range, you were deadly. Absolutely deadly.

"Impressive, very impressive, but now for your next challenge. It's time for that short recurve, and this time, you'll be shooting on the move, just to make it a little more interesting. Whaddya say?"

Shooting a bow and arrow, while standing on the flatbed of a pickup truck, is nothing like riding a horse, the arrows' flight vectors are.

"Okay, Joey, here we go again, but this time, no firecrackers. Not that they seemed to bother you anyway.

"In the flatbed, I have erected a waist-high cage for you to stand in. That way you won't fall out. Just wrap one leg around an upright, and you should be fine. By the way, this is how I taught Yul Brynner to fire from his chariot. DeMille was so paranoid about Yul getting hurt even riding around in a chariot that they shot the scene with a moving background. But Yul was a real gamer! He wanted to know if he could do it, so I rigged up this flatbed so that he could practice for real. Much like yourself, Joey, Yul was a real athlete.

"Now, what I want you to do is shoot as many arrows as you can before I stop the truck. There's a bunch in the can there. Try to nail those five targets out there as many times as you can. Got that?"

With a smile as wide as the Mississippi, Richards just nodded and climbed aboard the truck.

"Here we go!"

The setup was an old and uneven wheat field with the bales set up in a V-formation. With a crunch of the gears and a lurch, the truck was off and Richards began his withering fire, learning on the run, as Depuy drove the truck on a diagonal this way and that across the field, ever advancing on the bales.

After his fourth pass, he stopped the truck and got out to inspect the carnage. The first bale, at the bottom of the V, had four arrows in its target. The rest had three each. Out of arrows, Depuy judged that not bad, a tad better than fifty percent, for someone who had never before ridden in the back of his truck.

*   *   *

While Richards was off learning how to ride and how to shoot a bow, Vesna Gregorieva, a disarmingly beautiful and graceful dancer, was busy learning how to best gut, maim, bash, and dismember an enemy opponent. Why, do you say? If she was to accompany Richards on this deployment, then such deadly skills were deemed useful and necessary.

The real issue was who was to teach this energetic and frenetic young woman about the dark arts of close medieval combat and dirty tricks? As you might guess, no one modern soldier could, but Tuna Cartwright knew of at least five or six candidates that might fill the bill. So, the ex-Special Forces officer arranged to meet with Gregorieva in one of the conference rooms of the second sublevel of the Philology Annex to discuss the matter.

"You realize that this next deployment is not back *somewhen* to Egypt, but rather into the wilds of medieval Gaul. From everything that I have read and have been briefed on, you will not enjoy the many freedoms that you did in Egypt."

"Yes, so I have been told," stated the woman with long silky black hair, which now she had allowed to grow down to her wasp-like waist.

"In fact, Ms. Gregorieva, because of that fact, we have arranged for you no fewer than five trainers, each a specialist in their particular field, all to prepare you for the medieval environment. That, of course, is in addition to your language implants. So, are you still interested?"

"Is Joey going?"

"Yes, he is. In fact, he is in training right this minute."

"Well then," she said with a sultry and mischievous smile, "I guess that I will have to go as well. Gods only know what trouble he will get himself into."

*   *   *

Cartwright was suffering from some real heartburn as he reviewed Gregorieva's personal training curriculum:

Session One: Anti-rape training.
        Instructor: Ms. Marlene Carter

Session Two: Knife fighting.
        Instructor: Mr. Jack Matthews

Session Three: Short swords.
        Instructor: Mr. Jim Crowfoot

Session Four: Garroting and nerve physiology.
        Instructor: Mr. John Black

Session Five: Offensive soft tissue penetration.
        Instructor: Ms. Sun Zung.

Cartwright's issues began with the fact that he readily acknowledged that he was overly protective of the field agent, who fell within the age ranges of his own daughters. He also recognized that he was a social dinosaur, who believed that women had no place on the battlefield. And yet, here he was, trying to prepare Gregorieva for the truly awful unknown. But in so doing, would she retain her personal integrity, or would she develop some kind of antisocial behavior akin to Post-Traumatic Stress Disorder? Yet, not to prepare the woman would be just as criminal. In so many ways, this is why Cartwright was so miffed that this duty had fallen to him.

*   *   *

It had been two months since Gregorieva began her strenuous personal development training regime. Looking down at the five evaluations that were submitted to Cartwright for his review and his alone, he

239

read through them with some trepidation as he sensed that a seminal transformation of Vesna Gregorieva had occurred.

While her instructors had uniformly praised the performance of their charge, all had specifically noted an uncommon and misplaced sense of joy that was expressed by their student. Furthermore, each instructor genuinely feared her by their session's end, all except for Sun Zung. Instead, her marginalia mentioned that the candidate's longish fingernails were perfect for soft tissue penetration and that Gregorieva's intense motivation seemed to be based upon some deeply ingrained need for revenge and retribution.

"Jesus H. Christ!" Cartwright whispered to himself. "I was afraid of this! I have to get a copy of this off to Doc Allen ASAP! Only he is qualified to officially wash her out."

CHAPTER XVII
Multiple Drops

Aref's supervisor at SAVAMA was quite surprised when his well-connected subordinate requested to lead the assassination team. Usually, men of Aref's pedigree and caliber worked from behind the scenes, instead of standing among the common faithful in the front lines. In many ways, the request was a godsend, as it promised the removal from his side a very troublesome political and management thorn. On the other hand, he recognized that Aref's presence on the mission greatly enhanced its potential for success. And that too, was good reason for optimism.

While the Iranian agent's supervisor was glowing with his happy fortune, Aref was pleased as well. For he knew that if he was successful, then only he would know, as the time stream going forward would be totally changed, where modern-day Iran might not even exist. The agent even allowed himself to contemplate what it would be like, once he was raised to the exalted position of an Islamic prince of a new timeline.

*   *   *

Aref did not know what to make of the transition from his current time to the medieval *somewhen*. One moment, he was ludicrously standing atop a wooden ladder in the backyard of the French property. Below him, he watched as a strangely smooth and gray surface had formed within the hovering drop ring between its four field generating pylons. Then he jumped through the ring and landed squarely into the chaff of a freshly harvested field. His visceral sensation was a dirty and clammy feeling that reached him to his very core, and so he did the natural thing, he shivered. Then remembering his training, he immediately rolled away from beneath the brightly glowing, two-dimensional disk and into the bright glare of the noontime sun. And it was good that he had, for no sooner than he had gotten clear than he was joined by the arrival of the first of his six fellow assassins. As each fell through the field, Aref pulled them out from under the glowing disk of the temporal portal.

Now with all seven having successfully dropped, seven heavy military backpacks began to sequentially plop down near their collective feet, which were next followed by a near rain of holstered side arms, ammunition belts, and AK-47s. Finally, as the stock of the long fifty-caliber Barrett XM500 began to show itself as coming through the field, its operator, not wishing the scoped weapon to fall on the sun-baked ground, instead instinctively reached out and caught it, unfortunately while the end of its long barrel was still in contact with the temporal field.

The reaction to this grave miscalculation on the part of the sniper was instantaneous. A loud gunshot-like crack of sound was painfully heard by the team as the temporal field grounded and catastrophically collapsed. Then came the overwhelming reek of ozone and the total annihilation of the sniper's body, as the combined wattage and amperage of the four generators, liberated by the grounding, poured through his frame. As for the rifle, its barrel had been severed and end transformed into a glowing, molten mass of metal.

Unknown to the rest of the drop team, there had been inexplicably a round loaded in the rifle's receiver, which had discharged and cleanly cut in two their colleague who had been dropping their gear from atop the wooden ladder. With the grounding, all four generators were ruined, as without their governors they had literally melted themselves down. In that process alone, the engine of the Mercedes-Benz became mechanically frozen, as in magnetized, on account of the runaway electromagnetic surge. The drop ring, no longer suspended by the failed temporal field, fell and shattered on the parking lot's pavement. The four pylons, which projected the electromagnetic field, sagged into grotesque Salvador Dalí-like forms due to the extreme heat.

The duration of the entire drop of men and supplies took just about four minutes, all to travel some 1,278 years back in time. But Aref raged as they were already one fewer and minus their most effective long-range threat.

"Damn the infidels!" was all that he could muster.

Fortunately, dropping as they did on October 2nd, no one had witnessed their rather noisy arrival, which would have appeared as seven men in green camo BDUs, followed by all of their gear, falling out of thin air. Also fortunate for the assassination team, a sizable woodland thicket was close at hand, and so they made for that cover. The only evidence of their arrival was six sets of departing boot prints and one gnarled, burned, and unidentifiable husk that once was a man, grotesquely fused to a very misshapen rifle.

*   *   *

Ever since the first reports of the detection of the Iranian-built temporal field, Richards and Gregorieva had redoubled their training efforts. No longer just a possibility, they had to be ready to drop on a moment's notice. Since all at the Philology Annex had been in agreement that a temporal deployment from a location as far away as Tehran was extremely low, it had been decided that the pair should take up residence in the quaint French town of Poitiers and await further orders. Only some thirteen and a half miles from where the battle was to take place on October 10th, all agreed that this course was the most prudent. In the meantime, Richards continued to allow his hair to become shaggy and let his beard grow out, while Gregorieva, swallowing hard, allowed her hair to be cut in a more medieval manner, a shoulder-length pageboy cut. Her transformation from sultry to impish was simply amazing.

Also deployed in the vicinity of that picturesque town were Callahan, a full detachment of his security troops, Horizon Pass' only portable temporal device, and a PVC drop and retrieval tower. While some might have snickered at the location as a "really tough" duty station, Cartwright figured that if and when the Iranians dropped into the neighborhood, he wanted his people in position and ready to go within one hour's time. Fortunately, he successfully found and negotiated a secure location for the American deployment and much hoped for retrieval, within the fourth century Baptistery of St. Jean. As of their arrival, the revered location had been closed to the public due to recently discovered structural issues, fueled by a generous donation from an American architectural philanthropic organization.

*   *   *

During the weeks-long wait for the Iranian deployment, Richards and Gregorieva made it their business during their daily runs to discover every interesting nook and cranny in the town of Poitiers. Initially, the motivation was to keep fit and to acquaint themselves with the town's layout. Then the daily runs became more of a scavenger hunt for the odd and curious. Always starting at the Romanesque Baptistery of St. Jean, the pair began looking for the oldest parts of town, which they believed would become landmarks for them once deployed in the past. Then, as the runs extended and became more like mini-marathons, specific locations to stop and rest became favored, above all, ancient wells and springheads. They reasoned, "You always need water."

Entwined between the runs, Richards and Gregorieva tried to remain sharp on their new skills as well. For the American, it was the longbow. For the Russian, she basically picked a fight with one of Callahan's men on nearly a daily basis. While the retrieval of errant arrows was not much fun, Richards' skill was steadily improving. As for Gregorieva, after seven days' worth of sparing, the security force flat out refused to mess with her anymore, so Richards began teaching her how to shoot the bow, more to keep her out of their hair than anything else.

Sheer boredom, both for the drop team and the security force was the main obstacle to their operational preparedness, and only so many cultural tours, books, games, and videos could fill the void. With such sharply honed personnel, waiting became a unique torture of its own.

Then during a pleasant lunch of salad, bread, and cheese, the drop team learned of the Iranian deployment. Without having to say a word, they both got up and changed into their threadbare medieval attire of coarse linen shirts, vest-like jackets, and leather belted woolen pants. To save them from any undue scratchiness, all of the woolen garments had been carefully lined with cotton material. For shoes, they donned heavy leather, moccasin-like foot coverings that laced to a degree. Once so attired, Richards and Gregorieva boldly walked the two blocks from their flat to the baptistery. He with his longbow and quiver of period authentic arrows. She with three craftily hidden knives. Both also carried over their shoulders a small burlap sack with one loaf of fresh bread and a tiny pouch of silver coins, most of which were Roman in origin. Only four people witnessed this brazen display of period attire, and only one of them even bothered to turn their head in curiosity. It was the baker.

Once within the natural coolness of the baptistery, they were greeted by Callahan and four of his men. The rest, armed to the teeth, were sprinkled around the environs, all in their signature adaptive camouflage that allowed them to disappear into shadows.

Erected in the central nave, the engineers had set up the Soap Bubble's pylons along with the incongruous PVC platform standing next to it. Upon entering, there was a tangible buzz in the air as the charging up of the drop ring was in progress.

"Well, folks," Calli began, "per usual procedures, we will power up the Bubble every midnight local time for thirty seconds. If you don't throw anything through to signal us for a retrieval, then we'll just shut down for the next day.

"Any questions?"

Getting none, the lieutenant turned away and began barking out orders for the drop sequence. With the ring hovering at its nominal height of five feet above the floor, confirmation was made with Corporal Brown as to the temporal coordinates and time for the drop: October 2rd, AD 732, at 1200 hours. Next, Corporal Small inserted a nonmetallic, low-light, fiber-optic lens and cable into the still metallic gray surface of the temporal field. After about forty seconds of perusal, Small reported back that the surface on the other side was also about a five foot drop and that the coast was clear.

Mounting the platform, Richards reminded his partner to bend her knees, drop, and roll. Smiling nervously back at him, she said, "Just don't pass out on me again." An inside reference to Richards' notorious problems with PDS, or post-drop syndrome.

In a serious tone, Callahan said, "Okay, Robin Hood and Maid Marian, Cartwright and the rest of the gang send their best. Dump all your metals. Then, get out of here."

First Richards and then Gregorieva dropped through the ring's field, their arms and their personal sacks. Then, just as wordlessly, they each stepped out and soundlessly disappeared.

*　　*　　*

Landing clean and rolling out of the way, Richards was somewhat surprised that his head had remained so clear on the drop. *I wonder why?* He thought. *It's been some time since the last deployment, would that explain it? Or would it be that this time is so much more recent?*

The next thing that he knew he was being rather rudely shaken. Why? And then he came to.

"Willahelm. Willahelm. Wake up, damn you!" hissed a concerned and protective Gregorieva into his ear. "Get your damn fat ass moving!" she continued in her newly acquired Latin tongue.

Grunting his way back into the here and now, Richards had to brace himself on his elbow against the cool stone flooring, as the world seemed to be spinning out of control. Then, just as fast as it came, the nausea left him.

"Damn salts," Willahelm commented in perfect Latin. "How long have I been out, Veer?"

"Almost two minutes. You had me worried – again!"

"Understood. Now let us depart."

*   *   *

Having left the tomb-like quiet and the faint smell of sacred incense behind them, the team ventured out of the relative protection of the baptistery into the bright sunlit, blue cloudless sky, and the vile open sewers that served as the streets of eighth-century Poitiers. Holding their hands over their noses and mouths, they barely staunched the bile back into their throats. Looking quickly around to orient themselves, they made their way down slope toward the town's southeastern gate. Their goal was to reach the bridge beyond that went across the River Clain that surrounded and protected the town to the east, while the River Boivre, a tributary of the Clain, completed the circuit around the town to the west.

To the utter amazement of Veer and Willahelm, the town gate stood wide open as the rural population, with their carts and animals, flooded in to get behind the protective shadow of the town's ancient walls. Meanwhile, the gate's two near-dozing guards sat on their stools, as they carefully monitored the situation. With the remains of their lunch still decorating the fronts of their tunics, the Americans passed by them and through the hustle and bustle, made the old Roman bridge, crossed it, and turned left on an equally ancient stone pavement. It was the Roman road that led north toward Tours, where they hoped to find the main Frankish army.

After having taken only fifty paces on the road, an old man, carrying all of his life's possessions in a sack over his shoulder, stopped them.

"My son, do you not know that Saracens frequent this road, as if it were their very own?"

"I do, sir. But we are making way to join the Frankish army. We were told that this is the way."

Shaking his head, the ancient one murmured, "Indeed it is, my son, but armed with only with that old bow, your quest is madness, utter madness."

With those words of encouragement, they continued on walking in a direction that no one else was taking, all the time receiving glances mixed with fear and total disbelief from the passersby.

After about an hour's trek, Veer and Willahelm found that, while they were making excellent time, they also were alone and out in the open. As the road gently

rose and fell as it followed the natural contours of the
land, their sight lines were not always the best, and the
distinct possibility of a surprise encounter became very
real. Yet, for the moment, that was not the case.
Nonetheless, their heavy garments were warm in the
sunshine and from their excursions, which meant that a
water source had to be found. Instead, the thirsty pair
encountered a short marble pillar that stood alongside
the road. It was a Roman milestone that dated from the
early 270s, which proclaimed:

> The   Emperor   Caesar   Lucius   Domitian
> Aurelianus, |
> fortunate, invincible, august, |
> high priest, greatest conqueror |
> of the Germans, Goths, Carpi, Parthians, |
> reinvested with the power ||
> of a tribune for the [?] time, consul [?] times, |
> father of his country, proconsul, restorer of
> universal peace, restored it: 3 [or 4] miles.|

"A rather long-winded declaration just to say that
he fixed this section of the highway," Veer quipped.

"Actually, the stonemason was probably paid by
the word," smiled back Willahelm. "But we still need to
find some water, and soon."

*   *   *

"Colonel," a member of Aref's team named Vahid
dared to ask, "now that we do not have a sniper, what is
our plan? How are we now to kill the Satanic Frankish
warrior named Charles?"

Well-hidden in the woodland thicket that they had retreated to, the question was a good one, as the team had lost its primary weapon.

Instead of berating the man, Aref answered reasonably, "Vahid, that is a very good question, but as soldiers of Allah, we must be creative in the face of such adversity. So, we must shift our focus, and first locate the main army of the faithful. And when we do, we offer ourselves as protectors and body guards for the governor of Al-Andalus, 'Abdul Rahman Al Ghafiqi himself.

"Why, you say? Because history tells us that it was his death that caused the premature withdrawal of his army from the battlefield. Because he, and he alone, held the Caliph's *fatwa* to command his vast army. So, we must protect him from all harm. Does that answer your question?"

"So, Colonel," Vahid again asked, "where is his army?"

Feeling his blood pressure precipitously rise, Aref hotly answered, "You stupid imbecile, he has not arrived yet!"

*　　*　　*

With the milestone a good hour behind them, Veer and Willahelm next came upon a small low-walled ruin. More a scatter of stone blocks and broken orange ceramic roof tiles, the structure had become overgrown with prickly holly bushes and an absolute riot of colorful wildflowers. But more importantly, they spied what probably allowed for such vegetative abundance, a stone trough bubbling over with clear water. After having filled themselves with its cool deliciousness until their stomachs were distended, Willahelm piped up, "This was once part of the Roman road system. It's a staging house for the change and watering of horses. That means that we are at least halfway to Tours."

With a furrowed brow, Veer said, "How can you be so sure?"

"Because that's the way the Romans did things."

As soon as he finished saying that, the pair distinctly heard the approaching sounds of horses. Lots of them. Glancing around, they quickly made for the *mansio*'s still standing low walls and forced themselves to literally burrow into and huddle beneath its holly bushes, which concealed them, and just in the nick of time.

Over the northern rise galloping along the road were forty heavily armored Islamic warriors. They were resplendent in their flowing red capes, domed helmets, and full chain mail from their necks to their knees. They were heavily armed with broad shields, spears, curved scimitars in ornate scabbards that hung from thick belts on their left hips, and short knives on their right.

From the look of them, they had been in a recent fight, as fresh gashes marked their shields and blood splatter was everywhere. Those who had been wounded sagged in their framed saddles, practically falling off despite their stirrups. Even in their dire physical need, the horses were watered first, and they did so greedily. Only then did their riders dismount with a grunt, drink their fill, and tend to their wounds. Veer and Willahelm lay motionless and silent, fearful, and just listening. Because of his early exposure to contemporary Egyptian Arabic, Willahelm managed after a time to pick up quite a bit, which he would then whisper into Veer's nearby ear.

"It seems that they are a raiding party, or a scouting party, who have just received a bloody nose by the Franks," he began. "The big one over there seems to be in charge. . . . There are four wounded. . . . They all want to get back to camp with their booty. . . . The big one doubts that two of the wounded can even make it back, so they are going to leave soon. One of the wounded keeps babbling the name of his wife at the camp, wherever that is."

After only about a half hour's respite, true to Willahelm's prediction, the forty rode off, heading south on the road that Veer and Willahelm had just walked. Clearly, that old man who had warned them knew what he was talking about.

Extricating themselves from their hiding place took a good ten minutes of colorful and linguistically mixed cursing and swearing. Even so, just as darkness began to fall, both looked like that they had been in a cat fight where the cat had won. With their scratches washed and guts again filled with water, they pressed on north toward Tours.

*　　*　　*

Sheer ferocity. Absolute, sheer ferocity. It was palpable.

That's what the Iranian team saw, when the heavily armored raiding party on horseback fell upon the Frankish infantry column. Initially, at least until the footmen had gathered themselves into a defensive square, thirteen of their number had been hacked down by the surprise attack.

As his men began to jump up and cheer on their distant cousins, Aref struck them with the butt stock of his weapon to silence them.

"Arash! Masoud! Farid!" he hissed. "You are not at a fucking soccer match! Be still!"

But during the intervening time that it took to deliver that poignant message, the Franks had turned the tables on the Muslim raiding band, who were accustomed to running down and trampling their prey. Now they were confronted with a united front, a square of determined men that bristled with spear points backed by an impregnable wall of shields. And the formation was on the move, feinting this way, retreating that way, and in the process had caught four careless riders out of position. All were gored with spear points, none lethal, but good enough to paint sheets of blood on their horses' flanks.

And then, as soon as it started, it was over. The raiding party headed south and the infantry column stripped their dead and carried off their wounded. Aref, seeing the tableau for what it was, a teachable moment, turned to his team and asked, "So, what did you just learn? You, Mohsen, what did you just witness with your own eyes?"

Surprised to be singled out, the young Iranian, with his large brown eyes and long eyelashes, blushed and just shook his head mostly out of fear than anything else.

"And you, Hossein, what did you see?"

"What I saw, Colonel, was an overwhelmingly successful surprise attack that was not disciplined. The horsemen did not press the attack and instead allowed the infidels to organize. Then the horsemen got sloppy.

Those four who got too close were more concerned about their over-weighted saddlebags than their own lives."

Smiling warmly back at Hossein, Aref said, "Well said, Hossein. You have sharp eyes. As for the rest of you, wake up! This is not the twenty-first century! This is the eighth! Where war booty is king and religion second.

"Yes, you heard me correctly. War in this day and age was how one made his daily wage in captured spoils earned in battle. Religion is only the trigger, the excuse to raid and pillage. Those Franks out there lost close to ten, maybe fifteen, of their fighting force and *still* they managed to organize themselves into an effective fighting unit.

"How did they do it? Because they are hardened, disciplined veteran soldiers, while those mounted raiders are just pretend soldiers. Their first and last consideration is personal greed.

"Men, this is why we must protect the person of 'Abdul Rahman Al Ghafiqi, because these Franks are seasoned warriors fighting for their own lands and families.

"I ask you, would any of you trust those raiders to cover your back? They're a collection of wild Berber tribesman, Moors, Libyans, Egyptians, and Arabs. This is why we must stay close to 'Abdul Rahman Al Ghafiqi, for he is the glue to this circus of an army.

"And as for Charles, he will succumb to the sword, as Allah himself has spoken it."

*   *   *

They reached Tours around midnight, and since the gates had been long closed and bolted, a nearly empty hay barn served as their hotel, where they ate some of their bread, huddled together for warmth, and not knowing whether this was their last evening, found great comfort in joining as only two desperate humans might: arm in arm, entangled, groaning in pleasure, and forgetting themselves in the moment. And finally, after much passion, they managed to grab some restful sleep.

CHAPTER XVIII
Preliminaries

To be clear, the decisive battle for the very existence of Christian Europe did not take place at Poitiers, or Tours. Rather it took place within the fork of two rivers to the southwest of Tours. There, a hilly and treed area, the Franks dug in with their collective backs against the water, and with a thin tree line before them. It was hoped that those trees would blunt the savage charge of the Muslim heavy cavalry.

Another mistaken idea is that the Battle of Tours took place on October 10th, AD 732, while in actual fact, as the main Islamic force slowly ground its way toward Tours, some six days of low-grade skirmishing, plundering, and raiding had been taking place in anticipation of taking the far greater prize, Tours itself.

Tours started out, as did so many towns in Europe, as a first-century fort, or in Latin, *castrum*, with the highly imaginative and therefore very Roman name of *Caesarodunum*, or Caesar's Hill. Its strategic importance was its bridgehead that spanned the Loire River. With such an available crossing point, trade naturally flourished, and the control of it waxed and waned with whoever was master of the bridge. By the fourth century, the *castrum*'s name, now a thriving trading depot, became *Turones* and was officially recognized by the Late Roman administration as *civitas Turonum*, and from hence it became Tours.

As Tours grew, it became more and more important, raised to the status of a metropolis of a province, and with such recognition, the town even had its own amphitheater. With the spread of Christianity to the region, St. Martin became its patron saint, and consequently the town was established on the great pilgrimage route through Europe. With the elevation of King Clovis, the first king of the Franks, his lavish largess and favor benefited the city greatly and also did wonders for the Abbey of St. Martin. In short, by AD 732, Tours was a very ripe and irresistible plum, which the raiders of Islam dearly wanted to pick.

As to why the Muslim forces were even in France in the first place, it is attributed to two main themes in the historical literature: religion and greed. A main tenet of Islam is the conversion of the infidel. The conversion process itself is a simple one, where one orally submits to Allah and acknowledges that Muhammad was his prophet. This fact explains in large part why the conquest of North Africa resembled a prairie fire before a stiff wind.

Christian Spain, however, was a far different story, as its conquest was a hard-earned one, but one that was very profitable in spoil and plunder for those involved. And so was the Muslim taste whetted, for beyond the Pyrenees mountain range lay even vaster resources, there for the taking. In fact, the main reason for the sluggish if not near-glacial progress of the main Muslim force, as it inched toward Tours, was because of its baggage train of loot taken from the sack of Bordeaux, now reduced to a burned-out shell.

Historical accounts of the battle differ, but perhaps the best source, whether Latin or Arabic, is the *Chronicle of 754*, written in Latin and composed in 754 by a chronicler in Muslim-held Spain. Here is the critical passage:

While Abd ar-Rahman was pursuing Odo, he decided to despoil Tours by destroying its palaces and burning its churches. There he confronted the consul of Austrasia by the name of Charles, a man who, having proved himself to be a warrior from his youth and an expert in things military, had been summoned by Odo. After each side had tormented the other with raids for almost seven days, they finally prepared their battle lines and fought fiercely. The northern peoples remained as immobile as a wall, holding together like a glacier in the cold regions. In the blink of an eye, they annihilated the Arabs with the sword. The people of Austrasia, greater in number of soldiers and formidably armed, killed the king, Abd ar-Rahman, when they found him, striking him on the chest. But suddenly, within sight of the countless tents of the Arabs, the Franks despicably sheathed their swords postponing the fight until the next day since night had fallen during the battle. Rising from their own camp at dawn, the Europeans saw the tents and canopies of the Arabs all arranged just as they had appeared the day before. Not knowing that they were empty and thinking that inside them there were Saracen forces ready for battle, they sent officers to reconnoiter and discovered that all the Ishmaelite troops had left. They had indeed fled silently by night in tight formation, returning to their own.

*   *   *

After waiting five days in the thicket of the wood, the Muslim main army arrived. Aref, ever anxious, decided that it was high time to introduce the governor to his new bodyguards. While it was a short walk to the edge of the Saracen encampment, they would still have to negotiate their way through hundreds of armed men and horses. So, loading up all of their gear, he gathered his five men around him in a protective ring and brazenly made themselves known.

Needless to say, the sudden appearance of these moderns on foot attracted some attention, but even more so when Aref shouted loudly out to them, "*Allahu akbar!*" which even with his Farsi accent was readily understandable.

"Who are you!" retorted several heavily armed men.

"That is not your concern. Take us to 'Abdul Rahman Al Ghafiqi the Magnificent! Immediately!" Aref said with his best command voice.

"No! Who are you!" said one particularly belligerent and self-important guard as he stalked forward several steps with his sword now drawn and at the ready.

To this, Aref answered with two quick shots from his 9mm handgun, which split the man's head nearly in half in spite of the helmet that he wore.

At the loud reports, the first of their kind ever heard in the eighth century, time seemed to stop as men and horses first froze at the foreign sound and then turned to face their origin in wonder and curiosity.

"Now that I have your attention, take us to 'Abdul Rahman Al Ghafiqi the Magnificent! Immediately! Or does some other fool wish to die?"

And a broad path through the morass of men and horse seemed to magically appear before the advancing Iranians.

*   *   *

Having spent the night in the hay barn huddled against one another to fend off the chill of the night, the American team awoke at dawn to the clattering sound of marching men banging their swords against the boss of their round shields. Rousing themselves, they beheld about one thousand of the most rough, tough, and battle-hardened human beings that they had ever seen. For Willahelm, it was like defensive lineman after defensive lineman, each big, easily six foot tall, and some even taller. Massive bodies swayed in cadence as they marched toward and through the now open gates of Tours, as its inhabitants cheered to them in greeting from atop the city's walls.

"Who are they?" queried Veer.

"By the looks of them, veterans. Germans to be sure. I see a lot of blue eyes and blond hair from beneath all of that dried blood, sweat, and filth."

Finally, after the last of the horde had passed, Veer and Willahelm fell in behind the last. And while they had so gained entrance to Tours, their next challenge was to make contact with Charles, the Mayor of the Palace. But logic suggested that following the soldiers would get them at least into the mayor's vicinity. And so, they did just that.

The interior of Tours was an odd mix of fine stone Romanesque architecture, massively built on truly a grand scale, and hovels built of mud and straw brickwork with sooty thatched roofs. Again, as in Poitiers, the unmistakably rank smell of an open sewer assaulted their nostrils, as these streets too were also precisely that. In fact, a narrow notch ran down the center to encourage the flow of the effluence.

In the center of the town, before the twin doors of a large stone edifice, the palace of archbishop of Tours, the soldiers gathered as one, standing and waiting in silence. But not for long, as a broad figure appeared, dressed as they were, in full battle armor, but lacking in only a shield. A shout rang out, accompanying the sound of one thousand swords being drawn as one, as those same swords were raised high in the air.

"Lord Mayor! We are here!"

As the echo of that call faded off the building's facade, the broad figure smiled, extended his arms wide as if to encompass the entire one thousand, and said, "My brothers. I see that you are well-bled by the look of you! Woe onto the Saracen devils!"

And again came that roar as one, "Lord Mayor! We are here!"

*　　*　　*

As Aref and his men proceeded through the vast Saracen camp, their goal became obvious, as the finest cluster of tents and largest number of deep green and powder blue battle flags flew directly before them. Finally, coming to a halt before a wall of heavily armored soldiers, Aref raised his hand in greeting and again in his best command voice, stated, "We seek audience with 'Abdul Rahman Al Ghafiqi the Magnificent. Stand aside, so we may pass."

Looking down on Aref, a swarthy soldier stepped forward and stood with his feet wide and his hands on his hips. Twin daggers crisscrossed his chest covered in armor made of fine Damascus steel. The worn, leather grip of a massive sword was visible within easy reach behind his right shoulder. His helmet, much dented, ended in a treacherous spike. Long of hair and beard, he first smiled a toothy smile and then demanded, "Just who are you, puny man?"

Aref, sensing that this was a crucial moment, smiled back and slightly bowed his head in the warrior's direction, but keeping his eyes locked on him.

"I am Aref the Brave."

Replying in a mocking manner, "Oh, so you say, puny man. Be gone before I split you in two!"

Aref, still smiling, just raised his 9mm and fired. Two quick shots removed the man's face. His head exploded and decorated the men nearby in a splatter of blood and gore. As the bold warrior slowly toppled to the ground, the shock of the gunshots and their effect stunned the immediate audience.

"Now. Again. I am Aref the Brave. I, and my fierce band of men, wish to speak with 'Abdul Rahman Al Ghafiqi the Magnificent. Take us to him. Now!"

And again, a passage was created through which he and his men were allowed to pass, this time into the tented mobile city, and this time, two of the outer guards led the way.

For the Iranians, what they were experiencing was like something out of a fairy tale. Silken walls dyed brilliant colors fluttered in the breezes and quaked at their passing. Veiled women with beautiful eyes watched their every move. Powerful soldiers beyond count watched them as well. Their feet tread no longer upon the packed and dried earth of October, but instead upon a vast carpeted expanse. Finally, their guides stopped, and one disappeared into the darkness of the next tented area. Several moments passed. Several of Aref's men began to nervously fidget, which earned a quick scowl from their commander to be still. When the guide reappeared through the tent folds, he held them open and indicated for the strangers to proceed.

Entering the tent, the Iranians momentarily stopped as their eyes adjusted to the low light. And there, on the far side of a carpeted sea, sat a lone man on a single cushion. With a neatly trimmed beard and his long hair drawn back in a knot, he wore a simple, black, ankle-length robe. His crossed feet were wrapped in the heavy leather boots of a rider. His face was gaunt and made leathery from the sun. But his blue eyes were everything, took in everything, and missed little as they approached.

"*As-salam alaykum!* (God's peace be upon you!) Abdul Rahman Al Ghafiqi! The Magnificent!" Aref intoned with a bowed head and open hands.

"*Wa-laikum as-Salam* (And God's peace be upon you)," came the emotionless reply.

"My Great Lord, we have come from faraway Persia to protect you from the heathen infidels. We bring powerful weapons to protect your person.

"I am Aref the Brave. I, and these five men, wish to sacrifice our very lives so that you may live to conquer the land of the Franks.

"We, Great Lord, are at your service."

Several moments of silence passed as the Saracen general rather pointedly looked over each of the Iranians.

"At my service, you say, but only after killing two of my warriors with your thunder weapons. How am I to trust that you do not turn your weapons upon my person?"

"Because, Great Lord," Aref responded, "we are here to make sure that you are victorious over the Frankish infidels. That is our purpose, nothing else. And with that victory, you will be forever known throughout history as 'the Magnificent.'"

*   *   *

As the Frankish troops began to noisily disperse after their acknowledgment of Charles, and he of them, Willahelm and Veer made for the double doors of the archbishop's palace. While they threaded their way through the milling crowd, they were noticed, but were forgotten, as calls for celebratory wine and mead were being made. Mounting the palace's stone steps, Willahelm brazenly pushed against one of the door leaves, which mercifully gave way to his pressure. Once inside the cool, low light ambiance of the building, the American sensed, more than saw, that he and Veer were surrounded within a large space. Stopping and standing stock-still, the Egyptologist firmly stated into the gloom, "I am Willahelm the True, and this is my faithful wife, Veer. We wish an audience with the Mayor of the Palace."

Only then did the team hear the shuffling of booted feet, and indeed, they were surrounded.

"And what might your business be with the mayor?" challenged a strong voice from directly behind the pair.

Holding his open hands up for their inspection, which Veer quickly copied, Willahelm answered, "I offer my bow and my knowledge of the ways of battle.

As for my wife, I offer her cunning ways with a blade and an even sharper tongue."

This last caused several chuckles and one rather lewd remark that told the pair precisely where all the guards stood.

"Careful, friend," Willahelm softly said. "My wife is not one to be trifled with. Trust me. I'm her husband."

More guffaws broke out, but the one guard behind them just couldn't resist the temptation and so made the colossal mistake of grabbing the Russian. It happened so quickly that it was over before it began. Veer threw the man over her right shoulder, put him on his back, and held him there immobilized with a single hand holding a painfully twisted wrist. The more the man squirmed, the farther Veer bent back his wrist, until he struggled no more.

"My good men, now you can see what I have to put up with every day. Veer, my sweet, let go of the man. He was only doing what his master has asked of him."

With a grunt, the fallen man got to his feet, rubbed the back of his head, and then attended to his wrist.

"Indeed!" boomed a voice filled with command. "Alberic was doing precisely what he was told. But he deserves his discomfort for not heeding a husband's own warning. Carefully bring them to my chamber, as I wish to speak to them."

*   *   *

Entering through a peaked key-stoned doorway, the American team stood before a pacing giant of a man. To say that Charles was big would be one thing. But to stand near him was another. Willahelm judged the man to be around two hundred and sixty pounds, all pure muscle and bone on a barrel-chested frame of six-two.

Veer saw the facial worry lines, the beginnings of gray at the temples, the intelligent brown eyes, and slab-like hands of pure callus.

Bowing at the neck, Willahelm stated, "Lord Mayor, I am Willahelm the True, and this is—"

"Yes, yes, I know, your 'faithful wife, Veer.' What do you want? Do you have a grievance? And if so, see your local bishop about it, as I have a war to wage."

"And what you want most of all is an appropriate place to do battle, perhaps a hilly spot, between two converging rivers to protect your flanks, and with trees before it to bedevil the Saracen cavalry. How am I doing so far, Lord Mayor?"

Willahelm knew for a fact that he was doing well, as the noble's raised eyebrows had betrayed him.

"So, Lord Mayor, what I and my wife want, is to join your army. I can offer you stratagems and my longbow. My wife is a superb scout and a silent and deadly raider.

"You, Lord Mayor, have a veteran and disciplined army that the Saracens have yet to encounter and will not expect. The Saracen leader's army is a haphazard mix of many tribes and nations. He struggles just to manage them, as their only true god is plunder. So they come for Tours. Lord Mayor, if during the battle, Veer and a select number of your men were to attack their camp, putting it in serious jeopardy, then who would truly command the battlefield?"

"For a man called 'the True,' I would wager that you are more wizard, as only I have considered such things and have never spoken them aloud.

"Now, Willahelm, do you have any more ideas as to how I should make battle?"

With a slight smile, Willahelm offered the following.

"Lord Mayor, I have only two other suggestions. One is an old ruse. It is called the field of pots. This stratagem causes the defender to dig holes, put pots or wicker baskets in them, and then cover them up with a light layer of soil. These holes should be dug between the trees where horses might find easy passage. As the Saracen cavalry gallop between the trees, their horses' hooves will find those holes, which will trip the horses, making them fall, and breaking their legs. After all, what good is a heavily armed Saracen without his horse?"

With a deeply furrowed and intent stare, Willahelm could see that Charles was considering this plan.

"As for my second suggestion, I wish to remain at your side throughout the battle."

"But you are so puny, Willahelm the True! What can you possibly do to protect me that my own handpicked friends and relatives cannot?"

Now smiling broadly, the American set the hook.

"Lord Mayor. Who in your army is an archer? Who in your army can kill a man from over two hundred paces?

"Lord Mayor, I and my bow represent an advantage that the Saracens do not know and have never tasted. If I hide in the center of your formation, I can wait until I see that their leader is within two hundred paces. Then I will kill him. And once killed, what will happen to his army of many tribes and nations? What will happen when this army learns that the enemy is plundering their camp, taking their gold, and ravaging their women?"

*   *   *

"Willahelm," Veer later asked, "what is this about the field of pots? I don't remember anything about that in the briefing back at the Philology Annex?"

Smiling, "That's because it wasn't in it. I just thought that I would help the Franks a bit and cause some low-tech chaos. But the idea is not mine. It's quite ancient actually. The Greek historian Herodotus recorded in his *Histories* that the Phocians had used the stratagem against the Thessalian cavalry. So why not use it here as well?"

*   *   *

"If you wish to serve me," 'Abdul Rahman imperiously stated, "then you must do two things.

"First, you, Aref the Brave, must choose which three of your men will protect this camp during the battle. The enemy is wily, and I will not have them looting that which is justly ours, taken with the spear. This is needful as my army is like a herd of cats who only wish to collect around bowls of warm milk. Therefore, three of your men must protect the camp with your thunder weapons.

"Second, you, Aref the Brave, and two others of your choosing, will protect my person with your thunder weapons, both from the infidels and any other who might threaten my person.

"Are my wishes made clear?"

Deeply bowing his head in acknowledgment, Aref

divided before the Saracen general his already meager forces, indicating that Vahid, Masoud, and Farid were selected to guard the camp and its vast booty, while he, Arash and Hossein, would join the personal bodyguard of the general during the actual battle.

"It is done, Great Lord, as you have so prudently specified."

Smiling broadly in satisfaction, 'Abdul Rahman continued, "Now, Aref the Brave, I require one last thing: a demonstration of your thunder weapons. While I have been told of their power, this thing I must see with my own eyes."

In answer to the Saracen general's reasonable request, Aref asked for eight of his strongest warriors and four of their stoutest shields to be brought to an open field near the camp. With a slightly worried look, Abdul Rahman scowled and, only after some thought, ordered this. Then, with his entire entourage, he walked to this open place and stood waiting with his arms folded across his chest as the preparations were being made.

Aref then arranged three of the heavy circular shields in a single-file row, one a foot behind the other with their edges resting upon the ground, supported by two warriors each, one to each side. The fourth shield was then similarly supported, but about two feet behind the other three. Aref then challenged all of them to grip their edges tightly as if their lives depended upon them.

Walking away from the first shield one hundred paces, Aref charged the receiver on his AK-47 and selected auto. Aref then suggested that the Saracen general put his hands over his ears. When he had done so, he turned toward the row of standing shields, aimed, and fired off the entire thirty-round magazine.

The effect was predictable. First, the absolute shock of the sustained rifle fire frightened all eight of the warriors. Two actually released their grip on their shield to cover their ears. Second, the first three shields were shredded into kindling wood, their center metal bosses left twisted and rent, while the fourth shield was perforated with thirteen gaping holes.

As the smoke cleared, shocked faces painted with fear and wonder faced the Iranian.

"So Great Lord, as I have promised you, I and my men will protect your person and your camp with our thunder weapons. And, at battle's end, you will indeed be called the Magnificent."

CHAPTER XIX
The Battle for Christendom

The early morning of the battle, Aref, Hossein and Arash, much to their surprise, learned that they would be provided with horses. After all, a member of the governor's personal guard stated, "How else will you keep up? On foot?" And then he fell into hysterical laughter.

What concerned Aref the most upon learning their mode of transportation was not his or his men's lack of experience on horseback, but how the horses would react to the unfamiliar sound of gunfire. He hoped that the sheer din of battle would help, but it was a variable that he had never before considered. Fortunately, the trio was fitted in very supportive saddle frames with stirrups that they could literally stand upon. This last, the stirrups, was a revolutionary Near Eastern innovation that Europe had yet to fully appreciate.

Discarding their field packs, the men transferred to their body webbing all of the AK-47 ammo and magazines, ten in all, and that did not include the personal weapon that each carried strapped to their thighs for easy access. Finally, all three had massive K-Bar knifes strapped over their left shoulders in their sheaths. These items were the only ones that their eighth-century compatriots truly understood, but even then, their distant brothers thought them to be too small.

Riding remarkably docile mounts, the Iranians quickly took up their posts near the Saracen governor of Al-Andalus, while their other team members prepared themselves within the camp.

For Aref, it was simply breathtaking. It was as if he were adrift in a sea of metallic men and horses, all who were facing in one direction – north. Distinct groups were easily spotted by their colorful war flags or the streaming pennants attached to their lances.

Men were going through their final preparations for battle, tightening this, loosening that, settling themselves deep into their saddles. Steam rose in the still morning air from the many snorting nostrils and freshly deposited dung heaps. And then Aref caught the heavy scents of leather, rust, and sweat mixed with fear. That he understood all too well.

Try as he might, he could not estimate how many men and horses 'Abdul Rahman had at his command, so he sat up in his saddle and quickly counted out a small nearby area, and then multiplied that by what he could see. Staggered, he came up with a cipher over twenty thousand.

"Aref, the Brave." A voice reached him. "How many do you see about my person?" 'Abdul Rahman quipped through the slight muffling of his full-faced helmet.

"Perhaps twenty thousand, Great One."

"Ha! Double your estimate, Aref! We are like an ocean. Nothing can stand before us!"

"Where are the infidels?" Aref countered.

"Ahead of us, to the north, just beyond that thin line of trees. They have trapped themselves between two rivers. Tours will be ours before sunset."

And then the governor signaled the nearby trumpeter, who promptly blew three blasts from his bronze instrument, which were echoed by many more up and down the line.

And then the ocean began to move and pick up speed.

*　　*　　*

Beyond the tree line to the north, Charles, the Mayor of the Palace of Austrasia, and some fifteen thousand grizzled veterans waited in a tight, rectangular formation with their heavy, rectangular shields grounded and their spears facing out like a prickly porcupine.

To Willahelm, standing near the mayor, it looked like the world's largest rugby scrum, except that each man carried nearly eighty pounds of armor and arms, including the heavy shield. Through it all, the former American football player nonetheless recognized the many signs of nervousness. There were the facial twitches, grim eyes, the banter between men, last-minute urinations, last-minute signs of the cross, and explosive flatulence. In short, the usual.

Then Charles broke his silence and conversationally asked, "Will, is this your first battle?"

"No, Lord Mayor. It's just the size that is new for me. My first was in the defense of our home – Bordeaux," Willahelm improvised.

"Well, my friend, I think that you will find this will complete your education. Although I can say that I have never been in such a dire situation as defending my own house. I cannot imagine such desperation. What was it like?"

"Beyond sanity. Your sword is never fast enough. Your quiver never has enough arrows. It is, my Lord, not for the fainthearted."

To this, Charles simply grunted in understanding.

Then they distinctly heard from behind the thin tree line three blasts of a trumpet, which was then answered at least twenty times. Unbidden, Willahelm looked down as he felt a subliminal vibration course through his feet.

"Will," the mayor quietly said. "Can you feel it? They are coming."

And then he bellowed loud enough for the entire troop to hear, "My brothers, the godless are coming! Now send them all to hell!"

And a mighty roar of deafening defiance erupted, while the men along the first line lifted and shouldered their shields and then dug into the earth the ends of their spears in anticipation of a god-awful impact.

*   *   *

By the time the forward elements of the Saracen horde had reached the tree line, they had reached full gallop with their lances at the ready and their war flags flying. It was like something out of Hollywood's *Wind and the Lion*, but real. Men gritting their teeth, leaning forward in their saddle racking, urging on their much-beloved mounts through the gaps in the tree line, up the subtly rising slope, racing headlong to either victory or paradise, come what may. They sounded like thunder. They shook the earth.

Then, within the tree line, something odd began to happen. Here and there, horses began to topple, fall, and scream as their legs were broken. Their riders, all thrown, fell awkwardly, some cart wheeling to an instant death. The stricken horses and their cries distracted others. Horses shied as they came upon those who had fallen. Collisions began to occur among the trees. Both horses and men were trampled by the continuous pressure of the Saracen surge. The many fallen had slowed and then clogged the Saracen advance. Those riders who successfully got through now had to charge uphill against the massed Frankish formation, which they did not expect. And the Franks were eagerly waiting for them.

*　*　*

A mere hundred paces beyond the border of the tree line, Charles had placed his porcupine-like formation. After their initial slowing to get through the trees, the Saracen cavalry now had neither time nor the real estate to recover, organize, and then muster a full charge against the Frankish formation. The field of pots had seriously degraded their momentum. Consequently, and not knowing how to attack such a mass of men, the riders just flung themselves and their mounts upon the phalanx, thinking that they would give way before their charge. They were wrong. The Frankish line held, and the truly grim business of close battle ensued. What the Saracen cavalry did not understand was for each mount that came into contact with the square, there were at the minimum four spears waiting for them. At impact, the front line subliminally and subtly dimpled, creating a momentary pocket where the Saracen horse and rider were briefly surrounded on three sides and hacked to pieces.

*　*　*

Prior to the battle, during the early dark hours of morning, Veer, and a select group of raiders all handpicked by Charles, had ventured out of a hidden postern gate in search of the Saracen camp. Avoiding all roads and byways, the group, with their faces covered with black ash and in dark clothing, wordlessly moved as one, in an almost snake-like formation, along a game trail near the river's bank. Moving in a southerly direction, within two hours' time they reached a point equidistant, and not far from, the still sleeping Saracen camp. There, they settled in to wait for the right moment in the high grass, forty-one raiders strong.

Veer, on her belly and peering at the camp at dawn's first light, could not believe her eyes, as the central cluster of tents alone seemed to cover more than two acres, while surrounding them were hundreds, no, thousands, of sleeping horse with their masters. Suddenly, the Russian wished for a Gatling gun, as her position would have made quick work of the immediate area. Instead, however, she had four period-piece knives, and she knew how to use them, as they had been her training tools.

A slight rustle in the grass announced that another had joined her. It was none other than Alberic, one of the personal guards of Charles and the one that Veer had so quickly bested at the palace.

"A truly intimidating sight to behold, my lady. All those tents, horses, and men."

Smiling, she answered, "My friend, think not on that, but instead on all the gold that we will find."

Truly liking her answer, he continued, "Do you really think that we will find some?"

"Without question. I can smell it. But before we think of riches, think on this. Somewhere among those tents are men who are dressed strangely. They bear strange and powerful weapons. If we encounter them, avoid them or you will surely die. Let the rest of the men know this."

"My lady, who then will kill them, if we all avoid them?"

"Trust in me, my strong friend. I will personally kill them all."

"Why such a dangerous and foolhardy plan?"

"Because this is personal. This is about *Wehrgeld* – 'man-money' – and I intend to collect it, all of it."

Momentarily breathless.

"My lady, are you always so . . . so fearsome?"

Now, for the first time in a long time, Veer smiled, bared her teeth for emphasis, and then creativity lied. Well, only half lied.

"My husband is Willahelm the True. I am called Veer the Bloody. I killed my mother in childbirth and was born in much blood. I fought beside my husband at Bordeaux, and we barely escaped with our lives. We both lost our entire families to the strange men in that camp. I claim them as mine. Now do you understand?"

"Indeed, my lady. I will pass the word."

*   *   *

It was not long after dawn's true break that the slumbering camp came alive.

"It's like the stirring of an ant hill," Alberic whispered in awe. "There are so many of them."

"Worry not. That camp will soon be far fewer once they mount their horses for battle. Then, my strong friend, fire will become our greatest ally," said the Russian as she took measure of the direction of the breezes across the field's long grasses.

And within the hour, her observations proved true in every respect, as hundreds upon hundreds of men moved off toward the north, organizing themselves under their colorful war banners.

After the passing of another hour, only a thin force seemed to mill about the tented area, and then Veer finally saw what she had been looking for. A shaggy-headed figure wearing green BDUs had appeared from one of the myriad tents to relieve himself.

"Alberic!" she hissed. "Spy that one? In the green? He is one of the strangers that I told you about. He and his kind are mine, all mine."

"Yes, my lady. I will pass the word of this as well."

*   *   *

Willahelm could not believe his eyes. Twice, fanatical Saracen horsemen had broken into the square in their attempt to reach Charles at its center, and twice they had been turned back. Frantic Frankish footmen poked, jabbed, and hacked away at any exposed horse flesh in the sure knowledge that a Saracen on foot was far easier to deal with than one astride a horse. The Saracen horses, mouths covered in foam, eyes huge with fear, and noses wide with snorting effort, impaled themselves one after another on Frankish spears.

One Frank, Theodoret by name, almost decapitated a horse with a mighty blow of his ax. As the hot blood flew, he was temporarily blinded, lost his footing, and was crushed by the fall of the very horse that he had just killed. Another Frank, named Sigamundus, attempted to block a Saracen's blow with his shield, which unfortunately split in two, leaving him defenseless. Instead of retreating, he grabbed the rider's leg, pulled him down from his horse, and pummeled him to death with his bare fists. As for Willahelm, he himself had slain two dismounted riders with his knife, cutting them both deeply in the neck, covering himself with their spurting blood. Twice, the field medics had thought him killed, and twice the American disappointed them and avoided their barbaric and ignorant ministrations, as their field dressings left much to be desired.

This once dry and dusty field of October had turned into a slippery, ankle-deep, brown morass of blood and entrails. Already, flies had become a nuisance and hordes of black crows filled the nearby trees in anticipation of a great feast. Locked into a virtual stalemate of bloodletting, Charles knew that a diversion would be much welcomed in order to turn the tide of battle.

*   *   *

"Alberic, see how far the tall grass grows?" Veer whispered.

"Yes, my lady. It looks to extend about thirty paces from here."

"Tell the men to slowly, quietly crawl to the point where it thins and then wait for my signal."

*   *   *

Charles was not blind to the fact that even this veteran force was taking quite a beating. Acts of heroism and valor surrounded him, yet men were men, made of flesh and bone. So he ordered that the formation move fifty paces back, and in the process they left behind the carnage of the first hour's battle. Quite literally, their short retreat left behind a square outline of fallen horses and men. No longer would the Saracens use their own as ramps to leap over his army's spears and shields. And, he thought, that planned distraction would be a helpful thing right about now.

*   *   *

Putting her two fingers to her lips, Veer let out a loud and clear whistle, and out of the tall grasses, as if by magic, forty Franks appeared and ran toward the nearest tents. All but one failed to reach their shade, as Alberic's own brother was impaled on a thrown Saracen spear.

Finding still smoldering heating coals and cooking fires, the firing of the tents began, which were accompanied by the screams of women and children and the sounds of grave hand-to-hand fighting.

While all of this raged around Veer, she began stalking the Iranians, and in the process surprised many a Saracen who had taken her form too lightly. Then she began hearing gunfire, undisciplined gunfire, which made her smile.

"Go ahead, waste your ammo. I'm still coming for you!" She snarled as she vectored in on the reports.

The first Iranian that she encountered had killed six of her raiding party. Veer distracted him with a knife throw. When he stupidly looked down at the hilt that was buried deep in his left thigh, Veer took him with a vicious slash across his throat that almost decapitated him. Now with her face and chest painted in blood, Veer stripped the fallen carcass of all its ammo, AK-47, and its two handguns, which she strapped to her thighs.

Looking down, she smiled. "Angelia Jolie, eat your heart out. It's time to hunt!" she said as she slapped in a fresh magazine and charged the receiver.

* * *

Over the tree line, Charles saw the first wisps of smoke and then heard the distinct sounds of thunder erupting in short, almost coughing, claps. Now smiling to himself, he shouted, "My brothers, we have taken their camp! Look toward the south. It burns."

As the men responded to his words, they began to cheer, their spirit renewed, and the force of their blows redoubled.

* * *

Veer at this point had taken the lead, as she hunted down the rest of the Iranians. Any Saracens unlucky enough to cross her path were efficiently shot twice to knock them down. Alberic and the others then finished whoever was still alive.

"All of them. Make sure that they are killed. We do not wish to be surprised from behind," she bellowed as they grimly went about their business.

Finally, Veer came across a tent that had three full backpacks, which were leaning together at its center. Bending down, she ransacked them all, looking for ammunition, which was not there. Emptying them of their personal effects, she tossed one to Alberic and the others to two to his men.

"Remember to fill these with any gold that you may find. That will be our offering to St. Martin for ensuring our victory."

*   *   *

As the smoke from the burning camp began to fill the sky, even 'Abdul Rahman could not ignore it, as he could tell that his composite army was faltering, their allegiances torn between fighting an unexpectedly tough and formidable force and the Frankish threat to their plundered fortunes. Seeing this, the governor called for yet another charge against the Frankish formation. And for the first time during the battle, with that impulsive act, 'Abdul Rahman had placed himself in harm's way, fully expecting his forces to follow.

*   *   *

Veer saw the second Iranian walking about as if in a trance, firing indiscriminately at anything that moved, even his fellow eighth-century compatriots. She made short work of him, stripped him of all of his ammunition and weapons, and moved on. They had yet to find any treasure, but the raiding party, now only twenty-one strong, naturally followed along behind Veer in an expanding V-shaped formation, with the Russian at its tip, slaughtering wantonly all who came in her path. It was extermination, pure and simple, and that fact was not lost on her comrades.

"Alberic!" said Grote. "She is most formidable with that thunderous weapon! It is like taking trout in a dammed stream."

The last Iranian, who had heard the approach of the disciplined shots, thought that one of his own team was fighting his way toward him. He was greatly mistaken, as Veer removed his face with two bullets.

Now with two rifles and the same number of

holsters slung over her left shoulder, Veer called to Alberic for assistance.

"My strong friend, I need your assistance. Carry these for me, as I cannot." And she piled twelve loaded magazines into his hands.

"What are these, my lady?"

"Flying death for the Saracens. Now, let's go."

To her great displeasure, Veer encountered no more Iranians, but she and her companions, had begun the slaughter of the first of the returning Saracen cavalry, which caused them to retreat back toward the Frankish formation beyond the tree line.

* * *

In comparison to the first two, the final Saracen charge was a feeble act. With about two hundred men and horses, the Frankish formation again readied itself for impact. Charles, noting that the Saracen leader was among them, called out to Willahelm to ready his bow, which he quickly did, but found that he could not see over the massed men before him to judge the shot.

"Lord Mayor! I am too puny! I cannot see over your men!"

Laughing, Charles called out to the front line, "Kneel and ground your shields! The puny one needs to see over you."

Sharing the dark humor of their mayor while the Saracen charge was underway, the line knelt as one, and suddenly all was clear for the archer. Quickly drawing his bow and kissing its string, Willahelm briefly paused to settle himself and loose the arrow. Without giving a second thought, the second arrow was away just before the first struck a horse full in the face, toppling it and its rider, to the cheers of the Frankish front line. The second arrow struck one of Aref's Iranians square in the chest, and because the man wore no body armor, only its feathers could be seen. The third struck another horse, which clearly faltered at the blow. The fourth hit the second Iranian guard in the face, and the cheers continued. The fifth embedded itself in the extended shield of 'Abdul Rahman and pierced his forearm, causing the shield to drop. The sixth found the Saracen governor's chest, causing him to sag like a rag doll, supported only by his saddle's racking. And at that, the roar of the Franks had become deafening.

Aref went totally berserk after seeing that both of his men and 'Abdul Rahman had been so mortally wounded. Flicking his rifle to full automatic, he goaded his horse into a charge at the Frankish formation and carved out a space for his horse to pass through the front line directly toward Charles.

As soon as Willahelm heard the rifle fire, he flung himself at the mayor, tackling him to the ground, as three of his surrounding body guards were felled by the twenty-first century technology. In so doing, Willahelm felt the searing sting of a bullet graze along his upper left thigh. Ignoring it, he rolled over to one knee. And while shielding the mayor's person with his own, the American loosed his seventh arrow squarely into the chest of the bloodthirsty Iranian, who fell from his horse into the middle of the square.

Going to him, Willahelm grabbed the dying man by his shoulders and looked deeply into his eyes.

Holy crap! He thought. *It's that damn fake imam!*

Now speaking to Aref in Arabic, Willahelm said,

"Look into my eyes, evil one. You know me. You interviewed me in Cairo."

The expiring, fluttering eyes widened with recognition and disbelief.

"Yes, it is I, an American. It was my e-mail you hacked. I am Joseph Richards. Remember this as you rot in hell's fires. Remember also that you failed."

And then Willahelm slit the man's throat.

* * *

With their leader dead, the charge quickly lost its energy, failed, and soon evaporated like an early morning mist over a still pond. Still, the reports of gunfire could be heard, and heard advancing. Realizing what this meant, Willahelm whirled to Charles, who had regained his feet.

"Lord Mayor! We must advance, as the raiding party is attempting to reach us!"

Accepting the Americans assessment of the situation, the formation rose and began to advance, catching and ruthlessly dispatching here and there the occasional Saracen. Along the way, Willahelm retrieved Aref's weapons and ammo and that of his fallen men, now clanking along looking more like a surplus weapons armory than an archer.

* * *

With the Saracen camp gutted and Alberic leading fifteen men and fourteen horses straining beneath their golden burdens, the hopelessly fragmented Saracen coalition beat a hasty retreat from the battlefield and even France itself.

Veer, quite a sight to behold, presented herself to her husband exhausted. The pair, dropping their weapons load, ran to each other. Holding her tightly in his arms and lifting her from the ground, Willahelm whispered in her ear, ignoring all the blood and gore in her hair, "I am most pleased, my wife, that you have survived."

"As am I for you," she whispered back.

*   *   *

On the short march back to Tours, long after the bone fires had finished smoldering, the fallen enemy plundered, their abandoned camp picked over, and the wounded carried away, Willahelm asked Charles if he knew of a blacksmith. Finding out that there were several, he asked which one the mayor preferred. Then Willahelm suggested to Charles that all of the Saracen saddles should be taken from the field as well.

"Why?" the mayor of the palace asked.

"Because," Willahelm hinted, "the next time the Saracens come, you, Lord Mayor, will want to field your own cavalry against them."

*   *   *

To say that the next three days of celebration and feasting were epic seems, well, an understatement. One tenth of the plunder from the Saracen camp filled the coffers of St. Martin's treasury in pious thanksgiving, and in repayment for the good saint's protection – albeit acknowledged after the fact. A portion of what was left went to Charles' veterans, as did several portions to the archbishops who initially had funded the standing army, in some cases under extreme pressure to do so. To say that the mayor of the palace had mended his fences would have been mild, proving, even during the Early Middle Ages, money does make the world go round.

But elsewhere in Tours, a blacksmith was hard at work. Seven gold pieces helped mightily with his motivation during such a celebratory time at this, as he stoked his fire to the highest temperature possible, all to melt six rifles and seven side arms into one, molten state. Fortunately, the blacksmith, a true craftsman, possessed many useful molds and into one in particular, he poured the molten river of fire. Several hours later, he had completed his sweaty labors, now seven gold pieces richer.

*   *   *

It was on the third day of celebration, Willahelm and Veer presented Charles with a battle trophy at a feast attended by his veterans. The trophy was a simple battle hammer, affixed to a stout oak handle wrapped in leather, complete with a leather thong for the wrist.

"Charles, Lord Mayor of the Palace of Austrasia!" Willahelm bellowed, while standing atop a table in order to get the full attention of the truly rowdy audience.

"I, Willahelm the Puny, and my wife, Veer the Bloody, present to you this battle trophy, this war hammer of Donar, forged from the captured thunder weapons. Henceforth, you, Charles, shall be known as Charles the Hammer!"

To this, a deafening explosion of boisterous cheers erupted, especially from his Germanic veterans, who fully appreciated the pagan reference and what it symbolized, the Romanized Hercules and Nordic Thor. And before they were finished toasting and boasting to their victorious mayor, both Willahelm and Veer had already begun their journey back to a certain baptistery in Poitiers.

*   *   *

While the retrieval of the American team went without a hitch, their appearance and smell was noted by Callahan's men, and one, the newbie Blackfeather, voiced what everyone else was thinking. "Those two look horrible and smell damn rank!"

But after a hot shower and a good delousing, just to be sure, the pair was judged fit to return to the States for their usual post-drop debrief.

The debrief back at Horizon Pass comprised a physical examination by Doc Allen and a detailed personal account of the deployment delivered to Naysmithe and Callahan. However, Doc Allen had in his possession a confidential e-mail from Cartwright, who wanted Gregorieva's psychological profile checked. In his very words, "Doc, check and see if her head is screwed on right."

Richards, excepting a mildly infected thigh from a bullet graze, various lice and insect bites, and a bunch of beautiful bruises, passed with flying colors. His post-drop syndrome, however, remained vexing and worrisome, as Gregorieva estimated in her report that this latest blackout lasted some two to three minutes.

As for Gregorieva, besides some bruising, she was physically fit and ready to go. In Richards' report, she had received only glowing praise for her ingenuity and combat leadership. But, as for her well-being, her demeanor, Doc Allen noted that she was noticeably calmer, more together, than he had ever seen her before. Gone was the chip on her shoulder, which was replaced with a calm that was markedly new for Vesna.

When asked why she was so relaxed, the physician Allen recorded that she just shrugged, sighed, and said, "My dear Doctor Allen, you know me so well. I am now at peace. I can live my life knowing that I struck back at the monsters of my childhood, who so brutally killed by parents during the First Chechen War. Doctor, you may not know this, but Iran greatly aided that Chechen uprising, much to my country's displeasure, and my personal pain. And so, with my actions during this last deployment, I had my revenge on those animals and on my own terms."

These words Doc Allen recorded and added to Gregorieva's medical file. His only comment was the following:

> It seems that whatever demons used to bedevil her soul have been banished. What has replaced them is a far surer sense of self. There's no question about it. This gal has been purged, and the dark side has lost. Thank God for her, and for that matter, the rest of us as well.

CHAPTER XX
Payback

"Typically, Dr. Young is the one who convenes such confabs as this, but he deferred that custom. "So," Cartwright primed his audience as he rubbed his hands together, "what do we know? Let's get it all on the table."

Sitting in the secure conference room of the second sublevel of the Philology Annex, only a handful of folks faced him, but they were a very motivated bunch.

Buddy McGuire's hand shot into the air.

"Yes, thank you, Mr. McGuire, for getting the ball rolling. What have you to contribute?"

Squirming with a bit of nervousness, the head of network security looked down at his yellow legal notepad and practically read from it.

"My first sniff that the Iranians were interested in us came to me by total accident. As part of Marla von Epping's interview process, the newest member of my team, I challenged her to break into the e-mail server of the Niroo Research Institute, an Iranian think tank in Tehran, and copy out their last six months' correspondence. Then I had her translate the data and search it for any references to high energy physics or electromagnetism. In those e-mail files, we were mentioned *a lot*. It really freaked me out at the time, so I told Dr. Naysmithe about it, and I still have Marla's take here on this thumb drive.

"Another item worth noting is that an Iranian hack copied six years' worth of Professor Richards' e-mails. It originated from the very same NRI think tank. While they were successful in doing that, and no doubt learned a shitload about us, the hack was a crude, quick, and dirty one, as it pointed back to this same Iranian think tank – the NRI.

"Lastly, and this refers directly to the hack on Horizon Pass, we have the e-mail address that the Iranian viruses used when they started their plunder of our database. This e-mail address does not match any those at the Niroo Research Institute. Therefore, it probably originated with the SAVAMA, or perhaps is even one connected with the Iranian Cyber Police and Communications Regulatory Authority. It is they who monitor Internet content and other online activities. But my money is on SAVAMA."

Cartwright nodded to the techie in gratitude for his contribution. Then he looked hopefully around the group for more input, and Callahan spoke up.

"I have bad news and good news. First, for the bad. For the past two months, we now know that the Iranians have been probing the neighborhood of Horizon Pass. No doubt, they were trying to get a fix on it. Several dirt bikes and one tracker later, we were able to crack their cell that led to the capture and deportation of that Roots creep.

"Now for my good news. Believe it or not, that wily Doc Allen pulled a fast one on that Iranian agent, Roots, who we had expelled from the country. While performing a blood draw on the perp, Doc Allen managed to insert a military ID chip in his arm. The guy didn't see it happening, as the wimp couldn't even bear to watch his own blood being drawn.

"So, with that chip in him, we should be able to track his movements from fifty thousand feet. And if he's really SAVAMA, then wherever he goes to work in Tehran is probably a SAVAMA location, if not SAVAMA central itself."

"Fine report, Calli," Cartwright said with some pride. Rubbing his hands again together, he added, "Now, anyone else?"

Richards raised his hand.

"Well, sir, as you already know, I was interviewed by perhaps the lead Iranian agent behind all of this. I was posing as an Egyptian Antiquities guard, and this guy with a Farsi accent wanted to know all about my odd and strange experiences while I was a guard at Karnak. Apparently, according to Dr. Sharil Moussa, this same man had already interviewed some thirty other individuals that we had come in contact with. He even abducted Sharil's father and interrogated the old man with sodium pentothal. Then, for some reason, he chose not kill him. This same dude, I killed at the battle, so he is permanently out of the picture. He and the remains of his team were burned. However, his ministry must pay."

"Anyone else want to get something off of their chest?" Cartwright prodded.

Gregorieva signaled Cartwright that she did.

"While I am the newest member of this gathering, I was nonetheless shocked by the series of hacks and what they led to. So I asked myself, what would my predecessor, Piankoff, do? What I believe is that he would call for the physical destruction of their research facility and the obliteration of their computers. That kind of action would appeal to him, something dramatic, something painful, and something everlasting. My Sasha would want this, as do I."

"Thank you, Ms. Gregorieva. I happen to agree with you and your channeling of your predecessor. We need to hit them and hit them hard. Anyone else have something to say?"

"I do," Naysmithe said, with his arms tightly folded across his chest. "I want to hurt SAVAMA. I am convinced the hacks were their doing. And I agree with Vesna. We have to turn the Niroo facility into a crater."

Cartwright then looked at the aging professor, Ernst Jung, a physicist by trade, gray-haired and slightly stooped in posture, complete with a tweed jacket and leather elbow patches. "Do you have anything, Professor?"

"Yes. Yes, I do, Commander. From what I have just heard, it seems we can damage this SAVAMA and the Niroo Institute in several ways, some that are within our direct ability to exercise, others, where we will need a helping hand.

"First, we can hurt both the Niroo Research Institute and SAVAMA through a cyber attack, the likes of which no one has ever seen before. Mr. McGuire, I believe that the von Epping girl will be the one to orchestrate this act of wanton destruction. I have read about her. I have heard about her. She is most formidable.

"Second, any damaging information that we harvest from the NRI and SAVAMA files, we publish on the Internet. It is well known that Iran controls all access to it. Iran also controls its media through the Islamic Republic of Iran Broadcasting, an organization that is responsible for censoring information and using state-media transmissions to trample dissent, filter out unwanted television content, and as a means to broadcast its own propaganda. Nonetheless, that control cannot be as airtight as their government believes. If played well, the youth of Iran could ignite a new revolution. Allow me to be clear, I am not speaking of the dissemination of misinformation, I refer only to the truth.

"Now kindly allow me to be crystal clear about something. Iranian Islam is of the Shi'a variety, and as a consequence, has engendered many militant strains. Iranian Islam is the ideological epicenter, the womb from which was born the Muslim suicide bomber. They thought it up, religiously justified it, and then exported it. Now, while all of this is troubling, Iranian Islam has one more feature to it that is most disturbing. It is something that no other Muslim country believes in. The Iranian leadership believes in an apocalyptic End of Days. To bring on this apocalypse, Israel, the little Satan, and the United States, the great Satan, have to be annihilated before the Islamic messiah, the Great Mahdi or Twelfth Imam, can rule again on the earth.

"In short, the Iranians do not play by our rules. The loss of ten million of their people in a nuclear exchange with Israel means nothing to their leadership, as those lost would be raised to martyrdom status. So, if we generate a psy-op against SAVAMA and the NRI, we must squarely attack their leadership's ideology.

"Third, I believe that money should be one of our cyber targets as well. Not on a national basis, but to ransack the coffers of the SAVAMA and NRI budgets. Then we place those funds in such a way as to make them look religiously and morally corrupt in the eyes of the Iranian population at large.

"Finally, there is the issue of their temporal device and their computer storage. And the only way that I can see us, this very small group, removing them from Iranian soil is to put the Gulf Stream V and its fair pilots in harm's way. I know for a fact that this airframe's rotary launcher can accommodate a small version of a cruise missile. Nonetheless, given the GV's naturally stealthy characteristics, I envision it flying to the brink of Iranian airspace before it unleashes its full fury. The military chip that the good doctor so thoughtfully implanted would provide the basis for some of the missiles' targeting. In short, I vote to give them a bitter taste in their mouth."

At the conclusion of Jung's dissertation and snap analysis based upon such underdeveloped data, all the former head of security could do was shake his head in admiration.

"Professor Jung, did you ever know John Milson?"

Smiling kindly at the mention of the late Egyptologist's name, Jung responded, "Indeed I did, Commander. Johnny Milson and I were very close friends. We both lost our wives in the same year to the same cancer. We first met in some nameless hospital waiting room. What I just said is what I would imagine Johnny would have proposed. A well-timed, well-calculated attack, designed to specifically injure and paralyze the enemy."

Sitting back, Cartwright announced to the group, "Well. It seems that we all have some homework to do. Let's meet here again in two days' time for some serious planning. We need to build a schedule. Now don't disappoint me. Dismissed."

*   *   *

Cartwright noted that their cadre had grown. McGuire had brought along a his entire tech team of Ron Marston, Stan Fielding, and even Marla von Epping – the former summer hire, now temporarily on loan as a consultant, as it was the middle of the fall semester. Lieutenant Callahan was accompanied by two of his sergeants. Young, Richards, Gregorieva, and Jung had all arrived separately. Observing them, they were a somber bunch with a lot on their minds. All possessed a burning desire to do something calculated, as soon as feasible. In short, they needed a game plan to execute.

"All right, everyone, here's the deal as I see it," Cartwright began.

"We need a phased approach to this operation and what I suggest is the following. Phase One is the cyber stuff. Phase Two, we cash out their bank accounts. Phase Three is the dissemination of whatever dirt we find. And Phase Four is an aerial assault on their facilities.

"As you can imagine, all of these phases are extremely interdependent. Therefore, we must establish priorities and their timing, so that the execution of these phases will be successful and cause the most damage possible.

"To make things easier, may I suggest that we divide up into fields of interest? McGuire's cyber team, Jung, Richards, and Gregorieva are psy-ops, Young will head the financial team, and I the aerial strike team.

"So, cyber team, what are your priorities?"

So it began, a room full of grim, creative vengeance.

* * *

Phase One began on an early Friday evening during the fourth call to prayer, the *azan*, just as sunset fell over Tehran. The e-mail servers at the Niroo Research Institute were penetrated and their contents copied. While that exercise was underway, a worm had been released into the general network that discovered a sloppy access point into the institute's main data storage areas. These storage areas were also copied. The hack of both network regions took several minutes. The copying process, however, took a very tense thirty-four minutes of download. When the download of the two regions was completed, they unleashed a 256-bit encryption process. It burned through the entire network like a wildfire, rendering it useless and highly infective to any computer or device that subsequently connected to it.

While the NRI network was so assaulted, defeated, copied, and fried, it had been discovered that the three inbound e-mail addresses, which had been logged during the raid on Horizon Pass, led to a single IP address. Under Marla's scrutiny, the IP trail led to a series of virtual private networks, each of which demanded authentication, each of which she rapidly defeated. Now in, she found herself inside an open network with seventeen separate databases. The download of fourteen of them went rather briskly, but the last three alone took a full fifty-four minutes. Again, as with the NRI network, once finished, Marla shut the entire network down with an encryption worm that was extremely infective.

In all, the cyber team's take from the two sources was close to two terabytes of data. When all was said and done, McGuire quipped the data cables almost sizzled during the downloads. While elated by their success and pleased with the downloads, the cyber team now had to pick through it, translating as they went. Long nights would have been in store for them, but for the surprise arrival of an expert in Farsi that Professor Jung just so happened to know. Now with the Farsi specialist scanning the directories, progress was greatly enhanced.

*   *   *

Phase Two began the next day, a Saturday, again during the early evening hours Tehran time, also during the *azan*. Dr. Young, an Oxford trained economist, was assisted by the now bloodshot-eyed cyber team, who had such success the previous evening. Young's brazen plan was twofold. First, they would attack the financial center of Iran through a back door, and then to deposit the purloined funds in the most unexpected of places.

The back door that Young intended to exploit was the Society for Worldwide Interbank Financial Telecommunication, or SWIFT, an electronic financial transactions network that almost all major banks and financial institutions used. SWIFT sends financial data and messages, making it akin to a globally accepted postal service for financial transactions. This network is supervised by the central banks of the ten leading industrial nations, as well as Belgium's central bank, and facilitates the flow of most electronic financial transactions. Key to Young's planned hack was that SWIFT had been disconnected from about thirty Iranian banks, including that country's central bank, after the European Union placed a ban on its shady dealings, soon followed by additional UN sanctions. So, while Iran's access to SWIFT had been severed by the Western financial world, the banking codes for the Central Bank of Iran, while secure, were not being monitored. Hence, the back door.

As for the Central Bank of Iran (CBI, also known as *Bank Markazi Jomhouri Islami Iran*), it was established in 1960 as the Iranian government's banker, with the responsibility for issuing currency. In 1972, legislation further defined the CBI's functions as a central bank, responsible for national monetary policy, foreign trade transactions, maintenance of the country's balance of trade, regulation of gold transactions, and foreign exchange. After the Islamic Revolution, it continued on in these capacities, but its monetary policies were modified to reflect Islamic sensibilities regarding interest-free regulations. Young's keen interest in CBI was that as the Iranian government's banker, it was mandated to keep government accounts, grant loans, and credits to state enterprises and agencies, while providing other banking functions and operations.

The cyber team had already done its homework on the structure of the SWIFT bank coding system, which was unique for each financial institution, and the authentication processes involved. In Marla's hands, getting past that process, while tricky, was *swiftly* accomplished. And once in, the fall of the bank's own internal security measures occurred three minutes later.

As most of the directories were in Farsi, the team again relied on the translation assistance of Professor Jung's "friend." As a result, four government accounts were identified that had SAVAMA's stain. Just as quickly they were plundered as the funds were transferred into ten separate Swiss bank accounts, which Young had previously set up for the purpose. Interestingly, one of the four accounts was in U.S. dollars, while the other three were reckoned in Iranian rials. Clearly, at least in Young's mind, the dollar-denominated account had all the earmarks of an "external extracurricular activities account," while the rial accounts were established for domestic expenditures. The rial, valued at only one, one-thousandth of a Swiss franc, made for a poor exchange, while the U.S. dollars did far better. When everything was said and done, the financial haul amounted to more than eighty-nine million Swiss francs.

"A quite tidy sum," the economist chuckled to himself. "That's more than ninety-five million U.S. dollars."

Next on Young's agenda, as he expansively cracked his knuckles, was the fun part – the distribution of all the ill-gotten gains in the form of anonymous grants and donations to appropriately embarrassing causes and organizations. But while he could load the many transfers "in the can" as it were, their distribution would have to be carefully timed events, designed to catch maximum media attention. So with great glee, the Dean of Humanities began allotting funds from this or that Swiss account to transfer notices, which to chronologically trigger in a very particular manner. After about an hour and a half of such magnanimous philanthropic diligence, Young exclaimed, "Damnation that felt good! And the best part, is that I have finally put to good use my Oxford studies in economics!"

*   *   *

Phase Three was timed to occur several weeks after the aforementioned database and financial mischief. It began with the publication of several well-placed press releases with *Al Jazeera*, the London *Times*, the *International Herald Tribune*, the *New York Times*, and the *Wall Street Journal* that outlined Young's well-placed surprise endowments. The printed editorials that resulted predictably ranged from "sheer blasphemy and a total betrayal of the Qur'anic teachings" to "adroit portfolio management in the steamier and seamier sectors."

Meanwhile, many local and international cable networks aired the news across the airwaves like so much dirty laundry, while their commentators damned or wryly smirked about these significant investments in corporate gambling, pornography, alcohol, and swine production.

Within the week, a very righteous Sunni imam of the Saudi Kingdom openly declared that the Iranian government had been laid low by their greedy pursuit to fill their coffers with such ill-gotten gain. That pronouncement alone opened the floodgates of indignant regional criticism in that part of the world.

Even one Western economic minister quipped at the situation, "Now that's one creative way to stimulate the funding of their secret service, while at the same time so skillfully avoiding UN sanctions."

In fact, the feeding frenzy was so blindly participated in that no one had bothered to check the source of this media windfall. And if they had, then they would have found that a minor Iranian commercial bank's IP address was the culprit.

Once all the financial news had hit the street, it was now the psy-op team's moment to subtly play it in the most visceral and raw way possible. To make the most impact, the right chord had to be plucked. The theme had to be shaped in purely Islamic terms, tailored specifically to an Iranian's Shi'a sensibilities.

The conjunction of shocking financial revelations, followed by the release of internal Iranian secret files, graphically portrayed the greed, hypocrisy, and obscenely venial nature of the SAVAMA. Yet more dire news was leaked in the form of internal memos, surveillance reports, and secret directives that revealed SAVAMA's own insecurity regarding its relationship with its masters.

One such document, clearly a blue-chip blackmail piece, recorded the questionable predilections of several members of the Iranian Supreme Council when they were traveling outside of Iran. Another told of SAVAMA's grisly practice of abuse, murder, and imprisonment of Iranian citizens, who, at the whim of the Iranian High Council, were deemed unsavory. What struck Tehran's population the most were that these kinds of activities were usually associated with the infamous SAVAK of the Shah and not that of the current revolutionary regime.

Then the team exposed a publically unknown Iranian organization's charter regarding the Internet and television broadcasting access. Hearing about this for the first time, albeit second-hand via outside sources, Tehran's highly educated inhabitants found out that their own government had put in place a near-secret organization called the Islamic Republic of Iran Broadcasting. Its stated mandate listed, among other things, the responsibility for censoring information on the Internet and using state-media transmissions to crush dissent, filter out unwanted television content, and broadcast only state-approved programming.

The gig was up, and the Iranian people now knew that their Islamic government was lying to them, deceiving them, plotting evil against them, and betraying their trust – all Qur'anic sins and offenses against Allah.

So had the psy-op team used the uncovered surfeit of materials from within the SAVAMA files. But, in the end, it would be the long legacy of domestic abuses that would call down upon the Iranian revolutionary regime. Not only the wrath of its people, but also that of several United Nations' agencies. The key to the psy-ops team's success was their canny timing and presentation of both the heinous and the disgusting, which fed the building storm of demographic frenzy. And no one could deny the authenticity of the published documents, for to do so was to dig their graves even deeper.

*   *   *

Phase Four, without any doubt, was the most difficult to conceive, much less execute. It involved a very special Gulf Stream V, a costly Horizon Pass asset, and its mortal flight crew.

For the second time, the airframe's distinctive ventral bulge would be put to use. Not for defensive purposes as it was initially conceived, but rather for quite the opposite – offensive measures. Who knew?

Although sculpted nicely into the plane's overall lines, this bulge had three parallel seams that betrayed the presence of doors to a depressurized bay. This cavity could accommodate a variety of items that ranged from a photo reconnaissance and ground-mapping radar suite to a rotary missile launcher. In this particular application, the latter was installed.

This phase placed in harm's way human assets as well, highly trained ones, that just could not disappear off the grid for a couple of days and expect their absence to be unnoticed. Further, special arrangements had to be made for remote fueling locations, landing and takeoff clearances in foreign locales, specialized munitions, fuel purchases, and bribes paid. It was a tall order.

The magnitude of the logistics alone were numbing, as in backside numbing. Holloman AFB via Chicago and Gander, Newfoundland, to Lajes in the Azores was some 4,400 miles. The next segment, from Lajes to Larnaca, Cyprus, was another 3,300 miles. From Larnaca to a turning point south of Baku, Azerbaijan, was almost another thousand. And from there across the Caspian Sea to a launch point just southeast of coastal city of Ramsar, Iran, another three hundred. In all, the GV's crew had to fly some 8,400 plus miles *one way*.

Given that the Gulf Stream V had an advertised commercial range of some 7,400 miles, not counting its two auxiliary wing tanks, the mileage did not seem so insurmountable from a purely mechanical point of view, especially given the two scheduled refueling stops. Human endurance, however, was another issue, and so Cartwright figured into his plan two flight crews instead of one. In so doing, he consciously put at risk twice the manpower.

However, the procurement of the desired payload, four U.S. Navy AGM-84K "SLAM-ER" cruise missiles, was another story altogether. The Standoff Land Attack Missile is described as "a long range, air-launched, precision sea and land cruise missile." Manufactured by Boeing, they are not cheap. With its Teledyne turbojet engine, the missile cruised at high subsonic speeds for more than one hundred and fifty-five miles. A little more than fourteen feet in length, the SLAM-ER just fit the rotary launcher in GV's belly. Weighing in at around 1,500 pounds each, four can be accommodated, but a fuel penalty. Hence Cartwright's planned need for several inbound refueling stops.

A "fire-and-forget" weapon, the SLAM-ER packs quite a punch with its penetrating eight-hundred-pound, blast-fragmentation warhead. Given that the weapons' release point was only ninety miles away from their targets, any remaining fuel aboard the missile would additionally create a fireball effect upon impact. Two such missiles were tasked for each target and their combined effect was calculated to be epic.

Before any of this could be contemplated, Cartwright received access to a global positioning satellite to track the subcutaneous military-grade chip that Doc Allen had implanted in the arm of Jahan Manu Rabiei, the expelled Iranian. At a minimum, two weeks' worth of observation was needed to establish the man's movements, and ultimately, his place of employment, SAVAMA. That requirement did not take long.

The plan called for a missile launch while the GV was still in international waters off the northern coast of Iran, while flying at low-level. The droning cruise missiles, unerringly guided by their preprogrammed GPS waypoints, were to first climb and then cross the crest of the Elburz Mountains between the villages of Elit and Alit located to the southeast of the15,000 plus foot peak of Alam-Kuh. From there, they were to descend directly toward Tehran's city center, porpoise to one thousand feet, and then be steered by their onboard sensors to their designated targets.

*   *   *

During yet another early evening post-*azan* meeting, two religious colleagues met, initially to discuss Fardoust's abject mission failure. Again beginning with the standard formulaic pleasantries, the men discussed the immediate and dire subjects of catastrophic network failures, financial break-ins, and now the damning international press. Under such pressure, the hot topic of Aref Fardoust had been long forgotten. What these two imams did not realize was that their nation was under a seriously prosecuted attack. The aggressor organization that launched it acted far beyond their nation's foreign policy constraints, much less established international law.

Then the two men heard something that was quite arresting. It was the split-second, high-pitched whistle and whine of a rocket motor descending down their building's ventilation shaft. At thirteen and a half inches in diameter, a SLAM-ER was doing just that, for that was what they were designed to specifically do.

The many demonstrators who had been voicing their outrage outside the seven-story concrete structure stopped to view the arrival of the first cruise missile. It took on an almost majestic pose, as it gracefully traced its fiery ascending parabola in the dark sky. Then, as it descended, they all turned and ran for their lives, for at some innately primitive level they recognized danger.

It was well they had, as the initial warhead detonation within such a confined space created a concussion wave that sundered all of the structure's glass. That was immediately followed by the ignition of the missile's unspent fuel. Consequently, the lowest stories belched fireballs of flame and debris in four directions. Then the second SLAM-ER hit, this time penetrating the concrete roof and obliterating the upper section of the now teetering structure, held together by its rebar alone. Almost four miles away, the same ruthless havoc rained down upon the main building of the Niroo Research Institute.

*   *   *

(Tehran, Iran) *Al Jazeera* – Yesterday evening an unprecedented attack upon the sovereignty of the Islamic Republic of Iran occurred, when four missiles struck the Iranian capital city. Heavily damaged was the main administration building of the Niroo Research Institute and, in a similar attack, an unidentified governmental structure, said numerous eyewitnesses.

While those who launched the missiles remain unknown, a source from within the Iranian Air Force said that the missile launches originated from somewhere within international airspace above the Caspian Sea.

Iran, a country that has recently been racked by extremely provocative public revelations regarding the activities of its government officials and the domestic policies of its security ministry, has been left in a spiritual, emotional, and political turmoil.

Widespread demonstrations have been reported throughout Tehran over the past week as well as a harsh governmental response. The magnitude of the upheaval was perhaps best expressed by an unidentified imam, who was quoted among the demonstrators. "The total and complete destruction of these accursed buildings proves that a righteous God willed this act, forever ridding the people of Iran of their inhabitants' shameful pestilence."

*   *   *

The return flight of the very special Gulf Stream V took place without incident. In fact, at no time did any nation realize that its airspace had been over flown throughout the entire exercise. At the refueling stops, both on the inbound and return legs, no questions were ever asked or papers requested, as Cartwright had greased their way so well. However, upon landing at Holloman Air Force Base, its crew of four was "greeted" by four military police Hummers, who escorted the exhausted men and the flight recorder to the base commander's office for a thorough debriefing.

* * *

Throughout the entire execution of Phase Four, the core team of Cartwright, Callahan, Jung, Gregorieva, Richards, and Young had remained glued to the four massive flat screens that McGuire and his team had set up in the second sublevel's conference room. Due to national and internal security, however, none of the cyber team was allowed to witness this phase, especially von Epping, as they had been linked to the GV's telemetry in real time via several USAF satellites.

Initially, the tracking of the aircraft on its inbound leg had been displayed on only one of the flat screens, while the other three remained idle. Watching the slowly moving cursor as it moved across the Atlantic seemed to drag on endlessly as they sat, stood, and stared glassy-eyed from cots that had been thoughtfully set up for the duration. But once the plane got past its refueling point in the Azores and delicately weaved its way through the Mediterranean's airspace, Cartwright's succinct dialogue explained what the pilots were doing and why, and what they were evading and why. It all hit his audience like triple shots of espresso coffee.

"The idea, folks, is to split the Straits of Gibraltar, fly within a neutral area over the Med, and avoid any islands with sophisticated radars. That way we don't piss off anybody who might blunder into looking our way, which is very doubtful, given the airframe's tiny radar signature, and its chameleon-like, camouflaging skin. Even so, the trickiest part early on is slipping by Cyprus and the airfield at Nicosia, as it has powerful military radars."

The GV went "feet dry" at the head of the Armenian Gulf just north of the city of Dörtyol on the southeastern coastline of Turkey. Now the second and third flat screens went live as they depicted the planned flight path over a topographical overlay that took the aircraft stealthily through Turkish airspace just north of Lake Van, south of Sevan Lake of Armenia, and into the wilds of Azerbaijan.

"Notice, folks," Cartwright continued, "that the flight plan calls for routes that avoid airports and heavily populated areas."

When the waypoint southwest of Baku was finally reached, a nearly audible intake of collective breath was heard as the GV banked southeast near the heights overlooking Qobustan and south of the airport at Sangachal. Once "feet wet" again, this time over the Caspian Sea, the flight crew began its preparations for the bombing run.

At a point twenty-three nautical miles from the Iranian coastline, the doors of the plane's fuselage opened, and the four cruise missiles were sequentially deployed from the rotary launcher into the aircraft's slipstream. Once clear, each missile's engine ignited and their scissor-like wings deployed. At the same time, the fourth flat screen came to life with four black-and-white in-screen images that were quite literally from the cameras of the missiles themselves, as they streaked across the waves inbound toward their distant targets.

While all of this was happening on the fourth screen, the GV had already bugged out and headed back to the relative safety of the Baku waypoint. Now lighter by some six thousand pounds of dead weight, the copilot dumped the empty external fuel tanks into the black waters below.

So lightened, sleeker, and now with a far more commercial look to the GV, the airframe just got up and went. But frankly, no one really watched the second and third screens anymore as the aircraft made good its escape.

All were now transfixed as they watched in the low-light conditions the constellation of lights that represented the Iranian shoreline settlements as they blurred by, followed by those of inland burgs and villages. It wasn't long before the terrain-following missiles left the green vegetation of the coast behind as they crossed inland toward the rocky crags of the higher elevations. Then, just as quickly, the missiles crested and began their dip down the rocky backside of the mountain chain.

What was helpful to the viewers was the launch-to-target clock that was counting down in the lower right corner of each of the four mini-screens. At three minutes remaining, of the approximately sixteen-minute flight, the illuminated streaks of settlements began to pick up noticeably as the northernmost suburbs of Tehran were being rapidly over flown.

At twenty-one seconds, the pop-up, or porpoise climb to one thousand feet was initiated by the missiles' onboard computers.

At seven seconds, a mixture of onboard radar and thermal images clearly depicted the two targets from directly above. Almost comically, missile two of the upper right screen seemed fixated on a massive cooling vent on the roof of its target. And then it flew directly into it. Unconsciously, all took in a deep breath at the shock of the maneuver.

As the four in-screen images went sequentially blank, all eyes blinked in surprise and only then in recognition of what had silently occurred. Only then did everyone's eyes finally notice on screens two and three that the GV was already halfway across Turkish airspace on its return leg, and by the way the cursor was moving across the screen, the pilots were pushing their engines hard.

Once the flight had gone again "feet wet" at the Armenian Gulf, Cartwright stated for the record, "Ladies and gentlemen. You have just witnessed history in the making. I don't know about you, but I could really use a cold beer right about now."

Then he got up from his chair, stretched, audibly cracking several vertebrae, and then rolled the tension out of his neck.

"Calli," he said, "do me a favor and watch those screens carefully. If anything bad happens, you can find me in the head puking my guts out."

"Yes, sir. I've got your back."

Jung just sat there, staring wearily at screens two and three, chin in hand, wishing the returning aircraft to go faster and get home quicker.

Young, with a dark set of rings around his eyes, looked exhausted, but triumphant.

Gregorieva, during the tension of the missile assault, had latched onto Richards' bicep and had not let go. Finally peeling her fingers off, clear red blotches appeared where they had been.

"Time to crash, Vesna," Richards quietly said as he took her hand and stood up to leave.

CHAPTER XXI
The Second Teleconference

As had happened before, Dr. Young requested of his Russian counterparts a convenient time for "a frank chat." With a time and date agreed upon, the secure teleconference was scheduled with the U.S. Air Force, as it was that organization, after all, who owned the satellites and the translation software that made it all possible.

As that date and time arrived, Dr. Young opened the proceedings.

"Good evening, gentlemen," the Dean of Humanities said as he quickly glanced at his wristwatch to confirm that fact. "As always, we here in Chicago thank you for your flexibility."

Okay, thought Rosovec. *Get on with it, you overly polite Brit!*

"I am sure that you are monitoring the current internal turmoil that is breaking out in the capital of your Islamic neighbor to the south. I am of course referring to the Islamic Republic of Iran. The reason for this teleconference is to inform you that it was us who orchestrated the many document leaks and press releases. And yes, even the missile strikes."

At this news, wide-eyed and with their mouths agape, Popev and Rosovec almost stood out of their chairs, while their usually uninformed and oblivious colleague Sokolovska just sat there with an extremely intense look on his face.

Young then continued.

"Needless to say, I share this information with you with the clear understanding that it will remain within our circle. Do we have that understanding?"

Three Russian heads nodded in assent.

"Now you are probably wondering why we undertook this action. For that, I ask Dr. Naysmithe here to fill you in."

"Good evening," Naysmithe said. "Our attack on the Tehran Niroo Research Institute, and the Iranian SAVAMA building in particular, was precipitated by their successful hack of files associated with Soap Bubble."

My, my, thought Rosovec, *our southern neighbors do have some brass after all.*

"It began with the interrogation of some thirty Egyptian Antiquities personnel who told a SAVAMA agent of our joint participation in some odd events, first at Karnak and later at Sakkara. Even an Egyptian high official was abducted and subsequently questioned under the influence of sodium pentothal.

"Then we experienced several cyber assaults, both here in Chicago and in New Mexico. Both were perpetrated by the Iranians.

"What finally pushed us into doing what we did was an Iranian temporal deployment, which we had to subsequently deal with."

Now all three Russians looked to one another rather meaningfully.

"Also, as a result of the Iranian hack, they located and successfully raided Horizon Pass itself. We lost almost one half of our personnel in New Mexico. Make no mistake, this was totally an Iranian operation, and we have the bodies to prove it. Therefore, we have decided to totally dismantle and shut down the Soap Bubble project. What that means to you is that there will be no more databases to hack, as they no longer exist. What that also means is that our two temporal devices have been dismantled, and their components destroyed, so there is nothing left to steal. And, my dear colleagues, most importantly, we both are out of the temporal exploration business.

"I sincerely apologize for my rather curt demeanor, but under the circumstances, I am sure that each and every one of you can appreciate my position and current state of mind."

With Naysmithe's concluding remark, Young then added, "Again, thank you for joining us. Have a good day."

And then with relish, he signaled the videographer to abruptly cut the transmission with a slicing finger across his throat.

Damn I enjoyed doing that!

* * *

Now mutely staring at the snowy white haze of their teleconferencing screen, Rosovec was the first to recover and signaled his technician to also stop the feed.

"Well, that was rather abrupt, but it also explains a lot."

Pause.

"It would appear gentlemen that we will have to adjust our future departmental budgets accordingly."

* * *

"Well," said Naysmithe as he looked over at Young still glowing with his schoolboy's grin and Cartwright with his best Louisiana gambler's smile.

"Do you think that they bought it?"

"Hook, line, and sinker," said Cartwright while he slowly crossed his arms across his chest in confident triumph.

"Their faces were so transparent with shock at the news about the Iranian temporal device, their deployment, the supposed raid on Horizon Pass, our response, and then that we had the balls to unilaterally shut the whole damn thing down. Well, for what it's worth, I believe the last part is well worth a replay.

"But on a far more serious note, we owe the United States Air Force big time for their satellites and all the operational paperwork that they either conveniently overlooked or outright sanctioned with the running of Phase Four. And, quite frankly, I do not know how or when those jokers are going to ask us to pay up."

At that moment, for some reason, Young interrupted the group's train of thought.

"Gentlemen," he said, nodding to his two colleagues, "I do believe that now is the time for a rather well-timed telephone call. Sorry to rush off, but I see a delicious opportunity." And with that the Dean of Humanities bolted for the door.

"I wonder what that was all about," Naysmithe said.

"Haven't the foggiest, but Young is not one to quibble with," the retired soldier said. "At times, he is an absolute witch doctor on wheels."

*   *   *

Once back in his palatial office, Rosovec felt small, tiny, and emasculated as he sat behind the vast surface of his desk beneath its matching baroque ceiling.

I have been feeling this way for far too long, the director of Advanced and Theoretical Technological Research for the Russian Academy of Sciences thought. *Perhaps I should retire to the private sector and make my millions there while I still have my contacts in place. I must think on this. No, better, I think that Popev and I should have a quiet talk about this in private, perhaps dinner somewhere. I'll call him.*

*   *   *

Meanwhile, Sokolovska, the head of the Institute of Theoretical Biology, was also on the phone.

"Yes, Dr. Young, I greatly appreciate your kind offer, and yes, I will most happily join your very prestigious faculty.

"By the way, I really think that your group did a very fine job recently."

"Yes, it was most extraordinary."

"You will? That would indeed be most generous! I can assure you that my wife has never flown in a corporate jet. She will be most impressed, and perhaps that will help her to make the correct decision as well."

"Yes, thank you again, and good afternoon to you too."

Sitting behind his massive office desk, Young smiled a very satisfied smile.

Damn, I enjoyed doing that!

*   *   *

After Young had deserted them, Naysmithe and Cartwright left the secured conference room and sought out Marla von Epping, who was chatting with Ms. Kelly on the first floor.

"Marla," said Naysmithe, "may we have a word?"

Looking up and feeling like a cornered squirrel, the college senior nodded once and stood up in helpless resignation, while Ms. Kelly looked on, nose a-twitch, wondering what was up.

Finding the neighboring book stack devoted to Phoenician philology empty, the trio sat down at an old and much-worn reading table, all the while Marla chose to closely examine her nails.

"Marla," Naysmithe gently began, "please look at us. We're not going to bite. Both Tuna and I know that you have been through a lot, put in some really long hours, and shouldered a ton of stress. We want you to know that we're very proud of you and how you handled yourself."

"Marla, dear," Cartwright continued. "I am the father of three ladies who are not much older than you. While I love 'em all to pieces, none of them can hold a candle to you. You are one tough, scary bright cookie."

"So," Naysmithe concluded, "I would really appreciate it if you would consider us in your future plans beyond graduation. Frankly, we really need you. I know for a fact that Buddy, Stan, and Ron all have your back. And for your information, all of them have privately cornered me on this subject."

Now with huge eyes, Marla said, "You mean that you want me back? Like for real? Like permanent?"

"Indeed, Marla, like yesterday," said Naysmithe with a catch in his throat.

CHAPTER XXII
Actions and Their Consequences

Anapa was a sleepy Russian resort town located along the sandy beached eastern coastline of the Black Sea. Located as it was, just a short drive north of Tsemess Bay and its bustling city of Novorossiysk, Anapa's sixty thousand or so inhabitants truly have few needs or wants. Perfumed with many varieties of subtropical flowers and shaded with palm trees, it was hard to believe that this was Russian soil. But it was. Apparently, the ancients thought that the area was special as well, as a series of lush third and second century BC Greek villas have been recently discovered in the area.

Outside of Anapa proper, the coastline is studded with a hodgepodge of small beachfront properties, some constructed as far back as the 1940s, while others dated to more recent decades. Paradoxically, it was the earlier beach houses that were the most coveted on the real estate market, with their exquisite quaintness and superior build quality, entirely made of wood. Just seeing an example instantly catapulted one to a storybook land of intricate gingerbread houses inhabited by Hansel and Gretel, or the remote and gabled redoubts that one might find in the Tyrolean Alps. Then add in the many riotous two-story floral waterfalls all canopied by palm fronds and the resulting image was quite extraordinary. How this curious juxtaposition of southern European carpentry and beachfront property came about was not a secret. The beach houses were exclusively built by Austrian and

German master carpenters, prisoners all from the Second World War. The beneficiaries of their industry were the Soviet Party's bureaucratic bigwigs, who did not buy or sell these properties but rather bequeathed them for a considerable amount of money to their bureaucratic successors. Hence the origin of their exclusivity and near total absence from the real estate market.

Two men resided in such architectural elegance and subtropical splendor. They had, after all, given over their entire lives to the care and protection of mother Russia – the *Rodina*. They had sacrificed much in ways that today's Russian bureaucratic would never even contemplate, much less understand. Regardless of that unfortunate fact, these two men met at least once every week to discuss world events over tall iced teas or pleasant fruit drinks. To drink anything stronger from their youth would have put their delicately medicated metabolisms into conniption fits.

Both men were now old and were enjoying their much-deserved retirements. They had done much, seen more, and probably had forgotten more secrets than anyone else of their vigorous generation. In their distant youth, Vasily had been of middle height and blond hair with the bluest of eyes that betrayed his connection with the Urals. Karlov, however, was a polar opposite, being of a swarthier complexion with dark curly hair and stocky build. Both had fought and survived the Fascist War. Both had been heavily decorated.

They now sat on Vasily's porch facing the beach and the sea. A very pleasant morning offshore breeze cooled the pair as they sat in the shade.

"You know, Vasily," Karlov began, "it has been some time since we last heard from our respective counterparts to the East. Hell, it's been nearly a year now. Perhaps you have heard something of consequence?"

Vasily, who had been sipping a delicate blend of fresh orange and lemon juice, finished and smacked his lips in total satisfaction before he answered.

"Well, Karli, I cannot say that I have, which makes me wonder. The last news had been about two failed attempts at acquiring the American temporal device. After that, nothing. Absolutely nothing."

"Yes, I know," Karlov darkly confided. "And those failed attempts came at some cost, as I remember. Five men and a Libyan airframe asset in the first. An entire *Spetsnaz* squad vanished in the second, with only pools of blood and shell casings as evidence of their passing. As the former Head of the Special Projects Directorate, I can tell you that such incompetence would not have been tolerated," a now agitated Karlov emphasized with a tight fist that pounded the wooden table.

With a wan smile, Vasily, the former Director of the Institute of Theoretical Biology, responded mildly.

"Now, Karli. Relax, my friend. Be mindful of your heart. And besides, what's done is done. I think that we both know that our successors, while technically savvy, do not have a clue about wet work. Certainly not as well as you do, and certainly not as well as I have come to understand it.

"So, and consider this, my dear colleague," the Russian biologist said with a wage of his finger, "a time will come when one or both of us will receive a call. And when that happens, we must have a plan for them.

So, let's us begin to theorize the way we used to, back when we young, impertinent, and still thought of ourselves as immortal."

*   *   *

In the center of his Moscow office sat a man behind a massive antique desk that matched in every proportion and detail the foil of the gilded, ornate, and baroque, pre-revolution two-story ceiling overhead. Instead of being a separate piece of furniture, it seemed more a thing that had been organically grown in place or something that had once been part of the ceiling, but had fallen.

Disheartened. Dejected. Shocked. And perhaps several other well-chosen words could only begin to describe the sudden downward course that his career had taken. Stefan Rosovec, the Director of Advanced and Theoretical Technological Research for the Russian Academy of Sciences, actually, for the first time in his life, felt trapped, and he really didn't like that strange and creepy feeling. Ever since he had not so gently "nudged" out his former colleagues on the basis of their complete technological backwardness, Rosovec's accomplishments had been few and far between. In fact, of the three operational failures that had taken place under his watch, any one of them would have been reason enough for his summary execution during the previous Soviet regime. Furthermore, Rosovec was honest enough with himself to admit that all of these operational failures were the direct result of his own overblown ego, impatience, and total lack of operational experience in such clandestine adventures – items all that his processors had excelled in. And it was all because the Americans were the ones who controlled the temporal device known as the Soap Bubble. First came the Icelandic misadventure along with an aircraft and its pilot. Then came the loss of a full squad of *Spetsnaz* without a trace. Next came the defection of Vesna Gregorieva to the West. That was a game changer in so many ways. Just how often do you have the chance to mold an orphan's anger and desire for vengeance into such a deadly and subtle weapon? As if that were not enough, the Americans made the unilateral decision to dismantle the Soap Bubble Project, courtesy of the Iranians. And now this, the defection of Sokolovska to the States.

Frankly, I can't blame the lucky bastard.

*　　*　　*

"Karli, did you hear about what happened in Tehran?"

"*Da*, someone with really big brass balls finally erased from the planet some Iranian scum, and along the way, served up several of their leadership on a platter as well. I could kiss them!"

"But, Karli, it was not Israel or the U.S. that did it."

"Who then was it, Vasily?"

"Horizon Pass."

A pause of wide-eyed surprise.

"Who told you?"

"My successor did, who by the way, is now living in the United States."

"Damn, they really do have big ones," murmured Karli.

Chapter XXIII
Vault No. 17

It wasn't a surprise visit on the part of the American Egyptologist to the director of the Cairo National Museum. In actual fact, it wasn't a social visit either. Instead, it was all business.

"So, Sharil, I find that you have been holding out on me, and I want to know why."

Genuinely perplexed by Richards' challenge and accusatory tone, "Joey, whatever do you mean that I have been holding out on you?"

"What I mean is what happened to a certain spherical object, reference Sakkara ZF9321. What is it? And where is it?"

Sharil frowned her best fake frown. "Joey, I am sorry, but I don't know what you're referring to."

Smiling a gambler's smile, who just saw through a phony tell, Richards continued. "I understand. You are the director of this vast museum. God only knows how many artifacts are under your care and protection. But Ulli Schachermayr and I are good colleagues. His father and John Milson were also quite close. So needless to say, I carefully went through Ulli's field report on the Imhotep Galleries, and the description of one item was glaringly missing. Ulli too knows this to be the case. He was even specifically waved off the subject by your very own Dr. Ahmed Rashid, this museum's head of conservation.

"So, Sharil, do you remember Sakkara ZF9321?"

With a firm and steely demeanor, the cornered Egyptian admitted it, but only after several moments of careful consideration.

"Yes, Joey, I do know what that object represents and where it is located."

A relieved sigh from the American Egyptologist.

"Well that is very good news, very good indeed."

"Why?" queried the director.

"Do you remember the deployment that took place in the open desert just west of the Step Pyramid?"

"How could I forget it! From what I recall, wasn't there a skirmish with some Russian Special Forces?"

"Sharil, your memory is as sharp as ever. That deployment went back to Predynastic times. Gregorieva and I actually managed to interview Ptah, the man, in the flesh. He turned out to be an Old One, one of those ancient entities that the author of the Annex Papyrus referred to, the papyrus that you and John studied and translated."

"This I did not know. An Old One, you say?"

"Yes, Sharil. Now flash forward to about four months ago. This same entity, this same Old One, paid me a visit at my office."

Total disbelief broke out on Sharil's face, then acceptance as she realized who this information was coming from.

"And?" she dared.

"And we discussed his current mission to Earth, his purpose for visiting us, not once, but three times: first, during the Predynastic Period as Ptah; second, during the early Third Dynasty as, ready yourself, as the architect Imhotep; and finally, four months ago, as an Italian named Alfonso Ricardo Russo."

"Joey," she whispered, "you must be kidding. Both Ptah and Imhotep . . . were the same entity?"

"No, Sharil, sadly, I am not, and yes, he was. Here is a photo of him." Richards extended the Vatican Library pass across the director's desk.

"What?! A pass to Vatican Library! How?"

"That's a long story for another time. Now for the real reason as to why I am here. This Ptah-Imhotep-Alfonso fellow, take your pick, has helped along the development of this planet's civilizations in various ways. But during his most recent visit, the lesson that he was trying to teach us, was to share, specifically to share with the rest of humanity a certain embargoed artifact."

"You're serious, aren't you?"

"Drop dead serious. Sharil, your museum is sitting on something that was given to humanity, something that was meant to be shared on a global basis. What that something is, what specifically is to be shared, I frankly don't know. But I suspect by your reaction, you don't know either. So, come on Sharil, old friend, share what you have."

*   *   *

It is generally believed that every major museum in the world, on average, has on display only about eight percent of its permanent collection. That means that the remaining ninety-two or so percent is in storage, on loan, or in restoration. Given that the British Museum reckons that it holds some eight million works in its permanent collection, this would suggest that *only* about six hundred and eighty thousand objects are on display. Furthermore, it is rumored that the underground storage beneath the British Museum is so cavernous that no one person really knows what is where with any reliability. Images from Indiana Jones movies, *National Treasure*, and the television series *Warehouse 13* come readily to mind.

Then there is the Cairo National Museum and its collection, which is spread out all over hither, thither, and yon in sealed magazines. But there exists, nonetheless, a storage area within that early twentieth century pink edifice where very special (i.e., embargoed) artifacts are to be found. Located beneath the building's main basement, this storage area is so secret that it doesn't even have a name, nor does it appear in any architectural drawings. It just is.

* * *

Opening her top left desk drawer, the museum's director reached in and teased out into the palm of her hand a brass key from its hiding spot. Looking down at it evoked several memories. Some exciting, some less so, but all filled with equal parts of awe and trepidation.

Curtly, the Egyptian said to Richards, "Kindly follow me. And please do not remember how we got to where we're going."

"Understood," the American Egyptologist replied.

Leaving her office, the pair walked down the long corridor that was the administrative wing. They then made a right turn toward the general collection on the First Floor. But before reaching the many exhibits that millions have viewed with intense interest, Sharil stopped at a modest wood door on the left, inserted her key, and beckoned Richards to quickly pass through. Entering, the Egyptologist quickly realized that he was standing in a deep and rectangular elevator cab that reminded him of ones in a modern hospital. Closing and locking the door behind her, Sharil pressed the bottom of two black buttons and the cab began its herky-jerky descent. After what seemed to Richards several minutes, but was only about forty-five seconds, the elevator came to a stop. Once again, Sharil unlocked the door, which allowed them to exit the lift.

The atmosphere was extremely dry and stuffy, to the point that the American was sure that the moisture in his nose was being robbed as he breathed. Sharil, reaching into the darkness with her right hand, found the light switch, and turned its archaic porcelain knob, which illuminated a simple row of caged lights that spanned an unadorned, but broad, corridor that stretched out before them. Richards stood shocked with a sense of *déjà vu. It's just like the Amen Re treasury, only smaller.*

At this point Sharil turned to Richards and flatly stated, "What you are about to see has never been seen by any American. Not even Breasted or Milson. A few French and Germans, yes, but you are the first American."

Turning abruptly on her heel, she led Richards down the long corridor past locked doorway after locked doorway, each spaced about thirty-five paces apart.

"What's in all of these, these rooms?" Richards asked.

"Lots of stuff," Moussa replied. "Most of it is erotica that my country's cultural sensibilities are uncomfortable with, mostly papyri and artifacts. They are all invaluable for understanding and appreciating the ancient Egyptian culture, but we as a nation are not ready for them quite yet."

Stopping about mid-way, Sharil turned to the right and began turning the knob on an old combination lock that secured this particular steel door. The number painted upon it said No. 17.

"How many rooms are down here?" Richards tried to casually ask in a conversational tone.

"Far too many, about twenty-five in all, I think."

Opening the door with a creak coming from its hinges, Sharil again groped for a light switch, found it, and illuminated the rectangular magazine. Along the walls stood low wooden tables, and down its center a racking of sorts. Looking up, the Egyptian noted that one of the light bulbs needed changing. This caused her to mutter and remember to bring a fresh one the next time that she was down.

"This way, Joey," she said as she took him down the left-side aisle. "Here against the wall is the original Annex Papyrus, conserved in its own frame and mounted against an acid-free backing. This is a truly magnificent document."

Now indicating with the little finger of her right hand, Sharil continued, "Note here, Joey, how carefully written this papyrus was. Believe it or not, there is not one erasure or errant drop of ink anywhere on it. Remarkable, simply remarkable."

Moving away, she stopped before a set of ceramic jugs with perforated lids on them. Out of one of the holes a thin bronze bar peeked out.

"Joey, have you ever heard of the Bagdad battery?"

Shaking his head in the affirmative, Sharil quipped, "Well, here's our version. It was found in a noble's tomb that dated from the mid-Eleventh Dynasty. Dr. Rashid tested it with a vinegar solution, and it produced a steady eleven volts at one amp. Again, simply remarkable. Probably was used for the electroplating of fine jewelry."

Now nearing the corner, the director stopped at a long cedarwood coffin.

"Joey, I'm afraid that you might recognize this. These are the remains of the high priest Meryptah. Your good friend and adopted father."

For the first time Richards removed his hands from his sport jacket's pockets and gently, no, reverently, laid them upon the coffin, while his fingertips unconsciously read the hieroglyphic inscription. His eyes suddenly, unbidden, filled with tears.

Sharil, noting this emotional moment, remained silent and still. After several moments passed, Richards broke out of his trance-like concentration, sniffed, and wiped his eyes with the cuff of his jacket.

"Thank you," was all that he cared to say.

Now reaching the center of the short length of table opposite the doorway, there stood on a low wooden tray what looked to be a heavy round object. Resting on a bed of natural cotton batting, the artifact was covered with a blue cloth. Pulling from a nearby box a pair of latex gloves, Sharil put them on and then rather dramatically removed the blue cloth.

"Joey, I present to you Sakkara ZF9321."

Bending over to carefully examine the spherical object, Richards took a moment and then whispered under his breath, "Oh, my dear God!"

*   *   *

The pair, returning to the public part of the museum, then sought out the office of the institution's chief conservator.

"Dr. Rashid, kindly tell Professor Richards about your experimental results with the embargoed Sakkara artifact."

Nervous, Rashid first looked deeply into Sharil's eyes before he began, just to make sure that she really wanted him to inform this American on the truly odd qualities of the object. Receiving a nod to continue, he then began.

"Well, once one can get beyond the fact that 9321 is an exact replica of the planet Earth, both in its extraordinary geographical depictions and quantitatively in its dimensions, its other 'qualities' seem almost miraculous.

"What I mean is that 9321 possesses a hidden mystery unto itself. What seems obvious is clearly not."

At that particular turn of phrase, Richards politely put up his hand to stop the chemist and glanced meaningfully at the museum director as he clearly remembered a similarly vexing phrase that was found in the Imhotep galleries.

"Precisely, Dr. Rashid, what do you mean that 9321 is more than what is obvious?"

"That the object is a replica of our planet, and yet, I fear, it is something else.

"Dr. Richards," Rashid continued now with a thin layer of perspiration on his upper lip, "that object vaporizes water on contact. In a rather reckless test, I totally submerged it into a partially filled fifty-five gallon drum of distilled water, while suspending it from plastic netting. Even though 9321 is hollow, it sank easily into the water, and in mere moments, the entire contents of the drum had come to boil!

"Furthermore, when I lifted 9321 out of the drum, it instantly dried itself, and its surface was cool to the touch."

Richards, fascinated, stroked his chin, and said, "Did 9321 change in any way as a result of its immersion?"

"No."

"Did it weigh the same?"

"Yes, absolutely to the gram."

"Huh. Well, I am certainly not a physicist, but it seems to me that heating water that quickly requires a lot of energy. Is 9321 radioactive?"

"Absolutely not."

"So, what you are telling me is that an artifact that is, what, some five thousand plus years old, can boil water for tea faster than a microwave oven."

"Well . . . well, yes, I am."

Now looking over to Sharil, Richards softly said, "Madam Director, your face is well known, your reputation well established after the Treasury of Amen Re's discovery.

"What this object represents is a revolutionary source of clean energy. Just off the top of my head, can you imagine 9321 suspended within a controlled, self-contained, high pressure steam environment? It could run God knows how many steam turbines for free and without any exhaust products. So, I would make the following suggestion. Have Dr. Rashid demonstrate 9321's boiling of water before an international panel of high energy physicists. Let them poke at the artifact. Let them worry about how it works. But to sit on this potential technology and not share it with the rest of the world community, I think would be a dire mistake.

"It could be Egypt's gift to the world, something to be shared openly. Imagine, for a moment, Sharil, the possibilities! And . . . and then imagine this. You reveal 9321 to the world. Where? There's only one place in Egypt, Alexandria, the home of Hero and his ancient steam device, the *aeolipile*. Book a reservation at the Biblioteca Alexandrina complex right now.

"Sharil, for the love of God, you have to do this!"

Ancient Egyptian Chronology

During the third century BC, King Ptolemy I of Egypt commanded Manetho, high priest of the sun god of Heliopolis, to write a history of Egypt. Unfortunately, that work now only exists in the form of tantalizing fragments, which merely list kings, how long they ruled, and their dynastic divisions. Fortunately for Egyptologists, they have at their disposal several papyri and temple inscriptions, which help to fill in the blanks.

But truth be told, the principal chronological benchmarks, the Royal Turin Canon, the King List at Abydos, and the Sakkara King List are just that – lists, which do not provide us with an absolute chronology. Further, some lists, while completely preserved, are suspect in their content, while others have been handed down to us only in a fragmentary state. Meanwhile, none of these lists alert us to the possibilities of kingly interregnums or co-regencies.

Occasionally, however, hints do appear in the historical record, specifically the recording of exceptional astronomical phenomena, from which can be calculated an absolute date for a given event. Consequently, the absolute dating of precisely when such and such a king ruled has become a sort of scholarly contest between who can count the most accurately between these astronomical benchmark events.

As if these considerations were not enough to trouble the mind of a conscientious historian, one must contend with the difference between the established Egyptian civil calendar and our own. Unlike our modern calendar that begins on January 1st, the first month of the Egyptian civil calendar began at the Inundation of the Nile River that occurred between June 15th and June 30th. Then there is the tendency among some Egyptian dynasties – and in our case, the Third Dynasty – to employ the use of a regnal calendar, meaning that time was recorded in years from the date of a pharaoh's accession to the throne.

In the case of the chronology at the end of the Second and beginning of the Egyptian Third Dynasty, the death of Khasekhemwy in 2686 BC seems to be more firmly grounded than most with the length of his reign judged between seventeen and a half years and eighteen years, two months, and twenty-three days. For the first king of the Third Dynasty, Djoser, it was long held that a certain Nebka preceded him; however, subsequent research has since upheld Djoser's primacy. But for the length of his reign, once again there are conflicting schools of thought, as one supports a reign of nineteen years and another one of some twenty-eight. Currently, the latter estimate seems to hold the most favor.

Recent discussions of early Egyptian dynastic chronology have been published by Ian Shaw (ed., *The Oxford History of Ancient Egypt*, Oxford University Press 2000, p. 480) and Toby Wilkenson (*Royal Annals of Ancient Egypt. The Palermo Stone and its associated fragments*, Kegan Paul International 2000, pp. 79, 258).

On the basis of these two readily accessible English language sources, the following general chronological outline has been constructed. It is by no means to be considered authoritative. All dates are understood as BC.

Second Dynasty (2890-2686)

Hotepsekhemwy – 2890-2860 (? Chronology uncertain)

Nebra – 2860-2848 (? Chronology uncertain)

Nynetjer – 2848-2808 (? Chronology uncertain)

Senedj – 2808-2788 (? Chronology uncertain)

Seth-Peribsen (? Chronology – Individual uncertain)

Sekhemib-Perenmaat (? Chronology – Individual uncertain)

Khasekhemwy – 2704-2686

Third Dynasty (2686-2613)

Djoser – 2686-2658

Djoserty – 2658-2649 (? Chronology uncertain)

Nebka – 2649-2643 (? Chronology uncertain)

Huni – 2643-2613 (? Chronology – Individual uncertain)

On Egyptian Priests &
Their Priesthoods

The duties of Egyptian priests and their many priesthoods, varied during the three thousand years of pharaonic history. By the time of the New Kingdom (1567-1085 BC), the vast majority of religious functions were performed on the behalf of the king by the priests devoted to each god. As one might expect, due to the formation of so many religious organizations, priestly bureaucracies formed to manage the resources of the god's estate. Just as naturally priestly hierarchies developed in order to apportion and manage the many tasks associated with the care and maintenance of a specific deity. At the top of this priest ranking stood those who served the god, the high priest, literally "the first servant of the god," who in turn was followed by the "second," "third," and "fourth servant of the god" as well.

In opposition to these administrative rankings, the vast majority of Egyptian priests who undertook the day-to-day temple duties were the common priests, the *wab*-priests, literally "the cleaners." This is not to say that specialty priesthoods did not exist, for they did, especially those devoted to mummification and the necropolis. But one class of priests, the *sem*-priests, appears to connote a ranking of importance unto their own. While certainly not as powerful as high priests nor as lowly as *wab*-priests, the *sem*-priests were those associated with cultic activities and even the royal palace itself.

A Note on the Vocalization of Ancient Egyptian

Regarding the vocalization of ancient Egyptian, the fact of the matter is simply this: the language is a very, very dead one – meaning that what it sounded like has been long lost. Its closest linguistic cousin, Coptic, is itself a dead language, but at least one that included vowels within its script. On this shirt-tailed basis, Egyptologists have carefully compared the vocabularies of the two languages and have constructed a scientific vocalization scheme to approximate what the Egyptian tongue might have sounded like. But even if the assigned vowel placements are accurate, their quality remains just as uncertain as is their emphasis, or where the accent falls on a particular word – not to mention that there is evidence to suggest several regional dialectics during the course of any given dynasty. To add even more fuel to the fire, different vocalization schemes have been put forward by the dominant Egyptological schools of thought be they American, British, French, Italian, or German. As a consequence, the vocalization of ancient Egyptian becomes more a matter of one's cultural preference than anything else. In short, just what the language really sounded like during a given time period and within a given region is up for grabs.

With the above caveats and considerations in mind, the author offers the following possible pronunciations for the ancient Egyptian names and words that appear in this manuscript.

Ankhtowe – Suburban village of Men-nefer: *ankhh-towee*

Djoser – First king of the Third Dynasty: *zo-ser*

Ephiphi – Third month of the Egyptian summer (late June–late July): *ephi-phi*

Imhotep – Royal architect: *im-hotep*

Ipi – Royal administrator and confidant of Djoser: *ii-pee*

Kanofer – Adopted father of Imhotep: *kan-o-fer*

Khasekhemwy – Last king of the Second Dynasty: *ka-skeck-hem-wee*

Khereduankh – Adopted mother of Imhotep: *kher-edoo-ankh*

Mennefer – Early capital city of Egypt: *men-nefer*

Nekhem – *Wab*-priest of Ptah: *neck-hem*

Ptah – Memphite god of creation and civilization: *pp-taah*

Sekemka – *Sem*-priest of Ptah: *seck-em-kha*

A Note on the Editing of Papyri & Inscriptions

The study of inscriptions, known as epigraphy, possesses a well-known philological shorthand for the recording and interpretation of such ancient monuments – be they handsomely carved stone inscriptions, painted surfaces, or hastily scratched-out graffiti. This methodology was first established by Theodor Mommsen, the founder of the *Corpus Inscriptionum Latinarum*, or *CIL*, in 1853. The *CIL*, which celebrated its 150th anniversary in 2003, is a vast compendium of nearly eighty volumes of inscriptions that relate to the Roman Empire. The continued study and publication of newly discovered inscriptions from this period of history is the patient and laborious task of the Berlin-Brandenburgische Academie der Wissenschaften, Corpus Inscriptionum Latinarum's staff, and its most able director, Prof. Dr. Manfred Gerhard Schmidt.

Needless to say, with such a ready tool available historians and philologists of other ancient time periods naturally gravitated to the *CIL* methodology of philological criticism and commentary and either wholly adopted it or did so with few exceptions.

Consequently, all of the ancient Egyptian texts contained within this book follow the *CIL*'s editorial conventions and use the following symbols to indicate:

| | Single bar indicates one line of text

|| Two bars indicate the fifth line of a text

a|bc Breaks in the text, usually a line break

a||bc Text located outside of an inscribed field or displaced text

(vac.)	The presence of a gap in the text
[[abc]]	An ancient erasure of text
<<abc>>	Ancient text inscribed on an erased background
abc (!)	An ancient grammatical error, misspelling, or philological irregularity of some kind
abc (?)	Uncertain reading of the text
(abc)	Either the modern explanation of an abbreviation or philological convention
a[bc]	A modern editorial addition, explanation, or change to the text
{abc}	A modern editorial deletion of text
<u>abc</u>	Letters once read by previous editors, which are currently lost or unreadable

ABOUT THE AUTHOR

To craft such a tale takes wit, a love of science and science fiction, and above all a deep reverence for ancient history and archaeology. All of these qualities are stitched together beautifully in his books, because Cherf has been there, dug that. This is a guy who has seen the sun rise from atop the Great Pyramid.

Needless to say, Cherf's books have been generously reviewed by his readers, who have in turn eagerly shared their joy. The *Historical Fiction Society* in 2013 rated *Bow Tie* an Editor's Choice. For an author, such sentiments are an embarrassment of riches – precious words like honey deliciously, drizzled.

At his core, Cherf is a teacher and his books do just that. They are a passionate sharing of a much-beloved subject. His readers tend to be adults who are looking for an adventure, who enjoy lively description, an involved plot, and the intellectual satisfaction of learning something new.

Cherf has excavated in Israel and Greece and toured and photographed many of Egypt's ancient sites firsthand. He is a big fan of vintage Tom Clancy and Michael Crichton.

Degreed in Anthropology, Egyptian Archaeology, and with a PhD in Ancient History, Cherf remains a member of Denver's Egyptian Study Society.

Living with his beloved wife, Sue, they keep Foxbat 1 out in the garage. They enjoy playing golf, road racing (that's where Foxbat 1 comes in), jawing around a fire pit on a cool evening while sampling craft beers, and rooting for the Cubs – clearly Cherf is a hopeless romantic.

Visit www.wjcherf.com to access free sample chapters to all of his eighteen works, and continue following the temporal adventures of Egyptologist Joseph Richards.